REJECTS PARADISE

Cover Design: Covers by Aura
Photographer: Valua Vitaly
Proofreading: Danielle Stansbury
Editing: Heather Fox
Editing & Formatting: Sheridan Anne

RIDE
or Die

Ahhhhh…. the final book is here!

Who am I supposed to dedicate it to? I guess that would be you, the reader who has come along on this epic journey with me and fallen in love with Ocean, Colton … and maybe Nic just as much as I have. If that's you, then THANK YOU! Without you, I wouldn't be able to keep doing what I love and that means the absolute world to me!

I love you all!!!!

To Heather - You're freaking awesome! I give you impossible deadlines and you're always like yeah, hit me with it!

To Danielle - Without you, I'd be crying on my kitchen floor! You keep me sane!

CHAPTER 1

Dominic

Tears well in his pathetic eyes as he stares up at me, silently begging me to spare his life, but I'm not about that shit here. I'm Dominic Fucking Garcia; I'm un-fucking-touchable. No one gets away with turning their back on the Widows. *No one.*

He knew the rules. All the fucking Widows do. My father ran a tight ship, but I'm not him. He used to let his men run wild; he used to let them get away with all kinds of shit as long as they came home at the end of the day. But loyalty means something a little different to me, and unfortunately for this fucker, he don't got it.

I crouch down, studying his face and taking in the black widow tattoo that sits just below his eyes. He doesn't deserve our mark. He's a traitor to his family.

The light of the small warehouse flickers above and sends shadows soaring over his already terrified face. I love that fucking flicker. It's why I use this warehouse. There's something about a flickering light that sends an already scared man into overdrive. Maybe it's the small buzz and zap when the light finally gives out and sends the room into darkness. It could be the way that it slowly rocks from side to side as the breeze comes in through the back door, casting shadows back and forth across the warehouse, playing mind games.

I grin as the light flickers back to life. The fucker looks absolutely terrified.

What can I say? I'm all about the dramatics.

Murder isn't something to take lightly. If you're going to end someone and send them to the darkest pits of hell, then it's always best to do it with a little terror in their system.

Fuck, I can only imagine what someone on the outside looking in would think of me—that fucker needs therapy. They'd be right. I'm all sorts of fucked up, and it only gets worse, but what's more, I fucking love it.

Respect. Power. Domination. It's all fucking mine.

This is exactly what my father wanted for me, and it's exactly what I took. I'm a fucking king and no one will take that away from me. I'm a god among my men, I'm a monster to the outsiders, and feared by the enemy.

No one can touch me.

"Come on, bro," Kairo's soft whine comes from the back of the warehouse, killing my vibe. "You've been playing with him for hours. Get it over and done with so I can get home and find a tight pussy to sink my dick into."

Always thinking about his fucking dick.

My jaw clenches. Had that been anyone else interrupting my fun, they'd be on the ground beside this traitor, ready to hand over their life. Kai is my boy though, my best fucking friend, my brother, and my second. There are only three bastards in this godforsaken world that could get away with this bullshit—Kairo, Sebastian, and Elijah.

They've had my back since day one. They've witnessed all the bullshit and know me better than I know myself. They're the reason I'm not rotting in jail; they're the reason my fucking father didn't rot in jail. Without them, I don't know where I'd be. They reel in my crazy. They think they know just how far I'll go, but they don't. If they did … fuck. I don't even want to think about that.

If they knew the shit that I did, they might just turn their backs on me too, and that's a blow that I wouldn't be able to come back from.

I groan and ignore Kai's comments. He needs to live a little; he's such a fucking robot. I swear the guy's never allowed himself to have just a little bit of fun.

Keeping my eyes on my traitor, I pull my knife and bring it toward the fucker's black widow tattoo. He doesn't deserve to wear our mark on his skin.

His eyes zone in, carefully watching the tip of my blade. "You fucked up," I murmur, my voice low and threatening.

"I … I … I know. I'm sorry," he says in a cold sweat. "I swear, I'll never do it again. Please, I …"

"You'll what?"

The front of his jeans darkens with piss, and I scrunch my face in disgust. There's nothing worse than a man who can't handle fear, and judging by the shame that flashes on his face, he knows it. He's not worthy of being one of my men. Had Russo been the one to take him, this bitch would have squealed in seconds. He would have told him everything there is to know about Dominic Garcia and the Breakers Flats Black Widows, and that shit is unforgivable.

I slice the tip of my knife through his tattoo, making a point that he doesn't belong. "You wear this tattoo with pride, yet you're fucking the enemy," I say, watching as he flinches with the sharp sting of the knife.

A fat drop of blood begins running down the side of his face. I can't take my eyes off it as it slides over his jaw and down the column of his neck. It's fucking thrilling and within seconds, it's staining the top of his already bloodied shirt. "I'm sorry," he cries, fearing his time for begging is up. "I know. I fucked up. Please, Nic, I'll—"

"You did fuck up, and you did it willingly," I laugh. "You turned your back on your family for what? Some cheap pussy?"

"I love her," he cries making anger pulse through me. "Kian knew about her. He was okay with it. He gave his approval."

A sick grin twists across my face. "Well, Kian ain't here no more, and I'm not okay with my men fucking some slut Wolf. So, what's it going to be?" I question. "Are you a traitor to your family, or are you one of us?"

His eyes harden, knowing exactly what I'm asking. Is he going to be labeled a traitor and killed on the spot? Or is he going to give up the girl and be a part of our family, even if that means he will never earn my trust back, and probably get himself killed anyway?

He nods viciously. "I'm a Widow," he declares with tears in his eyes, viciously nodding his head, almost as though he's trying to convince himself. "I'm always a Widow."

I straighten out of my crouch and look down at the pathetic excuse of a man at my feet. "Right, then what's her name?"

His face instantly drains of blood and I grin wide, knowing damn well this fucker isn't about to give up her name. He's kidding himself if he thinks I'm about to let him back into my family. We're built on loyalty and trust, without that, we have nothing.

He starts shaking his head, proving once and for all where his loyalties lie, but it doesn't matter. I don't need her name; I already have it. Veronica Davies—though she's better known as Roni Russo around here. The one girl who broke free from this world and just happens to be the guidance counselor at a fancy private school for rich kids in Bellevue Springs. She's also the woman who gave my girl the big idea that she could get out too. That bitch has her own crimes to pay for, and she will in due time. But first things first …

"What's wrong?" I question, crouching down again and trailing the tip of my knife over his skin. I meet his eyes, letting him see just how fucked up I really am. "I promise, I won't touch her."

"Nic," Kairo snaps from behind me, bored of my games. "Get it over and done with so we can get the fuck out of here."

My eyes sparkle in excitement as I watch the traitor on his knees before me. His jaw is clenched, staring up at me as though Kairo isn't even in the room. "Leave her the fuck alone," he spits through his teeth, giving one last half-assed attempt to save the woman of his dreams. "She did nothing wrong. Leave her out of this bullshit. She's not even a Wolf. Her brother is."

"Ahhhh, you see that's where you're wrong," I tell him, knowing that girl better than he could possibly know. "I hope you told her that you loved her when you left this morning."

His eyes go wide just as the swinging light above us flickers and sends the room into darkness. I can't help the grin that takes over my face.

That fucking light never ceases to amaze me.

I sink my knife into his stomach and slice a deep curve just like my father taught me. His screams are strangled and filled with agony, but I tune them out in favor of listening to the soft, splashing sounds of his intestines sliding out of his body and hitting the cold concrete ground.

Fuck, that's satisfying. Wrong, but so fucking good.

I have to be honest, this really wasn't an easy trick to learn. I had to practice … a lot, but my father kept on me until I had it down to a fine art. It's ironic, apparently, he'd learned it from Louis Munroe, Ocean's father, back in the day when the two of them actually got along. You know, until the bastard got jumped in as a Wolf.

The lights flicker above and restore light to the warehouse just in time to see the bastard crumble to the ground, and as he does, I hear Kairo's disgusted groan from behind me. "Fuck, man. You just keep getting sicker," he grunts, slipping his phone from out of his pocket.

I laugh and clean off my knife against the fucker's jeans until it's sparkling clean before turning back to Kai. I shrug my shoulders and laugh. "What can I say? He had it coming."

Kai rolls his eyes as he brings up our cleaner's number. "What's wrong with a simple bullet between the eyes? It's so much easier…" he looks down at the mess of intestines, looking a little green. "And cleaner."

I consider his suggestion and instantly know that a bullet between the eyes would have been too easy. A traitor should always go down with a little effort, sending a message to all the other bastards who want to cross me. I save the easy kills for the fuckers I don't give a shit about.

I'm just about to tell him that when the cleaner on the other end of Kai's phone picks up and Kairo falls into conversation. "Yo, clean up at the old warehouse. Bring a fucking team for this one," he says, eyeing me. "It's a mess."

The guy responds and Kai meets my stare before giving a firm nod, telling me that he's on his way. The call ends, and knowing damn well that the cleaner will do his job to perfection, we head for the doors, leaving the fucking traitor behind.

We drop down into my car and take off, heading back towards the Widows compound when Kai's heavy sigh draws my attention from the road. "What?" I grunt, knowing this guy better than anyone. He's not much for talking. He's the suffer in silence type, and sometimes a sigh is the only indication that there's something on his mind.

"It's nothing, man."

"Fucking spit it out, bro."

Kai glances at me and rubs his hand over his jaw, deep in thought with regret heavy in his dark eyes. "I don't think I can do this anymore."

"The fuck?" I demand, turning my glare on him as my brows pinch in confusion. There's a lot of shit I expected to come out of his mouth, but that wasnt it. "You want out?"

His eyes widen and his arm slams out against my chest. "No, fuckwit. That's not what I mean. I'm a fucking Widow through and through. I'm talking about the fucking killing. It's getting to me, Nic. It's too heavy."

Understanding dawns, and I take a slow, deep breath, letting it really sink in. "You're struggling with this shit?"

"Yeah, man. I'm at the point of no fucking return. If I cross over it …"

"You'll be like me," I murmur, finishing his sentence, knowing all too fucking well what it feels like. I crossed over that line years ago, and I've never been able to come back from it. It was a hard fucking pill to swallow, and I don't want that for any of my boys, especially if it's a road they're not willing to travel.

"Alright, man. I'll sort it out," I tell him, glancing across at him as we race through the streets of Breakers Flats. "You're still my second though. Nothing will change that."

He nods. "I know."

Silence falls through my car as I knew it would. Kai's good like that; he doesn't need to fill the empty spaces with mindless chatter. That's what Sebastian and Eli are for.

We pull up into the Widow's compound and the massive roller doors are opened for me. I drive on through, and just as I'm bringing my car to a stop, my phone rings in my pocket.

I get out of the car and close the door behind me while pulling out my phone. I glance down at the screen to find Eli's name flashing up at me. I let out a heavy sigh. What does this idiot want? He's been giving me a hard time for the past few weeks, ever since I slipped up and let Ocean know about the fucking cameras we had installed in her pristine fucking mansion. Ocean ripped into him, and I'm man enough to admit that it's completely my fault, but he won't let it go despite the many times we've talked it through. When things aren't right with Ocean, they aren't right anywhere, that's just the way it is, the way it's always been.

She's the light in all of our skies, but lately, our worlds have never been so dull. Though, that could also have a little something to do with the fact that I killed her father … so, there's that.

"What's up?" I say, walking deeper into the compound with Kai at my side.

"WHAT THE FUCK DID YOU DO?"

The fuck is his problem?

I stop in the middle of the compound, not liking his tone one bit. Not because he's fucking screaming at me but because of the heavy betrayal lacing his voice. My brows instantly dip. "What the fuck are you talking about?" I question, making Kai stop and look back at me with his brows drawn, only to have Sebastian step in behind him and look at me in the same curious way.

"Ocean," he demands over the sound of his car engine roaring. "What did you do to her?"

Great. What have I done now?

I clench my jaw. I haven't exactly been upfront with these guys about killing her father or Charles Carrington. If they knew what I'd done … fuck. I'd lose them all. I let out an irritated sigh. "Not this fucking bullshit again," I snap, getting ready for the same old argument. "I fucking told you; we had a disagreement."

"A disagreement?" he scoffs, his voice quickly rising into hysteria. "Fucking bullshit. A disagreement doesn't lead my fucking girl to waltz into the Wolf Den."

I snap my gaze back to Kai and Sebastian and just like that, they know exactly who this is about. "What the fuck are you talking about? What do you mean she went to the Wolf Den?"

Sebastian's head snaps up. "What?" he demands as Kai stares with wide, horrified eyes, a million different scenarios flying through each of our minds.

"I mean what I fucking said," Eli snaps, his following growl more vicious than I've ever heard him. "What did you do to her? I've been with her all fucking morning. She said you didn't give us the full fucking story, and when she went to leave, I followed her only to find her pulling up in Blaxlands Grove and walking straight to their fucking door like she owned the place. WHAT. DID. YOU. DO?"

FUCK. Fuck. Fuck.

The betrayal slices through me like a warm knife through butter, and I might as well be the traitor bleeding out on the cold ground. If they knew I went there and held a gun to her head, forcing her to choose between me and Colton … FUCK.

My silence speaks volumes, and as Kai and Sebastian stare at me, knowing whatever I did would have been awful, Eli's voice comes rumbling through the phone. "You're fucking dead."

The call goes silent and my hand instantly clenches around my phone. "FUCK," I yell before launching my phone across the compound. It smashes against the brick wall and splinters into a million pieces.

"What the fuck did you do?" Sebastian demands, stepping right into me and blocking me. "Where's O?"

I slam my hand against his chest, forcing him a step back. "What does it fucking matter now? That bitch betrayed me. Betrayed us all. She's the fucking Wolves problem now."

Sebastian pushes me right back, and within seconds, we have the eyes of every fucking Widow in the compound on us. Slowly they creep in, waiting for the moment they're needed to protect their leader from a threat. But they should know, if any other fucker lays a hand on one of my boys, they'll have me to deal with, even if one of them has a gun against my head.

Oceania Munroe is a fucking goddess. She's the love of my life, but the fact that she's in the arms of that rich prick has me going in-fucking-sane. None of that matters right now. All that matters is how badly I screwed up. I pushed her too far; sent her straight into the arms of the enemy. They have her right where they want her now, ready to squeeze every last ounce of information out of her, and then fuck her over for fun. She'll give them what they want with a fucking smile on her face, just to stab me in the back.

She's the real traitor here. She turned her back on her family and I will never forget it. If I didn't love her, she would have been finished when she chose him over me. Why doesn't she understand that she belongs with me? We'd be unstoppable together.

Sebastian steps into me, crowding me as his eyes narrow to slits. He's the fun-loving one, but when he needs to be, he can be dangerously lethal. "What the fuck did you do?" he growls, repeating himself so low that Kai flinches, getting ready to jump in to pull us apart.

My hands curl into fists, more than ready to lay his ass out when a high squeal of tires comes to a screeching halt just outside the roller doors. Eli comes tearing in, ignoring all the Widows who now have their guns out, ready to face down any threat.

Eli comes storming up to me and grabs the front of my shirt, hauling me away from Sebastian, and within the blink of an eye, his fist smashes against my jaw like a fucking freight train. I stumble back and crash into Sebastian, who pushes me right back at Eli, who's ready with another punch, this time straight under my ribs, instantly winding me. "FUCK," I grunt, spitting out a mouthful of blood before straightening up.

I throw myself right back at the fucker and we go crashing down against the hard concrete floor of the compound. I nail him back, right in the eye, knowing damn well that the dick is going to have one hell of a black eye for the next few weeks. The fucker bruises like a peach.

We go punch for punch until we're both panting for breath, and only then does Kai get sick of it, commanding Sebastian to help tear us apart.

Two minutes later, we sit at the bar of my compound with ice-packs chilling on our battered bodies and a bottle of rum sitting between us.

"Alright," Kai finally says, walking around the other side of the bar so that he can have all of our attention as Sebastian moves in on the other side of Eli. "You have two fucking seconds to tell us what the fuck is going on."

I grab my shot glass and let out a heavy sigh as my finger traces the rim. I take the shot and then finally look up at the boys. I can't get away with this much longer. They have absolutely no issue with torturing the information out of me. "I fucked up," I tell them with a cringe, finally admitting it out loud. "On Wednesday, when O was chilling at my place, I sort of demanded that she marry me. Then when she told me no, we got into it and she went back home."

"Her friend was hurt," Sebastian throws in.

"Yeah," I continue, filling up my shot glass and throwing back another. "I kinda followed her home and cornered her and Colton in the hospital parking lot. Then with a gun against her head, I forced her to choose, and well, she chose fucking wrong."

I take another shot just moments before Kai's heavy fist slams against my cheek, instantly fracturing the bone. I fly back off my chair and crash down to the fucking ground, but I relish in it. I thrive on the pain. It's like a drug to me.

I get to my feet, wiping a hand down my aching face and spit out another mouthful of blood, glad that I took those few shots to help dull the ache.

"Fix it," Kai demands.

I scoff, scrunching my face in distaste. "No. She fucking chose. She's done with us."

"No," Sebastian snaps. "She's fucking done with *you*. She's like a little sister to me and I'm not going to let your bullshit stand in the way of me mending my relationship with her. We have to go and get her. She's not safe in the fucking Wolf Den."

"You're not going anywhere," I tell him, eyeing him and reminding him who's the fucking boss around here. "It's a fucking suicide mission. She walked in there on her own. This is her problem now, let her clean up her own mess for once."

Eli throws himself to his feet, fuming as he stares at me while struggling to keep in control. "Are you fucking kidding me? This is O we're talking about. Oceania fucking Munroe, not some dumb bitch."

"She. Chose."

"Get the fuck over it," he snaps, throwing his hand out and knocking the bottle of rum off the side of the bar, letting it crash to the ground and smash into a million little pieces. "She told you from day one that she wanted out of Breakers Flats. She hates gang life. She doesn't want to be anywhere near it, so why the fuck would she want to come back here to play your little traumatized wife? She's stronger than that, and you know it," he says. "You want to know why she was here in the first place? She was looking for help and she fucking came to me. She may have chosen to be with Colton, but she still chooses to have us in her life."

I flinch at his words. They fucking stung.

Kai steps around the bar, keeping his narrowed, jealous gaze on Eli as he moves in toward him. "What kind of help would she need that made her come all the way out here?"

In other words, why the fuck did she go to Eli and not him?

Eli drops his gaze, and I watch as he clenches his jaw, unable to keep the curiosity off my face. I might be angry as fuck with Ocean right now, but that won't change that I'd lay my fucking life down for her.

Eli's hands go into his hair, and he instantly starts pacing in front of the bar. "Shit," he spits through his teeth, fighting whatever inner demons are creeping up on him. "I fucking promised that I wouldn't say anything."

Sebastian grabs Eli by the front of his shirt and pulls him into his chest. "What the fuck is going on?"

Eli sighs, looking sick to his stomach. "She's fucking pregnant," he sighs, self-hatred flooding through him. "She asked me to go with her to get checked out."

My hands ball into fists as my jaw clenches hard enough to crack a fucking tooth. "I'm going to fucking kill him."

"No," Eli says, rushing in, slamming his hand against my chest. "It's not him. I've been at the fucking doctor's with her all morning. She's seven weeks. That makes it Jude's baby. That fucking rapist knocked up our girl and now she's in the Wolf Den with a death wish and a baby to look out for."

Kai grabs a bottle of bourbon from the bar and takes a long swig before looking at me. "I don't give a shit what you have to say," he tells me as Sebastian and Eli move in to flank him. "We're going after her and you're either with us or against us."

I clench my jaw and watch them. "It's a fucking suicide mission."

"She's worth it," Sebastian snaps.

The longer they watch me, the heavier their stares become, but it doesn't take them long to realize that this time, they're out on their own. They're right, Oceania Munroe is fucking worth it, but I can guarantee that the next time she sees me, she'll be putting a bullet right through my head, and that's not something I'm about to risk.

If they knew, they'd fucking understand, but then, they'd also be fighting over who gets to pull the trigger. What it really comes down to is that she ran to the Wolves instead of coming to us. The boys might think that she's there because she's too scared and doesn't know what to do. The truth of the matter is, I know her better than any of these fuckers. She is strong enough to handle the baby on her own. She walked into their world because she wants to go to war. So, instead of fighting for her, I take a step back and wave my hand toward the exit. "Fuck off then," I tell them coldly. "Go and save that traitor and her rapist's baby. You're on your own."

The boys gape at me in horror before shaking their heads and turning on their heels. They stalk right out of the compound, and within seconds are in Eli's car, turning their backs on their family. But they'll be back soon enough. Once a Widow, always a Widow.

I used to tell her, 'No friends, only family.' That saying used to hold weight between us, but not anymore. Oceania Munroe is no longer friend or family, and if it's a war she wants to bring to my doorstep, then it's a fucking war she'll get.

She better be prepared because I don't lose.

Ever.

CHAPTER 2

Ocean

The smell of rust and blood lingers in the air of the dark Wolf Den. It smells something like the wine cellar dungeon in the bottom of Colton's mansion, making me wonder what kind of secrets lay hidden in this place. Though, maybe wondering about that really isn't the best idea. I'm sure the secrets this den holds would be far worse than anything I've ever seen before.

I've only been here for twenty minutes, and that's more than enough time to realize how badly I screwed up. Well, sort of. I should never have come here. I never should have walked through the door and signed myself up for a lifetime of gang violence, but I had no choice. I had to do it. I didn't take this decision lightly, and despite how stupid it sounds, there's a method to my madness.

No one will understand, but hopefully, one day they will. I'll probably have destroyed all my friendships before then anyway. If the boys knew I'd come here, they'd be broken. Standing with the Wolves is the ultimate betrayal. They'll never forgive me for this.

How am I ever going to face them knowing that I stepped through this door with the intention to go against Nic? But, on the other hand, how could I bring a child into this world while up against a constant threat? I don't know how I feel about this child yet, but one thing is certain, it's half mine, and that means that I have a responsibility to give this child the best life possible.

Colton is where it gets complicated.

I'd do anything to have an easy life with him. He's going to be the one who takes this betrayal the hardest. I can just see it now. Had I gone home and explained this all to him, he would have played the role of my white knight and he would have done it flawlessly. He would have told me that he'd take on this baby as his own and to forget about Jude. He would have tried to deal with Nic himself, and he would have done everything in his power to take my fear away, but Colton doesn't know Nic like I do. Nic doesn't like to lose. He will keep going, hit after hit until he finally gets what he wants, and I can't bring that shit to Colton's door. It's already bad enough as it is. I need to face this head-on, and I need to do it with an army at my back who isn't afraid to get hurt.

I have to end this before it's too late.

There's a sinking feeling in my gut. I know this war is going to end with someone getting hurt and it terrifies me. Hell, even if it's Nic … no. I can't have anyone getting hurt. I should want Nic dead for everything he's done. He killed my father and then lied about it. He held me while I cried and promised me vengeance. All this time I've wondered if I'm becoming a monster, but the truth is, the monster has been right there by my side the whole time.

Nic killed Charles in response to a threat. He took away my right to privacy when he covered the mansion in cameras. He sent the DeCarlos to our doorstep. He hurt me, dragged me down the stairs, and bruised me over and over again. And then comes the killer; he held a gun on Colton and then pressed it against my temple, demanding that I choose.

I honestly thought there was a good chance that I could have died in that parking garage, but I wasn't about to lie to myself and tell Nic that I was still his special little girl. I was never going to ride off into the sunset with him and become his little gang wife. Surely, he must have known that. Colton is where my future is. He's my ride or die … assuming I can get through this and assuming he doesn't look at me like used goods when he discovers that I'm pregnant with my rapist's baby. He wouldn't though, he's too good.

Nic has to go down. There's no other option. For my sake, for Colton's sake, and for my unborn child's sake.

Had anyone suggested such horrors to me six months ago, I would have had them committed. Never in my wildest dreams did I think Nic was capable of all of this, but everyone changes and everyone has their secrets. I nearly killed a rapist who was locked up in a dungeon, and Colton shot a cold-blooded murderer in his kitchen. I guess everyone is capable of shit like this. The question is, how well they can keep it hidden?

I sit in the Wolf Den, cautiously looking around. There are strange men everywhere and not another woman in sight. I feel their eyes on me, watching me as though I'm a cheap stripper who just got invited to the bachelor party. They look at me like a treat, like they're about to bow down to Russo for bringing me in here for their enjoyment. It sends chills shooting down my spine. I shouldn't be here. I should have figured out another way.

Russo led me through the door and told me to sit my ass down before walking away, leaving me to fend for myself. That was twenty minutes ago. I never thought I'd utter these words, but I actually preferred him standing by my side. I felt oddly safer though I shouldn't. I'm sure Russo is worse than them all. His closet would have the worst kinds of skeletons.

The Wolf Den is remarkably similar to the Widows shitty little clubhouse. It has a crappy living area, which is where I am now. There's a bar filled with everything brown under the sun, the concrete floors have bullet holes and skid marks, while there are at least three smashed windows which have been pathetically boarded up.

This place would be all kinds of fun, you know, if I was a maniac.

I watch everyone with a sharp eye, keeping track of their movements, watching what they're drinking and who they're talking to.

It's like a puzzle that I need to work out. It doesn't pay to be stupid in places like this.

I watch as a man steps through the same door that I'd only come through. He's covered from head to toe in tattoos and does everything in his power to look dangerous. His gun is at his hip, being shown off for every motherfucker to see. A nasty, red scar sits under his eye and stretches down to his lip.

He doesn't look like the kind of guy I want to fuck with. When his eyes come to me, he licks his lips as though he's about to indulge in an afternoon snack. I have no choice but to make him my business.

I feel the eyes of the Wolves track his movements, and the way they watch him sends my blood cold. These guys are afraid of him and seeing as they're Wolves, that speaks volumes.

Scarface strides toward me, mentally undressing me. He shoots his hand out, pointing toward the guy behind the bar. "Drink."

The bartender instantly gets on it, and I swallow hard as he continues coming my way. He steps up close, hovering above me, and I look up at him from where I sit on the lone couch of the living area. "Get up," he snaps, licking his lips.

I narrow my eyes, more than aware that I need to play this carefully. "I'm not interested in being your little play toy. Get lost."

He steps closer, and I can feel his heavy boot pressing against my shoes. "I said, get up."

"Why?"

"Because if I grab you, these fuckers are going to try and stop me. Now, get the fuck up and start walking your ass out back before you cause a scene."

I laugh, standing to give myself leverage. "You're fucking insane if you think I'm about to go anywhere with you." His hand shoots out, and I slap it away with a sharp smack that sounds throughout the whole den. "Keep your dirty fucking hands off me, or I will become your worst fucking nightmare."

Scarface snaps. His big hand curls around my throat and squeezes, lifting until I'm barely hanging on by my tippy-toes. "You don't think I know who you are, Widow?" he demands, leaning in closer and whispering in my ear. "You don't think I see you hanging around Garcia and his boys all the time, whoring yourself out? You have a lot of fucking nerve coming in here and telling me who or what I can't fuck. If I say I want to fuck you, then you better get on your fucking knees and start begging for it."

I slam my knee up into his groin and watch as the fucker falls to the dirty floor before me. "Trust me, dickhead. You don't want to see what happened to the last motherfucker who thought he could put his hands on me."

"You little bitch," he roars, diving for his gun, only he doesn't find it because it's already resting heavily in my palm and aimed right at his chest.

"Just fucking try me," I dare him, watching as he raises to his feet.

"Give me my fucking gun, bitch."

"You know," I say, spinning it in my hand, the same way Nic does. "I think I might hang onto this."

He dives for me, and I let a bullet fly free, shooting at his feet and watching as he comes to a startling halt, only now just realizing how far I'll go to protect myself.

"Back off, Leon," comes a voice from across the room. I glance across the room to find a man watching me, though it's not with the same curiosity as the rest of them. There's something oddly soothing about him, something that tells me that he's the good kind while also someone who needs to be watched out for. "You don't want to fuck with her. That's big Lou's kid. She could probably fuck you up a million ways before you even knew what was going on."

Scarface looks back at me, his eyes raking up and down my body before he spits at my feet, forcing me back a step to avoid getting any of that shit on me. "You got off lucky this time, whore. Mark my words, you won't be that lucky next time."

Leon backs away, and I keep my eyes on him until he's completely out of sight. I turn back to my savior with a small, grateful smile. The guy nods and then looks away as though it never happened in the first place.

I stay on my feet, my body too pumped up and alert to be able to relax back into the dirty couch. I glance around, unsure of what to do with myself. Does Russo want me to make friends, or am I just supposed to sit here and look pretty until this shit gets sorted?

With nothing else to do, I find myself edging toward the guy who saved me despite the fact that I had it more than under control … at least I think I did. He probably doesn't want my company, and I don't want his, but so far, he's the only guy in the room who hasn't looked at me like a cheap whore or like someone who can be used in their wicked games.

I tuck Leon's gun in the back of my school skirt and get halfway to him when Russo's booming voice sounds behind me. "Where the fuck do you think you're going?" he demands, making me spin around with wide eyes. "You were told to sit."

I raise a brow and silently watch him, waiting to see what the hell he's going to do about it. I might have come here looking for help but that doesn't mean that I'm about to bow down and start kissing his damn feet. My hands fall to my hips, and for a seventeen-year-old girl, I must have bigger balls than anyone here in this room. "Are you done?" I question, raising my chin, taking a step toward him. "You may have branded me with your mark and stolen my freedom, but I'm not about being disrespected, and I sure as hell am not about having your men try to assault me. I've already put up with enough of that shit, and I'm not about to go through it again. Are we clear?"

Eyes widen all over the den, waiting for me to get my ass handed to me. But Russo just stares through a narrowed gaze, taking in my posture, more than aware that I will fight my way out of here if I have to. The seconds tick by, and with each passing one, the need to fidget grows, but I hold strong and don't let him see my fear. "Good," he finally says as though I just passed some kind of test. "I was worried you were weak. Maybe you're a little more like your father than I gave you credit for."

"That's not a compliment," I tell him.

"Wasn't meant to be," he says. "Now, follow me. It seems we have a few things to discuss."

Russo turns his back and almost on queue twenty men follow him, one of them being the guy, Snake, who had held his gun to my head in that damn alleyway. I'm shoved in the back, and as I go to curse out the fucker who dared touch me, I find the man who had saved me, the man with the kind eyes. "Just walk," he grunts in my ear, pushing me along.

I do as I'm told, and I follow the group of men into some kind of meeting room. There's a massive table, but no one seems to stand behind it, they just hover, waiting to hear what needs to be said.

Russo clears his throat once the last of his men have entered the room. The door is closed for privacy, though I have a feeling that privacy is something that I won't get much of around here. "This is Oceania Munroe, Big Lou's kid. She's a—"

"A fucking Widow, that's what she is," one of his men spits, staring at me with hate in his eyes. "I've seen her with those pricks. She's their little plaything. Why the fuck is she here? She's not our problem. You're just bringing more bullshit to our door."

Russo eyes his man and the look sends chills sweeping down my spine. He takes his gun and gently lays it on the table in front of him. "Did I ask for your input?"

The guy clenches his jaw, keeping his eyes on his leader. "No, boss."

"The next time you question me, you better be prepared to fight for it. Is that understood?"

The guy nods and takes a hesitant step back, folding into the line with the other men surrounding him, trying to hide away like a fucking pussy.

"As I was saying," Russo continues. "Oceania has come to us for help. Her father was my second, and we owe it to him to hear her out. Oceania is family. She bears our mark and has vowed to honor our mark. So you will give her the respect she is due."

Russo falls silent and all eyes look to me, waiting expectantly for me to come forward. "Oh, umm … am I supposed to make some kind of speech?" I question, having absolutely no idea what's expected of me right now.

Russo raises an expectant brow, daring me to get on with it, so I shrug my shoulders and do just that. "Alright then," I say, glancing around at the twenty or so men. "As a woman, I feel it's my duty to educate you all on the importance of washing between your ass crack and under your balls. It's imperative. You can't just let the water rush over it and expect it to be clean. I can not stress this enough. The two in one shampoo and body wash is not okay. It does not get the job done. Believe me, chicks do not dig a man with a stanky ass."

A hand slams down on the table, making me jump. "Do you think this is a joke?" Russo demands as the Wolves all seem to creep in closer, each and every one of them with a disgruntled scowl on their faces, all except my friendly guy who looks to be hiding a smirk.

"Oh," I say, sucking in a breath. "So, is this not a little 'get to know the new chick' thing?"

"You have two seconds to explain why you're here before I'm forced to get the information out of you."

I let out a heavy sigh and raise my chin, ready to get it over and done with. "Eight months ago, Dominic Garcia killed my father, and then he killed my boyfriend's father as well. He's done all sorts of unspeakable things toward me, and yes, up until a few days ago, I was loyal to Nic. He's been my best friend for years but killing my father? He needs to pay. I won't let him get away with it, and as of a few days ago, I turned my back on him."

Snake scoffs from across the room. "And I'm assuming you want us to do your dirty work?"

I scowl at him, unable to even pretend to be happy that I'm in this room. "Don't act as though you guys haven't been searching for my father's killer too. If you knew it was Nic, you would have gone after him ages ago. My father was a Wolf and not just any Wolf, but your second in command. That's gotta mean something." I take a breath and look around until I come back to Russo. "This morning, I found out that I was pregnant with my rapist's baby, and no, I have absolutely no fucking idea what I plan to do about that. But, I know that if I decide to go ahead with this pregnancy, I need to have this finished. I will not bring a child into this world that will be a target for Nic."

Russo leans forward on the table, keeping his eyes on mine. "What do you expect us to do about it?"

I shrug. "I expect your help. You said this was supposed to be a family, and I'm counting on that. From now on, Nic will pay. But, I must be clear about this; no more lives will be lost."

Scoffs are heard all around the room, and a booming laugh comes tearing out of Snake. "What do you think this is? We're not hired help. If we're going after the Widows, then you can guarantee that it'll be a fucking massacre."

I shake my head, horrified by the thought. "No. There are good guys in there," I insist, thinking of Sebastian, Kai, and Eli. "No one will be hurt. Take Nic and deal with him but leave the rest of them out of it."

Russo smirks. "You think that's how it works, sweet cheeks? You want us to go in there and take their leader, expecting the rest of them to just sit back and watch? Don't be so naive. If we go in there, men will be lost, both Widows and Wolves. Are you prepared to have that on your shoulders?"

I clench my jaw and instantly start shaking my head, horrified by the plan that's coming into place but knowing that I have to stay strong and stand by what I've said. It's either me or Nic, but there's that part of me that can't be responsible for the deaths of innocent men. If any of my boys were to be hurt … fuck. No, I couldn't handle that. This isn't what I wanted. "No, if that's the outcome, then no. I won't kill my friends. Thanks for nothing." I start walking to the door, ready to haul ass out of here. "I'll find another way to get at Nic."

"Well, well," Russo says in a tone that has me rooted to the spot. "If only it were that easy. You've given us Lou's killer on a silver platter and unfortunately for you, you're not the one who calls the shots around here. We don't play by your rules, Miss Munroe. Now, sit your ass down and tell us exactly what we need to know."

Shit.

CHAPTER 3
Colton

I slam the phone down after calling Ocean for the hundredth time, and just as I expected, there's no fucking answer. Where the hell is she?

I find myself staring at the security monitors again, and by now, I can't tell if it's out of habit or worry. I know I'm not going to see the Audi pull into the drive, it's all I've been hoping for the past few hours, but I know better. She's not coming back.

There was something off about her when she left this morning. There was an odd fear in her eyes, but she insisted that she was okay.

That was nearly fourteen hours ago, and no one has heard from her since.

Ocean should have been home ages ago. She was being shady and said that she needed to go and see someone before school, only she never fucking made it to school. She was a no-show, and I have no fucking idea where the hell she is. I feel sick. I need to know that she's okay.

I should have gone with her. She didn't look right. I should have trusted my gut, and now she's gone. I asked if she wanted me with her, but she blew me off. I should have insisted.

I hope I'm over-exaggerating this bullshit, but there's just something deep inside me that tells me to be worried.

I'm trying really fucking hard not to panic and to give her the space she needs to do whatever the fuck it is that she's doing, but I'm running out of patience. I can't take it anymore. I just need a text or something from her telling me that she's alright.

If something happened to her, if Nic got to her … fuck. I don't give a shit how she feels about him, I'll fucking kill him if I find that he's laid a hand on her. I don't care if it means the end of my relationship with Ocean. There's absolutely nothing that I wouldn't do to protect her. I know I'm only eighteen, and I'm not supposed to be thinking about this shit yet, but she's the one. I'm going to fucking marry that girl one day, and when I do, it's going to be the best goddamn day of my life.

I get up from my couch and instantly start pacing the living room, focusing on taking slow, deep breaths to stop me from grabbing the crystal vase that sits on the coffee table and launching it across the room.

Not being able to calm myself, I grab my phone off the armrest and scroll through until I come across Milo's number. I hit call and wait impatiently as it rings. Once. Twice. Three fucking times.

"Colton?" Milo says, not used to having me on the other end of a call. "What's up?"

"Have you heard from Ocean? She never came home today."

"The fuck? What do you mean she never came home? She texted this morning, checking that my nurses were playing nice."

"Did you hear from her after that?"

There's a slight pause, and I can almost hear the questions and horrors flying through his mind. "No," he finally says, his voice low and tortured. "What's going on? Did something happen? Where is she?"

I press my lips into a firm line and let out another slow breath. "That's what I'm trying to figure out."

I end the call and am about to try Hendrix when chaos down the hall has my phone dropping to my side. What the fuck is that? It sounds like a herd of elephants running through my house, and if Maria's loud shriek is anything to go by, I'd say it's anyone but Ocean.

I dart out of the living room and fly up the hall, following the sound of random men storming through my home. "Where is he?" someone calls through the house as I hear Cora shriek and fly back up the stairs, telling me that whoever these people are, they're no friends of ours.

The last time someone raided my home, the only motherly figure in my life was brutally shot and murdered, and I'm not about to sit back and allow that bullshit to happen again.

I move faster, determined to figure out why these people are in my home, but Maria's yells have my fears easing. "I don't care who you think you are. You can't just storm through here like you do back home. Besides, Ocean isn't even here. This isn't some trashy bar, this is a private home, and you need to leave."

"We're not here for Ocean," one of the guys snap back at her. "We know exactly where she is, which is why we're here."

"What's that supposed to mean?"

No response comes as I turn the corner and finally find them. Ocean's three little bodyguards; Sebastian, Elijah, and Kairo. They look pissed. "Where is she?" I demand, walking straight up to them as Maria hovers beside us looking lost and confused.

Kairo doesn't stop, just keeps walking straight into me, slamming his hands against my chest and pushing me back a step. "What the fuck did you do to her?"

"Excuse me?" I spit, pushing him right back into his friends and watching the astonishment on their faces that I was capable of moving him. But, honestly, if they think I'm about to sit back and let them go on with this bullshit, then they are sorely mistaken. "Where the fuck do you get off coming into my home and demanding some bullshit explanation out of me? I haven't done shit to Ocean. I have no fucking clue where she is, but clearly, that's not the case with you."

"What on earth is going on here?" Maria demands, pushing

herself between us. "Someone tell me where my daughter is right this very second."

Elijah cringes and drops his gaze to Maria but not after sending a glare my way. "She walked into the Wolf Den this morning and hasn't come out since."

My eyes bug out of my head as my heart begins to race for my girl. "The fuck? The Wolf Den? As in the fucking gang that her father was a part of? The fucking pricks who branded her in the street?"

Maria instantly starts shaking her head, her face growing pale as fear floods through her. "Keep up, rich boy," Elijah says, stepping forward as though he's the one playing point tonight. He gets right in my face, his jaw clenched and hands balled into tight fists, instantly setting me off. "I'm not here to give you a history lesson on Ocean's life, I'm here to find out what the fuck you did to her that made her make such a fucking stupid decision."

I push him back, demanding my space. "I didn't do shit. Everything is good between us, but if you're looking for a reason, perhaps look at yourself. You fucking Widows have done nothing but cause shit for her over and over again. Your overprotective and possessive bullshit is killing her. She just wants a fucking break from the drama."

"Don't fucking start with me," Elijah says, completely on edge. "She wouldn't just walk in there like that unless you freaked out over the fucking baby. What did you say to her?"

"Baby?" I question. "What fucking baby?"

The Widows go quiet and glance around at each other, confusion marking their faces. Sebastian turns to Kairo. "She didn't tell him."

He shakes his head. "No, then it's got to be something else. Some bullshit argument with Nic isn't enough to have her risking everything and walking in there."

My mind spins. Wolf Den. Baby? What the fuck is going on?

Maria grabs hold of Eli's shirt and pulls him right into her chest. "You have three damn seconds to tell me what the hell is going on with my daughter before I call your mother and tell her all about the things you've been getting up to, Elijah. You don't get to come into this home and throw around words like Wolf Den and baby without an explanation. Now, get talking."

Maria releases her grip on him but judging by the look in Eli's eyes, she's more than capable of making his life a living hell. He glances back at his dipshit friends before looking down at Maria with sympathy in his eyes. "I really don't want to be the one to have to explain this to you."

"The clock is ticking," she warns. "Two seconds left."

Eli looks up at me, fixing himself with a harsh scowl. "Ocean came to me this morning," he starts, making my brow raise straight up. She told me that she had to go and see someone but never in a million years did I think it was this guy. "She asked me to go to a doctor's appointment with her because she was scared."

"The fuck are you talking about?" I question as a fierce jealousy cuts through me. Why would she trust him with a doctor's appointment and not me? I would have had the fucking doctor come straight to her if she wasn't feeling well. "What doctor appointment?"

"If you fucking shut up and let me finish, maybe you will find out."

"Eli," Sebastian says. "Just tell them what's going on so we can sort this shit out."

Elijah shoots his heavy scowl at his friend but then finally sighs and looks back at Maria with his heart on his sleeve. "I'm sorry," he murmurs, his voice thick with pain. "The appointment was with an obstetrician. Ocean's pregnant."

A weight drops down on my chest as Maria sucks in a sharp gasp and turns to me in horror. "My baby," she cries before her hands start hitting against my chest. "What have you done? She's only seventeen. She's just a baby herself."

I shake my head, feeling as though I'm about to pass out. A fucking baby? Pregnant. Shit. "I … I… fuck. I'm sorry. I didn't—"

"Get off your fucking high horse," Elijah spits. "It's not your baby."

What?

Maria stops and whips her head around to Elijah just as I do, staring at him in confusion. "What?" she demands. "What are you talking about?"

Eli's face somehow breaks even more than it already was as the boys behind him grow impossibly still. That weight on my chest sinks to my gut, and an awful feeling comes over me as I wait for what I already fear to come out of Eli's mouth. "The doctor did a dating ultrasound on her," he explains, reaching out and taking Maria's hand. "She's seven weeks pregnant. That makes the father Jude Carter."

Maria's eyes go wide, and I fall against the wall of the hallway, sinking down until I collapse onto the floor. My head falls into my hands as I hear Maria's soft sobbing in the background. Sebastian pulls her into his arms as we process the news.

He fucking knocked her up. That bastard touched my girl and has now left her with scars that she's going to have to relive every fucking day. She deserves so much better than that. "How'd she end up at the Wolf Den?" I murmur, my voice strong despite how fucking weak I feel.

"That's what we don't know," Sebastian says. I pull my head out of my hands, looking up to meet his eyes, sensing there's more to this. "Eli said she looked odd after dropping him off. She said she needed to talk to you about what she was going to do and then took off, so he followed her to make sure she was safe, and instead of turning off for the highway, she turned back and pulled up outside the Wolf Den. She walked in before he could stop her."

I glance to Eli and he nods. "She was too far away. I couldn't even call out her name. If the Wolves had seen me on their territory ..."

A distasteful grunt pulls from deep within me. "So, you saved yourself instead of her?"

"It wasn't like that," Elijah snaps.

"Then what was it like?" I demand. "Because from where I'm sitting, it sure as hell seems that way."

Eli clenches his jaw, his hands balling into fists again, but Maria's soft cry steals the spotlight. "Why?" she whispers, tears gently falling down her face. "She's so strong. What would push her to do this?"

Kairo shakes his head. "That's what we don't know. We figured she must have called this rich pick in the car and he told her to fuck off."

"What?" I demand. "I'd never fucking do that to her."

They all shrug. "That's what I thought," Sebastian says. "But nothing else made sense."

I watch the three boys, scrambling for reasons, desperately trying to figure out what would push Ocean to such extremes. That's when I realize these fuckers don't have a fucking clue. "Tell me, what did Nic have to say about this?"

Their eyes scan to me, each of them narrowed and deadly. "What's it to you?"

"You said they had an argument. I'll take one fucking guess and say that you three have absolutely no idea what that argument was about."

Sebastian steps forward. "What the fuck is that supposed to mean?"

"It means that your boss, the guy who's supposed to be your friend, is a fucking liar."

Sebastian grabs me by the front of my shirt and pulls me in close. "Watch your fucking mouth."

"Then tell me, what did he say the fight was about?"

"That's none of your goddamn business."

Kairo sighs, done with this bullshit. "Nic proposed. She said no and told him to fuck off. Nothing out of the ordinary and certainly nothing that would send her running into the arms of the Wolves."

Maria shakes her head, already knowing exactly what it is that Nic did to push Ocean away. "You boys are so blind," she finally says. "You trust that man so blindly, but let me ask you this. Do you have any idea who killed my husband eight months ago?" Their brows furrow as they glance around nervously, not liking where this is going. "That's right," she continues, sensing their nervousness. "Dominic killed my Lou in cold-blood and then stood in my home, vowing to help bring his killer to justice. That's the kind of man you are serving."

Each of the Widows start shaking their heads. "No, that's not true. Nic would never do that to Ocean," Eli says. "He knows what that would have done to her. He loves her."

I scoff. "Yeah, he loves her so fucking much that he drags her down stairs and bruises her skin. He doesn't love her. He just doesn't want any other sorry bastard to have her. You know he's capable of this. You've seen him with your own fucking eyes. He killed Lou, and then he killed my father. Ocean found the fucking dagger in his room and he admitted it to her. That's what their argument was over. He came here Thursday morning, held a fucking gun to her head after she ran from him, and then demanded she choose. When she turned her back on him, he told her she was dead to him. That's why she walked into the fucking Wolf Den, and I can guarantee that she'll be doing everything she fucking can to build an army against Nic and take him out once and for all. So, when she comes asking what side you're on, you better know your answer."

They stare at me in horror as if only now just realizing how fucking serious this bullshit is going to get, but I don't have time to sit around and play the 'how fucked up is Nic' game. I have a girl to save.

I push myself to my feet and walk into my kitchen with the three Widows and Maria on my heels. I take my car keys off the counter and turn back to them. "Now, seeing as you three are here instead of at the Wolves fucking door, I'm assuming that you're too fucking pussy to fight for her. So, get out of my way, I have a girl to bring home."

"Don't be a fucking dickhead," Kairo says. "They're going to kill you on sight."

"Well," I say, raising a brow. "I'm ready to take that risk for Ocean. Are you?"

Not one of them budges, and I shake my head, disappointment raining down over me. If only Ocean knew where their priorities really stood.

With that, I walk through them, leaving them all behind with their fucking tails between their legs, knowing damn well that they won't risk their own lives to go in there and save her, despite how often they say that they will. If anyone is going to save her, it's going to be me, and I won't stop until I have her back in my arms, safe and sound. Right where she belongs.

CHAPTER 4
Ocean

I sit at the bar, sipping soda, and taking in everything around me. This place is one horror after another. It is well after seven at night, and the things I have already seen are terrifying. After the little 'meeting' that decided Nic's fate, I promptly threw up. Though honestly, the mental images of all the ways the wolves were going to end Nic had way more to do with feeling sick than this absurd pregnancy.

I need to stop this. I need to find a way out while making sure that no one gets hurt. I can circle back to revenge on Nic, but no matter what I do, they're going to attack. I gave them my father's killer without thinking. I thought maybe they would have already known.

Big. Fucking. Mistake.

With that one sentence that came out of my mouth, I sealed Nic's fate, and I don't know how to deal with that. Yes, he's an awful man, a liar, and a killer, but he's also my Nic. I thought maybe they'd go ahead with a little torture to make him feel really sorry for what he did, but not this. I never wanted to be the reason so many lives were lost, both Widows and Wolves.

What have I done?

Not only have I brought this bullshit down on Sebastian, Elijah, and Kairo, but I've also sealed my own fate. Russo will never let me go. I have a slim to none chance of getting out of this, and after the attack goes down, that slim chance will only get smaller.

Glancing around the Wolf Den, I see my future. This is my home now, not with Colton and not with the Widows.

What am I going to tell my mother? Not only do I have to tell her that my rapist got me pregnant, but I have to tell her that I came running in here without really thinking it through. All I knew was that I had to end Nic's bullshit before I brought a baby into the world.

She's never going to forgive me. She'll understand the whole baby thing even though it will destroy her, but deciding to go to Russo? Yeah, that's going to sting. She's going to feel betrayed, and she's going to hurt for the future that I won't be able to have. College and a happy, safe life with Colton? I can kiss that goodbye.

There has to be a silver lining here somewhere. I just have to find it.

I turn in my seat and watch the den around me just as I've been doing since I walked out of that meeting five hours ago. I've seen at least three fights, one that ended with a glass bottle being shattered, and a man nearly bleeding out on the ground. Judging by the way everyone just sat around and watched, I'd dare say this bullshit is a regular occurrence. The whole scene threw me back to being in that wine cellar with Jude. I was the raging lunatic with the smashed bottle in my hand, and to be honest, I really could have done without that reminder today. I've already got enough on my plate.

I've watched two men bring a girl through the doors and then get her off in the corner of the room, though thankfully, she appeared to be a willing participant. I've seen some loser with a needle, shooting himself up at the other end of the bar and then passing out twenty minutes later. But the best of all was when four guys came running through the door, each with a duffle bag, dropping them to the ground to take inventory. I don't know what they were expecting, but the stacks of cash, jewelry, and weapons seemed to surprise them.

I noticed the man who helped save me from Leon when I first got here hasn't stepped out of my sight, it's the only thing reassuring me that I might just get out of this alive. Don't get me wrong, he's not sitting beside me, and we're not playing footsies under the bar. He's keeping his distance while silently letting me know that he'll have my back if shit goes south, and I think I need that more than I could ever fully understand. I don't even know his name, but I appreciate him. I plan on making it my mission to get to know him, just not tonight.

Tonight is completely reserved for freaking out, panicking, and hating myself for making ridiculous, spur of the moment decisions.

This is my life now.

One foot out of place, and I'm a dead woman. Not to mention all the wandering eyes I've had to avoid over the past few hours. Scarface was put in his place, but new guys keep coming who have no idea who I am. It's only a matter of time before someone tries something again.

I hate the feeling of not being safe. I had everything with Colton. I should have just gone home and let him handle Nic like he said he would, but the thought of having him up against Nic makes me sick. If something was to happen to him? Fuck, I couldn't handle it. At least if one of these guys were to get hurt going against the Widows, I wouldn't feel so bad about it.

Maybe I have made the right decision …

"Here," a voice says from behind me. I swivel around in my barstool just in time to see the bartender slam a shot glass down in front of me. He instantly fills it up with a clear liquid that I'm not exactly sure I know the name of. It could be vodka or it could be fucking acid for all I know. "You look like you could use a drink. The soda you've been sipping on clearly hasn't been doing the job."

I slide the shot glass back toward him while taking in the tattoos, piercings, and scars covering his toned body. He has kind eyes, and that's the only reason why I don't throw the shot right back at him. "Can't," I tell him. "I'm seventeen and knocked up with my rapist's baby."

He sucks in a sharp breath and instantly slides the shot back toward me. "Shit. That's rough. Sounds like you need this more than you know."

My eyes drop to the glass. I'd do anything to get fucked up and forget this all happened. Yet, despite me being stupid enough to come here in the first place, I'm not stupid enough to allow myself to get fucked up around a bunch of sick, twisted men with less than honorable intentions.

"Really," I say, sliding it back again. "I can't."

"Suit yourself," he says, grabbing the shot and raising it to his lips. He throws it back and then slams the glass down on the bar again. He refills it and quickly takes another before tossing the glass over his shoulder and letting it smash against the back wall of the bar.

I can't help but stare. I don't know whether to be impressed, shocked, or scared of this guy, but for now, he's someone standing in front of me who doesn't seem all too bad, and because of that, I'm willing to give him my attention ... just not all of it.

His eyes drop to my stomach. "So," he says, grabbing some glasses and filling them with beer. "You keeping it?"

My hand automatically falls to my stomach as I feel a massive weight drop down on my shoulders. "I have no fucking idea," I tell him honestly, shrugging my shoulders and watching as he slides the beers down the bar to the men sitting at the opposite side. "I've always been pro-life. I mean, it's a fucking baby, but then at the same time ..."

"It's a rapist's baby," he says, finishing my sentence, his voice low. "Look, kid. You're only seventeen. I doubt any motherfucker is going to judge you for getting rid of it. It's not like you asked for it. You're young, you still have a shitload of living to do. You don't need to be held down by some cunt's kid."

I stare off to the wall behind him, taking in his words. I mean, he's not wrong. I didn't ask for this. If I did have this baby, I'd spend the rest of my life looking at it and remembering what happened to me. I'd never forget Jude's face because it would always be staring back at me through my child's eyes. I'd resent it for the rest of my life. But at the same time, this is an innocent baby who didn't do anything wrong. It's not it's fault that it's sperm donor is an awful man.

"To be honest," I tell the bartender. "I only found out this morning. I have no idea what I should do or what's right or wrong. I haven't even talked to my mom about this. She'll know what to do, but then, she'll probably tell me that I need to make this decision on my own, which is a load of bullshit."

"To be fair," he says, glancing up when another fight breaks out behind me. "Your mom would be right. This is your decision. It's your body, and you're the one who will have to live with it for the rest of your life."

I prop my elbows onto the bar and drop my face into my hands. "It's too much to think about. I should be freaking out about the History assignment I haven't done—which is due next week—not rapists and babies."

"Fair point," he says, leaning down on the bar and getting uncomfortably closer. "Look," he says. "I'm going to tell you something that I haven't told anyone in a while."

My brows furrow, and I take another sip of my soda, my curiosity burning within. "Go on then."

"When I was nineteen, I knocked up this chick. I met her in a bar, took her home, and fucked her until we couldn't walk. By the morning, she was gone, and I figured that was it. I'd never have to see her again. Until two months later, she came knocking on my door, claiming she was pregnant."

"What'd you do?"

"Freaked the fuck out."

I roll my eyes. "After that, dickhead."

"Look, I wasn't ready to be some kid's father, and she wasn't ready to hand over her lifestyle for breastfeeding and shitty diapers. I told her to get an abortion, but she wasn't down with that either. So, we looked into our options."

"You didn't leave her to figure it out on her own?"

"No," he says, pulling back and dropping his brows in annoyance. "That kid was my responsibility too. I was the one who knocked her up, so I was the one who needed to make sure she got out of it okay. I'm not one of those guys who just ditches a chick after getting her in trouble, like most of the fuckers in this place."

My respect for this stranger jumps up a few levels, but all I do is nod. Honestly, it's not my business to have an opinion on it. "So, what did you do?"

"We found a family that was ready."

"What do you mean? Adoption?"

"Mmhmm. A husband and wife who had been trying for a few years, having miscarriage after miscarriage. All they wanted in this world was a kid and we could give that to them with no strings attached. They paid for all the medical bills and took the responsibility off our hands. Gi had the baby seven months later, and that was it. That little boy would be twelve years old now."

"No shit?" I question, raising my brow as the idea settles into my mind, making me feel as though I'm not completely helpless.

"Yep," he says, nodding. "Take my advice or don't. It really makes no difference to me. All I'm saying is that you have options so before you start thinking that your life is over, look into them. This might feel like hell for you, but this hell could be someone else's miracle."

"Thanks," I say, glancing up at him. "That's actually … kinda helpful. What's your name?"

He nods and holds his hand out. "I'm Jaren."

I take his hand and give it a quick shake, not wanting to touch him any longer than necessary. "I'm Ocean."

"I know. You're the Widow chick. We've all heard about you around here."

I narrow my eyes at him, but murmurs and movement behind me have me spinning around to find out what the hell is going on. Everybody walks to the windows, glancing out and watching whatever the fuck is going on outside. "What's happening?" I ask, glancing back at Jaren.

He shrugs his shoulder. "Beats me."

"What's happening," Russo's deep, booming voice comes tearing through the den. "Is that it looks like you have a visitor."

"What?" I demand, throwing myself out of my chair. "Who? No

one knows I'm here."

"Well, you've been found."

Panic surges through me. Only a handful of people would be stupid enough to come here to get me, and they're all Widows. It's going to end in bloodshed, and I can't have that. I have to get rid of them.

I start surging toward the door, more than ready to tell them all to fuck off, praying to whoever exists above that this goes smoothly. "Stop right there," Russo demands. "Where the hell do you think you're going?"

I look back at him, still making my way to the door. "I'm going to get rid of them."

"I don't think so," he says, nodding to his men who instantly fall in front of the door, blocking my way. "If your boyfriend would like a minute of your time, then he will come inside."

My eyes bug out of my head. "Boyfriend?" I question, and the panic only intensifies. No, he can't be here. He'll get hurt.

I run to the door and try to barge my way through Russo's men, but it's impossible. "Move," I demand. "Get the fuck out of my way before I make you."

They laugh at my pathetic attempts, and I start looking around in a panic. What am I going to do? I don't even have my phone to call him. Russo took that from me the second I walked in here.

I hurry over to one of the many windows and barge my way to the front only to find Colton standing out front, leaning against his Veneno and staring at the Wolf Den. His arms are crossed over his chest, and he looks like the baddest kind of motherfucker around. He's lethal and terrifying and it has a thrill rushing through me, but what's more, he looks as though he's ready to wait all damn night.

Fuck. The idea of Colton coming in here? No. I can't allow that to happen. These guys won't hesitate to hurt him and attempt to drain him of every last cent he has, and only then will they finally kill him. I couldn't live if they took him away from me like that. I would never forgive myself. There are too many of them, and I can guarantee that he'd go down fighting. He'd never survive against numbers like this.

"Please," I beg, turning back to Russo. "Just let me get rid of him. I swear, I won't run. Just ... I'll make him leave."

Russo meets my eyes, and with a firm shake of his head, he walks away.

Fuck.

I look back out the window, watching as Colton pushes off his Veneno. He opens his arms out wide, daring the Wolves to make a move. "Jade," he calls, his voice loud and strong enough that it carries through to the den. It's only been a matter of hours since I saw him last. How is it possible for that one word to fill me with so much hope? "I know you're in there, baby. Come out here, and we won't have a problem."

Silence follows, and minutes slowly tick by. "I can wait all fucking night, baby girl."

Shiiiiit.

He leans back against his Veneno, knowing damn well that I'm not the reason I can't walk out that door, but he's fucking stubborn, and

I don't doubt that he'll stand by his word. I guess it's a matter of who tires of this bullshit game first.

It's impossible to tear my eyes away from him, watching as he paces back and forth, then leans back against the car. It quickly becomes a torturous routine. He'll call out, daring someone to come out and face him. He'll call for me to call off this bullshit, and then he'll pace, run his hands through his hair in frustration, and then lean, only to start all over again.

An hour quickly turns into two and then to three before Russo finally emerges from somewhere deep in the den with Snake by his side. All the other Wolves quickly got bored with the rich kid outside. One by one, they left the windows in favor of drinking out the bar. Until, eventually, I was left standing here alone to watch the guy I'm madly in love with offering himself up like a fucking buffet.

By the time Russo and Snake step into my side, my nerves are at their peak.

Snake steps in far too close, pressing his arm up against mine and leaning into the window to see Colton standing out in the dark. He shakes his head, more than annoyed by his presence. "This has gone on long enough," he growls, his voice low and spiteful as he slips his hand behind his back and pulls out a gun. "I'll get rid of him."

Fear surges through me as he pushes away from me and starts striding toward the door, then without thinking, I sprint after him. There's no way in hell this motherfucker is going anywhere near Colton with a gun. I'd sooner die.

In the blink of an eye, I fly in front of him, and before he has a chance to pull himself up, I grab his shoulders and slam my fist into his stomach as hard as I possibly can. Snake doubles over in pain, struggling to catch a breath, and as he goes down, I rip the gun from his hands and jam it up against his temple. For a moment, I forgot about the gun I stole from Leon, already tucked in the waistband of my skirt. That would have been easier, but this way, he's left without a weapon to fight back.

That's two for two. Maybe these dickheads will quickly learn not to mess with me. Though, they're all a bit dense for that.

Snake goes impossibly still, knowing I'm more than capable of pulling this trigger after the bullshit these guys pulled in that back alleyway. "If you even think of stepping out of this fucking den and going anywhere near Colton, I swear to you, I'll fucking end you right now. Trust me, you don't want to push me on this, not where he's concerned."

Snake's jaw clenches, and he glances back at Russo, probably wondering if he can disarm me quicker than I can pull the trigger. Russo meets my eye, narrowing his own, considering the situation.

"I swear," I tell him, not above begging. "I'll tell you anything you need to know or do anything you want me to do, just spare him. Let me send him away."

Russo clenches his jaw, still considering me and making the seconds tick by painfully slow. "Okay," he finally says, seeing something in me that he likes. "You have ten minutes with the boy. Snake goes with you. A second longer and Snake will put a bullet through his head. Is that understood?"

I swallow hard past the lump in my throat and nod before shoving the gun back into Snake's chest and turning on my heel, terrified of how the next ten minutes are going to go.

CHAPTER 5

Taking a breath, I push through the massive metal door of the Wolf Den and watch as Colton's head snaps up. He takes me in with wide eyes, almost as though he doesn't believe what he's seeing. Darkness covers Blaxlands Grove but, I could make out the concern in his eyes from a mile away.

He lets out a heavy sigh and pushes off the side of his car, desperate to get to me as the relief washes over him. "Fuck Jade, you—" He pulls himself up, his eyes snapping to the door as Snake follows me out. "Jade?" he questions, his voice low and full of warning as he continues to move toward me, now at a cautious creep. "What the fuck is going on?"

Knowing Snake won't attempt to do anything until my ten minutes is up, I make my way toward Colton. The second he can, he pulls me into his arms and instantly starts dragging me toward his car. "No, stop," I tell him, trying to pull back. "You can't be here."

"What the fuck are you doing? I need to get you out of here," he murmurs low, gripping my arm tightly. As he pulls me towards his Veneno, he keeps me right by his side, more than ready to pick my ass up and toss me in if that's what it comes down to.

"You can't," I insist, speaking through my teeth to try and keep our conversation private. "If you try to take me, Snake will kill you. Just please, you have to go."

Colton finally stops tugging at me as we step in beside his car, and he glances up at Snake, watching him cautiously. "What are you doing, Jade? Just get in the fucking car, we can sort this out later. I'm not about to leave you here."

"You have to. I walked in here and gave them my word. If I go back on that ... just please, Colton. You don't understand. I know you hate this but, you have to trust me."

"Trust you?" he questions, taking my shoulders and giving them a tight squeeze, silently letting me know how badly this is killing him. "Are you insane? You just walked straight into the fucking Wolf Den without even thinking about it. Forgive me, but trusting you isn't exactly high on my list of priorities right now."

"I know," I murmur, reaching up and taking hold of his hands on my shoulders. "I'm sorry, okay? I'm just ... I don't even know. I haven't had a chance to really process everything that's going on, but I swear,

I'm safe here. They need the information that I have, and they know that if I was to get hurt, I'd never give it up."

"Babe," he groans with pain in his eyes. "Please just get in the fucking car. We can sort it out later, just let me take you away from here. You don't belong here."

"It's too late," I tell him. "The second I stepped over the threshold, I accepted my place as a Wolf. I'm one of them now, and there's no going back. If you try to take me away, they'll see it as an attack against them, and they won't hesitate to come at you." I step in closer to him, needing to feel his body close to mine. "I'll never forgive myself if you were to get hurt because of my bullshit drama."

"Hurt?" he scoffs. "If getting hurt is what it takes to get you free from all of this, then I'll fucking do it. I'd give it all up, Jade. I fucking love you and seeing you here … you don't fucking belong here. You belong with me."

I shake my head, willing my eyes not to fill with tears. "I can't," I tell him. "I'm sorry. You wouldn't understand. Too much has changed. A lot has gone down today and I haven't even had a chance to process it all but if you knew what was going on, I promise, it would all make sense. You just need to trust that I'm doing the right thing despite how fucking crazy it sounds. Believe me, if I could have settled this any other way, I would have."

Colton's hands run down my arms and over my body until they come to a stop at my waist. He meets my eyes, holding me close. "I know about the baby, Ocean," he finally tells me his tone filled with the deepest kind of agony.

My eyes bug out of my head as I study him in horror, feeling my world begin to crumble around me. How could he know but more importantly, what could he possibly think of me now? I'm tainted, used, and abused. "What? How do you … I haven't …"

"I know," he says, his thumbs moving back and forth over my waist. "Eli, Sebastian, and Kairo came to see me today. Eli told me."

Betrayal slices right through me. That dickhead promised he wouldn't say a word. He hovered just outside my car door and gave me his word that he wouldn't say a damn thing, but apparently, the promise of his word doesn't hold the same kind of weight that it used to.

"Don't," Colton says, cutting off whatever bullshit was about to come flying out of my mouth. "He was worried about you. They all are. He followed you after your appointment this morning. He said you were acting strange, and he wanted to check that you were going to get home alright, but you made a stop that he wasn't expecting."

Fear races through me. "They know I'm here?" I question, knowing damn well that if they know I'm here, then Nic would know, and if anyone was able to figure out why I'd come, it'd be him, which means that we're all in trouble.

He presses his lips into a tight line and nods. "Yeah," he murmurs. "Eli saw you walk in there, but before he could do anything about it, it was already too late. That's why they came to me. They assumed that you must have told me about the baby and I didn't take it well. They're pissed, babe."

"I … I don't even know what to say," I whisper, struggling to meet his eyes as I try to come to terms with the fact that Nic could potentially know that I'm plotting against him. "Why aren't you running? I'm pregnant. Normal eighteen-year-old guys would be running so damn fast, especially when it's not their kid."

"If you think I'm the kind of guy to run away when things get hard, you don't know me very well," he says, offended. "I get it, and yeah, it's probably going to take a while to wrap my head around, but I want you in my life. If that means playing the role of baby daddy to your kid just to keep you by my side, then I'll do it."

I pull back and stare at him in shock. I surely didn't hear him right. I could have sworn that he just said that he'll be the father of my baby, despite knowing that this child's biological father is a rapist. "You'd do that?"

"I'd do just about anything if it meant hanging onto you."

A fat tear rolls over my cheek and drops off my chin, splashing onto my white school blouse. I can't find the words to tell him how much his admission means to me, but I don't have to, he gets it. He tugs me into his body, and he holds me with everything he's got. His big hands claim my skin and make me feel alive for the first time since peeing on that damn stick this morning.

"It doesn't make sense to me, Jade. Why'd you come here?" Colton asks after a moment of silence, making me realize that I was standing in his arms far too long. The minutes are quickly counting down, and I don't doubt that Snake wouldn't hesitate to take Colton out. In fact, he'd probably enjoy it just to spite me.

I run my tongue over my very suddenly dry lips. "It's Nic,"

I explain. "I don't know what came over me, but after my doctor's appointment this morning, a fierce protectiveness for this baby just settled inside of me. I realized that I can't bring a baby into this world while I'm still at war with Nic. He would use the baby against me, and I can't allow that to happen."

I let out a heavy sigh and meet his eyes, knowing how much the fact that I'm currently pregnant with someone else's child must be hurting him. "This baby is innocent. It didn't ask for any of this, and while we're on the topic, you need to know that I didn't purposefully keep this from you. I only found out this morning, and I was freaking out. I didn't want to tell you until I knew for sure, so I went to the doctor's appointment with Eli, and he told me that I was seven weeks along, making it Jude's baby. I just … I couldn't think clearly after that. My head is literally a mess. I don't know what to do, if I'm going to keep it or what my options are. But, I know that I have a responsibility to keep this baby safe until I can finally make that decision, and having Nic against me is not safe. I have to end this, Colton, and I have to do it without bringing you into it either."

He shakes his head. "Jade, no. What were you thinking? I told you that I could handle Nic. Call this shit off, and let me take you home. I swear to you, Jade, I'll handle this, and you'll never have to think about him again. I won't let him get away with it."

I clench my jaw and just as I'm about to explain myself a little more, Snake's deep, rumbly tone carries across the gravel drive. "Two minutes," he warns, making a show of already having his gun out and ready to go.

I take Colton's hands and squeeze. "I wish I could," I tell him, letting out a heavy breath and wishing that I was anywhere but here. "Thinking that they already knew, I said that Nic was the one who killed my father, and it all spiraled out of control from there. They want me to hand over every little bit of information that I have on Nic and the boys, and then they're going to go to war. I told them that's not what I wanted but it's too late. I fucked up. I should have trusted you, but I hated the idea of you getting hurt in all this. Eli, Sebastian, and Kai are going to hate me when they find out what I've done."

"They'll be fine," he says, his tone filled with distaste. "Don't worry about them. We just need to worry about getting you the fuck out of here."

I shake my head, lowering my eyes to his chest. "Nic is never going to let this go."

"I know," he murmurs. "Which is exactly why you need to let me handle it. You're too close to this, to them. You're—"

"Colton, please," I say, looking up and meeting his concerned stare. "I need you to go."

"I … no. No way in hell. I'm not leaving you here."

"Please," I beg, allowing him to see my desperation. "They're going to kill you if I can't make you go, and without you … I just … I can't. Please, just trust me to sort this out. I'll come home as soon as I can."

"Jade," he whispers, pulling me in again. "I can't leave you here."

"You have to."

He stares at me in horror as though I'm asking him to do the impossible. I press up onto my tippy-toes and brush my lips across his.

"I love you, Colton. I promise you, when all of this is over, I will come home. I won't let them break me."

"You know that I can't just stand back and let you do this."

"You have to," I whisper. "It's already done. I'm a Wolf now."

I step back out of his arms, and despite it only being a small space between us, I've never felt so far away. I take another step. "Babe, don't."

"I'm sorry," I whisper.

He groans, the frustration quickly taking over. He takes a step toward me, and I instantly step back again. "Fuck, Jade, please. Don't do this." He rakes his hands through his hair, and I see the exact moment where he fears he's losing me, but he should know better, that would never happen.

I take another step, and he holds his hands out, fearing that I'm going to go before he gets a chance to say everything he needs to say. "Wait, don't go yet. Just … call me back, okay? We can talk about this."

I shake my head. "I can't. Russo took my phone the second I walked in there. I haven't been able to call anyone."

He slips his hand into his pocket and glances over my shoulder at Snake. With his attention elsewhere, Colton quickly tosses me his phone. "Keep this on you and turn it to silent. Call me the second you can and we'll work something out. I'm not just going to give you up like this."

"Thirty seconds," Snake threatens, making a show of playing with his gun. "Please, draw this out. I fucking dare you."

Fuck.

I back up another few steps. "Please, Colton. Just get in your car and go. They won't hurt me. I have a gun, and you know that I'm capable of protecting myself. I'll be okay. I promise."

He looks up at me, completely helpless, and as Snake pushes off the brick wall of the den, Colton lets out a sigh, his chances of getting me out of here quickly dwindling to nothing. "I fucking hate this," he tells me, keeping a cautious eye on Snake.

"I know," I murmur. "I'm sorry."

With absolutely no choice left, he walks around to the driver's side of his Veneno and watches me over the top of his car. Pain and heartache shine in his hazel eyes. "I'm going to fix this," he promises me as the suicide door opens. "Mark my fucking words, Jade. I'll fix this."

"I know you will," I tell him, needing to give him that tiny bit of hope to keep him going. "I love you."

He clenches his jaw, and then just as Snake steps in beside me with his gun on display and a sick smirk on his lip, Colton tears me to pieces and drops down into his Veneno. The engine roars to life, and within a split second, he takes off up the road, his tires screeching along the tar.

"Well, well," Snake says. "I don't know whether you're too brave for your own good or just fucking stupid. You know he's never going to get you out of here, right? Once a Wolf, always a fucking Wolf."

I clench my jaw and turn away, stalking back to the door, all while Snake's booming laughter follows behind. "This is going to be fun."

CHAPTER 6

Snake pushes me through the door with his gun pressed against my back, forcing me to move my feet faster than they can naturally go. I get over the threshold, narrowly avoiding throwing my elbow back into his junk. Now that I'm in and Colton is well and truly gone, I won't be holding back.

I spin around so fast that he flinches, and I instantly knock his gun to the side, only being able to get one up on him out of sheer surprise. "Are you about done?" I demand, getting in his face. "You're a real big man waving your gun around every thirty seconds. I wonder how fucking tough you are without it."

His jaw clenches, and he doesn't hesitate to step in closer, lowering his voice to appear intimidating. But after having to send Colton away, I'm more than ready to take down dickheads like this. "Those are some real big words for a bitch in your position."

"Who's the fucking bitch around here?" I laugh. "I've been here for less than ten hours and can already tell that you're Russo's 'yes man.' Tell me, does it hurt being shoved so far up his ass?"

He growls, and I can practically see the steam puffing from his ears like some ridiculous animation. "You're going to regret ever walking in here."

"Why? You think you can hurt me? You think I'll ever give you that kind of power over me? Keep dreaming. While you lay awake tonight, thinking of all the ways you could get to me, I'll be sleeping like a fucking baby."

I laugh as I turn on my heel and walk away, straight back to the bar to where Jaren is busy filling glass after glass.

Snake remains behind me and luckily keeps his distance. He stalks off, pissed that the pregnant seventeen-year-old has probably seen more shit than he has.

Jaren turns back and eyes me curiously. "Are you okay, kid? Was that your boyfriend?" he questions, watching me over his shoulder as he effortlessly continues to work.

"Yeah, I'll be fine," I say, shrugging it off and feeling Colton's phone vibrating over and over again against my left tit as it remains squished inside my bra.

"Just keep your head up around here," he warns me. "You're welcome at my bar anytime, but this isn't the place you want to come to lose yourself. Keep your wits about you."

"I will," I tell him, straightening my back and trying to figure out his meaning, but it's completely lost on me. What's he trying to tell me? That if I turn my back for one second that someone is going to try and hurt me?

He gets back to work, and twenty minutes later, a plate slides down on the bar in front of me. "Eat," comes a low, intimidating voice from behind. I whip my head over my shoulder to find the guy who had helped save me from Scarface settling into the vacant barstool beside me.

He drops down and silently places his own plate on the bar. He gets comfortable and not a second later, digs into his meal.

I gape in confusion. What the hell is this about?

"Eat your fucking food, Oceania," he warns, pointing at my plate with his knife. "You're pregnant, and you haven't eaten a single thing since you got here. It's not good for the baby."

I raise a brow, unable to stop staring at this over-protective stranger. "Who are you?"

He lets out a sigh and focuses back on his plate. "Eat."

I glance down at the food, assuming I can trust him. My stomach constantly grumbles, taking in the steak and veggies that have been thrown together on the plate. It's definitely not restaurant-worthy, but it smells damn good and has me reaching for my knife and fork.

I dig in, and the second my fork hits my tongue, I groan in satisfaction. I should have eaten hours ago, but my day has been an absolute mess. Seeing that I'm being a good little girl and doing as

I'm told, the perfect stranger beside me lets out a relieved sigh. "I'm Christian," he mutters into his plate.

I glance over at him while forking another bite into my mouth. "Um … well, thanks. You know, for this and for before." He nods and gets back to eating, but I'm not quite done yet. "I'm Ocean."

"I know," he says. "You're the princess of Breakers Flats and Bellevue Springs. Even before you walked your stupid ass in here, we've all known who you were. We've been watching you since you were just a little girl."

My brows drop. "What? What do you mean?"

"You're Big Lou's baby girl. It was our job to keep you safe, and then Nic and his friends moved into your life, and you became a priority."

I stare, my mouth hanging open in surprise. "You've been watching me for that long?"

"Mmhmm. I know it doesn't seem like it, but we're family here. When it comes down to it, we have your back."

I scoff and start working on my dinner again. "I'll believe that when I see it."

Christian nods, knowing that was a fair call. "You'll understand soon enough. There's a lot to learn about being a Wolf."

"You mean, figuring out the best method to hide your joint up your ass before getting strip-searched and frisked?"

A smirk pulls at his lips, and he shakes his head in amusement. "Just stick with me, and you'll be alright."

I can't take my eyes off him as he focuses on his dinner. "Why are you being so nice to me? No one else around here gives a shit about me except for maybe Jaren, but I think he's just talking to me out of boredom."

"Probably," Christian agrees before taking a deep breath. "Look," he starts. "Don't take this the wrong way, but for some fucking reason, I feel very protective of you." I gape at him, but luckily he continues before I can think anything else of it. "You remind me of someone I used to know."

"*Used* to know?" I question, suddenly a little more intrigued by this mystery man.

He nods. "My little sister, Roni. She's about five years older than you."

"Why do I get the feeling that this isn't a good story?"

"Oh, it is," he tells me. "It's the best story. She's living the dream and did the impossible, but doing the impossible means that she can't be in my life."

There's pain in Christian's voice, and it has me leaning in, more desperate to know about this sister of his and how the hell she managed to pull off getting out of Blaxlands Grove. Doing that is just as hard as escaping Breakers Flats. I got lucky by moving to Bellevue Springs with Mom. But even living two hours away, I'm still attached to this place and unable to completely break free. If Colton was smart, he'd ditch me and go and find himself a girl that isn't going to drag him down like this. He deserves so much better, but unfortunately for him, I'm a selfish bitch and won't ever let go of him.

"What happened to her?" I question, hoping I'm not crossing

some invisible line.

He looks over at me and gives me a tight smile. "She was always so smart. She didn't belong here like the rest of us. I don't know where she got them from, but she had brains like I've never seen before. She was too kind for this place. She needed to be somewhere that wouldn't destroy her. So, after she graduated high school, I gave her my car and every cent I had to my name, and I told her to drive until she found a place that would accept her."

My brows shoot up. "You just let her leave?"

He nods. "Sometimes, when you love something, you have to let it go in order for it to shine to its best potential, and that's exactly what she did."

"What do you mean?"

"She got herself a job and worked her ass off for four years while she put herself through college. I can't say that I really loved that part. She was working at Hooters for three years, and it drove me insane, but she suffered through it like a fucking boss. She rented this shitty little apartment with a few girls, and they supported each other all the way through to graduation when she came out top of her class."

"Wow," I say in awe, thinking of my own acceptance letter sitting on the kitchen counter in Colton's pool house. "Girls from around here hardly ever get into college, let alone graduate at the top."

"I know," he says, pride shining brightly in his eyes. "She did amazing. I stood in the back and watched her accept her diploma. It was the best moment of my life. She made it."

"That's amazing," I whisper as an agonizing jealousy tears through me. I was so close to having a future like that. I glance down at my plate, assuming I can trust him. "What happened after that?"

"She worked her way up. Last I checked, she was working as a school guidance counselor in one of those rich, private schools."

Rich, private schools? "Wait," I say, scrunching my brows and staring at him as though he just grew a second head. "Did you say Hooters?"

"Umm … yeah," he says slowly, his eyes narrowing to slits.

"You're not talking about Miss Davies, are you? The guidance counselor at Bellevue Springs Private school?"

He pulls back ever so slightly, watching me with caution. "Yeah. You know her?"

My eyes go big as excitement tears through me. "Holy shit," I laugh. "Yes, I freaking know her. I'm a student at her school. She's the reason that I got into college. She pushed me to be better because she didn't want to see another girl from Breakers Flats with the same, boring generic life. She's the first person to have believed in me in a really long time."

"No shit?" he questions, a proud as fuck smile stretching across his face.

"Yeah, she told me all about you. You're the brother who got jumped in so she wouldn't have to."

He nods. "Damn fucking straight, I am," he says, leaning back into the barstool as though he can hardly believe what he's hearing. "How was she? Did she look alright? I haven't checked in with her for a while."

"She's doing great," I tell him. "Super cocky about being the one girl who made it out of Blaxlands Grove, though I think she was putting it on just so I'd want to be better. She told me that she bought her own house."

His brows shoot up, and he laughs as the pride begins to overwhelm him. "No fucking way," he says, shaking his head in disbelief. "She really fucking made it."

"She did, and it's all thanks to you. Now she's helping other girls that were in her situation do the same. She turned my life around at least, for a while she had, and because of her, I was actually looking forward to my future. You know, until now."

"I'm glad to hear that," he tells me, moving straight past my last comment. "What's her situation? Does she have a boyfriend? Married?"

"I don't know," I say with a shrug. "I didn't see any ring on her finger, but that doesn't mean that she doesn't have someone." He nods, lost in thought. "When was the last time you checked in with her?"

"It's been a while," he tells me. "Maybe two years. I try to keep my distance. The less I'm in her life, the less reason she has to come back."

"I get that, but don't you think that—"

"Ocean," Russo's deep, booming voice calls across the bar. My head whips his way as Christian presses his lips into a tight, disapproving line. "With me, now."

I swallow back fear, hating the uncertainty. What does he want with me? I hesitate for a moment before Christian nods, silently telling me that it's not wise to keep him waiting. I scoop my drink off the bar and start following Russo out of the bar when Christian calls back to me. "Ocean," he says. I glance back to find his eyes on mine before he mouths, "Lock your door."

I nod, letting him know that I've understood him and consider running for the door when Russo snaps at me. "Keep up. Your boyfriend's pathetic little pissing contest has already wasted enough of my time tonight. There will be consequences for any more lost time."

Fuck.

I hurry to keep up with him and follow him through a maze of doors until we come to a long hallway. "These are the living quarters," Russo explains. "These are for Wolves who find themselves without a place to sleep."

"I already have a place to sleep," I remind him. "And it's in Bellevue Springs."

"I appreciate that," he tells me. "But until I can be sure that you're not about to go running back to Dominic or his friends, here is where you'll stay."

"But what about school? I go to school in Bellevue Springs. I can't go all the way there and back every day. That's insane."

Russo presses his lips into a tight line. "Well then, you better gain my trust fast."

He comes to a stop outside a bedroom door and slips a key into the lock. He gives it a quick jiggle before finally getting it unlocked and pushing the door wide. "I suggest you get a good night's sleep tonight. You have a lot of talking to do tomorrow."

With that, he hands me the key and leaves me to fend for myself.

I step over the threshold into the dark room, feeling around on the wall for the light switch. After what feels like far too long, I get the light on, and the room floods with a dull brightness. I instantly close the door behind me and lock it, just as Christian had said.

I start looking around the small room. There's a single bed with sheets that look used, a dresser that's missing its handles, and a single bedside table with a shitty lamp. It's like a cell in here.

There's a small bathroom attached to the room, and I'm honestly terrified of walking in there, but I haven't peed since the doctor's office this morning. After sitting at the bar all day, I'm getting a little desperate.

I start making my way toward the bathroom door when I hear someone walking toward my door. Panic settles into my soul—deep and terrifying. Without thinking, I throw myself across the room and shove my shoulder into the dresser. I push it hard, over and over again until the heavy wooden piece of shit is firmly in front of the door. Then just to ease my fear, I pull Scarface's gun from the back of my school skirt.

I find myself standing still, listening out as the footsteps come closer. My heart races and my palms begin to sweat.

When I came here, I never imagined that I'd have to stay the night. There are a lot of things that I can deal with. But being caught alone in a warehouse full of predators is not exactly something a normal seventeen-year-old is experienced with.

The footsteps sound right outside my door, and I hardly hear them over the sound of my pulse beating right in my eardrum. There's a short pause before the footsteps pick up again and continue down the hall.

The relief is so heavy that I fall to my knees, still clutching the gun tightly in my hand.

Seconds turn into minutes and by the time half an hour has ticked by, I can finally breathe easy and remember my desperation for the toilet.

I get myself sorted out, and a few moments later, I sit on the floor, too disgusted to go anywhere near the bed. I pull out Colton's phone and quickly put in his passcode before staring down at the screen. There are a million missed calls, and I don't doubt that they're all from Colton.

Knowing that when I call him back, he's going to refuse to hang up, I go through the messages and realize that Colton must have told Eli, Sebastian, and Kai, that I have his phone. I can guarantee the unread messages from them on Colton's phone are certainly not for him.

I open up the messages from Eli.

Elijah - Ocean, I'm so fucking sorry. I failed you. What did you think you were doing walking in there?

Elijah - Please answer me, girl.

Elijah - You fucking hate me, don't you? I told them all that you're pregnant. I'm sorry, I had no fucking choice. I had to break my promise. They needed to understand why you went there.

Letting out a sigh, I move onto Kai.

Kairo - You should have come to me. If you were hurting or

needed help, I would have been there. Not them. Do you have any idea what kind of trouble you've just gotten yourself in?

Kairo - I know you got that rich boy's phone. Don't act like you haven't got my message.

Kairo - Fuck, Ocean. Just tell me that you're still fucking breathing.

My jaw clenches as I read over his texts twice and then three times. If only he knew what Nic had really done. I wonder if he'd change his tone. Surely he must know that after everything we've been through over the past few months, coming to them is just not an option anymore.

Not wanting to linger on it, I move along.

Sebastian - I don't even know what to say to you. I want to hate you for going to them. I've never felt so fucking betrayed by you, but at the same time, you're hurting. I don't know how to help you. Eli told us about the baby, and I swear, if you decide to keep it, I'll be there. I'll do whatever you need. Just don't shut me out.

Sebastian - I love you, Ocean. We all do. Please come home.

His text has a tear coming to my eye, and I want to hate him for it. How is he so good at getting me right where it hurts? Sebastian knows me too damn well.

Needing to get this over and done with, I create a group text with all three of them and start hashing out a response.

Ocean - I'm sorry. I know you're all hurting and can't understand why I came to the Wolves. Please know that I love

you all and would never intentionally try to hurt you, but I'm out of options. If only you knew the full story, knew what I knew … then you might understand. I never intended to hurt you guys. You're always my family, and I hope that one day you'll be able to forgive me for this, but I stand by my decision. I have to see this through. I have to end this. Not only for my sake, but for yours and Colton's, but most of all, for my baby.

Taking a deep breath, I hit send and watch as the message shoots up the screen.

Fear rattles me as I watch the little notification, telling me that each of them has received the message and are reading it, but I don't linger on it. I exit out of the messages app and bring up the number that Colton had been calling me on.

I put the phone to my ear, and as I curl into a shivering ball on the floor, I listen as the phone rings.

"Jade," Colton rushes out, barely allowing the phone to complete a whole ring before answering. "Are you okay? Are you coming home?"

"No," I murmur, trying to keep my voice low so that I don't alert the rest of the den to the fact that I'm alone in a bedroom with minimal exits. "I have to stay here for a while. He won't let me go until I've earned his trust. He thinks I'll run back to the Widows if I leave."

"That's fucking bullshit. Doesn't he know what happened? As if you'd ever go back there."

"I know, but they've been watching me for years. They know how close I am with the boys."

"Really? How close are you? Because this morning when I said that I was coming after you, not one of them was willing to come with me. They were too caught up with the possibility that they'd get a bullet through their head. But they should know that if they ever fail to fight for you like that again, that the bullet will be delivered by me."

"No," I argue, knowing that couldn't be true. "If given the chance, they would have come for me. I know they would have."

"I'm sorry, Jade, but they didn't."

Pain tears through me at the thought that they wouldn't risk coming in here for me after all the times that they've told me that they had my back. "Not even Sebastian?"

"Not even him."

A tightness constricts around my chest, squeezing until it's nearly impossible to breathe. I guess they've chosen their side in all of this, but they don't know what Nic did. They probably thought I came here because of the baby, and they just don't understand.

I let out a sigh, not wanting to focus on it any longer. "Tell me that I made the right decision."

"I can't do that, Ocean."

"Then tell me something else."

"I love you, no matter what. I'm so fucking angry with you right now, and although I understand why you went to Russo, I can't accept it."

"I stand by what I did, Colton. I have to. This can't all be for nothing. Nic killed our fathers, and despite the fact that they were both really shitty men, he took something from us, and I have to make this right. Nic won't stop until I'm gone. I turned my back on him, and he'll never be able to forgive that, but I'll never be able to forgive myself if I let you get involved and you ended up hurt or worse."

"I get it, Jade. I understand why you did it, I just don't like it. I wish you'd have come to me first."

"I know," I whisper as a yawn pulls from deep within me. "I'm kinda wishing that now too."

"Are you safe?"

"I don't know," I tell him honestly. "I'm in a bedroom, but I've locked the door and put the dresser in front of it just in case. I also stole some douchebags gun, so there's that. I just … I have a bad feeling."

"I know, baby. Me too," he murmurs. "Why don't you try to get some sleep?"

"I doubt I'll get any sleep here tonight."

"You need to try," he tells me. "You don't know when you'll need your energy. I'll stay on the line with you until you fall asleep."

I nod and somehow feel just a bit safer, more content with my fucked up situation. "I love you," I tell him. "I promise, I'll come home as soon as I can."

"I know you will," Colton murmurs. "I love you too. Now go to sleep and dream about me."

With that, the room becomes all too silent. I listen to his soft breathing as he types away on his computer, hopefully searching for something we can use to get me out of here or at least something to keep me safe.

CHAPTER 7

Saturday morning comes all too soon and quickly morphs into Sunday. Colton's phone died on Friday night as I shivered on the cold floor, making myself sick. It was worth it to hear his voice through the night though, soothing me and telling me that it was all going to be okay, but I admit, when the phone died and his voice cut out, I'd never felt more alone.

I'm not going to lie, while his voice certainly eased me, it didn't help. I didn't get a wink of sleep, and I sure as hell didn't get any last night either. I heard drunk morons outside my door all through the night, trying to entice me to let them in. The door handle has jiggled a total of seven times over the last two nights, and I can guarantee that it wasn't someone showing up to check on my well being.

I stayed in my room all Saturday, refusing to exit. For a while, I wondered if I was playing hostage, or if I was really a part of this bullshit 'family.' Christian came by with lunch and dinner but didn't stay. Jaren slipped a few old books under the door, all of which were non-fiction and not exactly to my taste. Though, I highly doubt a place like this has a library filled with all my favorite authors.

I'm surprised that I haven't had Colton trying to bust down the doors. I'm sure he's worried after not having heard from me since Friday night, but it's my mom that I should really be worried about. She is probably losing her mind and thinking the worst.

My stomach grumbles and I curse it out. Why do I have to have basic human needs? Hiding out in this room would be so much easier if I didn't have to eat and drink.

Peering out of the cracked door, I find the hallway clear and swallow back fear. I can do this. I sat out there all day on Friday, and I survived. Yesterday was terrible being locked in that room, I can't do it again. I'll go insane.

I step out of my room and make sure to pull the door closed behind me then lock it. After all, if I get thrown in there again tonight, I don't want to find any little surprises waiting for me. Keeping Scarface's gun firmly in my hand, I begin making my way down the hall, hoping that I don't take a wrong turn and make an even bigger mistake.

The hallway is dark, with the majority of the fluorescent lights above either smashed or blown. No windows are lighting the way, and I'm left to follow the sound coming from the main part of the building.

After two wrong turns, I finally find where I need to be and follow the smell of food only to find Jaren sitting up at the bar with two plates. I eye the plate and lick my lips, the hunger begging to send me crazy. "Ah, there she is," Jaren says to himself, sliding the plate toward me and making me sigh in relief. If that had been someone else's lunch, I'm pretty sure I would have shot someone. "Sit your ass down and eat."

I warily glance around and take note of the people around me, take in the eyes on my body and figure out who among these people would be a threat. For the record, it's nearly all of them.

My survival instincts kick in, and I hesitantly slide in beside Jaren, keeping myself extremely aware. "I don't see Christian anywhere," I comment, grabbing my fork and looking over the massive bowl of spaghetti. I barely know the guy, but he very quickly became one of my only allies in this place. Without him here, I feel vulnerable, and I don't like it.

"He's out on a job," Jaren says, glancing across at me and giving me that one explanation that I've been looking for. Why the hell didn't he come and deliver me food like he'd done yesterday? I guess that's settled, though I don't know why I suddenly felt entitled to that from him. He was only doing me a kindness yesterday. It's not as though it's his job to make me feel at home in this dump. "Why? Have you got a bit of a crush on the guy?"

My eyes bug out of my head, and I gape at Jaren as though he just told me that he fucks pineapples on his days off. "What? No."

"Hey, no judgment. I just think maybe he's a little old for you and no offense, but don't you have a little much going on right now? Besides, I doubt Christian would be down for raising some other cunt's kid."

I stare at him for a moment before dropping my gaze down to my lunch. "You're insane if you think I'm into him. I just like having him around because he seems like one of the only people in this place who aren't looking to fuck me over."

"Good point," Jaren laughs. "Christian is a good guy but be careful, he's fucking lethal when he needs to be."

I think of the story he told me about his sister on Friday and realize that he's right. I've been around guys like Christian all my life, and I don't doubt that there's absolutely nothing he wouldn't do when it came down to protecting someone he loves.

I nod, silently letting him know that I understand his warning to be careful, but for some reason, I don't think it applies to me. I get the feeling that I'm one of those people that he'd do anything to protect … At least, I think I am. Maybe that's stupid to think like that. I only met the guy on Friday. How can I rationally expect him to be on my side?

I keep my mind busy with thoughts while I eat my lunch, being grateful for Jaren's silence beside me. I can't say that I've met many bartenders in my life, but the few that I have always seem to know when to put their two cents into a conversation and when to keep quiet. I've honestly never appreciated that trait more in my life.

I'm busy scraping up the last bits of my lunch when Russo appears at my side. "I thought you might have run off when no one saw you yesterday."

"Can't get rid of me that quickly," I tell him, feigning confidence. "You promised me payback, and I need to make sure that you come through."

He raises a brow. "Do you assume that my word is not trustworthy?"

I slide my empty bowl away and look Russo right in the eye. "In all fairness, the first time I met you, you branded me while I screamed to be released. I don't trust easily, and so far, you've done nothing to earn my trust or prove that your word has any weight."

Russo leans against the bar, studying me with curiosity. "You have balls for a chick your age," he tells me. "But those balls will get you in trouble one day."

I wave my hand around the Wolf Den. "Take a look around you," I tell him. "My balls have already got me in trouble."

Russo laughs, and the sound is chilling. "Fair point," he tells me. "You want to know if my word is trustworthy, then now's your shot. I'll make a deal with you."

I narrow my gaze, not trusting him one bit. "What kind of deal?"

"I'm assuming that you'd like to go home at some point and attend school. Is that still the case?"

"More so than ever."

"Alright. You tell me everything I need to know, and I'll allow you to go home tonight."

I watch him for a moment. "What's the catch?"

"No catch. You'll be watched just as you were before, and you'll be expected to abide by the terms you agreed to when you first walked into my Den. You are a Wolf, and that must always come first. So as long as you can live with that, then you're free to come and go as you please."

I slip off the barstool and quickly glance at Jaren, who nods, insisting that this is as good as it's going to get. "And all I have to do is give you everything you want on Nic?"

"Correct."

"Haven't I already given you everything you needed on Friday?"

"Yes, you gave me everything I needed, but now there's all the stuff that I *want*."

Understanding dawns. He wants me to completely give him up. Tell him every little piece of information that I have on Nic so that when they take him down, he stays down. Nic will never be able to crawl his way back up after Russo is through with him, and as I think over everything that I've lost because of Dominic Garcia, I find myself holding out my hand.

Russo takes my hand with a firm grip and shakes it. "You have yourself a deal."

Two hours later, I stand in Russo's office, watching as he unlocks a desk drawer while feeling like a complete bitch. I told him everything he asked for; Nic's birth date, his mother's name, Nic's address, his family pet as a kid. Every last thing was shared, and I feel completely sick about it, but in the end, Nic killed my father. He lied, he cheated, he tore me to shreds, and I hate that I've had to go against my morals to make this happen, but Nic needs to be stopped. Despite what Colton says, this is out of our league.

Colton thinks that fire is fought with fire, but in reality, all that's going to do is make us burn. If you want to beat fire, you need water, and you need to drown the motherfucker until it can't possibly ignite again.

Russo gets the drawer unlocked, and as he pulls it open, I find my phone, car keys, and everything he'd taken from me when I first walked in here. "If you run ..." he warns, leaving his threat wide open as he takes my things from the drawer.

"I know," I tell him, resisting rolling my eyes, but what can I say? 48-hours with no sleep tends to bring out my inner bitch. "Your guys are watching me."

He nods and hands over my things. "Keep your phone on you," he tells me in that same warning tone. "I'll be checking in on you."

I nod, and he finally hands over my freedom, and without a backward glance, I all but run from his office.

I keep Scarface's gun in my hand and barge through the throng of Wolves, knowing that what I did here really sucked, while also knowing that in the end, Nic is going to get what's coming for him. He has too many contacts within the justice system, and this was my last option. I'm not going to pretend that I know what Russo is going to do, but I know that it will make up for his crimes. Whatever happens to him now, it's in Russo's hands. I just have to hope that Nic doesn't come for me in the meantime.

I beeline for the front door but keep my eyes on Jaren, giving him a nod as I pass. I don't feel like we're friends, but I also don't feel like we hate each other. Allies? Maybe, but all that matters is that when I get out of here, and Christian comes back from his run tonight, I trust that Jaren will let him know what's been going on.

I don't know why I feel that connection to Christian, but I feel like I've somehow taken on the role of his new little sister. It's almost like he's using me to fill the void that Miss Davies left when she escaped this town, and for some reason unknown to me, I'm kinda happy about it.

I break out through the door, and my feet take me faster than I could ever imagine. The Audi has been moved, and for a fleeting second, panic surges through me until I notice a small parking lot off to the side.

Relief settles through me, and I race toward it, hoping to god that nothing has happened to it. Around here, when someone sees a nice car, it doesn't take long for them to decide that it's theirs to do with as they please, but I guess being a Wolf has its advantages. Anyone would be stupid to steal a car from this lot.

I unlock the Audi in record time and start the engine before my ass has even hit the seat. I reverse out of there, and within moments, I'm flying down the very highway that I should have taken Friday morning instead of stopping here, but as it is, I can't bring myself to regret my decision even though I know I should. I just hope the other Widows are left out of it.

After half an hour of driving, I calm myself enough to realize that in the center console, there's a phone charger, and I let out a soft sigh. Why didn't I realize that sooner? Of course there's one in here. Colton wouldn't have it any other way.

I feel around on the passenger's seat for my discarded phone when

I come back with Colton's. I know I should probably charge mine and figure out what I've missed out on, but the curiosity of the boy's responses to my message on Friday night has been sitting heavy on my heart. I never got a chance to read them after speaking to Colton, but a part of me was grateful.

I've been fearing their responses because I know they're going to hurt if they were to turn their backs on me.

I plug in his phone and wait the agonizing few minutes for it to charge enough to power up. Why can't someone just invent a phone that never dies?

It finally comes to life, and within seconds, his phone starts buzzing with all the notifications. I struggle to enter his passcode with one hand, but I'm determined. I need to know what they said.

Realizing there's a mess of messages he's missed over the last few days, I have no choice but to pull off on the side of the road to find what I'm looking for. After scrolling through the unread texts, I finally find the group message I sent on Friday night.

Opening it up, I find Kai's response first.

Kairo - O, come on. Don't be stupid. Just walk out of there, and we'll sort this out. We love you. We can fix this.

Next up, Eli.

Elijah - Understand? I don't fucking understand. You walked away from us, from everything we had. You're supposed to be a little sister to us.

I skip over the rest of his response because I know how Eli gets, and it's not good. It's only going to tear me apart as he works through his anger at me. So instead of letting it cut me like he'd hoped, I move onto the final message and find five simple words that hurt me more than anything else ever could.

Sebastian - We will always love you.

A fat tear rolls down my cheek and splashes against the dirty school uniform that still dons my body. I haven't showered in three days, simply because I have nothing to change into, and I'll be damned if I was to ask any of the Wolves for help. Besides, getting naked in that place? No thank you.

I can't wait to get home and feel human again, but before I can do that, I have to ease their minds. They have to know how much I care for them. I hit reply on the text.

Ocean - I'm on my way home. Maybe we can talk things through and I can tell you everything that's been going on.

I watch the message go, and as all three of the guys receive and view it, I wait, hoping for even the smallest olive branch from just one of them. One minute, two minutes, three, four, five.

Nothing.

My heart shatters, but I hold back my emotions, not allowing them to take over as all that matters right now is getting home to Mom and Colton.

Putting the phone down, I hit the gas and pull back onto the highway, fighting my tired eyes the whole way. As I'm finally pulling into the Carrington driveway, I lean out my open window and hash the code in for the massive iron gates.

They slowly peel back as my patience wears thin. Finally, when they're wide enough for me to squeeze the Audi past, I fly down the long drive in desperation.

By the time I finally make it and cut the engine, my mom is halfway down the grand stairs of the Carrington mansion. I hurry out of the Audi and race around to her, feeling the exhaustion of the past few days beginning to catch up to me.

Mom crashes into me as Colton stands at the top of the stairs, leaving us to have this moment. Her arms wrap around me, and for the first time in years, I feel like a little girl who desperately needs her mother's comfort. "Oh, honey," Mom cries into my shoulder. "Don't you ever scare me like that again."

"I'm sorry," I murmur into her neck, my words hardly audible by how hard I'm holding her. "I had to do it. We're finally going to get justice for dad."

Mom pulls me back, holding onto my shoulders, and gives me a pained smile. "I know, sweetie. I just hope getting justice doesn't mean giving up a part of yourself."

A single tear rolls down my cheek as I give her a brave smile, her words heavy with their honesty. "I think it's a little too late for that," I whisper.

Mom's hands drop to mine and she squeezes them tight. "Come on," she tells me. "Let me get you inside, then you can tell us exactly what happened."

I nod, unsure that I actually have the strength to get the words out. "Okay," I finally say, allowing her to pull on my hands and lead me up the stairs to where Colton waits for me, more than ready to pull me into his loving arms and never let me go.

CHAPTER 8

Monday morning comes around far too quickly, and Colton is curling his arms around me, reminding me that if I want to make it to school, now is the time to get up and make it happen.

I curl into his body, hating that I pulled away from him during the night. But after not sleeping for two nights straight, I can't take responsibility for what I did once my eyes finally closed.

It was just after four in the afternoon when I'd gotten home, and it was well after six before I finally finished explaining everything that had happened. To be honest, I was expecting Mom to be really upset about it all, but she understood and accepted every word I said, almost as though she'd been considering doing the same thing herself. Colton however, still wasn't on board with the plan—not that he has much of a choice at this point. Though, I know he can't deny that he's happy I'm home unscathed.

Colton kept his hand on my body from the second I walked through the front door until I fell asleep at the dinner table. I can't explain the power he holds over me with just a single touch, one that both soothes and excites me all at once. When his hands are on me, I feel as though everything will be alright, and I'm more than grateful to finally have it back. It doesn't matter if the world is falling down around me as long as I have Colton by my side, then it's all going to be okay.

"What do you want to do?" Colton murmurs, his voice thick with sleep. "I can take the morning off and spend a few hours with you if you need me too."

I let out a sigh and sink further into him, keeping my eyes closed as I refuse to believe that it's already morning. "Can't I just stay in bed all day and forget that anything ever happened?"

"I'm down with that," he tells me, holding me a little tighter. "I'm sure I could make you forget your own name if you want me to."

I groan against his chest. "No. I can't even think about getting naked right now. I haven't showered in days, and for the record, I'm pissed with you for letting me go to bed without showering last night. Do you have any idea how gross that is? You should be disgusted. How are you even touching me?"

I can practically hear his eyes roll. "Don't be ridiculous. Besides, what was I supposed to do? You were asleep on the fucking table. The whole house could have burned down around you and you wouldn't have known. I've never seen anyone do that before. Did you even sleep while you were there?"

I shake my head against his chest. "Nope. It was torture. I've never been so tired, but I don't know … I just couldn't force myself to give in to the tiredness."

"Shit, Jade. I'm sorry. If I knew you hadn't slept that whole time, I would have snuck out and let you sleep until you were ready."

"No," I groan, rolling out of his arms and stretching, feeling my consciousness really start to come back to me as the fogginess of my sleep begins to clear. "I need to get to school. I've missed too much of it over the last few weeks … and … well … I don't know what's going to happen with the whole college thing, but if this is my last shot at an education, I shouldn't waste it."

"It's not your last shot," he tells me, sitting up in bed and watching as I try to convince myself to get to my feet. "I swear to you, Jade. I'm not going to let that happen. The University of Bellevue Springs wants you, and I know I don't like to share, but I won't stop until they get you."

"But …"

"No buts. You're going to college, and that's final."

I roll my eyes as I finally get to my feet. The rejection letters I'd received Friday morning sit heavily on my mind, but I can't tell him yet. Now's not exactly the moment to shoot down his hopes and dreams for me. And I really don't want to get into the 'I'll pay for you to go to college' argument that seems to be a regular occurrence around here.

I make my way across the room, and just as I go to step into his bathroom, I look back at Colton, finding his eyes all over my body. "I missed you," I tell him. "I know it was only a few days, but those few days without you really sucked."

A soft smile plays on his lips, and I watch as his eyes shine with joy. "I'm never letting you go back there again," he tells me. "You'll have to pry yourself out of my cold, dead hands."

I laugh. "That can be arranged," I tell him, winking before I disappear into the bathroom, closing the door on the shocked expression on his face.

I lean into the shower and turn on the water before stripping out of my clothes. I've never been so happy to be naked in my life. The water hardly gets a second to completely warm before I throw myself under it and instantly fall victim to its comfort.

Fuck, that's good. I'll never take for granted a good shower again.

I let the warm water wash over my face, and as the minutes pass, I don't move an inch. I kinda expected Colton to come in ages ago and take over my shower. Though I have to admit, for once, I'm enjoying the privacy, and I'm grateful that he's given me a few moments to myself. I know how hard that must be for him.

I realize that if I don't speed things up I'm going to be late for school, so I get busy washing my hair and scrubbing the memory of the last few days off of my body. The loofa roams over my skin, and when it passes by my nipples, I cringe as a shock of pain tears through me.

What the fuck was that?

I glance down at my tits and scan over them, but there's no cuts or bruises, nothing that could bring me any pain. My brows furrow as I take hold of them, feeling around and pressing my fingers into the soft flesh. I let out a long sigh, finding them both extremely tender and beginning to swell.

I really am pregnant.

I don't know why I hadn't expected any of this, but I should have known. I'm fucking lucky that I haven't been hurling everything I eat with that dreaded morning sickness.

Maybe it's about time I start googling these things. I mean, what's supposed to come next? When will I start to get a bump? I should sit down with Mom tonight and discuss it all. After all, she's been through it with me. Who better to ask?

I finish up in my shower and wrap my towel around me just as Colton barges through the bathroom door with my phone in his hand. "Here," he says, handing me the phone with an annoyed expression on his face. "Please talk to Milo so he'll finally stop calling me."

I laugh and scoop the phone out of Colton's hand and hold it to my ear. "What do you think you're doing bugging my boyfriend at this time of the morning?" I question as Colton steps in behind me and curls his arms around my waist, studying my face through the mirror.

"Girl, where the hell have you been?" Milo questions, most of his perky attitude back in force after it took a hit when he was attacked on Wednesday. "What are you doing today?"

"Umm … I was planning on going to school."

"Don't," he says. "I just got discharged, and now I have to spend the day sitting in bed with no one to talk to."

"Really?" I question, my eyes going wide. "That's the best news I've had in days."

"Tell me about it. I've never been so happy to get out of there. The dude in the next room snores like a fucking trooper, and no matter what I do, I can't seem to get the sound of it out of my head. So, what do you say? Are you coming? I'm halfway through the Vampire Diaries, and I'm a little obsessed right now, but I'm going to need you to stop and get me some popcorn."

"A day in bed watching *The Vampire Diaries?*" I ask, glancing up and meeting Colton's eyes through the mirror. "I'm so down for that. I'll be there in twenty."

Colton's mouth drops open as he stares at me in horror. "What?" I laugh once Milo has ended the call.

"Let me get this straight," Colton teases, his lips pulling up into a cocky smirk that has me desperate to kiss him. He releases his hold from around my waist and turns me so that I'm staring straight into his perfectly hazel eyes. "You'll spend the day in bed with Milo but won't spend it with me?"

"What can I say?" I laugh, taking a step back from him and edging toward the bathroom door. "Milo has a bigger dick."

Colton's jaw drops again, and he stares at me as though I've just committed a heinous crime. I don't give him a chance to defend his honor before I'm slipping from the bathroom and hurrying into his massive closet.

I start searching for something to wear and settle on one of his shirts that nearly drops to my knees and a pair of his sweatpants that I have to roll at my hips three times just to avoid them falling to my ankles. If I'm going to spend the whole day in bed watching *The Vampire Diaries,* then I should at least be comfortable. It's the only way to do it.

I hear Colton in the shower, and just as I finish getting ready, he meets me back in his room. "I'm going to go," I tell him, stretching up onto my tippy toes and brushing my lips over his.

"Alright," he tells me. "Try not to make any unplanned stops this time."

"Okay," I laugh as he wraps me in his arms. "I promise. I'll be a good little girl all day long."

He drops his lips to mine before murmuring the sweetest words I've ever heard. "Only if you promise to be a bad one when you get home."

Well, shit. Maybe I should stay here with him today.

"No," Colton says, stepping back from me. "I know that look in your eyes, and if you don't show up at Milo's place in twenty minutes as you promised, he's going to end up here, and then he'll never leave."

"But ..."

"Nope. Go. Get your sweet ass out of here, and when you get home tonight, I'll show you exactly what you were missing."

I let out a sigh, but he's right. If I don't show up on Milo's doorstep with popcorn in hand, there's going to be trouble. "Deal," I finally tell him, stepping into him and kissing him one last time before marching my way to the door. "But I swear, Colton Carrington, you better make it worth my while, or you and I are going to have problems."

With that, I step out of his room and get my ass to Milo's place as promised.

Thirty minutes later, my arms are laden with ice cream, candy, and popcorn as I barge through the Queen's bedroom door. What better distraction from my troubles than falling more and more in love with *Ian Somerhalder?*

"Take your time," Milo grumbles as I climb into his bed beside him and study his face. He still looks like he's in a lot of pain but he seems a million times better. I still can't believe he was attacked purely because he likes guys. It makes me sick, and had the boys not gone and handled it, I would have been more than happy to handle it myself.

Though the swelling on his face has gone down, the bruising has come out, ready to take the spotlight. I scrunch up my face as I look at him and he instantly cuts me off. "Don't even say it," he says, holding up a hand to stop me. "I know how it looks and trust me, with the pain meds I'm on, it looks a million times worse than how it feels."

"Are you sure?" I question, glancing around his room for some kind of way to help him.

"If you even think about fluffing my pillows or fussing over me, I'm going to whoop that fat ass of yours. I've had nurses in and around my business for days—constantly poking and prodding. All I want is to be left alone to watch *Damon* and *Stefan* fight over *Elena* as though she isn't a whiny bitch."

I roll my eyes and scoot closer into his bed, making myself

comfortable. "Fine, have it your way, but just so you know, this ice cream isn't going to stay frozen forever, and I have absolutely no plans to get up and put it in the freezer. So unless you want it melted through your bed and making everything all sticky, then we have to eat it now."

Milo laughs to himself. "It's not the first time my bed's been all sticky."

"Gross," I say, wanting to be anywhere but in his bed after a comment like that. But considering his father's high standards for his staff, I'm sure his bed had clean sheets put on before he came home. "You're disgusting."

"You like it like that," he tells me before struggling to sit up and grab the bag of goodies I brought along with me. "Ooh, chocolate chip."

He dives into the bag and cracks open the ice cream before digging straight in. I won't lie, ice cream at nine in the morning is exactly the kind of bullshit I need in my life right now.

Just as promised, *The Vampire Diaries* gets turned on, and we watch in silence for half an hour before the dreaded question comes shooting through the room. He glances over at me, holding the ice cream in one hand while the spoon awkwardly points at me. "Do you want to talk about it?"

I feel my good mood plummeting, and as I look at him, I press my lips into a hard line, trying to not allow the emotions to well up inside of me. "What do you mean?"

"Ocean, you disappeared for three days while I was in the hospital. Something happened. Otherwise, you would have been in my stupid hospital room demanding that my doctors find a miracle cure to make me heal overnight. You were gone, and judging by the way you've been avoiding looking into my eyes since you got here, it's bad."

"I … fuck. How do you do that?"

"It's called being observant. If any of your other friends cared about you half as much as I do, they would have been able to tell. Now, like I said, do you want to talk about it?"

Letting out a sigh, I realize that Milo has become so much closer than I ever expected he would, and I absolutely love him for that. Seeing the pain ripping across my face at everything that's been going on, he offers me his hand. I take it eagerly as he watches me, waiting to hear whatever it is I need to get off my chest. So without wasting another moment, I give it to him straight. "Nic killed my father."

Milo's jaw drops in shock, and he stares at me as though the words I just uttered make absolutely no sense at all. And just like that, the whole torturous story comes out. I tell him every last detail, right down to everything that happened while I was staying with the Wolves. Though, I skip over the whole rapist bun in the oven thing. That's a story for another day.

We talk and talk until there's nothing left to say, and only then does he start with his own issues, all revolving around the fear he's felt since being attacked on Wednesday.

We completely forget the TV, and the hours fly by lost in conversation. It's after five in the afternoon by the time Milo's parents are shoving me out the door, desperate to allow Milo a chance to rest.

After saying goodbye, I promise him I'll be back tomorrow, and the next day, and then every day after that. I make my way out to Colton's Audi, and just as I'm about to unlock the car door, my phone rings deep in the pocket of my borrowed sweatpants.

I ignore it, assuming that it's Colton or Mom checking in on me for the millionth time today. I'll be home in five minutes, and then they can check on me in person. I get into the Audi, and when my phone instantly starts ringing again, my stomach drops. No one rings me twice quickly like that unless there's some kind of problem.

I dig into the deep pockets of my sweatpants, and as I pull my phone out, I find an unfamiliar number flashing on my screen. My brows drop but realizing that it must be a Wolf issue, I unlock the screen and hesitantly accept the call. "Hello," I say cautiously.

"Kid, it's Christian."

Relief surges through me, but I'm not going to lie, I'm still far too on edge for my own good. "What's up?"

"Listen," he says, his voice low and muffled as though he's hiding away to make this call. "You need to watch your back. Snake held a vote today."

"A vote?"

"Yeah, that fucker has it in for you. He put it forward that if you want to be one of us, that you need to join how the rest of us did."

My brows pinch as confusion begins to baffle me. "What's that supposed to mean?"

"We all got jumped in, Ocean, and now they're going to do the same to you."

Well, fuck.

CHAPTER 9

I drive through to the garage of the Carrington mansion, and as I go, I can't help but look around in fear. They wouldn't really jump me, would they?

Fuck. I've been around guys like this since I was a little girl. Of course they would go through with it. They don't give a shit that I'm female, and they certainly don't care that I'm knocked up. All they care about is making a point that they're on top, and I'm a nobody. I'm nothing to them, just another person they get to exploit and hurt in the name of 'family' and 'tradition.'

This is bullshit. I can only imagine what Colton is going to say about this. I still haven't heard from Eli, Sebastian, or Kai, but I'd assume that they'd be against it too. Though, who really knows when it comes to them? They're all wild cards now, and I hate that about them. Surely they'll be able to forgive me. Nic doesn't deserve to just sit back and watch all the chaos burning around him, he needs to burn too, and I'm going to make sure of it.

I bring the Audi to a stop and I can't help but glance around the dark garage, feeling like I'm being watched, but that's the paranoia getting to me. They're not here. If they were going to jump me, it wouldn't be in my boyfriend's prestigious and expensive garage. When they come for me, it will be in some dodgy back alleyway or an abandoned parking lot. Though, maybe they should get to me here. With any luck, they'd get distracted by the shiny toys and give me a chance to escape.

Yeah … that's a long shot. They'd only jump me first and then steal the cars as well.

Slipping out of the Audi, I hit the button for the remote garage and watch it with a keen eye, making sure it gets all the way to the bottom before taking my eyes off it. Is this going to be my life now? Peering around every corner and constantly watching my back? To be fair, I probably should be doing that anyway when there are men like Dominic Garcia hanging around.

I must have done something really shitty in another life, and now it's all coming back to haunt me. No one deserves this shit. I guess the question is, how many hits am I willing to take to make Nic suffer for all that he's done?

Confident that the Wolves aren't about to jump out from behind Colton's parked Veneno, I take a breath and slowly let it out before making my way to the internal entrance into the mansion. It's eerily quiet in here, and I hate it. I'm used to seeing Harrison waiting by the front door and the sound of Mom busily running around, but today, there's nothing.

I make my way deeper into the mansion, and with every step I take, my heart slowly begins settling back to a normal rhythm. I hate the feeling of constantly being scared, but being with Colton is one of the few places where I can escape. He's my safety net, the one place I can find peace.

I walk through to the staff quarters, expecting to find Mom and Harrison fussing around as the rest of the staff gets everything done, but walking in, I find it completely empty.

What the hell is going on here?

I turn on my heel and stalk back into the main part of the mansion. Colton's Veneno was in the garage, so he's definitely home. It's rare that he ever takes any of the other cars, so I doubt that he's gone anywhere.

I hear soft clanging coming from the kitchen and I follow the noise, unsure of what I will walk in to find. I turn the corner into the kitchen and come to a standstill, looking in at the candlelit room while my boyfriend slaves over the stove, probably having no idea what he's doing.

I gape in awe, struggling to move my feet until he glances up and gives me one of those award-winning smiles. "I thought you'd never come home," he complains with that cheeky grin that I love so much.

"Oh, really?" I laugh, walking in and feeling the butterflies taking flight in my stomach. "With everyone out of the house, it sure seems like you were expecting me."

He shrugs his shoulder. "What can I say? I had Milo text me when you were leaving."

"That little rat," I grumble, finally stepping into his arms. I can't help but look around the room and feel like the most loved woman on the planet. "What is all of this?" I ask, taking in the flowers on the table, the stunning candles flickering in the dim light, and the soft music playing in the background.

Colton pulls me into his arms and drops a kiss to my lips. "I figured you could use a night to forget about all the bullshit."

I push up onto my tippy toes and slide my arms around his neck. "I think you'd be right about that."

Colton looks down into my eyes, and a moment of seriousness passes between us, one that has him reaching for the stove and turning it off. "I really hate that you're going through this," he tells me. "I feel like I'm letting you down. Like I'm just standing back and watching you make a mistake."

I shake my head, hating how pained he is over this. "You're not," I insist. "Stepping in and not allowing me to see this through would be the mistake. I need to do this. You'll understand when it's all over."

"I get that," he says. "I don't like it, but I get it. I just wish there was something I could do to take away all your suffering. There's nothing I wouldn't do for you, Ocean. I'll fucking pay for your freedom if that's what it takes. I'd give it all up just to see you safe."

"I'd never ask that of you."

"I know you wouldn't. It doesn't mean that I wouldn't do it, though."

I brush my lips over his, loving the feel of his kiss against my lips. "You're a stubborn asshole, you know that, right?"

He nods, a smile pulling at his lips. "Right back at ya, Jade."

I can't help but grin up at him, and as our eyes meet, he pushes me back against the counter, caging me in with his hard body. My hands slide down from around his neck and travel over his strong arms, feeling the tight ridges of his muscles.

He drops his face into the curve of my neck, and I feel his lips brushing over my sensitive skin. "Fuck dinner," he murmurs, his voice low and filled with desire. "I think I'll eat you instead."

His words are my undoing, and everything clenches deep within me. How does he have such a profound effect over my body? One minute I'm happy in his arms and the next I'm desperate to feel him deep inside me.

Colton Carrington is zero to one hundred in the blink of an eye, and I wouldn't have it any other way.

Need pulses through my veins, and I press my body against his, desperate to feel his skin on mine. His hands slip under the fabric of my too-big shirt until they're tickling my skin and giving me only a fraction of what I need. "I love it when you wear my clothes," he tells me, slowly raising the shirt up my body. "But I love it more when you wear nothing at all."

The shirt comes over my head, and he drops it on the marble floor before putting his hands back on my waist. His fingers travel down as his lips return to my neck, driving me wild with need. His fingertips slip under the waistband of my sweatpants, and with a gentle push, they fall down my legs, leaving me standing before him in nothing but a black bra and a skimpy lace thong.

A groan tears from the back of his throat as he takes me in. The sound speaks to the devil living inside of me, spurring me on, even more so when his large hands curve over my backside and squeeze firmly, teasing me with their power.

Colton lifts me up onto the counter, and I instantly spread my legs, allowing him space to get even closer. I don't waste a second unbuttoning his shirt and pushing it open to see his sculpted chest. It's so perfect, my mouth waters. I push the shirt over his shoulders and lick my lips as the soft material drops to the floor behind him, leaving him standing before me with that warm sun-kissed skin begging to be touched.

Colton's hands roam over my body, and I lock my legs around his waist, pulling me in until I feel his hardness against my center. He grinds against me, and a soft moan pulls from deep inside of me.

The wait is torture. I need to have him now.

I reach down between us and unbuckle his belt then tear it free from his pants in one easy pull. Sensing my urgency, Colton's lips lift into an excited grin. He slides his hands around my body, taking hold of my lace thong at the top of my ass and tearing hard, ripping the flimsy material right off my body.

My lady bits clench, and I bite down on my lower lip. Holy hell. How is this even real? Men like Colton need to be arrested and detained. The power they have over the opposite sex should be illegal.

The second his pants are gone, his large cock springs free. I watch with desire as he takes hold, curling his fingers around his base and slowly working up and down.

Fuck me. I'm going to hell for this.

Colton's eyes sparkle as he watches me squirm. He knows what he's doing to me, and if he's not careful, I might just play the same game.

He finally takes pity on me and curls an arm around my waist before scooting me toward the very edge of the counter and lining himself up with my entrance. The tip of his cock rubs against my clit, teasing me and driving me wild.

I tighten my legs around him, pulling him closer. His lips drop to my neck, and he tsks me while swiping his impressive length over my sensitive skin again. "Patience," he murmurs against my neck, his lips working me and making me flood with desire.

I curl my hand around his back and up into his messy hair, fisting my fingers into it, dying for some kind of release. "I have many skills, Colton," I whisper, my thinly veiled desperation seeping through my quiet tone, much like the wetness between my legs. "But patience isn't one of them."

"I know. That's what makes it so good."

"Careful," I tease. "If you can't make it happen, I'll have no choice but to take matters into my own hands."

Colton pulls back, meeting my eyes and almost looking offended with my comment. "I dare you to try," he says, rubbing that heavy cock over my clit just for fun. "Then see what happens."

I reach down between us, taking his cock in my hand, loving the feel of his velvety skin on my fingertips. I work my hand up and down, curving my thumb over his tip with every chance I get. He groans and leans into me, meeting his lips with mine as his fingers finally find my entrance. He slips two thick fingers straight in and curves them just right so with that very first touch, he finds my G-spot, making me gasp in excitement.

He plays with me, torturing my body as I do the same to his, and then all too soon, his fingers pull out of me, and I watch as he brings them to his mouth and sucks them clean. I gape at him, loving every second of this, but I don't get a chance to linger on it before he pushes me down on the counter and grabs my legs, opening them wide.

Colton lines himself up with my entrance while watching my heated body. I feel so vulnerable, so exposed. Yet in this dim candlelit room, I've never felt sexier, that is, until he pushes into me and makes me feel more alive than I've ever felt in my life.

He fills me to the brim, stretching me as he goes. His hands slide over my body, gently pinching at my pebbled nipples. I can't help but tip my head back, feeling every nerve ending light on fire and begin to burn within me.

He draws back before sliding straight back in, and the soft, delicious groan that rumbles through his chest is enough to set me off.

He works me, treating my body like a blank canvas with all the potential in the world. He touches me just right, every brush of his fingertips, every scan of his eyes. It's intoxicating. His thumb presses down over my clit as he pulls out of me. I suck in a gasp, the feeling almost too much to handle.

Colton watches me with heat in his eyes, seeing my pleasure as his own. I clench down around him, feeling that familiar ache beginning to build deep within me, so strong and enticing. He meets me thrust for thrust, giving me exactly what I need and picking up pace as his thumb teases my clit.

"Holy shit," I pant, squirming beneath him, my orgasm building so strong that I don't think I'll be able to handle it.

Colton's hand slips into mine, lacing our fingers and squeezing hard. "Don't you dare come, not yet."

"I … can't," I pant, feeling my orgasm right on the edge.

He clenches his jaw, so fucking close. His hand tightens on me as he adds more pressure to my clit. I barely hold on, squeezing my eyes closed and silently begging him to launch me over the edge. "Fuck," he grunts. "You're so fucking perfect."

My head tips back further, and I arch my back off the counter, pressing my tits up into the air. I grab hold with my other hand, squeezing them, kneading, and pinching while feeling his burning gaze on my body. "Fuck yeah, baby," he groans through his clenched teeth, watching me play.

He gets even faster and then, finally, tips me over the edge. I clench down on him, feeling my orgasm tear through me like dynamite as he comes hard, deep within me. My body squirms, my toes curl, and my bottom lip is nearly shredded from my bite.

Maybe it's the pregnancy hormones, or maybe Colton is just that good, but I've never felt it so intense, so deeply, or so satisfying. My body is completely wrecked. I'm so exhausted and utterly spent that after he pulls out from me, I can't move. I just lay there, spread eagle on the kitchen counter until he returns to me, surprising me on the other side of the counter with his lips on mine. "Are you okay?" he murmurs, his lips stretching into a boyish grin.

I roll my eyes at his charm. He's like a kid who just saw his first set of tits, so proud of himself. "Mmhmm," I grumble, refusing to get up.

Colton sits me up and spins me around on the counter until I'm facing the massive living room. "What do you need?" he questions, scanning his eyes all over my face and body.

"After that? A joint."

He grins, that same boyish charm shining bright. "Seriously, babe. Do you need anything?"

Hunger tears through me at his question. I look back at the stove, knowing damn well I don't have the energy to cook. "Chinese take out would be good."

He slips his phone out of his pocket, and I momentarily wonder when the hell he had a second to put his pants back on, but decide that I don't care enough to ask. His phone goes straight to his ear as he winks at me. "You got it, Jade."

I smile wide and quickly lean in, kissing him before he pulls away with his call. When the guy at the restaurant answers Colton starts pacing the kitchen, putting in an order big enough to feed an army.

I glance out the window, but with the dim lighting, it acts more like a mirror and reflects everything that's happening inside the house. I watch Colton from his reflection before scanning over myself, still naked on the counter.

I should really get myself dressed. After all, Colton never actually specified where everyone is tonight. I just assumed that we had the place to ourselves.

I jump down from the counter and walk around to the other side of the kitchen to find my clothes. After putting on my bra, I search around for my panties but quickly remember that Colton had torn them from my body. I guess I'm going commando for the night.

I pull on the sweatpants that I'd stolen from Colton this morning and as I roll the material over at my hips to keep them up, I find myself walking toward the massive floor to ceiling windows, staring at my reflection.

My eyes drop over my body. My tits had been tender this morning but they seem fine now, my stomach though … My hands glide over my abdomen, unable to comprehend that in a few short months, it's going to be bulging with a child. It's still completely flat for now, but it won't be long until it starts to grow.

When does that even happen? Is it going to be weeks or months until my secret is revealed to the world?

Do I even have it in me to be someone's mother? I'm only seventeen. Given my birthday is coming up but magically turning eighteen and technically becoming an adult isn't going to change that.

Just like everyone keeps reminding me, I do have options, some scarier than others. The thought of abortion doesn't sit well in my mind. The whole pro-life thing really isn't something that I've ever had to consider before. I mean, what girl my age really has unless she's been in this exact situation? I really don't know where I stand but thinking about it now, I don't know if I'd be able to go through it, which leaves me with two options; adoption or being this baby's mom.

Glancing back, I find Colton watching me as he talks on the phone. As if sensing that I'm about to work myself up into a panic, he steps in behind me, curling his arms around my body, and pushing my own hands out of the way.

He finishes up on the call, and his phone gets put straight back into his pocket as he kisses my temple. "You're going to be just fine, Jade," he promises me. "Now, come sit down, then you can tell me why you looked like you were going to be sick when you first walked in here."

Christian's call instantly comes to mind, and I have to admit, the idea of getting jumped really does make me forget about the whole baby thing.

Colton pulls me along, and as he drops down into the massive couch and pulls me down on top of him, I meet his eyes, knowing that this is one of those things that I can't keep to myself. I have to tell him about this. "There's something you need to know," I tell him, dreading having this conversation but knowing that I need to prepare him … prepare me for the worst.

CHAPTER 10

My feet drag, one after another as I find myself walking through the halls of Bellevue Springs Private School early on Tuesday morning. It almost feels ridiculous being here with everything else that's been going on. I should be locked up at home in a padded cell where Nic or the Wolves would never be able to get me.

I spent the night talking it through with Colton. To say that he was less than thrilled about the call I'd received from Christian yesterday is an understatement—a massive understatement. I'm surprised that he didn't lock me in the wine-cellar dungeon just for good measure. It was hard enough just getting out the door this morning. He insisted on driving me, but I made the argument that if they were to come to the school, I'd have a better chance of escape if I had a car here with me. He tried, but there's no arguing with logic.

I'm not going to lie, the second I drove out of the massive gate this morning, the paranoia swept over me again. I've been looking over my shoulder with every step I take. Colton has already called me twice to check in with me. Though I have to admit, I think that's going to be the new normal now. Not that I mind because, for those few minutes, I feel that familiar safety net wrap around me.

Walking down the hall feels surreal. Everybody is just going about their day as though my world isn't falling to pieces, yet with every eye that wanders my way, I can't help but wonder if they know. Are they staring at my stomach? Do they know a rapist knocked me up? Hell, do they know a fucking gang is looking for me so they can beat the living shit out of me? How simple their lives must be.

I can only imagine the bullshit rumors that will spread about me. They'll be worse than the ones Casey and Cora tried to hit me with a few weeks ago, only this time, it'll be true, and it'll hurt like a blade slicing through my skin, a bit like what I did to this baby's father.

By the time I reach my locker, Hendrix is already there bursting from the seams with a cheesy as fuck grin on her face. "Girl, where the hell have you been?" she starts, diving into me and wrapping me in a quick, warm hug. "I've been trying to get a hold of you since Friday. Have you been sick or something?"

"Or something," I grumble, glancing away to avoid looking at the confusion on her face.

She stares at me for a quick moment before shrugging it off and putting it down to one of my many weird quirks. "Anyway," she continues, backing up a step to give me space to open my locker. "Has your mom said anything about my dad? I swear, he's so smitten with her. Our plan totally worked. We should have hooked them up ages ago."

I glance back at her, trying my hardest to give her the kind of enthusiasm that she's looking for. "Umm … yeah, definitely. They're great together."

"I know, right. It's like they're soulmates or something."

I resist rolling my eyes. I'd hardly skip right to soulmates. They've been on one date, which only came about because we forced it on them. I mean, I totally get it. It's insta love that burns so bright that it's impossible to ignore, but I'd like to see what happens six months down the track, a year or maybe two. If things are still shining brightly, then yeah, I'll consider the whole soulmates thing for them. Call me a Debby Downer, but there's a big difference between being happy for my mom and finding the love of her life after one date.

After getting my books out of my locker, I close it and lean up against it only to find Drix staring at me. "What's up with you?" she asks. "You seem really off. Like you're not even excited about it at all."

I let out a sigh. "I'm sorry. I am excited. I think it's great that they're hitting it off. I've just had a really big few days, and I'm kinda struggling to focus on everything. My head is just … a bit of a mess."

"Oh," she says, looping her arm over my shoulder and dragging me across the hall to where Jess is just arriving. "You should have said something. Do you need to talk about it? I know your life is all bat shit crazy, so I can't promise to keep up, but I can promise to ooh and ahh at all the right times, especially if it has anything to do with those tattooed gang guys that showed up here last week."

I groan at her attraction to Nic and Sebastian. I mean, I get it, I totally do. But if she knew the kinds of things those boys got up to, she'd be horrified that she even looked their way. "Those tattooed gang guys are not the kind of guys you want to be getting yourself involved with, trust me. Besides, aren't you screwing around with Charlie?"

Jess looks over at us as she finishes in her locker. "Wait. What's going on?"

Drix smirks and leans against the cold, metal lockers. "Don't change the topic," she warns me before glancing back at Jess. "Ocean here was just about to tell us what the hell has been going on over the last few days."

I shake my head, considering for the briefest second actually talking to them about all of this. In reality, doing that would only drag them down into a world that would break girls like them. Besides, even the slightest whisper of a teen pregnancy and I'll have every school in Bellevue Springs knowing my business before lunch. "I wasn't about to tell you guys shit," I laugh before leaning in. "It's gang business, and you know how they get about bitches who squeal."

Both their eyes go wide. "Oh, shit," Drix says. "Are you serious? Do they tell you all that stuff? Fuck, I didn't realize you were like … in with them. I just figured they were trying to get in your pants."

If only she knew that I wasn't even referring to the same gang that she's thinking of, but that's something that I'll never tell. It's one thing for her to know about the Widows, but if she was to start snooping around the Wolves, she could end up in trouble.

"They're just friends," I tell her, referring to the guys she's actually thinking of. "At least, usually, they're just friends. Right now, they're all on my shit list."

"Even the guy who came storming into the cafeteria? Because let me tell you, I don't think he thought you guys were just friends."

I look her straight in the eyes. "Nic is the worst of them," I tell her. "Stay far, far away from him. He's going to rot in hell for the shit that he's done."

Both of their brows drop, picking up on the pain in my tone. "Are you okay?" Jess asks. "Is something more going on that we should know about?"

I press my lips into a tight line and shake my head. "No, it's nothing," I tell them, even though referring to Nic's sins as 'nothing' feels wrong. They're absolutely everything. "I can't talk about it. Just know that when I get snappy today, it's not you guys. I'm just trying to work through some shit."

"Are you sure?" Drix questions, lowering her voice and stepping into me to keep our conversation private from the rest of the students lingering in the hallway. "Is there anything we can do to make it better?"

"You can change the topic," I say, desperate to move this right along. "What's going on with Charlie? Are you guys still smooshing your bits together?"

Drix gives me a blank stare as Jess tries to smother a laugh. "Do you really have to say it like that? You make it sound gross. What Charlie and I have is … romantic."

"Romantic?" I laugh. "Charlie is a lot of things, but romantic is not one of them."

Hendrix groans and rolls her eyes before a wide grin stretches across her face and she gets all flustered. "Alright, fine. He's not romantic at all. He's a total dork, like a super dork with this cheesy, but sexy grin, and when his eyes sparkle it's like a warning that I'm about to get my world rocked. He's …"

"He's Charlie," I finish for her, completely understanding where she's coming from. "You really like him."

"I mean, I don't *really* like him. I like him just the normal amount."

Jess scoffs. "Uh-huh. If you liked him the normal amount, you wouldn't have called me every night for the past four nights telling me all about the guy, and how he accidentally brushed past your hand, and it gave you butterflies, and how—"

"Okaaaaay," Drix cuts in, her cheeks flushed with embarrassment as she stares at Jess. "That's more than enough out of you." She looks back at me. "Don't listen to her. It's been too long since she got off with an actual penis that she's starting to hear things."

Jess rolls her eyes and steps around us. "Alright, bitches. I'm out of here. You two can suck my massive dick." We laugh as she goes, but she stops and turns back, aiming a daring smirk at Drix. "For the record, you're totally in love with Charlie, and I don't need to have a plowed pussy to tell."

Drix stares with her mouth hanging open as I howl with laughter, feeling as though that one comment was exactly what I needed to get my head back in the game.

I don't even know why I'm still bothering with school. It feels like a colossal waste of time at this point. It's not like I'm going to have time for college once I have a baby. Not to mention, if things don't pan out how I hope, I'm going to be with the Wolves for a while. I highly doubt that they're all about having a higher education. Sure, they might put me through a few training courses, but that would be more like, 'How to Kill Quickly and Efficiently 101' or 'Gutting: The How To Guide.'

The bell sounds and Drix loops her arm through mine. "So, things really are happening with Charlie?" I ask in all seriousness as we start making our way down the hall toward our homeroom classes.

She shrugs her shoulders. "I mean, I guess. Nothing official has really happened, but he's coming around every day and wanting to see me all the time. He texts me before bed and sends me ridiculous little things when I'm not feeling so great. He treats me like I'm his, but you know, nothing official."

"It sounds pretty official to me," I tell her. "Have you talked to him about it?"

Drix scrunches her face. "I tried," she admits. "You know, that day you were on the phone and he showed up. We talked a bit, but then I kinda jumped him, and then I forgot what fucking day it was so …"

I glance across at her. "I could talk to him if you want me to," I suggest. "See what's going through his head right now. I have a particular gift for getting information out of that one."

"No," she laughs. "We're not kids anymore. I can do it, but I just … I don't know. I'm kinda scared that he's going to say that we're just friends and having fun. I mean, isn't that what he said to you?"

"Not exactly," I say with a cringe, feeling slightly awkward. "It was the other way around."

"Oh, so you're the whore in that situation?"

"No," I laugh. "We were both whores just looking for a little fun, but he could tell that Colton had his eye on me and he just wanted to nail me down before Colton could steal his little toy away, but I'm not about that." I glance over at her to find her hanging on every single word. "Look, to be completely honest, it wasn't real between Charlie and me. It was just some innocent flirting, and he wanted to hang onto it because it was the start of our friendship, but we've both grown since then, and the friendship is still intact. It's over, like so over that I hardly even remember it happening."

"You're sure? There's not even a hint of feeling left inside you wishing you could take another stab at him?"

I shake my head. "Not even a little. In fact, I can't even remember the last time I saw him, and I'm pretty sure that makes me a really shitty friend."

"It does," she agrees with a teasing sparkle hitting her eye. We turn the corner, and she instantly unhooks her arm from mine as we near her homeroom class. "Alright, I'll see you during the first break. Try not to whore yourself out while I'm gone."

"Ha. Ha," I say blankly, continuing on past as she whips herself into the room.

I keep moving down the hallway, but for some reason, find myself stopping as I pass the library. Students bump into me as I stare into the massive room. I shouldn't be late for homeroom, but I'm edging forward anyway, knowing every step in the wrong direction is bringing me closer to detention.

I walk past the front desk and the quiet study area before slipping past the rows and rows of books until I finally find the office at the back. I glance up at the door and scan my eyes over the name. 'Miss Davies.'

What am I doing here? I should walk away. This isn't any of my business, and not to mention, if Christian knew I was standing at her door, he'd probably be the first to get in on jumping me.

Taking a breath, I raise my fist and gently knock on the door.

My hand falls back to my side, and within a second, her too chirpy voice calls through her office. "Come in."

Taking hold of the door handle, I push my way through to her office and watch as her brows raise as she takes me in. "Ocean, what a surprise," she says. "How can I help you?"

I glance around her office, not really sure how to say what I need to say. "I, uhh … I was hoping we could talk."

Miss Davies settles into her chair and leans back, watching me through curious eyes. "Is everything alright? Did all go well with your college applications?"

"Yeah, umm … that's all good. I got in, but then I got rejected for student loans, so that's a whole other issue I need to figure out. Not that it really matters anymore," I grumble under my breath, watching the excitement come to her face before it promptly fades away in confusion. "But that's not why I'm here."

"Oh?" she questions. "Well, my door is always open for my students. What do you need?"

"To talk, I guess," I say. "I kinda did something incredibly stupid."

"Go on …"

I swallow past the dread sitting in my stomach. "Well, the last time we spoke, I kinda lied to you."

Her eyes narrow in suspicion. "About?"

"You asked me about my father, and at the time, I didn't realize that the man I knew was the same one that you were referring to."

She gives me a warm smile as if she had known all along. "He really is."

"Yeah," I say, giving her an awkward smile. "But I was also Dominic Garcia's best friend, and over the past few weeks, a lot of bullshit has come to light." Her eyes darken at his name, it's clear that she knows exactly who he is, but this seems like so much more than gang affiliations. This is a deep hatred that comes from something horrifying, but it's not my business to ask, so I continue. "I was cornered by Mikhail Russo and a few of his guys in an alleyway. They branded me with their mark. He said I was one of his and will be brought into the family. At first, I was terrified because that meant turning my back on Nic, but then I discovered that Nic was the person who killed my father."

She sucks in another breath, almost struggling to hold herself together. "Oh, no, no, no. I know where this is going. Please tell me that you didn't go to the Wolves and get yourself involved in this mess?"

I press my lips together, regretting having to tell her this. "I did."

"Shit," she grunts, propping her elbows onto her desk and hanging her head. "What did my father do to you?"

"Your father?" I grunt, whipping my head up to meet her eyes. "What are you talking about?"

Miss Davies presses her lips into a tight line, giving me a sad and pained stare. "Mikhail, Ocean. Mikhail is my father."

I stare at her blankly. "What… What are you talking about? I came here to tell you that I met Christian and tell you how much he loves and misses you."

Her eyes go wide. "You what?"

We both sit in silence, lost in the revelations until she finally lets out a breath. "So, you're a Wolf, and you met my big brother?"

"Yeah," I say, unsure why I feel so shaky. "He's kinda awesome and told me all about you, though I have to admit, it took me a while to put the puzzle pieces together, but he misses you, like a lot. He didn't actually admit that, but I could tell."

She presses her lips together and gently shakes her head. "Then my brother is a better actor than I gave him credit for," she tells me. "He hasn't come to visit in over two years. I highly doubt that he's missing me."

"He told me that," I murmur. "He said that he stays away on purpose because of how well you're doing out here. He was so proud when he told me how you made it through college and have this big job at a fancy school. He's scared that if he was to come and see you, you might get close to him again, and he doesn't want to take away from everything you've achieved."

Her gaze drops to her hands. "If I got close again, my father would try to bring me back."

I nod, completely understanding. "You never mentioned that Russo was your father when we talked about it last."

She laughs. "It's not exactly something that I shout from the rooftops. I had my name officially changed to my mother's maiden name so that when I started going for jobs, I'd have no visible ties to gangs." I nod, and she continues. "Look, Ocean. I don't envy the position that you're in. Gang life is not for the faint-hearted, but you're strong. There's no way out for you now, so I can't help you, nor will I allow myself to get involved, but I can promise to be a shoulder to cry on when things get hard—because they will. But I think you already know that."

I nod and rise from my seat, keeping my eyes on her as I go. "Thanks, I should really get to homeroom before I get in even more trouble." I murmur, truly appreciating her gesture. "It'll be nice to talk to someone about it that actually understands."

"Trust me, I know the feeling," she laughs, getting up and walking around her desk. She instantly pulls me into a tight hug. "I'm rooting for you, Ocean. Play it smart and don't do anything stupid. It'd be a real shame if you were to get hurt. This world … it's brutal."

"I know," I tell her. "I'm being careful."

"Good." She pulls out of my arms and looks at me with a grim stare. "Do me a favor and don't mention me to anyone, and certainly don't tell Christian that we had this conversation. My father has wanted me back in the 'family business' for years now, and if he knew I was this close—"

"Of course," I tell her. "My lips are sealed."

"Good. Now, let me write you a note, excusing you from homeroom."

I grin wide. This might just be a friendship worth fighting for.

CHAPTER 11

The rest of the week drags by painfully slow, probably because I've spent every minute of it searching around corners and looking over my shoulders. Don't get me wrong, I'm thankful for Christian's warning, but a part of me is starting to wish that he hadn't called. That way when it finally happens, it'll be a surprise, and it'll be over before I know it. This way, while I can do my best to prepare, I'm also spending everyday living in fear.

Part of me wishes that the Wolves would just get their shit together and get it over with so I can get rid of this fear that lives inside of me. Who knows, maybe because I'm a chick and knocked up they might take it easy on me, but then, these guys don't give a shit about that.

What the hell have I got myself into? No, scrap that. What the hell did my father get me into? I was more than happy going about my days, looking at the Wolves as the enemy. That's what Nic had taught me to believe, and that's the truth that I stood by, but maybe they're not the enemy. Maybe they never have been.

My father was a good man, at least, I believed him to be. He was honorable to our family, always brought home money to pay the bills, always looked out for us, and always showed me and my mom all the love in the world. When he was taken from us, it was a tragedy. Learning about his secret life wasn't easy, but I like to think that even while he did these awful things, he was still a kind and loving man, and if that's true, then maybe there's more to being a Wolf that I'm not quite seeing.

Thoughts of my father have my fingertips brushing over the tattoo that sits over my right shoulder. I miss him so goddamn much. I don't think it's ever going to get easier, but I know I can get revenge. I just hope that when it comes down to it and Nic's eyes are staring into mine, that I have the strength to go through with it. It's going to be the hardest thing that I'll ever do and go against every moral that I've ever lived by, but I have to do this. Nic can't keep getting away with these things.

I guess I'm just grateful that Colton hasn't tried to take it into his own hands yet, though, with every day that passes, I see his patience getting thinner and thinner. He wants to do it, he craves it, but he won't, and I absolutely love him for that.

Walking out of the school on Friday afternoon, I find myself oddly excited. I've hardly had a chance all week to see Charlie and Spencer while poor Milo has been stuck at home in bed. I saw him yesterday, and I have to admit, he's been looking much better. He's even been walking around and ordering me to do ridiculous tasks for him, so I guess he's feeling more like himself.

Leaving Hendrix and Jess to argue over their Friday night plans, I slip out through the front gates and make my way down to the parking lot. Only after I have a look around and find the coast clear am I able to breathe easily.

I unlock the Audi and slip in, tossing my things onto the passenger's side seat before that familiar feeling of being watched comes over me. My head whips around to the back seat, and I double-check that there's no one about to jump out at me. I finally start the engine with a deep breath and back out of my spot. This paranoia is getting the best of me.

Trying to calm my racing mind, I turn on some music and focus on the drive. It's not that hard. All I have to do is get back home to Colton and make sure the gates lock behind me and then I'll be safe.

It's only a seven-minute drive. I'll be alright. Besides, they can't get to me here. This Audi would whip any of their cars, but I brush a finger over the lock button anyway, just to be sure.

Taking a shaky breath, I realize that I'm overthinking it again. It's all going to be alright.

I approach a red light, and just before I begin to start slowing the Audi, it turns green. I give myself a mental high-five for my perfect timing, only that high-five quickly drops from my mind when a familiar car pulls out in front of me from the side street. I have no choice but to slam on my brake to avoid smashing into the back of Sebastian's car.

My heart rate kicks up a few notches until it's in full-on panic mode. I haven't talked to the boys all week. None of them have answered my texts, and I fear that this time, I've gone too far to earn their forgiveness. I prepare myself for the worst, but when Sebastian keeps driving, I find myself staring at the back of his car. Perhaps he didn't see that it was me in the Audi and was just casually running a red light. It's not exactly something new for Sebastian. Breaking traffic laws is one of his favorite things to do.

His taillights begin to get further and further away and I let out a shaky breath. I'm all good.

Not wanting to hold up traffic, I hit the gas again. Just as I cross completely over the intersection, another familiar car pulls out from the side street, cutting in front of the other drivers until he's sitting right behind me.

What the fuck?

I glance up into my mirror to find Kairo staring back at me with Eli in the passenger seat, and I quickly realize that Sebastian driving past wasn't a mistake at all. He did it on purpose, even more so now that Sebastian is beginning to slow.

Wanting to get away, I change lanes and begin to speed up, only to have Sebastian cut in front of me and force me to slow.

Sebastian puts on his signal, and I watch him begin to make a turn, only when I go to drive straight past, Kairo is there, forcing my hand until I turn the goddamn wheels.

They're leading me somewhere, and I honestly don't know if I should be okay with this. But knowing these guys more than I know myself, I stop fighting it and allow them to lead me around until we're all coming to a stop in an empty parking lot in the next town over.

I watch as Sebastian gets out of his car and glance in my mirrors to watch Kai and Eli do the same. They start making their way toward the Audi, and unless I want them to break the window to get me out, then I better behave and do as they want.

After unlocking the door, I swing it open and slowly get out, unsure of what I'm about to be faced with. The door closes, and I stand right by it, not ready to move. The three of them crowd me, completely blocking any way of escape, each of them with the same look of disapproval and disappointment shining brightly in their eyes.

I glance around at each of them, really not sure what I'm supposed to say. "I, uhh …"

"No," Kairo says, holding up a hand to cut me off. "We speak. You listen."

I clench my jaw, wanting to let him know exactly what I think of his shitty tone, but I know better than to make matters worse right now. So I nod and wait to hear what they have to say, knowing that no matter how much they must hate me right now, they'll never hurt me.

Each of them remains quiet, and I realize that this isn't exactly a planned trip. None of them know what they want to say to me. All they know is that it has to be fixed.

Kai continues staring, shooting daggers at me while Eli just looks broken and sad, so I turn my stare on Sebastian, knowing that he'll be the first to break.

"You fucked up, O," he says, the betrayal thick in his tone. "You turned your back on us and went to the fucking Wolves. How could you do that? You're like a little fucking sister to me. You're supposed to be family."

I shake my head. "I am still your family," I tell him. "Apart from Mom and Colton, you three are the only family I have, which is exactly why I had to do what I did. I didn't fuck up. If only you knew—"

"That Nic killed your father?" Eli questions. "Yeah, we already fucking know."

My brows shoot up as the betrayal sinks in hard. They knew about this and didn't tell me. How could they? "You know?"

"Yeah," he scoffs. "We had to find out from your little boyfriend after you disappeared and joined the fucking Wolves. I was with you all morning. You should have been the one to tell me. You should have been honest."

"Are you kidding me?" I scoff. "You three have done nothing but lie to me since the beginning of time. What was I supposed to do? Come and tell you that your big bad leader fucked up and killed my daddy, only to have you fuckers tell me it's just Nic being Nic and still stand by his side? You wouldn't have chosen my side, and you know it. You would have tried to talk me out of it, and Nic would have gotten away with it, but I can't just stand by and let that happen. Nic is going down, and you three are going to stay out of my way. Otherwise, you'll only end up going down with him."

Kairo steps into me. "Is that a threat?"

"No," I snap back at him. "I'm just telling you like it is, and you know that. It's a fact. The Wolves are going after Nic, and if you get in the way, they won't hesitate to take you out. Don't act so surprised. You know that's how it works. I would never threaten you guys. I told them to keep you all out of it, but they don't play by my rules." I let out a sigh and push off the side of the car, stepping in closer to my boys. "I know it doesn't seem like it, but you really are family to me, and I really hate the disgusted way you're all looking at me."

Sebastian shakes his head. "Can you blame us? You went to the Wolves. We would have handled it. We saw how hurt you were after your dad died."

"Really?" I scoff. "You would have helped me even though my father was a Wolf? You would have gone against Nic?" All three of them give me guilty expressions, and just like that, I know the truth. "And that right there," I tell them. "Is why I had to go to the Wolves. You're all stuck so far up Nic's ass that you can't even see what's right in front of you."

"O…"

"No," I say, shaking my head at Sebastian. "You know it's true, and you know how much it kills me to go against Nic. I loved him so fucking much, and for him to do this to me … I just … I can't forgive him this time. It hurts too bad. This is my father we're talking about. My father. My blood. Surely that has to mean something to you guys."

Kairo sighs, taking on the role of the softie when we all know he's anything but. "Ocean," he murmurs cautiously. "Your father was a Wolf," he says cautiously, as though that's supposed to make a difference, as though that fact alone means he's not worthy of fighting for. "Even if we could have done something to help … it's not our place. We're only going to make things worse if we try to step in. All we can do is try to deal with Nic on our own terms. Let us do that."

I shake my head. "That's not good enough. What if this was your mothers, your little sisters, brothers? Would it be something you just shrug off then? You'd go to fucking war if he even thought about touching any of them."

Eli takes a hesitant step toward me. "They're our family. Nic would never …"

"Yeah," I scoff, feeling the hysteria beginning to rise. "Just like my father was my family. There was once a time that I thought Nic would never either. I know that I was never officially a Widow, but I thought that I had your protection. I thought I was safe."

With that, I turn and step back toward the Audi, only Kairo reaches out and grabs my wrist, spinning me back to face them. "Woah, Ocean. We're not nearly done with you yet. You turned your back on us. You betrayed our trust."

I tear my arm free of his grip and glare up at him as the anger begins pulsing through my veins. "You betrayed my trust first. You all did, yet I've stood by you and forgave you time and time again, making excuses for the bullshit you put me through when none of you deserved it, but it ends here. The cycle has been broken. From where I'm standing now, you're either with me or against me, but you're making your side pretty damn clear. Now, unless the only reason that you came all the way out here was to just run me off the road and make some kind of show about how you can still force me to do what you want, then I'm out. I'm not going to stand here and let you three try to make me hurt and regret my decision just because you all have bruised egos."

"Don't do this, Ocean," Sebastian begs. "It's not a war you can win."

"I'm not asking for a war," I tell him. "There's no reason for you all to get involved. Just hand over Nic, and I'll handle it quietly."

Eli scoffs. "You know that's never going to happen. You've already got the Wolves involved, and they won't stop until every last one of us are buried in the ground. It doesn't even matter how many of their own men have to die to make it happen. You're going to be responsible for a mass murder."

"Don't you dare try to put that on my shoulders," I demand. "I don't pull the strings, and you damn well know that. Russo is responsible for what happens now. All I did was give them the name of the man who killed my father. The rest is up to them. So, like I said, either hand over Nic or start preparing yourselves. Don't be stupid. I don't want to see any of you get hurt."

Kairo clenches his jaw, and I see his options swirling through his mind. Regret, hesitation, and indecision flashes across his face. I don't doubt that he's thinking about just taking me now and using me as a tool against the Wolves, but he wouldn't dare. His moral compass is too high for that, at least, there was a time that I thought it was. Who knows where we stand now?

I meet his eyes and gently shake my head, silently telling him that I know exactly what he's thinking. Guilt instantly floods his eyes, and for a brief moment, he looks sick with himself. That is until two cars pull into the empty parking lot and race toward us.

The three boys turn and step in front of me, proving that when it really comes down to it, they'll protect me with their life. The two cars come to a screeching halt, and within a second, four Wolves dressed completely in gang colors are standing in front of us, staring at the Widows.

There's silence as they all glare, waiting for someone to make a move. I've never felt tension like it.

How did they know I was here? Were the Wolves following me too? I shake the thought from my head instantly. Of course they were following me, Russo said as much.

Knowing how this is going to end, I try to step around Kai, but he throws his arm out like some kind of steel pole, blocking my advance.

The four Wolves seem to be shaking with anger, or maybe it's fear. After all, Kai, Sebastian, and Eli have a bit of a reputation for being some of the most lethal guys in the game. "She's ours now," one of the Wolves spit, his hand flinching by his side for his gun, but he shouldn't bother. No one pulls a gun or shoots faster than Sebastian. They'll all be dead before they've even got their gun out of their pants.

Eli scoffs. "She'll never be yours."

The Wolf who had spoken scans his dark gaze over the boys and then finally rests his glare on me. "Too late for that now, isn't it, princess?" he says with a sick smirk. "Call off your dogs. It's time for them to go."

Kairo steps forward, taking point. "The fuck did you say?"

No, no, no, no, no.

I race around Kairo and put myself between the two gangs. I meet the eye of the Wolf before looking at Kai and the boys. "He's right," I tell him, feeling the knife slice right through me. "It's time for you three to go. You've said what you came to say, and nothing has changed. Leave."

"You've got to be kidding me," Sebastian says, looking as though I just stabbed him in the back, which in all honesty, I think I did.

"Please," I say, desperate to keep the peace here. "Unless you've changed your mind, then there's nothing else that needs to be said. Just go before something happens."

Sebastian meets my eyes before shaking his head in disappointment. Without another word, he stalks back to his car, absolutely gutting me. I've never seen him look so broken and hurt in my life.

Eli is next. He looks at me just like Sebastian had, but he's more aware of the threat standing in front of him. "This ain't going to end pretty," he warns me.

"I know," I tell him before watching as he slinks away, leaving Kai staring straight ahead, more than capable of handling the four Wolves on his own.

"I know what you're fucking planning," he tells them, not bothering to look down at me. "Let this be your warning, if you touch even one hair on her body, I will personally end you."

The four Wolves swallow back fear and do their best to look confident, but they're fucking shaking at the thought of having to face down Nic's second in command. Not another word gets said, they just stare, the hatred between them thicker than anything I've ever felt.

I take a hesitant step toward the Wolves and turn to face Kai straight on, showing where I stand, and with that, he shakes his head and walks away.

I watch as the two cars pull away and drive out of the empty parking lot, but the second the Wolves step toward me, I retreat faster than my feet can take me. I race toward the Audi, terrified of being alone with these guys. After all, I am meant to be jumped at some point and after all that bullshit, I'm kinda hoping today isn't the day.

I dive back into the Audi and get my ass out of there, ignoring the twelve missed calls from Colton and the thirteenth that currently has my phone screeching through the car. All that matters is getting home.

CHAPTER 12

"Come on," Colton says, hooking his arm over my shoulders as we walk out of the shitty restaurant that just held the world's worst business dinner. I mean, there is no way that Colton is going to allow those douche canoes to get in bed with him. They were the dodgiest guys I have ever met, and that's saying a lot coming from me. "Let's get out of here before they come at me with more 'paperwork' to back up their ridiculous claims."

I laugh. "I mean, I'm not going to pretend that I understood anything that just went down in there, but even I can tell that those numbers weren't real."

"Exactly. They're just another company on the verge of bankruptcy.

They came here hoping that some stupid eighteen-year-old kid would fall for their bullshit and pull them out of the hole they dug."

I glance up at him, lacing my fingers through his as we walk out to his car, only after he was made to pay for the meal that we were just invited to. I mean, poor form. Again, I don't know shit about this world, but I can more than understand that if you request an audience with Colton Carrington to try and fool him into partnering with your broke ass company, the least you can do is cover the bill. I highly doubt anyone has slid a check across the table toward Colton and asked him to split it before. That kind of shit just doesn't happen around here and says more about them than we learned during the whole dinner. "Does that happen often?" I ask, referring to him constantly being asked to partner in businesses.

"More often than I'd like. I avoid three of these bullshit dinners every week, but these guys have been persistent. They have to be idiots if they think I'd be stupid enough to drag my company down into their bullshit. I get it though. If my company was failing, I'd be hoping the new kid with too much money to spare would be dumb enough to sign a contract. Their biggest mistake tonight was assuming my father didn't teach me the ropes … fucking idiots."

I laugh as I watch him. I love seeing him like this, absolutely dominating this world. He stepped right into his father's shoes, un-did all his dodgy deals, and made his company soar even higher. There's simply nobody like him, and I'm so damn lucky that I get to be the girl crawling into his bed at night. I mean, it also helps that he wears these suits that have all my bits screaming in desperation.

Colton grabs hold of his tie and pulls it until it's loose around his neck. He hooks it over his head and undoes his top button, all while saying something more about the dinner we just suffered through, but in all honesty, I'm stuck on the tie. I wonder how he feels about holding onto that for tonight?

"Jade?" he says, tightening his arm around my shoulder and stealing my attention. "Where'd you go? You disappeared for a second there."

My cheeks flush for the briefest moment before I remember who I'm talking to. There's no need to be shy about this. If anything, he'll be just as down for it as I am. "Well," I tell him. "I was just thinking about all the things you could do with that tie."

His brow arches and his eyes darken, telling me that he's more than down. "Oh, yeah?" he murmurs, leaning into me and brushing his lips over the sensitive skin on my neck before working them up and gently biting my ear lobe. "What'd you have in mind?"

Holy hell.

"Trust me," I whisper, squeezing his hand as my panties begin to soak. "There's not enough time in a night for all the things I have in mind."

Colton's lips twist into a cocky smirk, and I can't help but love it. "Anything you want, Jade," he says with fire burning in his eyes. "But first, there's something I wanted to talk to you about."

Both my brows raise in curiosity. "Like what?"

"Like something serious, something that I'm not about to bring up in a fucking dirty parking lot outside a shitty restaurant. I'll tell you when we get home."

"Come on," I groan, unhooking his arm from my shoulder just so I can glare at him better. "You realize that the whole drive home is going to kill me, right? I can't handle that kind of suspense."

He grins, his eyes sparkling with laughter. "I know."

I roll my eyes. "You suck."

He laughs a little more. "I know that too," he tells me. "But trust me, I know you, Jade, and you're going to want to put this conversation off for as long as you can."

I groan. "This better not be about the whole paying for college thing again."

"It's not."

My brows furrow. "Then what the hell could it be about? Is it bad?"

Colton shakes his head, but the amusement in his eyes is shining brighter than the sun. "I don't think it's bad at all," he murmurs, his voice dropping lower as a grin tears wide across his face. "But you will."

"Fuck, you know I hate you right now," I tell him, resisting having a full-blown tantrum as we finally reach his car. "I'm going to get it out of you."

Colton scoffs as he digs into his suit pocket and pulls out his keys. I walk around to the passenger side as he looks over the top of his car at me, making his way to the driver's door. "I really, really want to watch you try."

I shake my head, way too amused for my own good. I press the fancy little thing that opens the sleek suicide door, and just before I go to get in, I find myself glancing back up at Colton. His eyes are still on mine, so warm and loving, but in the blink of an eye, his face drops, and horror takes over him.

"JADE," he yells, but it's too late. Hands grab at me, and I scream out as I'm tugged back into the darkness of the parking lot. An arm is curled around my head, blocking my vision and sending my world into complete darkness.

Panic soars through me, and I try to pull myself free, but the fingers digging deep into my skin are too tight, too painful. "COLTON," I scream as I'm tossed around. "COLTON."

I tug and try to find purchase on the ground, digging my heels in and desperately trying to get free, searching around, but it's too dark. Disorientation rumbles through me. I don't know where I am, what direction they're dragging me in. How do I get back? How do I even fight?

Fear tears through me. Where's Colton? I try searching, desperately looking around. There are too many hands, too many people.

A familiar chuckle tears through the night, the sound tearing right through to my fears. "You want to be a fucking Wolf, well you got your wish, bitch."

Snake.

Fuck. This is it. This is the Wolves coming to hurt me, jump me into their world. There's no going back after this.

"Get off me, you fucking bastards." I hear the anger and desperation thick in Colton's voice as he struggles against someone. Where is he? There's a scuffle, and I hear flesh being pounded on before the sound of urgent footsteps approach. "If you even think about fucking touching her … JADE? WHERE THE FUCK ARE YOU?"

"COLTON." Tears stream down my face. Where is he? I need him. "I'M HERE. I'M HERE. PLEASE …"

"Shut up, bitch," comes Snake's voice again before a heavy fist slams down over my face, hitting the side of my nose. Pain rockets through me, and I cry out, feeling a warm trickle of blood seeping down from my nose and dropping into the curve of my lips. I taste it there, mixing with my tears.

I grab onto the arm around my eyes before digging my nails deep into his skin. The guy howls in pain, and with every ounce of strength I have, I tear his arm down and bite down as hard as I possibly can.

The arm is torn away from me, and my weight instantly drops to the hard concrete. I don't waste a damn second. I scramble to my feet as I see Snake launching toward me.

Not today, fucker.

I run, heading straight for Colton who's still coming at me. Three guys lay on the ground behind him, all struggling to get to their feet. I reach out and take his hand, and he holds onto it with every ounce of strength he possesses. "Fucking run," he tells me, spinning on the spot before taking off like a fucking bull out of a cage, pushing me ahead of him as the Wolves gain from behind.

I glance back over my shoulder into the night. There are at least twenty of them. We'll never win. I'll never get away from this. Snake bounds down behind me, and with a quick flash, I notice Christian chasing after me, and fuck, he looks sick at what he has to do. "We'll never make it," I panic, yelling across at Colton.

"I'm not about to let you get hurt." My feet pound against the concrete, my heart racing in fear, and then his voice comes again as a cold metal key is put into my hand. "Just keep running," he tells me. "Don't stop until you're in the car. I'll hold them off as long as I can."

"What?"

I look over at him, but it's too late.

Colton releases my hands and turns on the Wolves, ready to give his freedom for mine. "NOOOOOO," I scream, doubling back.

His desperate stare meets mine. "FUCKING RUN, JADE."

Tears stream down my face, but I do as I'm told, refusing to look back as I hear the sound of the Wolves catching up to Colton. There's a scuffle, shouts, and curses before an all too familiar pained groan.

Every fiber in my body screams at me to turn back, to help him, but I keep running, one devastating foot after another.

I'm only a few feet away as I fumble with the key fob, trying to concentrate enough to find the button to automatically open the door. I finally get it, and just as I go to launch myself through the door, a hand curls around my elbow and squeezes hard.

I'm tugged back with a hard yank and completely pulled off my feet. My ass hits the ground, and before I have a chance to pull myself up, my thighs are scraped along the concrete as Snake drags me back toward the darkness.

I scream out as I kick and flail about, doing anything and everything to try and get free. He drags me back past Colton, and as I meet his eyes, four guys struggle to hold him down while another slams his fists into his abdomen. His eyes are dark and wild, filled with desperation, regret, and failure. I can only imagine the things going through his mind right now.

This is all my fault, I did this. He shouldn't be involved. I was so stupid to assume that I'd be safe with him, that they'd leave him out of it. How am I ever going to make up for that?

"I'm going to enjoy this," Snake rumbles, adjusting his grip on me so that he's mainly dragging me by my hair.

I cry out in agony, and Snake laughs as Colton groans, hating nothing more than the sound of my despair. I try to meet his eyes again, but he's lost in a sea of Wolves. "No," I cry, around the sounds of my muffled pain. "Leave him alone."

Another hand grips my upper arm, this one gentle but firm. "Stop fighting it, Ocean," Christian's voice sounds right by my ear. "It'll be quicker that way."

Fearing just how right he is, my body crumples, and I'm thrown into a circle of Wolves as they cheer me on, but not for the reasons anyone would hope for. Colton is barely standing at the outskirts of the circle, restrained and being forced to watch.

I don't dare tear my eyes off his. Right now, he's my only beacon of hope that I might just get out of this alive. But the anguish in his eyes is something that I will never forget, and I despise myself for putting him through this. I've seen him hurting before, I've seen him begging on his knees, but this … this is so much worse than anything I could ever imagine. I've always seen Colton as the strongest person in the room.

Even from his knees, he's like a pillar of strength, an indestructible force. But the hopelessness clouding those beautiful eyes tears my soul right in two. "Don't you fucking give up," he begs me.

I shake my head, trying desperately to swallow past the lump in my throat. "I'm sorry."

His head hangs, and before I can start begging for his forgiveness, a heavy fist slams into me. One after another, hit after hit. Pain rips through me like never before, and I do everything I can to roll into a ball and protect my unborn child.

I scream in agony as the punches keep coming, delivered with hatred. The Wolves come at me with loud grunts and laughter, intent to cause as much damage to my already aching body as they can. Some are wearing rings, and they hurt the worst, tearing my skin right open.

Blood oozes onto the dirty concrete beneath me, and I do everything in my power to tune out Colton's groans and grunts as he tries to fight his way out and get to me.

Boots slam into my ribs, my skin is shredded, and my face is left for the taking as I keep my arms cradled around my stomach, pulled tightly into the fetal position.

Time escapes me, it could only be thirty seconds, or I could have been here for ten minutes before Christian steps in front of me, looking as though he's about to pass out. He meets my eyes, and I instantly clench them, not wanting to see what he's about to do to me, but knowing that if he refused right now, he'll be facing a much worse punishment than this.

He hesitates for the briefest moment. "Just get it over and done with," I grunt through a mouthful of blood, unsure how much longer I can take it. I'd do anything to be anywhere but here. On a tropical beach with Colton, in the darkest pits of hell, fuck, I'll even switch this out for the bullshit I suffered at the hands of Jude Carter.

I feel the brush of air against my skin as Christian steps into me, and with one devastating blow, his fist slams into my chest. I do everything in my power to hold in my grunts of pain, knowing that it's killing him just as much as it is me.

Christian instantly steps back, not willing to touch me again, and just like that Russo steps into the circle and raises his hand. I hadn't even known the fucker was here, but that's just foolish of me. Of course he'd want to see his little snitch taking a beating. Hell, maybe I even deserved it for betraying the boys.

"Enough," Russo says, stopping another Wolf from stepping forward. He meets my eyes, daring me to try and get up, but I don't move, I physically can't. He glances around and with one firm nod, the Wolves clear out of the darkness, leaving Colton to deal with the mess they left behind.

Colton dives toward me, scooping me off the ground and pulling me into his arms. "Fuck, fuck, fuck, Jade. Baby, please tell me you're alright. Can you hear me? Look at me, baby, please. Show me those fucking eyes."

With every last ounce of energy left within my body, I turn my head to look up at him. "I... I..."

"Shhhh, Jade. It's okay. I'm going to make it better," he promises me as a tear rolls down my cheek. "I'm going to make the hurt go away."

I nod, fearing the absolute worst.

"I love you, just hold on," he tells me, the very last words I hear before my world falls into darkness.

CHAPTER 13

A hand twitches in mine, and I'm instantly alerted to the soft rhythmic beep of the hospital room. I peel my eyes open into the bright clinical light while taking note of the agony coursing through my body. I've never felt pain like this. Everywhere hurts. The idea of moving is like some twisted joke.

My eyes scan the room. It's massive. The hospital back home was a piece of shit that I visited with the boys on far too many occasions. It was squishy with six beds jammed into the same room with cheap curtains between them. This here is different. This room is bigger than my whole kitchen and living room back home in Breakers Flats, and there's no doubt in my mind that Colton is paying top dollar for it.

Mom and Colton sit in my room, one on either side of me. Mom just sits, staring at my broken and bruised body while Colton holds my hand, his thumb rubbing back and forth over my fractured skin. His head is dropped down onto the bed beside me, and I can only imagine the bullshit running circles through his head.

I meet Mom's eye and as she gasps and instantly begins sobbing, Colton's head whips up. "Oh, thank fuck," he says, relief pouring over him in waves. He searches my eyes just as I do the same to him. "I thought the fucking worst," he tells me. "The way they were hurting you …"

"I know," I whisper, trying to squeeze his hand, but my strength is completely gone. I glance back at Mom, desperately needing to ease her worries. "I tried to run."

A loud, broken sob tears out of her, and tears stream down her face. "I know, sweetie," she cries. "You would have been so brave." Her words bring tears to my eyes and I do everything that I can to hold it together. If I break, I don't think I'll have the energy to pull myself back together. "How are you feeling? Are you hurting, or do you need some more pain meds?"

"I …" I shake my head, trying to take a mental catalog of everything going on right now. "I don't really know."

"Okay," she says, standing and wiping her tears on the back of her arms, trying to be strong when it's more than okay to fall to pieces. "I'll grab the nurse so she can check you out. You've been out for a few hours."

I nod as best I can, but the movement has a sharp, searing pain shooting down the back of my neck. I keep my pain to myself, not wanting to hurt her any more than I already have. Mom leans into me and ever so gently brushes her lips over my forehead. "I'll be back as soon as I can."

"Okay," I whisper, terrified of my voice breaking.

Silence fills the room as Mom looks down at me, struggling to convince herself to walk out of the room. She takes a heavy breath and then finally takes the few steps to the door, keeping her gaze locked on me until she steps out of the room, leaving me with Colton, who hasn't stopped watching me since the moment his head snapped up.

"How are you really?" he questions, gently squeezing my hand as his thumb continues rubbing back and forth over my skin. Despite the pain pulsing through my veins, his touch soothes me and gives me something else to focus on.

"It hurts so fucking bad," I tell him, finally allowing the tears to flow freely.

"Fuck," he panics, raising out of the stiff chair by my bedside and leaning into me. He props his elbow beside my shoulder and dips his head to mine. His lips brush over mine, and I do my best to savor it before he pulls away. "I'm so fucking sorry, Jade. I should never have dragged you out to dinner with me. I knew there was a chance they would come for you, but I didn't think it'd happen like that. I thought you were safe with me, and I fucking let you down. There were too many. I tried … fuck, Jade, I really tried."

Ignoring the shooting pain through my arm, I raise my hand to his cheek and force his lips back to mine. "Don't do that to yourself," I beg of him. "This is on me. I made the decision to go to the Wolves. I've been around gangs my whole life, I should have known that this was a possibility, but I overlooked it in my need to get revenge."

"I'm going to fucking kill them," he promises me. "Every last one of them who dared put their hands on you."

"You can't," I insist, hating the words as they slip off my tongue. There's nothing I want more than to end them for the fresh hell they just put me through, but without them, I'm left to stand against Nic on my own. I'll never get close to him like that, not now, not after everything that's gone down.

"I don't give a shit about that, not anymore. They took it too far."

"I can't just stop this, Colton. Look at everything that's happened. If I give up now, that means Nic wins, and after everything he's done, I can't let that happen. We've already come so far. Too much has happened for me to wave a white flag now." I gesture down my broken and beaten body, trying to ignore the millions of questions flooding my mind. "Look at me," I demand. "All of this would be for nothing. I can't let that happen, and I know deep down, you can't either."

"Babe…" he groans.

"Please," I whisper, desperately needing him to see this from where I stand. I take his bruised hand in mine and bring it to my lips, gently kissing his split knuckles. "Let this go. I want to have a future, and I want it so badly with you, but without this … we don't stand a chance. You don't know Nic like I do. He will not stop. He's obsessed, and now that I've turned my back on him and betrayed his trust, I'll never be safe. We can deal with the Wolves later, but I have to finish what I started first."

He goes to respond, and I see the objection in his eyes, but Mom comes back in with the doctor on her heels, desperately ushering him into the room so she can hang on every last word he has to offer.

Colton glances away, but there's a silent promise in the air that we'll be talking about this later. He doesn't dare take his hand from mine as the doctor walks deeper into the room and picks up the chart at the foot of my bed. "Miss Oceania," he says in a displeased tone. His eyes remain on the chart, scanning through the papers. "How are you feeling?"

I raise a brow and instantly regret it. "Like I just got run over by a train."

"I can imagine," he grumbles in a disapproving tone, making me wonder what the hell he knows. If I was an innocent victim, I'd assume that his attitude would be a shitload better. But at the end of the day, his attitude isn't what matters, it's what he has to say that does.

"Just rip it off like a bandaid," I tell him. "Give it to me straight."

Mom presses her lips into a tight line, more than inclined to hear the news in the soft, gentle way that she would have done it, but I'm not down for that today. Too much has happened to be wasting time with niceties.

"Okay," he tells me, letting out a deep breath and carelessly dropping the chart back into place before looking at me, making his disapproval more than obvious. "You nearly lost your life today by playing ridiculous games with gang members, so I hope that this will be a lesson to you." Colton flinches at my side, and I squeeze his hand to reel him in. "Three men are sitting in my waiting room, terrifying the patients, who are already being robbed of my attention."

Colton growls. "You're telling me that my girlfriend gets jumped by a fucking gang, and you want to start blaming her?"

"We had no gang activity in Bellevue Springs before this young lady moved in."

Colton stands, glaring at the doctor. "You'll be smart to remember who owns this fucking hospital and pays for your fucking penthouse apartment, your mistress, and the gambling addiction. Now, Ocean has asked you to tell her about her injuries. You have three fucking seconds to do that without the goddamn shitty attitude before I put in a call to the board and have your license revoked."

Well, well. If I wasn't stuck in a hospital bed, wanting nothing more than to bathe in a tub full of morphine, I'd be all over that fucking boss of a man. There's nothing sexier than Colton Carrington in alpha mode.

The doctor clenches his jaw, not taking kindly to threats from an eighteen-year-old kid, but not willing to risk his career on it either. He turns back to me and finally gets on with it. "You have severe, deep bruising all over your body and multiple lacerations. We've done a thorough check and are confident that you have no internal bleeding. You will be in quite a bit of pain for a few weeks. However, it will be manageable with some pain medication. You will need to stay a few days for observation."

I glance at Mom before looking back at the doctor. "And the baby?"

Colton's hand flinches again as we all seem to concentrate extremely hard on the doctor. "The baby seems to be doing well. There's still a heartbeat, however extremely weak. It is imperative that you rest and take care of yourself. Absolutely no stress permitted," he tells me, confusing me as a cloud of disappointment fares through me, making me feel like a horrible person. "There is quite deep bruising around your abdomen, which is why we need to hold you for observation. You're at a very high risk of miscarriage, so as soon as we can, we'll have a sonographer come and perform an ultrasound. It will also be wise to see an obstetrician who will see you through your pregnancy. I'm assuming you haven't looked into that yet?"

I press my lips into a tight line and shake my head. The doctor sighs as though my lack of attention to my healthcare is appalling, and honestly, he'd be right. But where I'm from, you're lucky just to have an obstetrician on call when you happen to walk through the doors with a baby falling out of your cooch. Otherwise, it's up to the ER doctors, and you just have to hope that they know what they're doing.

"Alright," he tells me. "I'll have a list of the best obstetricians in the area put together. Is there anything else I can do for you?" he questions, looking at me though I know the question is open for Colton as well.

"No, thank you," I tell him, nodding and watching as he excuses himself from the room, leaving us all nervously lost in our own thoughts.

I nearly lost the baby today, and for some reason, I can't find it within myself to be hurt about it. That must make me a monster. This is my child, my flesh and blood but at the same time, it's also Jude's, and that makes me resent this child. How will I have this baby and not see Jude in his or her eyes? How will I not always wonder if it'll turn out just like its father?

Is losing this baby really such a bad thing?

Fuck. I should hate myself for even having that thought. This child is innocent. It can't help who its father is, and it seems that I'm no better to have as a mother. If I was to have this baby, I'll fail it. There's no doubt in my mind. How could I be what a baby needs? There are much better parents out there, not me.

The room remains silent until a chirpy blonde comes striding through the door, pushing a big machine. She gives me a warm smile. "Good evening, Ocean. Are you ready to see your baby?"

Fear settles through me. It was a shock seeing it the first time, but seeing it again, now knowing that it's Jude's … yeah, I don't think I'm ready for that, but I really don't think I have a choice.

She shuffles in beside my bed, and Mom moves around her to remain as close as possible. She begins setting it up and looks over me with a sad smile. "I'm sorry this happened to you," she tells me before reaching over and gently peeling my blankets down. "Now, I'm going to have to lift your gown," she says, warning me, in case I need to send Colton or Mom out, but there's no way in hell. "Due to your state, it would be too risky to do an internal ultrasound, so we're going to have to settle for the good old kind and hope bub is strong enough to hear."

My brows furrow, not really understanding anything that's going on as she raises my gown over my stomach. It's still as flat as a pancake, but it sure looks different. My whole abdomen is covered in deep bruising, and it's a miracle that I don't have any broken ribs or internal bleeding. "Holy shit," Mom breathes at the state of my purple and blue skin, taking it all in while Colton looks like he wants to run out of here and beat the living shit out of the Wolves who have claimed the waiting room.

"Okay, this might be cold," the sonographer tells me before squeezing a clear gel onto my stomach. She presses the wand against my abdomen and cringes as she meets my eye. "I'm sorry, love. I'm going to have to press down. It may be a little uncomfortable."

I nod, holding onto Colton's hand a little bit tighter, and as the soft, rhythmic drumming of a heartbeat fills the room, all eyes turn toward the screen. "Ahh, there he is."

"He?" my mom asks, her eyes lifting to the chirpy blonde.

The sonographer shakes her head. "Sorry, I tend to refer to them all as 'he' out of habit. It's still a little too early to determine the baby's sex." Mom nods as the sonographer focuses back on the screen. Her brows furrow, and after a short moment, she looks back at me. "How far along were you?"

"Umm … I'm at eight weeks now."

"Hmm," she says, glancing back at the monitor. "I'm sorry, but I do this every day, and you're looking a little small for eight weeks. Do you mind if I take a few measurements?"

Colton straightens out beside me, his hand tightening in mine as the wheels begin to spin in all of our minds. "Are you sure?" I question. "The doctor in Breakers Flats assured me that I was seven weeks when

I got checked last Friday."

She shrugs her shoulders and gives me a gentle smile. "Well it couldn't hurt to double-check now, can it?"

"Actually, it can," Mom throws in. "It could mean the difference between the father of this baby being a rapist or not."

Her eyes go wide, and she looks back down at me, only to see the desperation and the sliver of hope her words have given me, and right now, that hope is a dangerous thing. "Okay," she murmurs, turning back to the monitor. "Then we better be thorough."

She starts taking her measurements, and the tension that builds in the room with every passing second is nearly enough to have me blacking out again. Two minutes become three, and by the time four minutes is finally approaching, she turns back to me and lets out a breath. "Alright, Ocean. I really hope this is good news for you. You're measuring at six weeks and five days."

Colton looks lost. "What does that mean? Is it mine?"

I shake my head, trying to do the math. Mom watches me in silent desperation, begging for a good outcome. I'd give anything for this baby to be Colton's. "I ... I don't know. We were together two weeks after Jude ... I mean," I look back up at the sonographer. "Does that mean he's the father?"

She shakes her head, looking doubtful. "Look, I'd highly recommend doing a paternity test in a few weeks. It's really very hard to tell unless you were tracking your cycle and can pinpoint when you ovulated last and can remember the dates in which you were sexually active."

"But I … I have PCOS. Tracking my cycle is nearly impossible. I mean, I … " I glance up at Mom, hoping for some kind of help. "I don't even know how to tell when I'm ovulating."

"Oh, honey," Mom says. "Don't stress. We'll do a test and get this sorted out, alright. There's no need to panic just yet. The doctor is going to set you up with an Obstetrician, and she or he will be able to guide you through this."

I nod, not feeling the panic ease one bit, but if I don't at least pretend for Mom, she'll start to panic herself.

"Alright," the woman says. "I'll leave you guys to it, but if you have any other questions, please feel free to shout out."

I give her a small smile as Mom thanks her for her time, all while Colton just stands and stares at the monitor with a frozen image of the baby growing inside my stomach. "It could be mine," he whispers with hope, finally dropping back to the seat beside me.

I shake my head. "I don't know. There's too much going on. My head is too sore to even begin trying to work out the dates."

"It's okay, honey," Mom says. "It's only a few weeks before you can take the paternity test. You just need to focus on healing. You've been through quite a lot these past few weeks." Her phone rings, and as she glances down, she cringes. "I'm sorry, sweet girl. It's Roman. He's been waiting for an update on your condition."

"It's fine," I tell her. "Take it. It's not like I can go anywhere."

She gives me a sad smile, and within seconds, she answers the call and hurries out of the room, leaving me with a still stunned Colton. I glance over at him and tug on his hand, forcing him closer. "I guess it's

Milo's turn to be my bitch."

A grin twists across Colton's face, and he shakes his head. "I can't believe you're fucking joking about this."

"Why the hell wouldn't she?" A voice rumbles through the room, sending shivers down my spine and fear pulsing through my veins. "She's a Wolf now. She's strong."

Russo welcomes himself deeper into my room, and I watch as Snake follows him in with Christian at his side.

Colton instantly flies to his feet and takes a step toward them, keeping himself as a barrier between them and me. "Get the fuck out."

Russo tsks him, shaking his head in disapproval. "You're lucky that I'm not sending you out of here, boy. She's one of mine now."

My jaw clenches at his words as I scan my gaze over my intruders. Russo watches me with a curious stare, almost as though I've surprised him, while Snake looks as though he's come to finish the job. Christian on the other hand, stands beside his father looking as though he's about ready to slice Snake's throat. It's clear that his only intention for being here right now was to check in on me and make sure that I'm still breathing. Keeping Snake in line in the process is just an added bonus.

Colton snaps back at Russo. "Over my dead fucking body."

"Careful, now," Russo warns. "You took quite a beating today. Ending you right here in front of your girl wouldn't be hard, but she's already gone through enough today, and I don't want to give her another reason to be distrustful of me. So, kindly step aside so that I may speak with my girl."

Colton laughs. "You're fucking insane if you think I'm about to leave her with you."

"Then, by all means, sit your ass down and shut up so that I can get out of here."

Colton glances back at me, and I quickly nod, letting him know that it's alright. Now that I've officially been jumped in, I'm considered family, and any hand laid on me, is a hand laid against Russo.

Colton steps back, keeping close to me but he refuses to sit down, a move that isn't lost on Russo. His gaze sweeps over Colton and I watch as Snake takes it as a sign of disrespect and goes for his gun. "Sit your motherfucking ass down, rich boy."

Christian clenches his jaw, almost as though he's embarrassed by Snake's recklessness all while Russo throws out his hand, barring it across Snake's chest. "Back off before I make you," Russo growls.

Snake looks back at Russo in astonishment, but Russo doesn't spare him another thought as his eyes come back to mine. "I've come to check that you were healing well."

"You mean check that you didn't kill me?" I demand.

Russo nods, not denying it in the least. "The rapist's baby?"

"Alive."

"Damn. That's a shame," he says, having the nerve to actually look as though he cares.

I narrow my eyes, giving him the stare that works so perfectly on the bitches at school. "Why are you really here?" I demand, not in the mood to pussyfoot around. "Just get on with it so you can get out of here and let me rest."

Surprisingly, Russo nods. "Very well then," he says. "I've come to inform you that now you are officially a member of my family, we can get to business."

"I thought we were already in business?"

Russo laughs. "Do you honestly think I would go out of my way for a child who was not one of mine to protect? You're a Wolf now, so I can give you what you're after, but I did it my way, and we'll be going ahead with an attack against the Black Widows."

My eyes bug out of my head. "No. That's not what I wanted. There are good guys in there. Just take Nic."

Russo shakes his head. "What did I tell you, pup? We play by my rules. Dominic Garcia took out my second, and he'll be paying for it with his life. I don't care who has to go down beside him. The more the merrier. With Dominic out of the way, the Wolves will thrive once again."

Fuck, what have I done? I can't be responsible for a mass murder. If Nic was under attack, my boys will jump in and lay their lives down for him. They'll do anything to protect each other's back, and that's going to be on me. The death of my boys is going to be on my shoulders.

I meet Christian's eyes and he gives me a blank stare before discreetly shaking his head, telling me to keep my mouth shut.

"When?" Colton demands.

Russo grins, his sick stare slicing across to Colton before coming back to me. "Isn't the unknown always a part of the fun?" he questions. "Be this a warning to you both, Ocean is a Wolf now, and she's expected to behave like one. I own her loyalty, and if that was to get betrayed, there will be consequences. Trust me when I say, you don't want to see what happens to somebody who betrays me."

With that, Russo turns on his heel and stalks out of the room, taking his son and his henchman with him while leaving me completely horrified with the mess I've created.

I glance at Colton and see the same horrors in his eyes, and as he looks at me, a silent message passes between us. We have to do something about this, but neither of us even know where to begin.

CHAPTER 14

The soft rainy drizzle splashes against the Veneno as Colton drives through the streets of Bellevue Springs, wanting nothing more than to get my ass home where I belong. It's been a long few days in the hospital, but the pain meds have more than helped to pass the time. I think I've slept more over the last few days than I've ever slept in my life.

The few days of rest saw the baby's heart rate strengthen to where it's supposed to be while the nurses did an incredible job of taking care of my bruises, cuts, and scrapes. Don't get me wrong, they're still there in fine form, but compared to Saturday night, they're a million times better.

Nothing has happened between the Wolves and the Widows, but one thing is for sure, my boys have been blowing up my phone since they were run off in the parking lot after school on Friday. I'm pretty sure they showed up at Colton's place, and after Mom had explained that I'd officially been jumped in, they've been keeping their distance.

I have to admit, not having to worry about getting jumped anymore is definitely a relief, but now there's another whole thing that's weighing down on me, something so much worse. This is people's lives in the balance. How will I ever fix this?

"Are you sure you want to sleep in the pool house? You can hardly move around. I can have the living room turned into your own personal hideout so you can chill out there while you heal. That way you won't be lonely, and you can see what's going on."

I shake my head. "No, I'd prefer to be in my own bed where I can be a hermit and lock everyone out."

"Babe …"

"No. Don't 'babe' me. There's nothing worse than being stuck in the living room where I'm going to have maids coming in and out, vacuuming around me, and listening to your sisters arguing over what they're going to have for breakfast. Besides, in my room, I can just turn on Netflix, sleep, and be a pig until someone barges in on me."

Colton laughs. "There won't be anyone barging in on you because you'll have someone with you all the time. Not to mention, Milo's been past four times already, bringing over magazines, books, loading the freezer with all the wrong kinds of ice cream, and filling your bedside table with every kind of vibrator under the sun."

"What?" I laugh. "Why the hell would I need vibrators?"

Colton shrugs his shoulders. "I don't know. I guess he figures you'd be too sore to fuck. So this way, you can take care of yourself, but honestly, it's really not necessary. I can take care of every little need you have."

A grin tears across my face. "Well, he's kinda right," I admit. "My hip has been really hurting, so spreading my legs is kinda a no-go at the moment."

"Fuck, really? Why didn't you say anything? Do you want me to call a physio and have you checked out?"

"I didn't say anything because I knew you'd be like this," I say, gently shaking my head and resisting laughing at how right I was. "But no, It's been feeling better and better every day. I think it just needs time to heal."

"Fine," he groans as the drizzling rain begins to pick up. "But if I hear you complain about it just once, I'll be making the call."

I hold my hand up and salute him with a cheesy grin. "Yes, sir."

He glances across at me while navigating through the heavy rain. "That's more like it."

I roll my eyes, and before I know it, we're pulling into his drive. I watch as his window drops, and he sticks his arm out into the rain to hash in the code for the gate. The gate slowly peels open and I can't resist teasing him. "Geez, for being the richest kid on the block, anyone would think that you'd have some kind of high-tech sensor gate that just automatically opened every time you drive in. I'm disappointed. This shit you have here, this is gated community, low class style."

Colton's head slowly turns toward me, a sharp glare resting in his eyes. "What did you just say about my front gate?"

I hold back a grin. "It's lacking … and it's kinda slow too."

His mouth drops open just as the gate opens fully, patiently waiting for us to drive past. "We're not moving until you apologize to the gate."

"In your dreams," I laugh. "It's slow, and you know it."

Colton looks out the front window of his car, staring at the gate in question. "It's waiting," he grumbles, before glancing back at me with his eyes sparkling. "For the record, I've got absolutely nothing to do today. I can do this for hours while you're probably already cramping up and sore."

"I think you underestimate just how stubborn I can be."

"I think you're the one underestimating."

I sit back in my seat, crossing my arms over my chest, making a point of not being the one to budge while Colton leans over and grabs a packet of candies out of the center console, also making a point of all the time he has to waste.

One minute passes, then two, and then my ass begins to get sore.

I clench my jaw, feeling my resolve beginning to break. "Oh, fuck it. I'm sorry I hurt your goddamn gate's feelings, but you can't deny that I'm right."

Colton looks back at me, and with a cocky grin, he finally hits the gas, sailing past the stupid gate. We get up to the mansion in no time, and as the Veneno comes to a stop in the ridiculously packed garage, I try my best to get my ass out.

The door swings wide, and as I attempt to move around, Colton gapes at me. "What the fuck do you think you're doing?" he demands, hurrying out of the car and rushing around to my side. "Just wait. I'll help you."

"I can manage," I insist.

"Jade, you can't even scratch your ass without howling in pain. Just let me help you in. Once there are people around, then I'll let you pretend that you're a badass bitch, but until then, I'm helping, and that's non-negotiable."

I groan but as he takes hold of me and helps me to my feet, I've never been so grateful. Doing that on my own would have hurt like a bitch. Sometimes I really hate that stubborn part of me that screams to always be in charge. I mean, why is it always so hard to accept help?

Colton slips his arm around my waist and helps me into the house, only to find it nearly dead inside. "Where is everyone?" I murmur.

He shrugs his shoulders. "How am I supposed to know? I've been with your stubborn ass all day."

I resist rolling my eyes as he leads me through the mansion. "Good point."

We take all the shortcuts on our way to the pool house, and as we go, I can't help but look up at Colton. "Hey, on Saturday night before all of this happened … you said something about wanting to talk."

"Yeah …"

"Well?" I ask. "Spit it out. What better time than the present?"

"Trust me, any other time is better than now. You have too much going on, and honestly, it might not even be an issue anymore."

"You know, I really hate when you do that."

"Do what?"

"Give me little hints about what it is but keep it so freaking vague that it's nearly impossible to figure out."

"Exactly, that way you won't have anything to go by and won't be able to work yourself into a panic over nothing." He laughs, reaching out and opening the back door of his home before helping me out. We stand under a shelter, and he cringes as he looks out at the rain, knowing damn well that to get to the pool house, we're going to have to cut through the weather. "Are you going to hate me if I was to just toss you over my shoulder and run?"

"Considering the fact that if you were to toss me over your shoulder, I'd probably scream in pain, then yeah, I can't see that being a very good idea."

"It was worth a shot," he grumbles, tightening his arm around my waist so that I don't slip on the wet floors before stepping out into the rain. We pick up our pace, and within two seconds, we're completely drenched from head to toe. What was I thinking? I should have just let him set me up in the living room, but no, I had to insist on staying in the pool house so I can be a pig, living in my own filth. Okay, I probably won't be that bad, but the point is there.

The rush toward the pool house door seems to take forever, and I've never felt like such a drowned rat before, but the fact that Colton is right there with me, equally as wet, makes it all so much better.

I hook my fingers around the door handle, and with the speed of light, I swing the door open and get myself inside before I end up with a cold on top of everything else that's been going on.

The pool house is in darkness and in the blink of an eye, it floods with light, revealing a room full of people with the cheesiest grins stretched across their beautiful faces.

"HAPPY BIRTHDAY!" they all yell, scaring the absolute shit out of me.

I gape in surprise at Mom, Harrison, the twins, Jess and Drix, and of course Milo, Charlie, and Spencer. Hell, even Roman is here, standing by my mom's side with his arm curled lovingly around her waist.

"What the hell is going on?" I ask, my eyes wide as Milo sends streamers shooting up into the sky, only to get caught on the ceiling fan.

Colton steps into my side with an arrogant smirk. "What's going on is that you forgot to mention that it was your birthday."

I cringe. "Whoops. Did I forget about that?" He raises a brow, knowing damn well that I didn't just 'forget' to mention it. I didn't tell him or anyone else on purpose. "Sorry," I say when he won't stop glaring. "There's just a lot going on and celebrating just kinda felt … wrong."

He leans into me and presses a kiss to my temple. "I don't care. It's your birthday. You only turn eighteen once, and you deserve to celebrate. Who cares about all the other shit? It's still going to be there tomorrow, so there's no point hiding out today."

"Are you sure?"

"Yes, now go and see your mom. She's annoyed that you tried to keep it quiet."

"And what about you?"

"You don't want to go there," he warns me. "I wouldn't have minded a little heads up so that I could have gotten you something."

I stretch up onto my tippy-toes, ignoring the dull ache that still remains in my sore muscles. "But why would I want anything else when I have everything I need right here?"

Colton rolls his eyes, a scoff tearing from deep in his chest. "Don't be cheesy."

I pull back from him, meeting his eyes. "Promise me you won't go and do anything?"

He grins back with a guilty sparkle hitting his hazel eyes. "I don't know what you're talking about."

"Colton," I warn, raising a brow. "Whatever you have planned … don't. I don't want any elaborate gifts from you because I'll never be able to do the same for you."

"Like I said," he tells me, his grin bigger than ever. "I don't know what you're talking about. Now go and see everyone so they can curse you out for doing them dirty."

"Shit."

Colton releases his hold on my waist, and I take a second to find myself without his support before finally walking into my mother's arms. "How are you feeling?" she questions, wrapping me in a warm hug and giving me a gentle squeeze.

"How do you think I'm feeling?" I say, unable to hide the smile in my tone. "I know this party was all your doing."

She shrugs her shoulders, not sorry at all. "What can I say? You're my only child, and you reached a milestone. The Widows and Wolves can wait another day to declare war while my baby celebrates her birthday."

"You realize how insane this is, right? I highly doubt my douchebag doctor is going to approve of a party the same day I get released from the hospital."

Mom winks. "Don't you worry about that," she tells me, taking my shoulders and gently turning me to face the couch, which is currently set up with everything I could possibly need. "We have you sorted. So, go and sit that toosh down. I've instructed everyone to come and worship at your feet. Anything you want, it's yours."

I raise my brow as a grin tears across my face. I could get used to that.

Like the bossy, over-protective mother that she is, Mom pushes me right toward the couch before even getting a chance to say hello to anyone else, even the man who stands right by her side.

She gets me comfortable and fluffs a pillow at least twelve times before helping to slide it behind my back. She's hardly even straightened out before Milo and Drix are there, stealing my attention.

Milo drops to his knee and bows his head. "My queen. How dareth you not tell me about your eighteenth dayeth of birth. I'm wounded."

"Ugh," Drix laughs, bumping him with her ass and watching him fumble to the side, making me realize that the two of them are already white girl wasted. "And here I thought you were the only queen around here."

Milo laughs and hooks his finger through the belt loop on her jeans before giving her a hard tug and sending her crashing into the other half of the couch. "Please accept my sincerest apologies, milady. Do allow me to take out the trash for you."

The two of them giggle like idiots as Charlie and Spencer watch on with grim, exhausted expressions, making me wonder just how long they've been putting up with these two lightweights.

Jess strolls over and boots the two drunken morons out of the way before leaning into me and giving me a big hug. "Happy birthday," she tells me with a warm smile. "How are you feeling?"

"I'm alright," I murmur just as music starts blaring through the speakers and the two drunken morons begin doing the WAP with more than practiced moves. I can't help but laugh as Charlie and Spencer begin watching with interest, and just like that, a wide smile stretches across my face. "And I have a feeling it's only going to get better."

Cora and Casey get in on the action, leaving Colton watching on in horror while Roman gapes at his daughter, only now just realizing that maybe she isn't the good little girl he's always thought her to be. Mom watches on, for the first time being more than thrilled that her daughter is stuck on the couch.

It only takes her thirty seconds to look up at Roman with wide eyes, and without saying a word, he nods, and the parents quickly vacate the premises, leaving us to fuck around and have the time of our lives.

CHAPTER 15

One day turns to two and before I know it, a week has passed with me anxiously waiting on the couch, desperate to hear news on the Widows or the Wolves. The more time that passes, the more I become frustrated with the situation. Not knowing is killing me. I need to know when they plan to attack, and I need to make sure that my boys aren't around when it happens.

How can I be responsible for this? This has gotten so out of hand, so much bigger than what I was looking for. My only saving grace is that Nic won't want to see me harmed.

I have to admit, the last few days haven't been so bad as I've sat in bed and healed. Milo has come over to keep me company, just as I did for him. He instantly started comparing our battle wounds, subtly suggesting that he was left in a worse way after his attack. But honestly, two guys beating on him really doesn't compare to the twenty Wolves jumping me. I think he just wants to pretend that he's tough, and that's more than okay. We all need a little tough in our lives sometimes.

It's Saturday morning, and I've just spent the last hour spying through the bathroom window of the pool house, looking into the mansion and watching Colton working up a sweat in his home gym. I can't believe I've never noticed that the two windows line up before, but walking in here to find him dragging his shirt over his head and revealing his perfectly sculpted chest and abs was one hell of a nice surprise. I'll never get bored of watching Colton working his body. It's hypnotic. He's hypnotic.

Realizing how ridiculous it is to spend the day hiding out in my bathroom and spying on my boyfriend, I make my way back to my room, getting dressed in a comfortable pair of sweatpants and a cropped black tank. Hell, I even brush my hair before throwing it up. I've been holed up inside the pool house all week, and it's starting to drive me a little stir crazy.

I take myself into Colton's big ass home and give a quick smile to Casey, who I pass in the living room, not surprised to find her nose stuck deep in a book. She hardly looks up as I pass, just grunts out a quick 'hey' and looks more than happy to see me continue past.

I make my way down to Colton's home gym and lean against the door frame, looking in to find him lying on the bench with a weighted bar above his head. The bar slowly travels up and down, and I instantly become mesmerized by the way his muscles bulge.

"Are you just going to stand there and watch me, or are you going to walk that sweet ass in here?"

I grin as I watch him, and then push off the door frame, welcoming myself into his gym with a nervous cringe settling across my face. "I … um … I think I need to go into Blaxlands Grove today."

Colton instantly racks his bar up above his head and pulls up until he's staring right at me. "You're fucking insane, right?"

"I'm serious," I tell him. "I can't just sit back and do nothing. I need to know the plan, and I need to know how to fix it. Sitting back in bed all week is killing me. I have to change his mind somehow. I can't be responsible for a mass murder."

"Nic is a big boy, Ocean. He knew what he was doing when he killed your father. He would have been expecting this very outcome since the second he decided to go ahead with it. I know he's a fucking dickhead, but he's not stupid. He knew what he was doing."

"I get that," I argue. "But what about the rest of them?"

Colton stands, letting out a breath before grabbing his drink and taking a hard pull. He walks toward me and places his hands on my shoulders, making sure that I'm listening to his every word. "They're not your problem. This isn't on your shoulders. All you did was give Russo Nic's name. He's the one who's doing this. He would have eventually figured out who killed your dad, and he would have still gone to war. You need to stop allowing this to bring you down. The Widows know what they're doing following Nic just as the Wolves know what they're doing being in league with Russo."

I drop my haze, unable to meet his eyes. "I …"

"Jade, no," he breathes, desperate to keep me here where he knows I'll be safe. "What can I do to make you see that you're not guilty in this? You haven't hurt anyone, you've never taken a man's life, you've only ever been guilty of caring too much."

"I'm just … I'm sorry. I have to go down there and see what's going on. All this waiting to hear something is driving me insane."

"There's nothing I can do to change your mind, is there?" I press my lips into a hard line and gently shake my head before he steps in close and drops his forehead to mine. "You're going to do everything in your power to make this happen without me by your side, aren't you?"

I nod, realizing just how well he's come to know me. "I'm not going to drag you into this world, Colton. They'd drain you of everything you have. It's too dangerous for you."

"I can handle myself."

"Please, I just need you to trust me one more time."

He rubs his thumb over the faded bruising on my cheekbone. "I trusted you against my better judgment, and look how that turned out."

"They won't hurt me now. I'm one of them now. All they can do is tell me to fuck off. Anything other than that is going against Russo, and he won't stand for that. Besides, Christian and Jaren will be there. I'll be safe."

"Do I need to remind you that Christian was the guy who delivered the final punch?"

"Really, you don't need to remind me about that. I'm more than aware of what happened. I remember every little second of it."

Colton shakes his head. "I don't like it, but if you really insist on doing this, then I'm coming with you."

I raise my chin, letting him see the defiance in my eyes. "No, you're not. I understand that you're protective of me, and I know how much it killed you seeing me get hurt, but I can't have you there. Russo was lenient letting you stay in the hospital room while he talked, he won't offer that same leniency again. He'll take it as you shitting all over his generosity."

Colton scoffs at my use of the word generosity. He steps back from me and runs his hands through his hair. "I don't like this."

"I know, I don't either, but whether we like it or not, this is a part of my life now, and in the long run, saving face with Russo is going to be better than him thinking that I'm still loyal to the Widows."

"FUCK, OCEAN," he grunts, beginning to pace the room before turning back to me. "I really fucking hate it when you're right."

I walk into him and take his hands, lacing his fingers through mine. "So, you're not going to fight me on this?"

He groans, and it's obvious just how much this situation is hurting him, but it's better than me just slipping out the door and not telling him about any of it. "I want a call from you the second you get there, and then a text every five minutes after that until you're back in the car and coming home to me. Got it? If you even miss one of those texts, I'll be coming after you."

I press up onto my tippy toes and brush my lips over his. "Thank you. I promise I'll be as quick as I can be."

"Good. Try not to let any of those fuckers jump you again."

"I promise."

He groans again, his frustration coming out loud and proud before blowing out a deep breath. "Get out of here before I change my mind."

"Okay, love you," I tell him before slowly stepping back and allowing our hands to drop into the empty space between us.

He gives me a pained smile, and before I convince myself to stay, I hurry out of his gym and make my way to the garage.

Just as I've become accustomed to, I drop into the Audi and hit the button for the remote garage. It opens wide, letting the morning sunlight spill into the oversized showroom. I hit the gas, and two hours later, I'm bringing the Audi to a stop and trying to remind myself of why I thought that I needed to be here.

I give Colton the call he'd asked for, and after demanding that I keep my attitude to myself while I'm in there, I end the call and take a shaky breath. I shouldn't be so scared of this. I should be able to walk in there with my head held high. After all, I'm one of them now. There shouldn't be a reason for any of them to want to hurt me now. What a fucking joke.

I climb out of the Audi and slip my phone into my back pocket, right beside the gun that sits in the waistband of my sweats before locking the car and walking toward the Wolf Den.

I can only imagine what Nic and the boys would think of me voluntarily walking into a place like this.

Fuck, I miss them. I miss the relationship we used to have. It was so simple, so easy and full of love, and now it's just strained, broken, and pathetic. I have faith that Sebastian, Kai, and Eli will come around though. They have to.

Shaking the thought from my head, I push through the same door that I'd come through two weeks ago, only this time, I'm not met with a welcome party. The Wolf Den is just as I remember it—dark, haunting, and terrifying.

There are people scattered everywhere, all minding their own business. Nearly everyone glances up as I walk through the Den but instantly looks away. I pass a scowling Scarface who watches my every step, yet he remains where he is, and I can't help but wonder if that's due to me stealing his gun and kicking his ass or if it's because I was jumped in. Probably the latter.

Not wanting to engage with anyone but the people I know, I walk straight over to the bar and let out a breath of relief seeing Jaren busily working. I might have told a little white lie in telling Colton that Jaren and Christian would be here in case things went south, but if I was left to defend myself, I would never have been able to get him to agree to this. Actually finding Jaren here makes me feel a million times better though.

"Well, well, look who the Wolves dragged in."

"Ha. Ha. Funny," I tell him darkly. "What's going on?"

"Not much," he says, scanning his gaze over my bruises with disappointment shining in his eyes. "So it's true, huh? You got jumped in?"

"Unfortunately," I grumble, feeling ashamed of the bruises and wishing that I could somehow hide them away.

"You okay?" he asks. "Mine was brutal."

"I'll live," I tell him. "Have you seen Russo? I need to speak to him."

Jaren shrugs his shoulders. "Pretty sure he's in his office. He never really comes out of it during the day, only for special occasions."

"You mean when a knocked up seventeen-year-old girl shows up at the door with information on the one guy he's been trying to take out for years?"

"Yeah," he says, nodding as a grin spreads wide over his face. "That'll do it."

I roll my eyes and push off the edge of the bar, heading toward the side door and pushing through to the back rooms. It would be so much easier if I actually remembered which one of these doors was his office.

As I walk, I pull out my phone and send a quick text, knowing damn well that Colton would be watching the clock like a hawk with his keys already in his hands, assuming he didn't actually follow me here and is just waiting around the corner.

Ocean - I'm alive! You can relax.

Colton - Like hell, I'll be able to relax. Get what you're looking for then get your ass out of there.

I grin to myself, knowing I shouldn't tease him but finding it impossible not to.

Ocean - Really? Some of the guys mentioned having a rave in the Den tonight. I was thinking I could stick around and party

with them.

Colton - Home. Now.

I laugh as I slip my phone back into the pocket of my sweatpants, finally finding the right office. My hand curls around the doorknob, and I twist while gently wrapping against the wooden door.

I swing it open and step into the office, not bothering to wait for an invitation. After all, Russo certainly hasn't offered me the same consideration. "Hey, I … WOAH, FUCK."

I come to a startling stop, staring ahead at Russo, who stands at his desk with a platinum blonde, buried deep inside of her as her head is pressed down against the dirty desk.

I know I should scramble away and start apologizing. Yet I find myself unable to move, unable to take my eyes off the woman who looks as though she's seeing a ghost.

Laurelle Fucking Carrington.

A grin stretches over my face, and I lean back against the open door before I start howling in laughter. "Well, well," I say as she finally pulls herself together and fixes her designer skirt back into place. "There's a face I never thought I'd be unlucky enough to ever have to see again. This certainly is unexpected."

Laurelle shoots a fierce glare at me before turning back to Russo. "Do something," she shrieks in that over-privileged tone of hers. "Get rid of her."

Russo drops down into his desk chair, batting her out of his way as he shrugs his shoulders. "Not going to happen, love," he says. "She's a Wolf now. If anyone should be leaving, it'd be you."

"Excuse me? You made this little bitch a Wolf?" she demands, looking down at him as though she can kill him with just her stare alone, which obviously has absolutely no effect on Russo.

"You heard me," he says, pulling open his desk drawer and pulling out a cigar. He takes a moment to light it up, and soon enough, a cloud of smoke gets blown into Laurelle's face. "Now, see yourself out. You've done your job. I needed you to watch over Ocean until I could get to her, and you've done that. I'm finished with you now."

Laurelle's eyes widen in horror, just as mine do. Russo was the one to put her in my life? She never actually came back to see Colton? This is ridiculous. How does he have that kind of pull, you know, apart from the obvious stuff like being the guy who's currently fucking her?

Her glare falls onto me, and realizing that I'm not about to leave, she focuses back on her Wolfy lover. "Excuse me?" she demands. "No one dismisses me like that. Do you have any idea who I am? That bitch put me through hell. She cost me my son and humiliated me in front of the Bellevue Springs elite. I'm not leaving until she's dealt with. You promised that she would be dealt with."

"And she was, but let's face it, Laurelle, you came here to fuck and for nothing else," he snaps back at her, "I happily obliged, but now it's time for business." He glances back at me with curiosity in his eyes while waving his hand toward Laurelle. "I trust you can find your own way out."

Laurelle sucks in a deep breath and slams her hand down on his desk, making me jump while he doesn't even flinch. "I said that I wanted her dealt with. I haven't been coming here every week for the past four months and sucking your dick for nothing. Finish this."

Russo stands and grabs Laurelle by the throat. He shoves her up against the wall and leans into her, easily overpowering her and reminding her just how replaceable she is. I'm sure a guy like Russo would have a line of women waiting to have their turn with him, hoping he could offer them and their families some kind of protection from the outside world.

"You seem to forget who you're talking to," Russo growls. "I've put up with your bullshit for months now. If I knew you were going to be such a demanding little whore, I would have used one of those prissy daughters of yours instead. I wanted Ocean, and now I've got her. You're done here. There's nothing else for you."

Her eyes flick to mine, and I see the panic deep within them, knowing that Russo isn't above snapping her neck like a twig, but it's not my place. She cuts her gaze back to Russo and knowing my eyes are on her, she decides to play brave. "You said I'd get paid."

"You were paid, baby," he says, leaning into her and rubbing his groin against her hip. "If you wanted cash, you should have specified. My time and dick don't come free."

She stares at him a minute longer, clenching her jaw until he finally releases his hold on her. She sags once his tight grip is removed from her neck and with no other choice, she runs for the door, not sparing me another glance.

I stare at the empty doorway in shock. Did that really just happen?

Russo drops back into his desk chair. "Ocean," he says welcomingly, as though a scorned woman didn't just run out of here after having her neck just moments from being snapped. "Lovely to see you so soon. You seem to be healing well."

"I, umm … yeah."

"What can I do for you?"

I stare at him, unable to recall the reasons that brought me to his office as I'm still far too caught up on everything I'd just learned. "You put her in my life?" I say, completely baffled by the connection. I mean, how did they even meet in the first place?

Russo's brows furrow, confused about why I feel the importance to ask. "Yes," he states. "I thought that much was clear. I told you that I had people watching you."

"Yeah, but I figured you just meant your men, not those kinds of people. Who else is on your payroll that's been hiding in plain sight, pretending to be someone they're not?"

He shakes his head, deep in thought. "That's a very broad question," he says. "I'm not about to go telling you all of my secrets, but I guess now that you're one of mine, there's no harm in sharing the names of those who have immediate access to you."

"Names? As in plural? How many people do you have watching me?"

"There have been plenty. I've had eyes on you since the second your father was murdered. But let's see, in more recent months, Robert Rinaldi and the coach at that ridiculous school … what was his name?"

My eyes widen. "Coach Sylvester?"

"Yeah, that's the one. He's been on my payroll for years. It was a real hassle when you had him fired. That cost me a bit of money having him bailed out. That idiot just had to go and incriminate himself. I should have left him rotting in that cell. He's only ever caused me trouble, just like you seem to be doing. I had to go and get Dean Simmon's onside after that."

I gape at him. "Go back. Robert Rinaldi? As in Milo's father?"

Russo shrugs a shoulder. "I believe so. I can't say that I'm particularly familiar with the names of his offspring."

"Wait … just wait," I say as dread sinks heavily into my stomach. "Are you telling me that Milo was put in my life? Does he know about this?"

Russo looks to be getting bored of our conversation and leans back into his chair. "I can't speak for your friend. That's a conversation you will have to have with him. I'm not about to pretend to know about the conversations Rinaldi has with his son. Now, tell me why you're sitting in my office."

"I …" I shake my head, still struggling to wrap my head around everything that's gone down over the last few minutes, but I have no choice. After all, there is a reason I'm here, and it's a shitload more important than Russo having a few of his watchdogs on me.

I meet his eye and swallow back fear, showing him that I deserve to know every last fucking detail he has. "I need to know what's going down with the Widows, and I won't be taking no for an answer."

Russo watches me a little while longer, studying the sharp lines of my clenched jaw. His eyes narrow in consideration, and as he relaxes back into his chair and laces his fingers, the most unexpected words come out of his mouth. "Alright," he finally says. "Here's what you need to know."

CHAPTER 16

The Audi flies through the streets of Blaxlands Grove and into Breakers Flats. I'm doing anything and everything to try and be okay with what just happened. I drive on auto-pilot, not even sure where I'm going until I'm pulling up at the shitty little lake where I used to come with the boys.

I'd called Colton the second I got out of there but told him that I needed some space to breathe. He didn't object but seeing as though I was out of the Den, he really had no reason to argue. I could tell he wanted me home, but that's going to have to wait until I can begin to wrap my head around everything I just learned. I mean, Laurelle Carrington was screwing Mikhail Russo, and then on top of that, Milo might have been put into my life. Is our friendship even real, or is he being forced to remain by my side? I think I'd break if I discovered it wasn't real.

After pushing the seat back and swinging the door open wide, I prop my feet up onto the dash, and look out over the water. The breeze sails through the open door and watching the lake before me is so soothing and refreshing. I'd give anything to have the life of still water—drama free. The only thing it has to worry about is drying out in the middle of summer, but even then, when the kids come to play, all it ever sees is joy and happiness.

I just want it to be over. I'm sick of walking around every corner, only to be smacked in the face with someone else's bullshit on top of all the bullshit already circulating my life.

Ten minutes turn into twenty, and before I know it, a familiar car is pulling in beside me. That's my cue, telling me that it's time to go, only I can't find the strength to turn the car back on and get out of here.

I just sit, staring at the water and letting the breeze blow away my problems as Kai, Sebastian, and Eli come and lean up against Eli's car and watch me through the open door.

"What are you doing here?" I ask, not taking my eyes off the lake.

"We could ask you the same thing," Sebastian says. "I saw you flying past my street and figured that you'd be hanging out here."

I shrug my shoulders, too out of it to bother searching for the sarcasm that his comment requires. "Good job. You caught me."

"What's going on, O?" Kai murmurs, his voice filled with concern. "You look like shit."

I let out a sigh and climb out of the Audi before walking down to the lake and kicking off my shoes. I roll up the bottom of my sweat pants and step into the cool water. "It's just been an interesting morning," I tell them as all three of them follow me down to the water's edge, standing behind me, so they don't get their precious sneakers wet.

"Were you planning on elaborating on that?" Sebastian murmurs, his voice low as he tries to hide his curiosity, trying really hard to be mad at me.

I shake my head, breathing in the fresh air. "Can't," I grumble. "Wolf business."

Eli grunts. "Are you going to keep pretending that we don't see those bruises?"

I scoff, glancing back over my shoulder and glaring. "Are you going to keep pretending like you didn't already know? I'm not a fucking idiot. I know you have guys hidden deep in the Wolves. You knew they were planning on jumping me in, and I can guarantee that you knew exactly when it was going to happen. You showed up after school on Friday to stop it, didn't you? You had no intention of trying to clear the air. None of you did. You were there long enough to show the Wolves that they weren't about to touch me, and then you left."

"We had nothing to do with it," Kai says, stepping forward.

"That's bullshit, and we all know it," I tell him. "I practically grew up around you guys. I know how this shit works. You scared them off on Friday, and so they came with the whole fucking calvary on Saturday. The question is; why didn't you stop it then?"

"Babe …" Sebastian says, the guilt spread far and wide over his face.

"No, don't 'babe' me. I don't need your excuses because I already know the truth. It was too many for the three of you to go up against, so you asked Nic to use the Widows, and he said no, didn't he?"

The boys glance at each other before Eli finally nods. "I'm sorry, O. We really fucking tried but he said that you'd made your decision, and to let you do your thing."

I turn back to the water and kick my foot out, watching as the water sprays across the surface. "That's fucking bullshit," I tell them.

"You don't get it," Kai says. "Nic feels like shit. He knows he fucked up, and if you want to bring the Wolves in to fight your battles, then he's prepared to face the firing squad."

I shake my head. "You don't fucking get it," I tell them. "It's not just Nic that they're going to take down. They're fucking planning on wiping out the whole Widows name."

"What?" Sebastian says, looking at the other two boys before grabbing my arm and spinning me around. "What the fuck are you talking about?"

I cringe, feeling as though I could throw up. "I'm not supposed to tell you. I'm a Wolf now."

Kai steals my attention. "I don't give a fuck who you belong to. You're our sister first. What's happening?"

I drop down into the water and bring my knees up to my chest, curling my arms around myself and trying to find some sort of comfort there. "I fucked up," I tell them all. "You were right. I should have come to you guys first, instead of trying to stand against you, but I knew deep down that you couldn't go against Nic. He's too strong, he has too much power—"

"Ocean, what's going down?" Sebastian demands, crouching down to meet my eyes. "What did you do?"

I drop my eyes, looking down at my hands, far too ashamed with myself. "Russo is planning an attack. It's not just war but a full-on extermination. They're planning a fucking ambush."

Panic rises in all of their eyes. "When?" Eli snaps.

I press my lips into a hard line, feeling as though I'm only moments from throwing up into the lake beside me. "He doesn't know yet. He's been calling in all the boys and gathering ammunition. He doesn't have enough yet, which is why they haven't made their move, but I doubt it'll take a guy like Russo long to get what he needs."

Sebastian drops to his ass, staring out at the water as Eli begins pacing, his hands raking through his hair as he starts trying to put together a plan. Kai just stares at me as though I'm a stranger, and it kills me the most.

I look at Sebastian and meet his horrified stare. "I don't know how to fix it," I whisper. "What am I supposed to do?"

"Run," he tells me, his voice flat and void of all emotion. "If this goes down, Nic will kill you, but if it doesn't, and Russo finds out that you squealed on Wolf business, you're just as dead. You know how this world works. The Wolves won't protect you like we would have."

My head falls into my hands as my tears drop into the cold water around my waist, feeling absolutely helpless, and for the first time, I find myself doubting his words. Colton had told me that when they showed up at his place to tell him where I was, none of them were prepared to go with him to come and get me, not that it would have helped, but the boys I once knew would have walked through fire just to get to me.

We all sit in silence, lost in our own thoughts until Eli walks up behind me and scoops me out of the water. He walks back to a small bench and takes a seat, putting me down beside him. "I feel like we've let you down," he tells me, glancing up to look at the boys who are blatantly listening in on our conversation. "We should have known about Nic and your dad. Maybe we could have done something to stop it. He should have known that stepping against your father would start a war."

"I don't know," I tell him. "I always used to be able to read Nic so easily. I knew what he did … what you all did. You never hid that from me, but my father? I never thought he was capable of hurting me like that. When it happened and Nic held me, I never dreamed that I was standing in the arms of my father's killer. And right now, I can't distinguish between what hurts more; his betrayal or the fact that my father is gone."

Eli's arm falls around my shoulder, and I lean into him, hating how things are between us but loving his comfort. I've missed this so much. "To be honest, I think we're all still a little in shock. We suspected that maybe Kian had something to do with it, but when Charles was killed the same way, we figured we were looking in the wrong place."

"But the file in his office with the Widows mark…"

"I know," he murmurs. "That really threw me. It put the suspicion right back on Kian, but then he was killed, and I figured it was over."

"You were wrong."

"So fucking wrong."

Kai and Sebastian look back at us and slowly make their way over. "Look," Sebastian starts. "Nic is … he's been going through some shit. Some really dark shit. The things that he has to see and do in his position; it would fucking kill you, O. He's changing, and I think the power of being in control is really starting to mess with his head. He's not the same guy you once knew, but he's still Nic. The real him is still in there, we just have to find it, but you need to know that to him, the Widows will always come first. That's just the way his father made him, but to me, you come first." He looks nervously at Kai and Eli before glancing back at me. "If it comes down to it, babe, I'll have your back. I didn't sign up for a life with the Widows to become a full-time killer. I don't want to spend the rest of my life behind bars. I joined for the brotherhood and for the protection the Widows could offer my family, and I'll always stand by that."

He presses his lips together, showing me that he's done with his speech, and I get up from the little bench and instantly step into his arms. "You know I love you," I tell him, snuggling into his wide chest and feeling a piece of my soul finally return to me.

"I love you too, Ocean. I hate all this bullshit between us right now."

"Me too," I murmur. "But I feel like we're strong enough to see it through to the other side."

"I fucking hope so."

Kairo steps into my side and pulls me from Sebastian's arm. "Come here," he tells me, pulling me in and folding me into his warm embrace. "I'm Nic's second. You know I can't stand against him."

"I know," I whisper, and he presses his lips to my forehead.

"That doesn't mean that I don't love you, because I do. So fucking much. You're my family. You always have been, and you always will be. No matter what comes of this bullshit. You're my fucking girl, O."

"Thanks, Kai. That means a lot to me."

"You'll never fully understand how fucking sorry I am that I let you get all mixed up in this shit. If I could change things and put it back to the way it used to be, I'd do it in a fucking heartbeat."

I shake my head against his chest. "I wouldn't," I tell him. "If I didn't have to go through all of this, I never would have found Colton, and I wouldn't change that for the world."

Eli stands behind me. "Things really are serious with this guy, huh?"

"A little more than serious," I admit.

Eli nods. "Then go home to him. We have to go and have a club meeting and let Nic know what's coming so we can prepare."

I step out of Kai's arm and give them all a smile that doesn't hit my eyes. "Okay."

Eli takes my hand and quickly pulls me in for a short-lived hug. "You know Nic," he tells me. "Even during all of this, he's still going to do everything in his power to protect you. You're going to be okay."

"I'm not too sure about that," I tell him, taking a few steps toward the cars. "But I'll figure out a way to be alright on my own."

They all watch me, and as I start walking back toward the Audi, I feel their pained stares on my back as they follow me up. I get to the car and look down at my soaking sweatpants, realizing that I can't morally get into Colton's car like this. Carefully, I slip from the pants and toss them onto the floor space in the back.

"Here," Eli says, leaning into the backseat of his beat-up old car and pulling out an old hoodie. "Take this."

I give him a warm smile of thanks and take the hoodie from him before slipping it over my head and breathing it in. It smells just like him and reminds me of all the good times we've shared, and without a doubt, I know that I'll be sleeping in this tonight and every night until the smell finally begins to fade.

The hoodie falls all the way to my knees, and I climb into the car, pulling the seat back into place before turning on the engine.

I'm just about to start backing out of my spot when Sebastian leans into the open window. "Take these. They're the good shit from my personal stash," he tells me, handing me three perfectly rolled joints. "Maybe smoke one tonight and relax a little. God knows you could use it."

I raise my brow as I take them from him. "You remember the whole pregnancy thing, right?"

His face scrunches, and with that one guilty expression, it's clear that he's already completely forgotten about it. "Keep them anyway," he tells me with a wink. "You know … just in case."

He quickly leans in closer and presses a sloppy kiss to my cheek before stepping back with the boys and giving me space to drive.

Not wanting to prolong this anymore, I hit the gas and back out of my spot while listening to the soft beep of my phone, telling me about all the missed calls and text messages. I drive away from the lake, watching the boys in my rearview mirror, and as I go, I quickly call Colton back to let him know that I'm still alive.

After he ends the call, I toss my phone to the side and pump the music. While my life is currently burning to ashes around me, I know I'll always have Sebastian, Kai, and Eli. No matter what.

Two hours later, I pull into the garage of the Carrington mansion and park the Audi beside where the Veneno usually lives. Only Colton's precious little first love is nowhere to be seen.

I cut the engine, and after feeling around on the passenger side for my phone, I come up blank. Where the hell did that stupid thing go?

I have no choice but to get serious about searching. After cutting the engine, I get out and make my way around to the passenger side while pulling up the sleeves of Eli's hoodie. I can't possibly start searching for my phone while my hands keep disappearing under the thick, black material.

Opening the passenger side door, I slide the chair back and start having a good feel around until my fingers curl around papers hidden under the chair.

What the hell is this?

My curiosity gets the best of me, and I pull them out before leaning forward onto the passenger seat and propping my elbows on the center console. My eyes scan over the papers, and I quickly realize that these are the registration papers for the Audi.

Realizing that it's nothing interesting, I go to slip them back under the seat, only as I go, a name catches my attention, only it's not the name I expect to see. It's my fucking name.

My mouth drops open, and I gape at the papers for a little while longer.

"That motherfucker," I say under my breath, wishing more than ever that I could light up one of Sebastian's joints. That sneaky bastard went and put the Audi in my name. The fucker gave me a goddamn car without me even noticing.

I clench my jaw and shove the papers right back where I found them, making sure to crumple every little piece of them. Frustration pulses through me, and I all but shove my head down around the floor space until I finally find my phone.

I get back to my feet, and before the door has even closed, I open a new text message and march my ass back inside the mansion.

Ocean - You're in a world of trouble, Colton Carrington. I suggest you get your ass home right now so I can bust it wide open ... and not in a good way.

<h1 style="text-align:center">CHAPTER 17</h1>

My fingers drum against the dining table as I stare at Colton sitting at the opposite side. He's been home for two hours, and he's done his absolute best not to get anywhere near me, but his time has run out. There's no avoiding me now.

From the guilty smirk across his face, he knows exactly what I found in his car, and he knows damn well that I'm not about to accept it. It's too much. It's freaking insane.

"Stop looking at me like that," he tells me, leaning back in his chair with his arm casually thrown over the backrest.

My eyes narrow further while my fingers begin to drum faster. Casey looks between us, her drink hovering in the air, right in front of her lips. "What's going on with you two? You're being weird."

I snap my glare at Casey. "Your stupid brother gave me a goddamn car."

Her face lights up in joy as my mother gasps in shock, just as onboard the train to Shitsville as I am, completely understanding why this 'gift' is way too much. "Oh, nice," Casey beams, more than ready to start congratulating her big brother on a job well done.

"No. Not nice," I throw back at her before shooting my glare at the douche across the table. "You can't just go and give me a car. Do you have any idea how freaking insane that is?"

His lips press together as he shrugs a shoulder, not caring about my objections in the least. "Too late, Jade. It's done now, but what's the big deal? It's not like I went out and bought one like I wanted to. All I did was have one little piece of paper transferred into your name. Besides, It's not even this year's model, and It's not like you hadn't already claimed the car as your own anyway. You've put more miles on it than I ever did."

My eyes widen in horror. "Holy shit, you're right. I didn't even think about that. Did I devalue the car or something?" I panic, beginning to worry about how I'm supposed to make up for that. I mean, I already owe him so much after he shrugged off my father's diamond thieving debt and released me from being owned by his family.

Colton scoffs as Cora and Casey laugh at the show. "Seriously, Jade," Colton says. "Stop panicking about it. It's nothing. Just forget you even saw the registration papers. I won't even pick you up on it when you call it my car."

"Have you gone out of your mind? Do you actually get how crazy this is? You're not *Oprah*. You can't just go around giving people cars."

He sucks in a breath through his teeth. "Well … whoops. I guess I kinda did."

I glare at him as Casey looks back at me. "Seriously, girl. It's really not a big deal. I saw the car he was actually thinking about getting you and let me tell you, if you feel like shit about this, then you would have really hated that. I mean that car …. damnnn," she says, glancing back at her brother. "I mean, if the offer is still on the table, you could always get it for my birthday."

"No fucking chance. Buy your own damn car," he grumbles, smirking as he looks back at me. "I figured if I bought you one, I would have been in a lot more shit than I'm already in."

"Uh, yeah … you would have been right about that."

He shakes his head, deep in thought. "I still feel like it's not enough though. What else do you want? I have a great diamond dealer. Do you want jewelry? A ring, necklace, matching earrings? Just name it."

"I …" I shake my head. "I can't even with you right now."

He shrugs his shoulders again and winks. "Well, I'm already in shit, so I might as well go ahead and do it. I'll call my guy in the morning."

"I swear, Colton. Call your guy, and I can promise that I'll shove your phone so far up your ass that you'll never get it out."

"Ocean," Mom shrieks in horror, her eyes wide. "Apologize immediately. I didn't raise you to talk like that."

I groan and push up from the table before walking around to Colton's side. I drop down into an extravagant curtsey. "My king, I sincerely apologize for my appalling behavior. You have my word, next time, I'll threaten you in private."

Colton takes my hand and tugs hard until I fall into his lap. His arms wrap around my waist, and just when I think he's going in for a hug, his arms lock around me like a tight vice. "Quick," he says to his sisters. "Give me all your rings. We'll size her before she gets away."

"NOOO," I screech, but it's too late. Colton holds me down as the twins rush in, pulling all the rings off their fingers and jamming them onto mine until they find one that fits perfectly. Cora grins at her brother proudly before handing it over. He takes it from her and slips it into his pocket with a smug as fuck smirk across his face before finally letting me go.

"You're an ass," I tell him, shaking my head and hoping to god that this is all just his way of screwing with me. I can only imagine the kind of jewelry a guy like Colton would be purchasing, and I really can't accept that. It would be insane.

I get back to my feet, and as Colton goes to take another bite of his half-eaten dinner, I slip his plate out from under him, making sure to narrow my eyes in the process. "I'm assuming you're done with this," I say, taking his plate to the kitchen counter to be washed up, trying my hardest not to smirk as he glances up and stares at me with laughter in his eyes.

"Is that really the game you want to play?" he questions, watching me strut back to the table.

I grab Cora and Casey's empty plates and turn back around. "I don't know what you're talking about," I tell him. "I'm just being a good little employee."

I drop the plates onto the counter beside Colton's and turn back just in time to see him getting up from the table, his eyes heavily on mine. He stalks forward, and my face drops.

Oh, fuck.

I back up a step, trying and failing not to grin at him, but damn it, it's too hard.

He takes another step and then another, his pace slowly picking up, and then he breaks out into a sprint, and I take off like a bat out of hell. "NOOOOOO," I shriek, my scream being muffled by my laughter. I dart around the kitchen counter as he goes the other way.

I stop at one end while he stands at the other, watching me like a lion watching his prey. I brace myself against the counter, more than ready to use it as leverage to propel myself faster. "Whatcha gonna do?" he teases, his grin so powerful and tempting. I should just give myself up and let him have me.

I shake my head, enjoying myself too much to give in like that. "You'll never catch me."

"Jade, I've already got you right where I want you."

With that, he dives to the left, and I sprint through the other side of the kitchen. As I pass him on the opposite side of the counter, he launches himself over it, coming down right behind me. I squeal as Mom panics, shouting something about being careful and not running in my condition.

I hardly hear her because when a woman has Colton tearing after her, it's the only thought circling her mind.

He gains on me quickly, and I aim for the door, knowing I'll have more luck in the hallway. But as I go to throw myself out of the door, his arms wrap around me and he scoops me right off the floor. Instead of taking me back to the kitchen, he continues down the hallway and up the stairs, not stopping until he's closing the door behind him and throwing me down on his bed. Exactly where I want to be.

Colton drops down on top of me, catching himself with his elbows so that no part of his body actually touches me, but I can't help flinching anyway. The bruises are still there, though they're faded enough that I can finally start hiding them with makeup, but just because I can hide them away, doesn't mean that they hurt any less.

His lips drop to mine, and as his hand falls to my waist, roaming over my skin, I pull back, meeting his eyes. "Wait," I tell him. "I have to tell you about today."

His lips come back to mine again. "It can wait."

I push him back, somehow finding the strength to resist him. "No, trust me, you're going to want to hear this, and if we wait, you would have wondered why I didn't tell you earlier."

Colton groans, dropping his forehead to mine. "But I don't want to talk," he whines, sounding as though I just asked him to roast his balls over a fire like marshmallows. "I'd rather sink into you."

"I know," I tell him, struggling not to laugh at how serious he's being. I guess even CEO billionaires get a little whiny when they don't get what they want. "I promise, as soon as we're done, I'm all yours, however you want me."

He groans again but can't deny that the idea of having me anyway he wants is certainly alluring. He finally pulls back and behaves himself. "Okay," he tells me. "I'll be patient."

"Good," I laugh, struggling to sit up into a position that doesn't hurt. I meet his eyes and try to figure out the best way to tell him this. "I sort of ran into someone today."

Colton's brows furrow, finally being serious. "Who?"

"Your mom."

"The fuck?" he grunts, pulling back and looking me dead in the eye. "Where the hell did you see her? She wasn't still sneaking around Bellevue Springs was she?"

I hold back a laugh. "Trust me, you could only hope that's where I saw her, but no, I saw her bent over a desk with her skirt somewhere up around her head while Mikhail Russo fucked her within an inch of her life."

His mouth drops, and he seems to turn a little green as he struggles to find the words to say. I raise a brow watching him as he shakes his head, desperate to get rid of the mental image I just supplied.

I lean back against the headboard of his bed, patiently waiting for him to come to terms with the bomb I just dropped right in his lap.

"Umm …" he finally says. "The fuck?"

"Yeah," I laugh. "She's been screwing Russo, hoping for a payday, but that's not even the worst part. The reason she came back here was because Russo put her here to keep tabs on me. The good part, though, is now that I'm officially a Wolf, he's done with your mom and kicked her to the curb."

"I …I can't even wrap my head around that. My mom was fucking

Russo?"

"Yeah," I say with a cringe, remembering the exact scene I had walked in to see. "And honestly, it looked a little sloppy."

"Jade, fuck. I don't want to know that."

I shrug my shoulders. "Sorry," I laugh. "I just wanted to paint a realistic picture for you. I mean, it's only fair, right? If I had to be subjected to it, then you should too."

He shakes his head, looking as though he's about to be sick. He pulls his phone out of his pocket and leaves it in his lap as he starts scrolling through his contact list. "Go back to the whole, 'keeping tabs on you' thing. What the fuck is that about?"

"I don't know, but from what I could gather, Russo already had a connection to your mom before we met. When we started getting serious, he used it to his advantage. He had other people placed in my life too. Coach Sylvester, Dean Simmons, even Milo's fucking dad, and now I have no idea if my friendship with Milo is even real?"

Colton reaches out and takes my hand. "It's fucking real," he insists. "Anyone can see that. I know Milo has practice at hiding what's real, but you can't fake that kind of friendship. It's not possible."

A ringing cuts through the room, and I glance down at Colton's phone to find his mom's name on the screen. He puts the call on speakerphone as we wait far too impatiently for her to answer.

"Colton, darling," her voice finally comes through the phone, sounding far too optimistic. "Have you finally come to your senses and are ready to apologize to your dear mother?"

His eyes shoot up to mine. "Is it true?" he snaps.

Laurelle sighs, and I want to smack her for the disappointment she causes to flash in Colton's eyes. "I figured that little bitch would twist the story. What did she tell you?"

"Exactly what happened. She walked in to find you fucking Mikhail Russo."

Laurelle gasps. "That's absurd. I don't even know who you're talking about. I'm in England at the moment, so I can assure you that your little whore certainly didn't walk in on me doing anything."

Colton scoffs and pulls up an app on his phone, which instantly locates her position. "Mom, you're in a shitty hotel on the outskirts of Breakers Flats. I don't know who you're trying to fool. But tell me, if this were true, how would you know to accuse Ocean of something before even hearing what I had to say?"

Laurelle huffs as Colton shakes his head at just how pathetic his mom has become. "Fine, I was in a brief relationship with Mikhail. However, I ended things. He's not a very good man."

I grumble under my breath. "More like he kicked your bitch ass out because he was through with you."

Colton meets my eye, and a sparkle lights up his face. "Mom, just be real for once. Why the fuck did you come back here? It wasn't to rebuild a relationship with me, was it?"

She groans. "I came back because Mikhail asked me to. He had me watching that little slut of yours, and reporting back on her every movement. He was supposed to pay me but he didn't hold up his end of the bargain."

"Really? Because it certainly sounds like you got more than what you bargained for."

"Don't you speak to me like that," Laurelle snaps. "I'm still your mother, and you will respect me."

Colton scoffs. "Why did you do it?"

"Because I had no damn choice," she yells at him. "And honestly, I don't get his infatuation with her. There is absolutely nothing special about that girl. She has no redeeming qualities, and she's not even pretty. You can do so much better, Colton. I thought I taught you better than that."

"Goodbye, Mother."

"Don't you dare hang—"

Colton ends the call and tosses his phone to the bed beside him before pulling me into his chest and collapsing down into the soft blankets. "I'm sorry you had to hear that," he tells me. "I promise, you'll never have to have anything to do with her again, not if you don't want to."

"Thanks," I murmur, spreading my fingers over his chest. "I don't know how you came from that. She's such a …"

"Bitch?"

"Yeah," I laugh, though the joy doesn't last long and quickly fades away, leaving us both laying with nothing but our own thoughts.

Colton lets out a deep sigh and curls his arm around my waist, holding me close. "I have to tell you something," he murmurs, his voice low and full of guilt.

I push up onto my elbow and look at him, my brows drawn as I take in the expression on his face. I instantly narrow my eyes at him, knowing damn well that I'm not going to like what's about to come out of his mouth. "What did you do?"

Colton presses his lips into a tight line, almost as though he's trying to prepare himself for the worst. "I was the one who made sure your student loan applications didn't go through."

I gape at him, unsure that I heard him correctly. "What?" I breathe, pushing up until I'm sitting. "I swear that I just heard you say that you're responsible for making my college dream that much harder."

Colton sits up and takes my hand. "Trust me, Jade, I didn't do it to make your life harder—"

"No," I scoff. "You did it so that I'd have no choice but to come and ask you for help, so I'd have to rely on you instead of finally standing on my own two feet."

"Babe, no. It's not like that. They were going to deny you anyway. Your application wasn't looking good, and it was going to put a black mark on your credit score. I didn't want it to fuck things up for your future. I withdrew the applications and had them email you to say it was rejected so you wouldn't think I had anything to do with it. But the more I fall in love with you, the harder it is to keep my fucking mouth shut."

I stare at him, not sure what to say. "They were going to deny it anyway?" I ask, feeling the devastation wash over me.

"Yeah," he sighs. "I'm sorry. I know how badly you wanted to do this on your own."

My bottom lip pouts out and I fall back into Colton's chest. "I guess it really doesn't matter now anyway. It's not like I'll be going to college while I'm pregnant. I'm going to have to try again for the following year."

Colton's arms wrap around me, and he props his chin over my head. "Whatever you want to do, Ocean, I'm going to be right there, making it happen. I promise, this baby is just a temporary setback. Once you figure out what you want to do, we can make a plan. I promise you, Jade, whatever you want in life, you're going to get it. You fucking deserve it, and I'll do everything I can to give it to you."

"You know when that time comes, I'm going to fight you on it."

Colton laughs, and it rumbles through his chest, spreading warmth through me. "I'm fucking counting on it."

CHAPTER 18

This whole waiting to hear about the Wolf and Widow gang war is really starting to drive me crazy, but the less I hear about it, the easier it is to pretend that everything is normal in the world. You know, except for the growing child in my womb and the fact that I haven't seen or talked to Nic in weeks. I don't think I've ever gone this long without talking to him, and although it shouldn't, it still hurts. I still miss him.

I must be crazy to miss the guy who murdered my father, but he's been such a huge part of my life for so long. I should hate him, well maybe I do. The last time I saw him, I'd only just found out. All the facts hadn't had a chance to settle, but now they have, and I'm curious to see if I'm going to regret making the decision to see Russo. I guess I won't know until I see him.

Colton's hand travels up my thigh, and I bite down on my lip, trying my best to keep my composure as it slides higher and higher.

We sit at the best restaurant that Bellevue Springs has to offer while Roman stands at the head of the table, gushing about how fortunate he was to have met my mom when he did. It's sweet, and I wish I could concentrate, but I'm really struggling.

That warm hand creeps even closer, teasing me, full of promise and desire. With Drix seated directly in front of me, I find it impossible to meet her eyes, knowing that with one look, she'll know exactly what's happening here. There's a massive, beaming smile on her face as she holds her glass up to her gushing father. They're so cute. It's as though being here with a woman at his side is already a huge accomplishment.

Colton's hand squeezes my thigh, and I sink into the firmness. I love how he doesn't hold back with me. He's never afraid to push the boundaries, and it sends an electrifying pulse through my body.

"What else can I say?" Roman declares, glancing down at Mom as we wait for our meals to arrive. "I know it's only been a few short weeks, but you've completely bewitched me. I've fallen so head over heels in love with you that I no longer see my life without you."

Mom blushes, placing her hand against her heart as she looks up at the man who is quickly becoming her knight in shining armor. "And I you," she tells him, reaching up and lacing her fingers through his.

I smile wide, feeling all the emotions rushing in and overwhelming me. My heart is so full as I watch them completely loved up. She was never this mushy with Dad. I know she loved him on a deep level, but it was never the all-consuming, unbreakable connection that she clearly shares with Roman.

I meet Drix's eye across the table and she gives me a warm, proud smile. I can't help but return it. Setting Mom and Roman up was the best thing we'll ever do. They look so happy, so over-the-moon in love, and solid.

I know I wanted to give it a few months to see where this was going, but seeing them here together, it's obvious. This is an ever-lasting kind of thing, and honestly, I don't even think Mom realizes it yet.

Roman raises his glass, and we all do the same, watching as he looks down at her with that love-crazed smile of his. My glass sits high in the air, and as I bring it to my lips, Colton's hand travels deeper between my legs, making me choke on my drink.

I feign innocence as everyone turns to look at me with concern, even Colton, the dick. "Sorry, it went down the wrong tube," I say, desperately trying to regain control of myself as a large hand finds its way inside my underwear.

Mom reaches out and pats my back, trying to help, but there's no helping me now. I'm in God's hands. "Are you alright, love?" she questions, concern written all over her face.

"Yep," I say quickly, taking another sip of my drink. "All good, thanks."

Colton's soft, rumbly laugh beside me has my elbow discreetly slamming back into his ribs and sending a wave of satisfaction over me.

Take that fucker. But as his thick fingers slide into me, I can imagine him thinking the exact same thing.

My hand slams down on his thigh, desperately needing to do something, to somehow let him know just how badly he's affecting me. All the while, trying to remain calm and pretend that I'm listening intently to Roman's every word.

Colton's fingers flinch inside of me, and a low groan rumbles through my chest. How lucky does a girl have to be to get dessert before dinner?

He really begins to move, and just as I feel that familiar pull deep inside of me, Roman drops to his knee in front of my mother, and my whole world freezes.

Colton's hand stops.

My eyes widen.

Drix sucks in a gasp.

"What the hell?" I breathe, staring at the man who suddenly looks as though he's about to be sick with nerves.

Colton thankfully slips his fingers out of me and allows me this moment to really take in what's happening. Honestly, I think he's just a little too shocked to keep himself moving.

Drix flashes her shocked stare to me, and a million messages pass between us when Roman clears his throat and brings all the attention back to him. "Maria," he breathes, saying her name like a soft caress on his lips. He reaches out and brushes her hair off her face as she stares at him with wide eyes. "I know this has only been a short few weeks—which have flown by—but they've been amazing and have told me everything that I need to know about you. I don't want to spend another day without you by my side."

Mom glances back at me, unsure of what to say and hoping that I can somehow help her, but I can't. I can't make this decision for her. She needs to figure this out on her own. "I … I … I don't know what to say."

Roman takes her hand in his. "I know, dear. I don't expect you to say anything. Believe me, I know just how crazy I sound. Who proposes to a woman that he met only a few weeks ago? All I know is that I can't stop thinking about you. I can't breathe when you're not with me. I can't function without seeing your smile. Maria … I don't even know what to say myself, but if I don't ask for your hand in marriage, or let you know my purest intention is to stand by your side as your loving husband for all of our days, it might just kill me."

Mom gapes at him, completely speechless when he pulls out a black velvet box and opens it up, holding it out to her and showing off the biggest rock I've ever seen.

Drix stares in shock, her mouth literally hanging open as I do the same.

Who is this amazing man?

Mom's hand falls to her chest again as she sucks in a deep breath. "Oh, my word," she whispers, her eyes filling with tears. "Do you realize that I come with a whole lot of baggage?"

Roman laughs and squeezes Mom's other hand. "You realize that I have just about the same amount of baggage that you have."

Mom's gaze flicks to me. "I highly doubt that," she says with a shy chuckle, looking back at him. "Am I insane for wanting to say yes?"

"Just as insane as I am for asking."

Mom lets out a shaky breath, keeping her eyes on Roman. "Are you going to hold it against me if I said that I need to think about it? It's all so sudden."

"Of course not, my dear. I wouldn't have expected anything else. It's a huge decision, and I want you to be certain if you were to accept my offer. I just want you to know where I stand. I'm not messing around here."

Mom nods. "I know," she murmurs as a beaming smile spreads across her face. "Neither am I."

The waiter chooses this particular moment to show up at our table with our meals. Roman moves back to his seat, and the two of them find it impossible to tear their gaze from the other.

Our dinner is placed down, and an awkward silence follows as everyone glances around, wondering if that really just happened. I meet Colton's stare, and he raises a knowing brow as if to say 'you're next.' I can't help but roll my eyes. "You're an idiot," I tell him. "You're going to need a bigger rock than that to win me over."

Colton laughs, knowing damn well that it has absolutely nothing to do with the size of the diamond sitting on my finger. We're only eighteen, we have time. I try to ignore him as I look back across the table at Drix to find a cheesy as fuck grin on her face. She looks as though she can barely hold herself together, and despite my mother's lack of response, she throws herself to her feet. "WE'RE GOING TO BE SISTERS!"

Oh, fuck. This is going to be interesting.

Three hours later, I sit with Mom on the couch in our pool house as she stares at a blank wall, completely speechless and unsure of how to even react.

"Well?" I ask, knowing that she's been desperate to start talking about it since the second the words slipped out of Roman's mouth. "What are you thinking?"

"I'm thinking that it's crazy," she says with a scoff, turning to look at me. "It's crazy, right? I'm not just being dramatic?"

"No," I laugh. "It's totally crazy, but it's not completely insane. I saw the way he was looking at you, and I know it's only been a few weeks, but it's obvious that his feelings are genuine and real."

"Do you really think so?"

"Yeah," I say, leaning into her side as she puts her arm around me. "I really do."

"Would you be weirded out if I was to say yes?"

I shrug my shoulders, not really having given it any thought yet. "I mean, I don't know. I'd probably have to get to know him a little better to really know how I'd feel. I can't say I've really spent much time with the man, but he seems alright. At least, that's what Drix keeps telling me. But you realize that marrying this guy means that you'd be moving in with him?"

Her eyes bug out of her head. "Oh, I … um … I guess I hadn't really considered that yet."

"Do you think you're ready to live with another man?"

Her lips press into a tight line as she thinks it over. "I mean, I'm not really sure. I have a feeling that living with a guy like Roman Jennings isn't going to be like anything I've ever experienced before."

"You've got that right," I say with a grunt, knowing all too well what it means to have a rich, alpha male suddenly appear in my life. "Take a look at Colton and this big ass house. You'll be the boss of all that shit."

Mom shakes her head. "Oh, I hardly think so," she says, her voice low and a little horrified. "That's ... that's too much pressure. I'd be happy just being the woman at his side. Besides, I have a feeling that Hendrix is already running things over there."

"I don't doubt that," I laugh. "She probably has Roman wrapped around her little finger."

"Oh, she does," Mom says, gushing. "You should hear the way he talks about her."

A wide smile spreads across my face, and I hold Mom a little tighter. "You're going to say yes, aren't you?"

Fondness stretches over her face and as she meets my eyes, she nods. "Yeah, I think I am," she whispers. "But I'm going to wait a few days. I want to be sure. This is all happening very fast, and I don't want to rush into it. Your father only passed eight months ago... surely, considering this must be ridiculous."

I shake my head. "I don't think it is," I tell her. "I think he's looking down on us and can see how happy you are. He's not around anymore, and no one expects you to just sit back and continue pining over a man who you will never be able to see again. Live your life and be happy. That's what he'd want, and it sure as hell is what I want."

A soft knock sounds at the door, and we look up and find Colton standing there, watching us. "I didn't mean to interrupt," he murmurs. "If you're having a moment, I can come back."

"Oh, no, no, no," Mom says, pulling herself off the couch. "She's all yours. It's getting a bit too late for me, and I have a lot to get through tomorrow. I think it's time for a shower and bed."

"Good plan," I smile, getting up beside her and instantly giving her a big hug. "It's going to be okay. You'll figure out what's best for you."

"I know, sweet girl," she says. "I just hope it's not something that I regret a year or two down the track."

"You won't."

With that, she pulls out of my arms and slinks down the hallway towards the bathroom. I make my way over to Colton, and he instantly puts his hand in mine before tugging me out the door. "Where are we going?" I ask.

"You'll see."

I follow Colton as he leads me into the mansion and through the maze of twists and turns before we're finally walking through to his office. The door gets shut behind us, and for a brief moment, I think he's about to throw me down and get a little kinky on his desk, that is, until he walks around and sits in his desk chair, pulling me down on his lap.

"Seriously, what are we doing?"

He shakes his head and reaches across me to type in a password for his computer, and not a second later, his screen comes to life.

He opens an email, clicks a secure link, and before I know it, we're watching live footage of the FBI storming through someone's home.

"What is this?" I ask, my brows furrowed.

"Luca DeCarlo, the eldest of Vincent's sons."

"What?" I breathe, leaning in a little closer to the screen, wishing that we could somehow put this up on his flat-screen TV rather than the small desk computer. "What's he being arrested for?"

"There's a whole fucking list of things," he says. "But nailing him down has been the hardest so far."

"What's the worst of it?"

"Kidnapping of minors and trading them on the black market," he tells me, looking sick and pissed off with himself at the same time for taking so long to make this happen. "He's been selling children to fucking wealthy businessmen across the globe. I can only imagine what's been happening to these kids."

"Fuck," I gasp, watching with wide eyes. "Where are the kids now?"

Colton shakes his head before resting his chin against my shoulder. "Gone, Jade. We couldn't save them in time, but you fucking bet that he's going to pay for his crimes."

A single tear rolls down my cheek as I watch the screen, seeing the exact moment that Luca DeCarlo is found and arrested. Usually, in times like this, I'd be thrilled to see the bad guy being arrested, but the heaviness sitting against my chest is just too great."

"Is there anything we can do to try and find them?"

He shakes his head as his arm circles my waist. "I really don't know," he tells me. "It's a long shot, but I can look into it. Maybe there's a paper trail. These guys had to pay him somehow, and where there's money, there's a trail."

I nod, feeling the smallest bit of hope beginning to rise within me. "Do you think Vincent knew about this?"

"Yeah," he scoffs. "I don't doubt that Vincent was one of his first customers. Besides, an operation like that doesn't come cheap, Luca would have been funded somehow."

Fuck.

I tear my eyes off the screen, having seen more than enough of this bullshit. I curl into Colton, crushing my face into his chest as he sits silently, watching the screen over my shoulder, making sure that everything goes as planned.

As we sit in silence, I can't help but think about the baby growing inside of me. I'm going to be this child's mother, and unfortunately, things like kidnapping and child abuse happen on the regular. How would I feel if that was to happen to my child?

A fierce protectiveness comes over me, and while I still don't know how I actually feel about having this baby, I know that it's my job to keep it safe. And just like that, I know exactly what I want to do with my life, and I won't stop until I make it right.

CHAPTER 19

I walk down the steps of the Carrington mansion on Monday morning feeling, as though this is all just a bad dream. There's still so much normal in my life, while the rest of it has been flooded with insanity.

I try to put it all to the back of my mind. After all, it's Monday morning, and I'm going to school like a normal teenager should. There are no gangs, no murder, no terrifying life choices to make, just regular, old school.

Milo's Aston Martin comes to a stop at the bottom of the grand stair entryway, and I can't help but smile at him as he hangs his head out of his window and gives me a goofy, lopsided grin. "What's up, skank?" he calls. "Why do I still need to drive your bitch ass around? I heard someone went and got a sugar daddy who gave her a car."

I roll my eyes, and I race down the last few stairs. "First of all," I tell him, walking around the front of his car to get to the passenger side. "If my bitch ass wants a ride to school, then that's what my bitch ass is going to get. Secondly, I don't have a sugar daddy, I have a boyfriend who doesn't know anything about keeping his toys to himself. As soon as I can, I'll be putting that car back in his name."

"You know that's only going to provoke him."

I groan low, dropping into the Aston Martin and reaching for my seatbelt. "I know," I grumble. I was up all night trying to figure out a way to get back at him for 'gifting' me a car, but all I could come up with was being a stubborn ass and not actually driving it anymore. It's pathetic, and it's only going to have him laughing at my attempts, but if I don't drive it, then I can happily pretend that it isn't mine.

"You're an idiot, you know that, right?" Milo laughs, hitting the gas and sending us flying down the long driveway. "But I can't deny that I love this little thing we've got going on. I feel like driving you to school is usually the only time I get to see you anymore. You know, since you decided to bitch out and move to the chick school."

"That's bullshit, and you know it. I belong at the girl school nearly as much as you do," I tease. "Besides, you're the one always ditching me now for your super hot, douchey boyfriend."

"Hey," Milo snaps, a twinkle sparkling in his eyes. "If you're going to insult Spence, then do it right. He's not super hot, he's steamily hot, and he's only a douche on Wednesdays."

I roll my eyes. "Who's the idiot now?"

Milo laughs and relaxes back into his seat, enjoying the ride to Bellevue Springs private. He stops by Starbucks and orders us both a coffee that seems to hit the spot just right. I sit back and enjoy the ride, sipping on my drink, and feeling the weight of the world slowly begin to rest back on my shoulders.

I guess I was fooling myself by pretending that I could forget about it for a day.

Milo glances over at me and narrows his eyes. "What's going on? You look like someone just ran over your cat and then laughed about it while shaking their ass in your face."

I press my lips into a tight line as I glance over at him and see the concern in his eyes, and I can't help but realize that I've been completely overthinking this. Milo is a real friend, even if he was put into my life or not, there's no denying it. "There's something I've been meaning to talk to you about."

His face scrunches up. "Eh? Me?"

"Yeah," I say, fighting the smile that threatens to tear across my face at his ridiculous response.

He looks back at the road, focusing on where he's going. "Go ahead caller, you're on the air."

I roll my eyes again. This is supposed to be a serious topic, and yet he has me about ready to crack up into embarrassing snorts of laughter. "I, um … okay, don't hate me, but I sort of went and saw Russo a few days ago."

Milo's eyes bug out of his head, and he swerves off the side of the road as I desperately try to keep my coffee from spilling all over his Aston Martin. "The guy who did this?" he demands, pointing out the still visible bruising that covers my skin. Apparently, I did a really shitty job of trying to cover them up.

"Uhh… yeah," I cringe.

Milo looks at me as though I've lost my mind before throwing his hand out and feeling my forehead. "Are you feeling okay? You must be getting sick to have done such a stupid thing like that." He drops his hand and looks back out the windshield, shaking his head. "I mean, who's the fucking idiot now?"

"I know," I groan. "Colton's already given me the rundown of what he thinks about me walking back into that place, but will you just listen? I learned a few things, and I'm trying to work out if you already knew about it."

Milo's head whips back to mine. "What? What the fuck are you talking about? How the hell would I know anything about what goes on in a gang? I hardly know about the shit that's going on in my own life."

"You see, that's kinda where the two connect."

"Okay, you really are losing it. I can promise you that whatever it is, it's not true, because the thought of having anything gang-related in my life scares the living shit out of me."

"That's what I thought," I tell him. "But I have to be sure."

He shakes his head, looking more than confused. "What's going on, Ocean?"

I take a shaky breath, unsure what I'm about to do by telling him this. "When I went into Russo's office on Saturday, Colton's mom was in there … in a compromising position." Milo's eyes bug out of his head, but I continue with my explanation before he has the chance to start getting all Milo-y on me. "After she left, Russo explained that he had put all these people in my life to keep an eye on me ever since my dad died, and well, he was the reason behind Laurelle coming back to Bellevue Springs and you—"

"You think I'm one of those people?" he demands in outrage. "Holy fuck, Ocean. I can't fucking believe you. Is that really what you think of me? Even if I didn't know you, I'd never align myself with people like that."

"No, no, no," I rush out. "Not you. Russo said that your dad was on his payroll, and well, I guess I'm just wondering if that means that you were maybe put into my life and just didn't know it or … I don't know. I guess I don't really know your dad well enough to make any assumptions."

Milo shakes his head, looking lost. "My dad? Are you sure?"

I nod, reaching out and squeezing his hand. "Yeah, I'm positive. There were a few others on that list, but your dad was the only one worth mentioning."

"So, he's a Wolf or just works for them? What? I don't get it. My dad would never. He doesn't even run in those circles. He's a businessman, not a gangster."

"I know, but Laurelle doesn't exactly scream gang member either," I tell him. "I don't think they're actual members, but I think that Russo would have gone out of his way to make their silence worthwhile. He has a big reach, maybe even bigger than Nic's."

Milo lets out a heavy sigh and glances back at me. "I just … I can't wrap my head around this. I thought I knew everything there was to know about my father. I've always known that every now and then he'll indulge in a dodgy deal, but this? This is too much. He wouldn't. He's better than that."

I reach out and take Milo's hand. "I'm sorry, Milo," I whisper. "I hate that I was the one to tell you that, but maybe it's not as bad as you think. Maybe he was just asked to keep an eye on me, and that's it."

Milo scoffs, scooting down into his seat, looking absolutely devastated that his father isn't who he always thought him to be. "My father doesn't get involved in little bullshit games like that," he explains. "If Russo had contacted him, there would have to be a big payday in it for my father, and I can assure that he would have had more to do with it than just keeping an eye on you."

"What are you saying?" I question, keeping my gaze locked on his.

"You know my father is on the board of BSA, right?"

"Yeah," I say, nodding my head, remembering the conversation we'd had where he explained it all to me.

Milo sighs. "I think you're right. I think I was put into your life."

"Are you sure?"

Milo's lips press into a tight line, and he squeezes my hand. "Yeah," he murmurs. "On your first day at BSA, I wasn't supposed to be on office duty. I'd already had my turn the month before, and I couldn't work out why I had to do it again. I just shrugged it off, you know, it didn't really matter, and it got me out of classes. But now I think that maybe that was my father's doing. If he really is working for Russo, it's possible that he had me put in the office to be the first person you met. It wouldn't have been a long stretch to realize that we would have gotten along. He was always asking me about you, and when the rumor went around that we were dating, he was pushing it really hard."

"Damn," I whisper. "That's what I was afraid of."

"You don't need to be," he tells me. "We'll just be careful from now on. I won't tell him anything about you or when we're hanging out. I swear—"

"I don't think it really matters anymore, to be honest," I tell him. "I'm already a Wolf. Russo got exactly what he wanted. He doesn't need people hidden in my life anymore, he has his henchmen following me everywhere."

"What? Are you serious?"

I nod. "Look around. I bet you'll find at least three of them if you look hard enough. They've been watching my every move, assuming that I'm about to run or start spilling their little secrets to the Widows. I wouldn't be surprised if they've bugged my phone."

"What?" he demands, his eyes going wide as he looks down at the phone that's been resting on my lap since I first got in his car, staring at it as though it could explode at any second. "Then what are you doing? I'll go and get you a new phone right now."

I shake my head. "And risk him knowing that I'm trying to block him out? No way. I'd rather just try and play it safe."

"Good point," he murmurs. "So, what do we do?"

"Absolutely nothing," I tell him, trying to give him what I think is an encouraging smile though knowing I'm failing pretty damn hard. "We go to school, and then we come home from school. There is nothing that we can do. This whole Wolf and Widows bullshit is beyond us, all we can do is hope that we don't get caught in the crossfire."

"Yeah, well I think it's already a little too late for you."

"That's the understatement of the century," I tell him, this time with a genuine smile before nodding back toward the road. "Now, be a good little chauffeur and drive my bitch ass to school."

Milo laughs and checks his mirrors before pulling back out onto the road. "Is there anything else Your Highness requires?"

"Well, as long as you're asking, I wouldn't mind a red carpet to be laid out everywhere I walk."

"Jesus Christ," he grumbles under his breath. "Does Colton know you're this high maintenance?"

"Please," I scoff. "I bet you're worse than me. In fact, I can guarantee it. Tell me, how often do you have Spencer hand feeding you grapes in a gold speedo?" A smile tears across Milo's face, and as he glances over at me, I see the wheels turning in his mind. I don't doubt that a brand new fantasy will be played out the next time they're together. "You're such a dirty bird," I tell him.

Milo laughs, and as he pulls onto the street that will bring us to the end of our time together, he looks over at me with sadness in his eyes. "I hope you know that to me, our friendship has always been real. I don't want you thinking anything less. You really are my best friend. There's no one out there like you."

Love soars through my veins and instantly overwhelms me. I want nothing more than to curse these stupid pregnancy hormones that have somehow turned me into an emotional mess. "Thanks," I tell him. "You have no idea how much of a relief it is to know that you have nothing to do with it. I mean, I had a feeling, and Colton told me that there was no way. He knew it was real, but my mind wouldn't stop wondering," I tell him. "And for the record, I feel the same way. I love you, and I absolutely love having you in my life. I wouldn't change it for the world. There are so many things that I wouldn't have been able to get through if I didn't have you."

"Ugh," he groans, bringing his car to a stop outside of BSP. "Don't give me all that sappy bullshit. Get yourself and your whiny ass out of my car."

I laugh as I swing the door open. "Hey, you're the one who started the sappy bullshit, I just finished it."

He rolls his eyes. "Out, wench."

I climb out of his car and make a point of walking slowly around the front of the Aston Martin, making it impossible for him to get his ass out of here. I lock my eyes on Milo's through his windshield and watch the smile tear across his face before he lays on his horn and doesn't let up. I jump out of my damn skin, and within seconds, we have every eye in the school on us.

That asshole.

I get up onto the curb, and as I walk toward the school gates, Milo's voice comes sailing through his open window. "I freaking love you, you skank ass bitch," he calls out before hitting the gas and taking off, making damn sure that he had the last word.

I laugh to myself as I turn back to the school gates and walk myself in. There are girls everywhere. Within seconds, Hendrix comes bounding toward me, instantly gushing about her father's proposal over the weekend and all the wedding plans she's already put together.

I gape at her, knowing there's no point in reminding her that Mom hasn't exactly agreed to anything yet. When she mentions what her dad told her about planning to watch Mom walk down the aisle as soon as possible, my head spins. For a guy with the means to make things happen, he could be talking weeks, not months.

Drix goes on and on about all the things she'd like to see happen. Apparently, she wants to become an A-list celebrity event planner, and putting together a dream wedding is a big deal for her. I, on the other hand, hardly know what the hell a bonbonniere is. She's raving about the silk rose gold bridesmaid gowns, insisting they are non-negotiable, but all I can picture is the price tag. I'm sure it will cost more money than Mom and I have ever seen.

Before I get a chance to remind her that this isn't her wedding and that Mom will be the one making those kinds of decisions, my phone starts vibrating inside my bra. With a few minutes before the bell is due to sound, I pull it out and look down at the screen, my brows pinching as an unknown number flashes on the screen.

I stare at it for a moment before Drix rolls her eyes. "Either you're going to answer it, or I am," she tells me. "But whatever you decide, make it quick because I found the perfect dress that will look incredible on your mom."

Letting out a breath, I realize that she's right. What harm could a phone call bring me?

After accepting the call, I bring the phone to my ear, hating seeing unknown numbers flashing on my screen. "Hello," I say hesitantly, hoping that I'm not about to regret this.

"Don't use that fucking scared tone with me," Christian says, making me wish that I had saved his number from the last time he called. "You should know by now that I'm not going to hurt you."

I scoff, unable to help the comment that comes flying from between my lips. "You mean you won't hurt me unless your boss tells you to? Or you mean you wouldn't hurt me *again?*" There's silence on the other end and I let out a sigh. "Look, the last time I had a call from an unknown number, some dick was telling me that I was about to get jumped."

"Fair point," he says. "Listen, I need to know if you've seen Russo?"

"You mean your father?"

There's silence on the other end of the call, and for a brief moment, I'm left wondering if he hung up on me, until his sharp tone slices through the line. "How the fuck did you know that?" he demands, his tone terrifying and deadly. "No one fucking knows about that."

My heart begins to race.

What the fuck was I thinking spurting out that bullshit? I assumed it was common knowledge. What do I do? What the ever-loving fuck do I do? I can't lose Christian. He and Jaren are the only two allies I have in that place. Without him, I'm screwed.

I swallow back fear and decide that it's best to come clean than to lie to him and have him always questioning my word. "I, uhh … kinda talked to your sister," I tell him. "She's the only one around here that can really understand what I'm going through and I … Shit, I'm sorry. I wasn't meaning to start any trouble."

Christian lets out a deep breath. "Fuck, I should have known it was her," he says. "Just keep it to yourself. If Snake was to figure out that connection, then there would be real fucking trouble. We've kept it quiet for a reason."

"You have my word," I tell him. "I won't say anything."

"Good," he grunts. "You're going to tell me everything that got said with Roni, but first, Russo. Have you seen or heard from him?"

My brows furrow as I cut through the students to get to my locker. "No," I grumble, accidentally nailing some girl in the shoulder as I squeeze past her. "Should I have?"

"No," he says. "That's just the thing. No one has heard from him."

Well, fuck. That could only mean one thing.

Nic.

CHAPTER 20

Colton

Midday hits as I walk through the door of the old abandoned factory in Breakers Flats that my father had purchased a few years ago. I always wondered why the hell he wanted a place like this. It's a fucking dump, but as of yesterday afternoon, I finally got it. The walls are fucking thick, and the security on this place is like none other, meaning no one can hear a motherfucker scream.

The heavy metal door slams shut behind me, and I watch as the lone figure sitting in the middle of the empty factory floor snaps his head up. I don't know why he bothers though, he can't see shit under the blacked-out bag that sits over his head.

I walk toward him, knowing the rhythmic sound of my footsteps getting closer would be playing all sorts of tricks on his mind. He has no fucking idea who took him, no clue where he is, or what he's even in for. Though I'm sure he has plenty of enemies, all who would want him dead.

Mikhail fucking Russo.

The motherfucker who dared put his hands on my girl.

I figured that snatching him up was going to be hard, but I've come to learn that guys like Russo, the ones who think they're untouchable, are usually the easiest ones to take down. They think no one can get to them, so they lower their guard. Grabbing him and forcing him into my factory was a fucking walk in the park, and I bet getting what I need from him is going to be just as easy. Though, even if I can, he's fucked anyway.

I was mostly all good with Ocean's plan of getting at Nic and using the Wolves to do our dirty work, but then this fucker had to go and jump her in, claiming that she's his now. Bullshit like that ain't going to fly, not where I'm concerned.

From the second Ocean stepped into the Wolf Den, it's just problem after problem. While I'm more than happy to sit back and deal with it, I don't want that for her, not when it's not the life she wanted for herself. If it was her life's long dream to become a fucking Wolf, then I'd be standing here at the sideline, cheering my girl on. But this is far from anything she ever wanted for herself, and what can I say? I'm a man who sticks to my word. I told her that I'd give her the fucking world, and I intend to come through on that. When I'm finished here, Ocean will have her freedom, and there's no doubt about it. The question is, how long will it take to make it happen?

Fuck, I'd give anything to go back and be there to stop her from walking through those doors, and I'm sure she would too, no matter how many times she tells me that she stands by her decision. I think she's too scared to admit when she's wrong, too strong, and so fucking stubborn, but that's what I'm here for. I'll always be there, standing right behind her, lifting her up when she can't do it herself.

I don't know when or how it happened, but at some point over the last few months, Oceania Munroe became my fucking world. I breathe for her. Everything I do is for her, and I don't give a shit if that makes me sound whipped. I'll fucking admit it, I'm completely whipped by her. She walked into my life with that smart mouth, thinking she could take me down, and fuck, she certainly did, but not in the way she was intending.

Without her ... that's a world I don't want to live in, one I refuse to live in. Unfortunately for Russo, he's the one obstacle stopping me from giving Ocean everything she ever wanted. She deserves better than that. I just wish she could see that she doesn't need the Wolves at her back when she has me. I understand it though, she wanted an army and to feel closer to her father, but she got so much more than what she bargained for.

I step in front of Russo and grab hold of the black bag that sits over his head. I tear it off and watch with a smirk as he squints into the midday light that shines through the old windows. "I trust you had a comfortable night," I say, waiting for him to adjust to the light and figure out who the fuck stands before him.

Russo watches me through narrowed eyes, and the second he sees me, he lets out a breath of relief. Big mistake, but that's okay. He's about to learn who Colton Carrington is the hard way. "What do you think you're doing, kid?" he questions, watching me closely as I step away from him, sliding my suit jacket off and placing it over a steel beam. "You do realize that by now my men would have figured out that I'm gone, and will be hunting you down. They're going to fucking kill you for this, mark my words, boy."

I laugh. I fucking love it when bastards like this underestimate me. It always makes for the best kind of fun. "I highly doubt that," I tell him, walking back over and placing myself in front of him before rolling up my sleeves. "You see, your men are fucking morons who stood less than ten feet away while their boss was swept off the side of the road and didn't notice a goddamn thing. I have plenty of time to say what I need to say before they even get close to figuring out what the fuck is going down here."

Russo clenches his jaw, and just like that, he gives himself away. He knows I'm right, and it only serves to fuel his anger. "What do you want?" he snaps, more than ready to get the show on the road.

"It's really quite simple," I tell him, slowly circling him and watching as he tracks my every move. "I want Ocean's freedom. Give her up, and you can walk freely."

Russo laughs. "Come on, kid. You know it's not that easy. I wouldn't give up that girl for nothing, more now that I know how badly you want her. Besides, there is no fucking out. She's mine."

"You see, that's just the thing, I've already got her, and you know damn well that she wants nothing to do with you."

"All the more reason to hold onto her a little tighter."

His words grate against my every nerve, and while I want nothing more than to lunge out and tear his throat right out of his body, I smile, letting him see just how fucking far I'll go for her. "I'm going to ask you again," I tell him. "We can do this the easy way or the hard way. Your choice."

Russo scoffs, leaning forward in his chair, though he doesn't get far with his hands bound behind the plastic of the chair. "Try your fucking hardest," he tells me. "You know, I've been fucking your mom. She's all dried up, the old bitch, but I fucked her anyway. Took her ass harder than your daddy ever did."

A grin stretches across my face, and for a brief moment, fear flashes in his eyes. I pull out my phone and send a quick text before taking a step back and leaning up against the pillar in the center of the factory. "Really?" I ask as I wait patiently. "Is that the best you got? The old 'I fucked your mom' bullshit? Is that supposed to send me off the deep end? So fucking what? No wonder she's all dried up. She's fucked half of Bellevue Springs."

It's only a short, two-minute wait before a text comes through to my phone, and I glance down and smile before putting myself right back in front of Russo. "I trust that you've heard of a little company by the name of VC Holdings, you know, the company that you run your whole organization through?"

His face drops, his skin turning a sickly shade of white. "What did you do?" he spits through his teeth.

"I bought it." I turn my phone around, showing him the screen that shows confirmation of my latest purchase. "It seems some of your guys aren't as loyal as you'd always thought. It was all too easy to get your company credentials and buy it out from under you, and I have to say, it went for quite a good price, next to nothing. Oh, wait, it was for nothing."

"What do you want?" he spits, knowing that this company holds every last secret he's ever held. With just one audit, I'd have his whole organization torn apart until it's nothing but ash left on the ground.

"I told you my fucking price," I tell him. "I want Ocean's freedom."

Russo clenches his jaw, his glare digging into me like two, piercing laser beams. "Fine, have the fucking bitch. Now, get me the fuck out of here and give me my fucking company."

I laugh, unbuttoning the top button of my suit shirt before pulling out a pair of brass knuckles and sliding them onto my fingers, right where they fucking belong. "Oh, you think it's going to be that easy?" I ask. "You think you can have twenty fucking guys jump my pregnant girl, and I'm just going to stand back and accept that?" My fist slams across his face, sending a mouthful of blood spraying over the floor of my factory. Russo grunts in pain, and as he looks back at me, I continue, "You think I'm just going to forget the sound of her flesh being beaten." I step into him, bringing my fist around in a devastating uppercut, slamming it up under his ribs and watching as he gasps for breath. "You think I'm just going to let you walk out of here unscathed?"

I walk around him and untie the bounds on his wrist. He tries to stand, ready to run, but he's not getting away that easy. He won't be leaving this place until I've left him as black and blue as what his men left my girl.

I jump at him, instantly taking him down, barrelling my fists into him. I hit him in all the places his men hit my girl, listening to his grunts of pain like trophies awarded for the best kind of vengeance.

I beat him until he can hardly move, and then just a little bit more. Every bit of anger I felt watching his twenty men beat my girl, I took out on his body. All I can see is Ocean, curled up on the ground, nothing but a blur of fists and feet slamming into her over and over again. She couldn't even cry. I'll never forget it. Even beating the living shit out of Russo and ending him, it'll never make what happened okay.

Only when I can physically no longer keep going do I finally pull away, looking down at the beaten and bloodied man lying helplessly on my factory floor. "You stick to your word," I tell him, "And I'll stick to mine. Do it quickly, and I won't do anything to your 'company' in the meantime … take your time, and you never know what might happen."

Leaving my threat dangling in the air, I walk across the factory until I'm standing in front of an old sink. I turn on the tap and listen to the squeal of the rusted metal pipes as they turn on for the first time in years. The water spits out a dark shade of brown and, after running for a minute, finally runs clear.

I wash the blood off my hands and clean off my brass knuckles before slipping them back into my pocket. I dry my hands on my pants, and without looking back, I scoop up my suit jacket and head for the door, pulling out Russo's phone that I took last night.

I scan through his contacts until I find the one person who I know will come and take his boss off my hands. It rings three times before Snake's voice tears through the line. "We're ready to go boss. We're on our way," he says, his voice full of pride and excitement. "Those fucking Widows won't live to see morning."

I stop in my tracks, looking back at Russo as horror begins to fill me. Ocean had told me the Wolves plan, and as much as I hate Nic, I can't stand back and watch as Ocean's brothers are slaughtered. She'll never be able to move on from that, never forgive herself.

I drop the phone and fucking run.

CHAPTER 21
Colton

I slam Russo's limp body into the passenger seat of my Veneno, cringing with the way his blood drips over my expensive leather seats. He grunts and groans with every little movement, but if he can survive my beating, he can fucking survive a short car ride.

The passenger door hardly closes by the time my ass is hitting my seat. The engine kicks over, and I race through the fucking streets, pushing my Veneno as fast as it can go. I've never been to the Widows clubhouse before, but it's not hard to figure out where it is. It's the street that nobody goes down, the one people are terrified of, the one that comes with a promise of death.

I grab my phone and find Nic's number, calling it over and over again, desperate to get through to him but with every call comes no answer, which in hindsight is fucking smart of him. I'm Ocean's boyfriend, and she's a Wolf. In any other situation, talking to me could be considered risky business, but right fucking now, it just makes him a bigger moron than I already know him to be.

It's a fucking godsend that I decided to deal with my business in Breakers Flats. I'm only around the corner, but who knows how long the Wolves have been driving for. They could beat me there, or I might just make it in time to save their dumbasses. I lost precious seconds going back for Russo, but he might just be what we need to give ourselves a few extra minutes.

The call rings out for the fourth time, and I clench my hand around the phone, my anger rising higher than I ever knew it could go. I look back down at it, needing to get the message through to someone when I scroll past Kairo's name. I hit call and glance up, just in time to catch myself from running off the fucking road.

I swerve back into position, and within seconds, Kairo's sharp tone is cutting through my Bluetooth speakers. "What the fuck do you want? Is Ocean okay?"

"The Wolves are on their fucking way," I shout through the car, "And your goddamn boss ain't answering his fucking phone."

"FUCK. NIC, THEY'RE COMING. IT'S FUCKING GO TIME," Kairo hollers before coming back to me. "How do you know?"

"Because I just got done beating the living shit out of Russo for touching Ocean." I speed down their street and spot their stupid warehouse from a fucking mile away, but what I can also see, there are no Wolves here. I glance in my rearview mirror, thankful we still have time. "Open the fucking roller door. I'm coming in."

The call goes dead, and two seconds later, the door begins slowly rolling up. Inch by inch, it sets my fucking nerves on edge. Maybe Ocean is right about having a gate that will open and close quickly. Right now, it's the difference between life and death, and I damn sure don't want to give my fucking life for this bullshit.

The second I can, my Veneno goes screeching into the clubhouse to where I find Nic standing front and center, armed and loaded with his Widows at his back. His jaw is clenched, and he looks more than ready to face down any fucking army. No wonder Ocean was so into this guy.

I force my Veneno forward, not about to park it at the front of the shop to be target practice for any of these dickheads. Call it selfish and wasting precious seconds, but this thing set me back a couple of million dollars, and getting new parts isn't going to be a walk in the park.

Every Widow watches me, Nic in the center with Kairo, Elijah, and Sebastian right by his sides, ready to lay their lives down and protect their family at all costs. I roll out of my car and hurry around to the passenger side, grabbing Russo with both hands and hauling his ass out.

I get no resistance from him as he's too fucking out of it to even know where he is, but as I clear the back of my car and the Widows get a good look at the man in my arms, there's a fucking uproar. Men come at me, wanting to get their hands on Russo for all the bullshit that he's brought to their doorstep.

Nic's voice bounds through the warehouse. "LET HIM THROUGH."

The Widows reluctantly stop coming for me, and I pass by them, more than aware of the automatic weapon that each of them holds. As I make my way through the throng of people, I glance around. Men are hiding up in the trellises of the roof with rifles, ready to take out any threat. I can't help but feel that they're as ready as they're going to be, but the Wolves have been preparing for this. I'll bet my whole fucking estate that they're coming with bigger toys than these guys have.

"I need a fucking chair and cable ties," I call out, strutting past the widows and going right to the front of the warehouse, and passing through the massive roller door.

I pull Russo off my shoulder and dump his heavy body to the ground as Nic presses his lips together before deciding to play it smart. He nods at one of his men, and the guy goes running. "What the fuck are you doing?" Nic demands, shooting his glare back at me.

"You want to survive this without losing your fucking men in a massacre? Then I suggest you shut the fuck up and help me tie this bastard to the chair," I tell him, not bothering to flinch at the way the Widows begin to creep forward. They don't like the tone I'm taking with their boss, but in the end, who really gives a fuck? I'm about to save their asses. They're all just too fucking stupid to see it. God fucking knows Nic doesn't deserve it, though. Not only is his bullshit with Ocean's dad to blame for this, but he also killed my father, and for that, he still hasn't been forgiven, nor will he ever be.

Nic clenches his jaw, holding his ground but as his guy comes racing back with the chair and cable ties, he has no fucking choice. He's backed into a corner, and he knows there's no way to win this.

The chair gets put down at my feet and I grab Russo's limp body before slamming him into it. Nic instantly starts binding his wrists. "How the fuck is this supposed to help?" he demands, loud enough for his men to hear.

"When the Wolves come, do you really think they're about to open fire on their fucking boss when fifty Widows are standing behind him with guns pointing at his head?" I question, raising my brow at his blank expression. "Yeah, I didn't think so. They're going to have to cover themselves to get him out of there, slowing them down and giving us the advantage."

"Us?" he questions. "This ain't your fight. Get the fuck out of here, rich boy."

I scoff and look back at Kairo, Elijah, and Sebastian. "I'm not going anywhere," I snarl, stepping up to him. "For some fucked up reason, Ocean still loves you four dickheads despite the bullshit you've put her through. You're her family, and because of that, I stand with you."

"Even though she's one of them?" he demands, nodding at Russo.

"She's one of them because you forced it on her after killing her father. That doesn't mean that those other three dickheads aren't still her brothers. If you four were to get hurt in this, she would never forgive herself, even though some of you deserve it."

Nic stares at me for a short moment, before realizing that he's quickly running out of time and has to make a decision now. Whether he likes it or not, I'm staying, because that's the kind of man Ocean deserves. I'm not about to back out of this with my tail between my legs. I will stand and fight and save the lives of Ocean's brothers.

Nic gives me one sharp nod, and with that, I stride past him to join the boys. Sebastian meets my gaze, and as I fall in line beside him, he tosses an army grade machine gun into my hands. "You know what to do with that?"

I nod. "This might be my first gang war, but it ain't my first rodeo."

Without another word, Sebastian turns back to the roller door as Nic steps back into the center of the line, silence falls over the warehouse.

A minute passes, and then a second when we finally hear it; tires screeching down the road.

Everybody flinches, their bodies going rigid with their fingers hovering over their triggers. Some of these men are going to die today, but with Russo stranded out front, at least we'll have a chance.

The cars creep closer and I try to listen out as they turn the last corner, trying to figure out just how many cars are coming our way, but it's nearly impossible to figure out over the sound of their engines.

Within a blink of an eye, cars begin flooding the front of the warehouse, speeding in and coming to a screeching stop, guns are pointed out windows, and when the first shot rings out, all hell breaks loose. Men start dropping and scattering around as the Wolves duck down behind open car doors.

Kairo gets a bullet through his upper arm, but when it sails right through his flesh, it only pushes him harder.

Nic has the biggest target on his head, but he doesn't relent as bullets start getting closer and closer to Russo, the Wolves finally see what's right in front of their faces.

Only a few seconds have passed since their arrival, but it's already been enough for both sides to have fatalities. I take a second to thank whoever lives above that Ocean wasn't dragged into this. I can guarantee that she probably doesn't even know this shit is going down and for good reason too.

The Wolves stop firing and scramble to put together a plan, shouting curses at one another over their car doors while Nic holds up his hand, stopping his men from shooting. My chest rises and falls with rapid movements as adrenaline pulses heavily through my body. I take the brief moment to scan over myself, checking for any bullet wounds but so far, it looks as though I'll make it to see another day.

I look left and then right. Ocean's four boys seem to be fine. Kairo has blood running down his arm but he doesn't even notice. Nic has a cut on his face, and I have no fucking idea how it got there, but it doesn't look like a bullet wound. Sebastian and Elijah seem to be completely unharmed, just wide-eyed and alert, just like me.

Everyone holds their breath as the tension rises, and while the Wolves fight for a plan, one man lays down his gun and steps out from behind a car door. I recognize him from the hospital when Russo had come to meet with Ocean after she was jumped in, though I can't recall his name. I do know that from the way Ocean seemed to relax with his presence, he's one of the good ones.

Nerves rise within me. If this man gets shot down, it's only going to make things worse. He raises his hands, silently begging Nic not to shoot, but as he takes another step forward, Nic stops him with a step of his own. "Don't be a fucking idiot, Christian," Nic warns him. "You've seen my aim. I don't fucking miss."

"Let's make a deal," Christian calls back. "We'll take Russo and walk away. No one else needs to get hurt. We've both already lost men."

"Why should I make a deal?" Nic demands. "You fuckers brought this bullshit down on my doorstep. I don't owe you a fucking deal. I should end you all right fucking now."

"I know," Christian tells him. "But you know that this isn't going to end well for either of us. Hand over Russo, and we'll leave quietly."

Nic clenches his jaw before raising his chin. I silently beg him to make the right decision. This is his only way out, his only way for his men to see another day, and he knows it, but he's fucking stubborn and obsessed with winning.

Kairo grumbles low beside him, so low that the other Widows would never be able to hear. "Come on, man. End this. We'll hit back at them another day, but if we don't end this, you won't have an army to hit back with."

Nic growls low in his throat, and it's damn clear that he doesn't appreciate his boys telling him how to handle his business, but when it comes down to it, he respects what his friends have to say.

Sirens are heard in the distance, and I don't doubt that they're coming here, but no one moves an inch, not one of them scared of a badge.

Christian remains still, unrelenting in his stare and not prepared to give up on his boss as the rest of them cower behind their cars. "What's it going to be?" Christian asks. "End this now, and we can all avoid jail time."

Eli grumbles beside me. "Think about your mom," he urges. "All of our moms. If you're not there, she's got no one."

A sharp grunt comes tearing out of Nic, telling Eli to watch his mouth, and then finally, Nic raises his gun again, making the rest of the Widows follow suit. "Slowly," he warns Christian. "Get your boss and then get the fuck out of here."

Christian doesn't waste any time moving forward, but when Snake steps out from behind a car door to help, Nic fires off a warning shot, and the coward instantly retreats.

Christian keeps his eyes on Nic as he reaches his boss and instantly snaps the cable ties before hauling Russo over his shoulder in the same way I had. He backs toward the Wolves as the sirens get louder. The seconds tick by, and the closer Christian gets to his car, the quicker he starts to move.

The Wolves start packing themselves into their cars, and when Russo is thrown into the backseat of someone's shitmobile, they all start taking off, hightailing out of here and leaving me and the Widows to finally take a breath, but it's not over yet.

"Get out of here," Nic grumbles beside me as the sirens hit the end of the street.

"What?" I question.

Nic steps into me and snatches the machine gun out of my hands. "Get the fuck out of here. You saved my boys' asses. I won't forget that."

I glance back at Sebastian, Eli, and Kairo, who all nod, silently urging me to just go and not look back. So without missing a beat, I run to my Veneno and drop down into it before flying out the back entrance of the building.

I cut around the back of the warehouse and have to go around the block before finally coming up the side of Nic's warehouse. I can't help but slow the Veneno to a crawl and find seven cop cars all moving in on the Widows. Nic stands front and center just as he had during the whole shoot out with his hands up. He slowly places the machine gun down on the ground while keeping his eyes locked on the cops. His men follow suit, and with all weapons down, the cops make their move.

Nic is slammed down on the hard concrete as the rest of the cops make an impenetrable barrier, blocking the Widows from jumping in. Nic is put in cuffs, and within seconds, his ass is hauled into the back of a cop car. Lines of officers are collecting the guns from the ground, preparing to raid the warehouse for whatever else they could find.

Not wanting to be caught here, I hit the gas and take off down the road, wondering how the hell I'm going to explain this to my girl.

CHAPTER 22
Ocean

Two freshmen girls come running the wrong way through the hall as everyone tries to escape through the corridor to finally put an end to this long ass day. "Holy shit, did you see him?" one of the girls squeaks to the other, making her friend giggle and blush.

"He was so hot and that body. I'd let a guy like that plow right through me. Who cares about saving myself for Brandon next week. I should go back out there and offer myself up like a buffet. I wonder if he'd screw me right there on the front of his car. Hell, I'd even let you watch."

My eyes widen as I watch the two girls run past. Are they kidding? They're only freshmen, and they're talking like that for everyone to hear? Have they even hit puberty yet? Have their periods? Holy shit.

The girls and their comments instantly fall from my mind as I get closer and closer to the door and begin hearing their adoring, needy whispers.

"Holy shit."

"Did you see that?"

"What's he doing here?"

Dread instantly fills me. The last time some random guy was welcoming himself into the school, it was Nic, and the time before that, Sebastian. I mean, who else would get that kind of reaction from the girls of BSP?

I start preparing myself for the worst. Sebastian won't risk coming here again, and I highly doubt it's Nic coming to grovel on his knees or to beg for forgiveness. It's either Kairo or Eli and seeing as though it's been a pretty good day, I could probably get through a whole meeting with them without losing my shit or telling them to get fucked. Hell, I guess they deserve some brownie points for waiting until school let out.

I narrowly squeeze through the flood of desperate girls, pushing and clawing to get a glimpse of the guys they've heard so much about. Once outside of the gates, and I have the parking lot in view, I instantly begin scanning. Only I don't have to wait long. The Veneno is front and center with Colton Carrington leaning up against it, his eyes on me, looking every bit of the badass that he is.

I take him in, and everything south of the border clenches.

Fuck me, there's something about him today. Maybe it's the dangerous sparkle in his eyes or the way that he leans against his car with his strong arms crossed over his wide chest. His hair is messy, his sleeves rolled to his elbows, and his top button undone. He looks as though he's had the day from hell and that thought alone has me picking up my pace.

Girls all around watch him, and then they watch me watching him, all but drooling over the glorious sight before them. I hear his name whispered on nearly every set of lips around me, some groaning in delight while others wonder how quickly they could steal him away.

I tune it all out, desperate to get into his arms and make whatever pain he's feeling fly away, but as I get closer, I can't help but wonder why he's here. Is it just because he's had a shit day and wanted to pick me up, or is something going on? He never picks me up unless I specifically ask him to. Milo's not here, so I'm assuming that Colton told him not to bother.

Concern sets itself into my mind, and as I get just a few feet away, his bloodied knuckles become obvious. I start scanning just a little closer, really taking him in. His knuckles aren't just bloodied but deeply bruised, his shirt is torn, pants dirty, and he looks fucking exhausted. Not to mention the blood splattered all over his clothes.

Colton prides himself on being put together. When he's at home, he doesn't give a shit and will walk around half-naked, but in public, he makes a point of looking the part, even when his world is burning to ashes around him. So for Colton to be standing here, looking disheveled and broken, something's up, and for some reason, my gut instinct is telling me to run.

Whatever this is, it's big.

I slow my pace, desperately wanting to put off whatever bullshit bomb that I fear is about to be dropped on me.

By the time I reach him, I'm walking at a snail's pace, doing everything I can to avoid the inevitable. The worry must show on my face as he pushes off his car and instantly wraps me in his arms. "It's going to be okay," he murmurs, holding me close, neither of us concerned about the blood that stains his clothes and is now most likely all over mine.

"What happened?"

He releases his hold on me and takes my hand, leading me around to the passenger side. "Not here," he tells me. "Just wait till we're in the car without your whole school listening."

I look up and meet his eyes with concern, but he gives nothing away as he opens the door for me and helps me in. I drop into the seat, still slightly throbbing with the dull ache that remains in my muscles from last week's attack.

Colton closes the door and as I drop my bag to the floor. I watch him walk around to his side, a grim expression on his face, but I'm distracted as my nostrils flare with the strange disinfectant smell filling the car.

I've never seen anything like it. Colton looks as though he's about to be sick with whatever he has to tell me. If he was any other guy and

I didn't know just how deep his love ran for me, I'd be worried that he's about to end it. But the blood and torn clothes are kind of a dead giveaway that this is something different, something huge.

Colton gets into his car, and as his engine rumbles to life, I glance over at him, sitting as still as can be as he stares out the windshield. "Just rip it off like a bandaid," I tell him. "Whatever it is, I can take it."

Colton looks over at me and lets out a heavy sigh before finally hitting the gas and taking my ass home. "I beat the living shit out of Russo today," he tells me. "I bargained for your freedom and blackmailed him until he agreed before leaving him in a pool of his own blood."

"What?" I breathe, staring at Colton as though he's some kind of stranger. "Why would you—"

"Just wait," he tells me, pulling over on the side of the road to where we won't have any eyes watching us. "As I was leaving, I used his phone and called one of his guys to come and get him, but Snake assumed I was Russo and mentioned the Wolves were on their way to end the Widows."

I suck in a deep breath, my eyes widening in fear. "No," I say, shaking my head, begging for it not to be true as dead sinks heavily into my stomach. "No, no, no. Please tell me they didn't."

Colton drops his head, looking at his bloodied hands. "They did," he murmurs. "I was in Breakers Flats in one of Dad's old factories and took Russo to Nic. I couldn't get through to Nic, but I got a hold of Kairo on the way and gave them a heads up, but there were only fifty or so of them there."

Tears form in my eyes and instantly start trailing down my face. "No," I say, my voice broken as the words struggle against the lump forming in my throat. "Just … please just tell me they're not dead. Tell me they're still alive."

"They're okay," he soothes, reaching out and taking my hand and sending a wave of relief crashing over me, making it just a little bit easier to breathe. "We put Russo out front and used him as a bargaining chip, but that doesn't mean that there weren't any fatalities. From what I could tell, Nic lost three men while the Wolves … I don't know. It was hard to tell. Maybe two of them went down. Maybe three."

"What happened?" I whisper, my heart aching.

"Your friend, Christian. He surrendered and laid his gun down to save Russo. He made a deal with Nic to call it off, said that if he just handed over Russo, they'd leave quietly, and I think Nic could tell they were outmatched. He didn't want to give in, but he did. The cops were coming, and everyone just wanted out."

"Are they okay?" I ask, not needing to clarify who 'they' are. "Did anyone get hurt?"

"They're alright," he says, desperately trying to soothe me. "Nic has a gash on his face, and Kairo got a bullet through his arm, but it's just a flesh wound. Nothing he can't handle."

I nod, knowing that if anyone can tough it out, it's Kai. "Sebastian and Eli?"

"Fine," he tells me.

I take a deep breath, leaning forward and dropping my face into my hands. "This is all my fault," I whisper. "Those guys who died, that's all on me. They're never going to forgive me. How am I ever supposed to face them again knowing what I did?"

Colton reaches over and unbuckles my seatbelt before pulling me across the car and into his lap, he wraps his arms around me, gently rubbing circles, and silently telling me that it's all going to be okay. "They don't blame you, Ocean," he murmurs, trying to reassure me. "I saw the look in their eyes today, they love you so deeply, there's nothing that you can do wrong. Even Nic, despite all the bullshit, he still sees you as family."

I shake my head. "They can't … not anymore."

"Stop, Jade. You weren't there, you didn't see what I saw. They know this isn't on you."

I rest my head into his chest, trying to will the tears from falling. "Where were you during all of this?"

"Standing with your brothers," he tells me. "Right where I should have been."

My eyes widen. "You stood against the Wolves?"

"Uh-huh," he murmurs. "I know you're one of them now, but standing with your brothers is more important to you than standing against them, and I know you don't want to believe that right now because you're still so hurt by what Nic did, but I had to."

I nod, lacing my fingers through his and holding on tight. "Did any of the Wolves recognize you?"

He shrugs his shoulders. "Not that I noticed, but I don't think it matters, Russo knows it was me who warned the Widows, and he's going to have it out for me, especially after the shit I pulled on him today."

"Why do I feel like there's more that I need to know?"

"I sort of bought the business that his whole organization runs through. With the information I have, I could bring the whole thing down and more."

"Fuck, Colton," I breathe. "He's going to try and kill you before you can even do anything with it."

"I know," he whispers. "It's better that he focuses on me and not you."

I shake my head, not even knowing what to say. "I want to hate you so bad right now."

"That's okay," he whispers, pulling me back into his chest. "Hate me if you have to, but either way, your part in this is over. They stood against the Widows, and all your boys came out unscathed while Russo has agreed to let you go. You can have it all now, college, this baby, if you want it, anything."

"I ...I ..."

"Shhhh," he murmurs, his hand still running up and down my spine as his lips press against my temple. "It's okay, you don't need to say anything, just know that it's all going to be alright. They can't hurt you now."

I shake my head. "I think we're fooling ourselves to assume the worst is over."

"Maybe," he tells me, pulling back. "But for now, why don't we just go home and you can call the boys, check in on them yourself?"

"Are you sure?" I ask, searching his eyes.

"Of course," he tells me, pressing his lips to mine before brushing my hair back off my face. "They need your reassurance just as much as you need theirs."

"Okay," I breathe before pulling myself out of his arms and climbing back into the passenger seat.

Colton hits the gas again, pulling back out onto the road, reaching over and taking my hand in his "There is something you should know," he tells me, rubbing his thumb back and forth over my hand. "You know how I mentioned the cops showing up?"

My head whips back around to him. I'd completely overlooked that part of his story. "Yeah," I say in a panic. "What happened?"

"The boys were all holding firearms when they showed up, and Nic was arrested for possession of a deadly weapon. I haven't heard any details, but I've sent one of my lawyers down to the police station and he'll be taking care of it. So, we should hopefully know something more tonight."

I stare up at him, amazed by his generosity after Nic has done so much to hurt him. "You didn't have to do that," I urge him, "but thank you."

Colton nods. "I didn't do it for him," he tells me. "I did it for you."

"I know," I whisper.

"Alright," he says, letting out a breath and showing me just how nervous he was to share all of that with me. "Let me get you home, and then we can figure out what our next steps will be."

"I can't agree more."

With that, Colton flies down the road, and twenty minutes later,

I stand out by one of the many pools, staring down at my phone, and trying to find the courage to actually call the guys.

I drop down onto one of the sunbeds while glancing through the back window of the mansion. Colton stands in the kitchen with his phone glued to his ear and appears as though he's busily putting something together, but we both know that he's just standing close in case I need him.

Wanting to be stronger, I let out a breath and get on with it. The phone rings three times before Kairo's face appears on my screen, looking more pissed off than I've ever seen him. "Ocean," he says, instantly making tears well in my eyes.

I hate myself for being so transparent and do my best to blink the tears away. "Hey," I say, my voice low and filled with pain. "I just needed to check that you're alright."

He rolls his eyes but doesn't lift the pissed-off stare that seems to hit me right through the phone. "Besides the fact that I had one of your guy's bullets slice through my arm, then yeah, just peachy."

"Kai," I say, my tone dropping low as my heart breaks. I completely deserved that. "You have to know that I didn't know they were coming for you. If I knew … I would have been there trying to make it stop. I'm so sorry, so fucking sorry, and I know I don't deserve your forgiveness, but I'm going to beg for it anyway because the thought of you guys hating me is killing me, and I just … I can't lose you all. You're all that I have left."

"Stop," he says, his voice finally breaking as his heart appears out on his sleeve. "We don't hate you. We told you that no matter what, you're always our sister, and we meant that."

I shake my head. "How can you say that after what I did? If I hadn't gone to Russo, then this never would have happened. Your guys would be alive, and you wouldn't be hurt."

"Pretty girl," he soothes, using that old nickname that I feel I haven't heard in months. "Whether you went to Russo or not, we were already at war. All you did was give him the push to do what he'd already had planned to do, but thanks to Colton, their plan backfired, and for now, we all get to live to see another day."

"I … I really don't even know what to say."

"I know," he murmurs, "But when you figure it out, can you make sure all the bullshit whining is finished. I don't want to hear it anymore. It is what it is, and we've both said what needs to be said. End of the discussion, okay?"

I nod, despite us both knowing damn well that this will be brought up at every chance I get. I'll never stop feeling miserable for this, which in turn means that despite having their forgiveness, I'll never stop apologizing.

"Come on, bro," a familiar voice says in the background. "Let me stitch your arm."

Kairo grunts and glances back down at me as I see the side of Eli's face come into the screen. "Looks like you're about to get yourself a show."

"Huh?" Eli says before leaning in and glancing down at me. "Hey, O. What's up, girl?" he says in a too cheery tone that makes me wonder if he was even there today. I mean, where's the anger, the resentment, the need to tear me to shreds?

"Hey," I say with a fake smile. "Are you alright? You didn't get hurt?"

His brows furrow and a cocky smirk stretches over his face. "Who, me?" he asks with a soft grunt. "Baby, no one can touch me. I'm indestructible."

Kai slams his elbow back into Eli's gut, and he doubles over in pain. "Yeah, real fucking indestructible," Kai murmurs before waving his arm around. "Get on with it, this gash ain't going to stitch itself."

Eli rights himself and stretches out again before focusing on Kai's arm, and I watch as his eyes narrow, and the sick grin twists across his face. "I apologize in advance," he murmurs to Kai, his eyes glistening with mischief. "This might sting a little."

"Nope," Kai snaps, yanking his arm out of Eli's hold. "Sebastian, get your ass over here. This fool ain't going to touch me."

Eli laughs as Sebastian appears at his side. "What's going on? Why aren't you stitched yet? Oh, hey O. What's up, girl? Caused any shootouts and gang wars today? Oh, wait … yep, you did do that."

Fuck me.

I groan, dropping my forehead into my hand and watching the boys smirk through the phone, making it all too clear that Sebastian is just teasing, but either way, it makes me feel like shit. "I'm really sorry," I tell him as he focuses on shoving Eli out of the way and taking a good look at Kai's arm. "Do you hate me?"

"Not today," he tells me, grabbing the things he needs to mend Kai. "You're going to have to do worse than that."

"Worse?" I grunt. "How could anyone ever do worse than that? A wild shootout with hostages is literally as bad as it gets."

Sebastian grins, glancing up at the screen with a sparkle in his eyes. "Nah," he says with a scoff. "It could have been worse."

I roll my eyes and let out a breath before pressing my lips into a hard line. "Have you guys heard from Nic? Is he doing alright?"

The boys shrug. "Not yet," Kai murmurs, shaking his head. "But you know how these things go. They'll hold him for forty-eight hours and do as much digging as they can, but Nic keeps his shit locked up tight. They won't get him."

"Even though they walked in to see him holding a gun that you and I both know was stolen?"

Kai shrugs. "What can I say? Dominic Garcia is a special breed."

"You got that right," I say with a laugh while silently hoping that he does get locked up because at least that way, he'll be doing time for his crimes. Kai's right though, Nic will get out of it, he always does. I can't help but glance back at the kitchen and take in Colton through the big windows. The phone is still attached to his ear, but now his eyes are on me, silently asking if I need him. I shake my head and look back down at the boys. "You know Colton set him up with one of his fancy lawyers."

"No shit," Eli says from off screen, secretly impressed.

"Yeah, hopefully he can help Nic's case."

"Nic will be fine," Sebastian throws in, giving his two cents. "Now why don't—"

My phone beeps with an incoming call, and I scrunch up my face as Christian's name flashes on my screen. "Shit," I say, cutting off Sebastian and knowing damn well that now isn't the time to avoid this call. "I have to go."

The boys nod. "Yeah, I thought that might be the case," Kai says, almost as though he knows exactly why I need to end this call so soon. "Talk soon, O."

Kai ends the call before the others get a chance to say goodbye, but I don't get a moment to think about it as Christian's call is instantly answered. "What's up?" I say into the phone, silently begging for some kind of good news.

"Mandatory club meeting," he says with a grunt. "You have two hours to get your ass here, and do me a favor, don't bring your boyfriend."

Shit.

CHAPTER 23

The whole avoiding the Audi thing goes to complete shit as I fly out of the driveway. I can't be late for this ridiculous little meeting.

I can only imagine what's going to go down. Russo is going to be there and he's going to be pissed that Colton managed to steal his business out from under him and then threw salt on the wound by beating the ever loving shit out of him.

This meeting isn't going to go well.

Getting out of the house wasn't exactly a walk in the park. Colton hates it when I leave to go into Blaxlands Grove. I think it makes him feel helpless, but at least this time, he didn't put up too much of a fight. He must have been expecting this. After all, he's convinced that Russo is going to let me walk in exchange for his untouched business. Though, I can guarantee that while Colton waits for Russo to release me, he'll be going through everything with a fine tooth comb and making copies on every hard drive he owns. Either way, Russo is going down.

The drive into Blaxlands Grove seems to take forever, when in reality, I get there much quicker than I had expected. The whole drive, my mind swirled around today's bullshit, wondering what Nic is going to do when he gets out. Though I don't need to wonder too much, he will retaliate, that's a given. The issue is how?

Will he come for me, or will he let it slide? Nic is going to be pissed and unlike Kai, Eli, and Sebastian, he doesn't forgive as easily, but I'm not sure that I really want his forgiveness, he's the one who needs mine.

I bring the Audi to a stop outside the Wolf Den and take a second to breathe. Only I don't get as long as I'd hoped when Christian appears at the door and gives me a stern look, telling me to get my ass inside.

I climb out of the Audi and scurry to catch up with him, hoping that if all hell breaks loose that maybe I could use him as a human shield. "What's going on?" I question, stepping in beside him and trying to keep up with his long strides as we walk through the big metal door of the Den. "What's this about?"

Christian scoffs and grabs me, pressing me up against the wall and lowering his voice, reminding me that he's not a friend, just an ally. "Don't play dumb with me, princess," he says. "I saw your boyfriend there. These other fuckers might have been too fucking stupid to put it together, but I know what the fuck's going on."

I swallow back fear, wondering if I've just walked into a trap when I hear Russo's, deep booming voice flowing over the Den. "Let's get on with it, we've wasted enough time."

Christian doesn't release me, just stands there staring at me with a heavy scowl, almost as though he's accusing me of something. After a minute passes and all the bodies in the Den begin crowding around, he finally releases me, and we both hurry to catch up.

There must be at least a hundred and fifty Wolves crammed into this small part of the Den, and I have to admit, I'm impressed that they're all falling in line and doing exactly what they've been told. Whether that's out of fear or loyalty, I don't know.

Christian walks right around to the front to stand by Russo's side while I hide in the back, keeping close to the exit for a quick escape.

"Right," Russo says with a grunt, sounding as though he's in pain. "Where is she?"

Fuck. That could only mean me.

I take a step back when a hand curls around my wrist like a steel vice. My eyes snap up to find Snake's sick glare on me, and I try to yank my arm free, only he's holding on far too tight. "Let me go," I growl, but it's as though he isn't listening to a damn word I say.

He gives me a hard yank and shoulders his way through the crowded bodies, dragging me through until he pushes me into the center of the circle, to where I fall to my knees at Russo's feet.

"Get up," Russo says on a growl, staring down at me with distaste.

My head snaps up to take him in. Russo leans against the bar, hardly holding himself up, and fuck, he looks bad. Colton really went to town. There's not a single section of his body left untouched, and he looks more than miserable.

I swallow back over the lump of fear growing in my throat. He's going to kill me for this. There's no way he's going to let me walk out of here still breathing. The only way I'm getting out of here is in a body bag. What was I thinking coming here? I should have run. I should have left when I had the chance.

I shakily get to my feet and as Russo's heavy stare settles on mine, I instantly begin backing up. With the Wolves behind me, they shove at me until I'm front and center. Russo points to the empty space to his left and shoots daggers at me. "Now," he growls.

Not stupid enough to make matters worse, I move, slowly taking myself to the space at his side, fearing the absolute worst. Christian's eyes remain on me with confusion, and the small concern in his gaze tells me that no matter what, he's still on my side. I still have his protection even though he's questioning my loyalty.

Once I'm right where Russo wants me, an intense hush falls over the Den, and Russo pushes off the bar, doing his best to look strong in front of his men despite the pain he must be in. "There are a few things we need to discuss," he announces, looking around the crowded bodies. Russo's gaze flicks to mine before looking back to his people. "Last night, I was taken off the fucking streets by Widows," he says, sending the men into an uproar. "Dominic Garcia tortured me for information, but I didn't relent."

My eyes bug out of my head as I look up at Russo.

The big, scary, broken man says what?

I swear he just told his people that Nic was the one who did this. Why would he do that? Is he trying to protect me or fuel their hatred of the Widows? This doesn't make any sense, but I'm not stupid enough to speak up about it. For now, it's the only thing keeping me breathing.

Christian glances at me, and that one look confirms his suspicion, but just like me, he keeps his mouth shut, letting Russo play out what little game he's brought us all here to play.

Snake takes a step into the circle. "The Widows knew we were coming," he spits, looking right at me. "The little bitch squealed. What's she even doing here? She's a Widow lover."

Russo steps directly in front of me and grabs Snake by the front of his shirt. "That little bitch was given the impression that we were still weeks off from an attack. Your big mouth was the fucking reason they knew, so I suggest you shut the fuck up and stand back in line where you belong. Unless you'd prefer me to tell your fellow Wolves how you directly told Dominic Garcia that you were on your way to take them out."

Snake's eyes go wide, and he instantly begins to retreat as the Wolves around him start to murmur, but as Russo steps out of my way, Snake's eyes come back to mine, filled with hatred.

"Today was a sham," Russo spits at his men. "An embarrassment. You all failed me. Instead of standing strong, you bitched out to save my life, but you all know better. If you have a chance to take out the enemy, you take it, no matter what the costs, even if it means sending a bullet straight through my brain. Failures."

Cries of outrage and protest come shooting through the Den, until Russo holds up his hands, not about to deal with their rowdy bullshit. "SILENCE," he demands, bringing order back to his meeting. Once he has all of their attention, he continues. "Here's the thing, Dominic has possession of something very important to me, something important to us all," he says, referring to his company that is now actually in Colton's possession, but these guys don't need to know that. "Dominic will use this against us. He will retaliate. He will not sit back and accept that we came to his home. We need to be prepared because this isn't just war anymore, this is a termination."

The Wolves start chanting, showing that they're ready for this when Russo holds up his hands, telling them to shut the fuck up. "I will lay my life down for the Wolves, but Dominic has made it impossible for me to fight, and because of that, there's something that I must do."

Every eye turns his way, focusing with every bit of attention they have. "In order to keep every one of your asses out of prison, I have to step down. I made a deal, and unless I stick to my word, we're all going down."

My brows furrow as the murmurs pick up through the room again. That wasn't the deal that Colton made. It was my freedom for his company. What the fuck is he playing at?

"As of now, you have a new leader," Russo explains. I glance at Christian, wondering how the fuck this is supposed to work. Does Snake step up as his second, or is Christian supposed to take over the family business? What kind of side deals has Russo made?

Christian's brows furrow as Snake raises his chin, puffing out his chest with pride. He's assuming that today is the day he finally gets what he has always wanted, but when Russo reaches back and snaps his fingers around my wrist and drags me forward, dread sinks heavily into my stomach.

"No, no, no, no, no," I begin chanting, desperately fighting against his hold as Russo speaks over me.

"Effectively immediately," he says with a loud, dominant tone, daring anyone to question his authority. "Oceania Munroe is now stepping up and taking her rightful place as the leader of the West Side Wolves."

I gape, horror washing through me like a wave crashing into a brick wall, completely rocking me to my core. I start shaking my head, searching out Christian for help, who looks back at me in confusion, standing as still as a statue while trying to come to terms with what just happened. "No," I say with desperation, trying with everything in my power to pull my wrist free of Russo's hold. "I didn't ask for this. Pick someone else. This isn't my rightful place. I don't even belong here."

Russo pulls me into him, baring his teeth like an actual wolf. "Your father was my second for twenty years. You belong more than the rest of these fuckers do, now stop being a disrespectful little bitch and show your family that you respect them."

Outrage and pissed off protests sound all around the Den while Snake forces his way back into the circle. "What the fuck is this?" he demands, lifting a hand and shoving it into my shoulder, sending me falling back against the bar as he stares down Russo. "I've stood by your side ever since the beginning. That spot is mine. I haven't been your 'yes man' for nothing."

Russo growls as he reaches for his gun and presses it against Snake's head. "You're a fucking disgrace," he roars. "You betrayed your brothers today. It was your actions that had four of our men lying on the ground, perishing in front of the Widows home like animals. You will never lead my people."

Snake ignores the gun at his head as though it's a common occurrence and jams his finger into Russo's chest. "You're going to regret this," he announces before smacking the gun away and turning his back. He walks away, shoving through the crowded bodies until he's flying out the door.

Russo finally releases his steel grip on my wrist, and all eyes slice to me. Jaren and Christian instantly appear at my sides, getting a discreet nod of approval from Russo as we stand as one, facing the Wolves front on.

Some scoff at the sight while others narrow their eyes, not liking what they're seeing, and honestly, I don't fucking like it either. I can't be the leader of a fucking gang, let alone the one who's at war with the Widows. I don't belong here, and looking out at the men standing before me, they don't think so either.

I go to move away but Christian jams his hand into my back. "Don't fucking turn your back. Stand until the last man has walked away unless you'd prefer to get a bullet through the back of your head."

Fuck me.

Bile rises in my throat, and I swallow it down over and over again as I stand tall against these men. Neither Christian nor Jaren moves a muscle until the last Wolf has walked away. I choose to honor this fuckery purely out of respect for Russo, assuming that there are reasons for why he did what he did. Hell, maybe he thinks that Nic won't stand against the Wolves while I'm at the top of the leaderboard, but if that's what he thinks, he's fucking wrong. It will only push Nic further.

Once everyone is out of hearing range, Russo finally turns to me with a grin ripping across his face. "You better watch your back, girl," he says in amusement. "Your boy has fucked with the wrong man."

Russo turns his back as a chill sweeps down my spine.

I'm in fucking trouble here.

The second Russo is gone, the bile rises again, and this time, I can't hold it down. I race for the bar and throw myself over it before finding an old bucket and throwing up everything in my stomach.

Ten minutes later, I sit at the bar with my head in my hands and Christian sitting beside me while Jaren refills my third glass of water.

Jaren places the glass down in front of me. I take it with both hands, watching as the water inside jostles around with my movements. "I can't do this," I murmur for only them to hear as Christian scans the room again, waiting for the threats to come at me. "I only just turned eighteen, and I don't even want to be in this stupid gang. I'm fucking pregnant. Can't Russo see how fucked up this is?"

Jaren grunts. "I think he's counting on it," he tells me bluntly, not sparing my emotions. "He's hoping you fuck it up and the boys deal with you themselves. Keep it clean and private, so your rich friends can't get involved."

"That's ridiculous. If something happened to me, Colton wouldn't stop until every last one of you are dealt with, and the Widows … it's only going to make it worse. It's got to be something else. Maybe he's trying to use me as leverage to get his shit back."

"What the fuck does Dominic have on him?" Christian demands, thinking out loud.

"The deed to his company," I say, deciding to keep quiet about the real person behind that. "Apparently, it's the company that Russo ran all of his bullshit through. It holds every secret, every deal, every tiny little thing to bring this whole thing down in flames."

"Fuck," Christian grunts, leaning back in his chair. "We'd all go down if that was to get out."

Jaren lets out a heavy sigh and leans onto the bar. "What the fuck are we supposed to do?"

Christian shakes his head, not liking his own damn plan. "We play along. We put Ocean in power and make her the best fucking leader these guys have ever had. We need to win her loyalty over Russo's."

My brows pinch as I stare at him in confusion. "And how the fuck am I supposed to get a bunch of grown-ass men to follow me?"

"You make a move," he tells me. "You take down our enemies and show that only you could have done it. You make Russo look weak. End the Widows and make the Wolves the most feared and coveted gang this country has ever seen."

I shake my head. "I can't make a move against the Widows like that."

"Then you die. It's as simple as that," he tells me. "I'm not trying to be an ass, I'm telling you how it is."

"He's right," Jaren murmurs, looking up and meeting my eyes. "But whatever you decide to do, you need to figure it out fast because these guys aren't going to sit around and wait on you forever. Make your move and make it a fucking good one."

CHAPTER 24

Whispers turn into muffled protests filled with nothing but arrogance that has me desperately wishing I could cross this stupid Den and smack it out of the Wolfy dickwads. They're acting as though I stole the leadership out from under Russo rather than having it forced down my throat.

Fuck, I'd give anything to not be here right now.

The Wolves hover in small-groups, standing suspiciously spaced around the bar where I sit with Christian and Jaren. My back is to them, and it feels like the most moronic thing I've ever done as every few minutes that pass by, I feel them inch closer, more than ready to steal my crown away from me.

They don't want me at the top just as much as I don't want to be there, but unfortunately for every single one of us, there's not a damn thing that can be done about it. It won't stop them from trying, though. Judging by what Jaren and Christian have been saying, they're going to try their hardest to get me out of here, even if it means putting a bullet through my brain.

I've never felt so sick in my life.

It's only been an hour since Russo's ridiculous little announcement, and seeing as though no one has died yet, I'd say I'm doing pretty well. I wonder what the world record for the shortest time in power is because I have a feeling I'm about to be at the top of the list. Russo must have a game plan. Surely he's not stupid enough to put me at the top of the organization that he's been behind for the last twenty or so years. It's a ploy, he's playing some kind of game, and I have a feeling that I don't have much time to figure it out.

If I was smart, I'd be embracing this new change. I should be taking advantage of a shitty situation and making some big changes. I should be using this time to mend bridges between the Widows and the Wolves so that no one else has to lose their lives. Hell, maybe even save my boy's asses while I'm at it. I should be turning over all the shitty people the Wolves deal with and get them off the street. I should be getting the Wolves clean and helping Blaxlands Grove become a desirable destination once again. But instead, I'm sitting here about ready to shit my pants.

Ha. I'm an idiot for thinking that I could have the kind of pull to make a difference around here. I'll be lucky if I can somehow escape with my life still intact. The Wolves won't stand for it. They won't allow me to come through here and tear down their carefully sculptured castle from the inside. It'll never happen. I just have to hope that while I'm here, I don't get myself mixed up in any of their mess. You know, apart from the mess I'm already caught up in.

I feel the nerves beginning to roll off of Christian beside me as Jaren continues looking around, watching the Wolves as they slowly creep closer and closer. Time is running out. If I'm going to make a stand and demand their respect, then it needs to be done sooner rather than later. If I decide to wait … later won't be an option.

"What's the plan?" Christian urges, low and demanding, the desperation thick in his voice as he tries to figure out how I'm going to play this. I can see the doubt in his eyes. He doesn't think I have the balls to face these guys and say what needs to be said. Christian has somehow taken on the role of my protector despite how annoyed he is that I went behind his back to talk to his sister and happen to have a boyfriend who was seen standing with the Widows. My gut is telling me that he can be trusted, and being Russo's son, I feel as though that gives him an edge, an advantage. He knows how things work around here, he knows what goes on behind closed doors, and he's strong enough to stand against his father. It makes him perfect to be my second.

I nervously glance back over my shoulder to find the Wolves a lot closer than I had expected. I discreetly shake my head, wishing I wasn't knocked up so I could take a shot or six to ease my nerves. "I have no fucking idea," I tell him.

Jaren sighs, leaning forward onto the bar to keep our conversation quiet. "Hurry up and figure it out," he tells me, nodding toward the entrance of the Den to where Snake stands, scanning the room, and looking for a target, who I have no doubt is me.

Snake's eyes come to mine, and he instantly curls his hand into a fist, cupping it with the other and cracking every knuckle in his hand. He looks as though he's about ready to steal the crown right off my head by sending my brains flying out the side of my ear.

This isn't good. I wonder how well Christian and Jaren fight? Actually … maybe I should figure out if these two would even be down for throwing themselves in front of a fist for me. I mean, it's one thing to want to mentor me through it, but not a lot of people are willing to risk a broken nose for some chick that they've met only a handful of times.

I turn back to Jaren, not wanting Snake to see just how much his dominance is making my blood run cold. I take a sip of my water, desperately trying to calm my nerves, but when Jaren grunts, I realize that it's showtime. "Ten seconds."

Fuck.

"Five."

Christian gets twitchy beside me, and as Jaren slips his hand under the bar and places a knife down in front of me, I have no choice but to make my move.

I feel Snake's fingers curl around my arm, the same way they had done as he dragged me away from Colton's Veneno and then beat the living shit out of me. I won't be allowing that to happen again.

Like lightning, my hand flies out and my fingers curl around the wooden hilt of the knife. As Snake hoists me up from my seat, I spin around and slam the knife up against his neck, bringing us both to an immediate standstill.

Snake's hand loosens on my arm, preparing to make some kind of move, but I see the fear in his eyes, and after everything I've been through at his hands, he knows damn well that I won't hesitate, not this time. I have too much to prove.

"You don't want to do that," he warns me, playing the role of the tough guy.

I lean into him, pressing the knife deeper into his skin and meeting his angered stare as every Wolf in the room watches on with wide eyes. None of them know for sure just how far I'll go to prove a point. "Oh, I really think I do."

Snake clenches his jaw. "You don't belong here."

I can't help but laugh, feeling as though the real me has just stepped right out of my body and is currently letting the crazy version of myself take the reigns. "Ha. You don't think I've figured that out? Go ahead. Say something else. Let's see how many times you can state the obvious before I get bored and slit this knife right through your throat."

His eyes narrow, and I don't doubt that he's wishing he'd brought his gun along to this little chat we're having. "You think you're pretty fucking hot, don't you? Standing up here, acting as though these guys are going to have your back."

I press a little harder and watch as the blade finally pierces his skin, sending a red trickle of blood smearing over my knife and dripping down the thick column of his neck. "That's where you're wrong," I tell him. "They'll have my back just as surely as I know they won't have yours. Look around you, dickhead, how many of them are rushing in to save you from the crazy bitch? Not a goddamn one."

The small ray of fear that shines through his eyes gets a little bigger, and I laugh as I push my limits a little harder. "What did you think you were going to achieve out of this? You've already beaten me senseless and watched me rise from the ashes. I'm a fucking phoenix. There's not a damn thing you can do to me."

As I continue pushing, Snake has no choice but to lower himself to his knees. "This isn't over," he warns me. "I'm not about to fold and let some bitch Widow lover stand where I'm supposed to stand and lead my men straight to their deaths."

"I'm sorry, you must have me confused. Aren't you the guy who literally just led these men into a war against the Widows that you weren't prepared for and then lost four of your own? Hmm. Funny. All this time I've been saying to stop the war and get at Nic in a different way, but none of you fuckers wanted to listen to me. You're all just so happy to walk straight to your deaths and condemn your brothers right along with you. Wow, what am I even doing here? You're right, you'd make such a great leader."

Snake gets right down to his knees and I watch as the Wolves surrounding us begin to straighten out, maybe even listening to what I have to say. Though, I'm not stupid enough to think that they're suddenly going to tolerate me after one stupid little sarcastic speech.

Snake clenches his jaw as he gets right down to his knees, and only then do I feel Christian take a discreet step back, deciding that I finally can take care of this on my own.

"You're done," I tell Snake, bending to get right into his face as I watch him pathetically kneel before me. "You know why?" I taunt, lowering my voice to a whisper. "Because I'm your fucking leader now, and there's not a goddamn thing you can do about it. You answer to me."

"I'll never answer to you."

"Look at yourself," I say, a massive grin spreading across my face. "You're already worshipping me, kneeling at my feet." With that, I pull back from the man on his knees and slam my foot heavily into his chest, sending him sprawling back over the dirty floor. The other Wolves have to step back to avoid being run into, but I don't miss the impressed stares on their faces. They know that if I can get Snake on his knees and send his ass flying, that I can do much worse to them.

I stare down at Snake as he fumbles around on the sticky floor. I raise my chin. "You're welcome to leave. Walk out the fucking door and watch how quickly the Widows claim you. You've got nothing without the Wolves at your back."

"And you think you do?" he spits, rubbing a hand over his chest.

A wide smile stretches across my face, and I meet his eyes, letting him see just how wrong he is. "Maybe I'm a different breed," I tell him. "Even without the fucking Wolves, I still have the whole damn world."

As Snake tries to get back to his feet, I turn back to the bar and shove my foot right up onto the stool I'd only just been sitting on a moment before Snake decided to yank me off it. Only with my back turned, someone moves into my peripheral vision, and without warning, I reach over and grab the gun from the waistband of Christian's jeans. I whip around and let three bullets fly before I even take a second to figure out who's coming for me.

The bullets slam into the concrete floor at the man's feet, and he brings himself to a blinding stop, sending the Den into complete and utter silence. I take the second I need to raise my eyes from the three small holes in the concrete and scan over my latest threat to find Leon, the fucker with the scar, the same dickhead who thought he could put his hands on me.

Maybe keeping these bastards in line is going to be a little more fun than I had anticipated.

Leon meets my eyes, and with a clenched jaw and hatred shining in his own, he takes a step back, slowly raising his hands in surrender. "Yeah, that's what I thought," I say, deciding to keep Christian's gun for a little while longer.

I stand and stare out of the Wolves for a second longer before deciding that I'm good to turn my back again, and this time as I shove my foot up on the stool, I make my move quickly.

I push up and then step right onto the bar before turning and facing every man in the room, baring myself and letting them see the real me. Every eye in the room stares up at me, waiting to see what I have to say for myself. It's then that I notice Russo standing in the back of the room, covered by shadows and watching me through narrowed eyes, clearly not liking what he's seeing.

I stare out at the men who all look as though they're wanting to skin me like some kind of animal and then wear me like a trophy, and I realize that I only have one shot at this. "I didn't ask for this," I start, keeping my voice strong, my chin raised, and my attitude fierce. "Just as you guys didn't, but I'm not a fool. I'm not going to stand here and expect that I'm entitled to your loyalty. I know if I were standing in your position, I'd sure as hell not be giving it. But I can guarantee that I will earn it."

A few scoffs come from around the room before a deep voice tears through the silence. "You're just a fucking kid. How the hell do you think you're going to earn our loyalty?"

Well, that's a good fucking question.

I take a shaky breath and try to pinpoint the guy who had asked but come up with nothing so just keep addressing them as a group. "I'm going to be real with you, I don't know why Russo put me here. That's something you're going to have to take up with him. However, I do know that I came here with one goal and one goal only. I want to take down Dominic Garcia."

More scoffs sound around the room, and I quickly realize that's their arrogance talking. "Good luck, princess," someone says. "A kid like you couldn't even get within ten feet of the guy."

I raise a brow, actually able to find the guy who spoke. "Then it might come as a surprise to you to know that Dominic Garcia has been in love with me for over four years. I am his weakness, and I'm the only person on this fucking planet who is capable of getting close enough to destroy him. Up until a few weeks ago, I thought that I was going to need a whole fucking army to take him down, but it turns out that all I need is me. He killed my father and my boyfriend's father, so no, I'm not just going to sit back and let you fuckers walk all over me. I have a fucking job to do. So you know what, follow me or don't. It makes no difference to me. I came here with one purpose, and I intend to see it through with or without you."

All eyes watch me and after a beat of silence. I give them their choice. "Take your pick," I tell them. "Either stand with me, or turn your backs on your brothers and walk out the fucking door. But I can guarantee that if you walk, you won't be going free. Turning your back on me is turning your back on the Wolves and aligning yourself with our enemies. It's fucking ride or die, so what's it going to be?"

The silence is deadly and my nerves are at an all-time high. I've never felt anything like it, but when Jaren launches himself over the bar and stands in front of me, I feel things beginning to shift.

He drops to one knee before me. "I'll follow you."

Christian follows, sending a wave of pride soaring through me. "I'll follow you."

One by one, men begin dropping to their knees, realizing they have no choice but to give me their loyalty or to turn their backs on their brothers. I'm not stupid enough to think that from here on out it's going to be sunshine and rainbows. I haven't got their loyalty, I have a chance at gaining it, and I'm going to have to make some drastic moves to prove that I deserve it. Otherwise this is going to be a shitshow.

Within a moment, every knee is on the ground except for one, and I stare him down, knowing that this guy is going to be a problem.

Snake and I stare at each other in a fight for dominance, and our stare only breaks when a sharp tone cuts through the Den. "KNEEL TO HER," Russo demands, stepping out of the shadows. "She's your leader now. You will give her your loyalty."

"She hasn't earned it," Snake snaps back at him.

"Then walk."

Russo's words are said almost like a dare as Snake glances between the two of us, an understanding in his eyes. You live for your brothers, or you die by them. Snake looks back at me, reluctantly spitting the same words that every other man in the building has just vowed.

He drops to a knee, bowing his head. "I'll follow you."

And just like that, I've become the most powerful woman Blaxlands Grove has ever seen.

CHAPTER 25

It's well after three in the morning when the Audi comes to a stop in the massive garage. In a perfect world, I would have been home hours ago and already asleep in bed where I belong. Though in a perfect world, I also wouldn't be the leader of a street gang and planning a massive takedown. I guess we all can't get what we want.

I make my way through the internal garage door into the Carrington mansion, and I begin creeping through the house, trying my hardest to keep quiet. This place is huge, and the marble floors weren't exactly made for creeping. It's like an echo sounds through the house with every step I take.

I start heading for the hallway that leads me out toward the pool house, but when I pass the staircase that takes me up toward Colton's bedroom, I find myself taking a little detour. I'm sure he's been worried about me. After the bullshit that's been going down lately, I'd be worried about me too.

How the hell am I supposed to tell him that Russo made me the face of the whole operation instead of releasing me? This isn't going to go well.

By the time 7 pm came, Colton started calling. After a quick reassurance that I was alright, he backed off and allowed me to do what I had to do, but that was assuming that when I came home, I'd be free. Fuck, he's going to shred Russo to pieces for this.

I make my way up the stairs and creep along the marble floors until I'm standing in front of his door. Grabbing the handle, I give it a gentle turn and open the door into a dark room.

Light from the hallway streams through his room and shines upon Colton like a spotlight, showing me exactly what I came here to see. I find Colton sitting up in bed with his arm propped behind his head. His shirt is nowhere to be seen, but that's the way I like him. I'm smacked in the face with his handsome beauty. He's so fucking edible. I could lay in bed and lick my way up and down those abs all day and never get bored. But what's really got me by my balls of steel is the way his bicep bulges as it rests behind his head.

He's simply delicious.

"Jade," he murmurs, adjusting himself in bed and making me drool over the way his abs crunch with his movement. "It's late."

I walk into his room, leaving the door slightly ajar so that I can keep drooling over his body. "You waited up for me," I comment, moving toward him and noticing the way his bedsheet hardly covers all the goodness hidden beneath.

He grins, his eyes darkening with desire as he watches me move across his room, striding toward him as though I can't breathe without him near. "And let you get home to celebrate all on your own? I hardly think so."

I walk around the side of his bed, propping my knee beside his thigh as I climb over and straddle his waist. "I missed you," I tell him, grabbing hold of the headboard on either side of his wide shoulders.

I grind down against him, feeling his hard cock rubbing against my clit. I groan deep in the back of my chest, needing him so much more than I even knew. His hand falls to my waist, and as I grind against him, his fingers dig into my skin, urging me on. "I missed you too," he tells me, his voice deep and full of seduction.

I moan, leaning into him and letting my lips brush over him. "I can tell," I murmur as he catches my lips in his and kisses me deeply. His warm, inviting lips move over mine, and I wonder why the hell I stayed so long at the Wolf Den when this was here waiting for me. I could have spent all night with Colton buried deep inside of me instead of fending off dickheads and making claims that I'll earn respect, trust, and loyalty.

Colton's tongue sweeps through my mouth, and I can't help the needy groan that escapes me. Why is this so good? It's as though my body was made just for his. Ever since the day I met him, the chemistry between us has been off the charts. Our bodies respond to one another's with a fierce need and longing that I will never find with another man. It's perfect. No wonder it was so easy to fall in love with him. It was inevitable.

The breeze from his open window blows against his door, slamming it against the little metal lock and leaving it open just a crack. The room is so dimly lit now that I barely see him, and I have to focus on just his touch alone.

Colton's fingers roam over my body, pulling my shirt over my head and then finally coming down on my skin. He teases me with his fingertips, gently brushing them over the sensitive parts of my body, the places he knows drives me wild with need. His touch tickles, and despite the growing need to pull away, I stay, allowing him to do it because his touch is so damn intoxicating.

Every place he touches me leaves a wake of goosebumps, which only makes my skin sensitive to his touch. He pulls back from me ever so slightly, but before I get a chance to protest, he drops his lips to my neck, making my fingers dig into the soft fabric of his headboard.

My hips continue rocking back and forth, grinding over him until neither of us can take it any longer. The bedsheet is torn out from between us, and within seconds, Colton rips my pants off my body. My flimsy thong disappears with it, and as I settle myself back over his waist, he lines himself up with my entrance, allowing me to slowly drop down on top of him.

He fills me so perfectly. So tight and hitting every fucking wall. Every time it just gets better. I sink down until there's nowhere left for me to go, clenching my eyes as the undeniable pleasure rocks through me. Colton's fingers tighten on my ass, gently rocking me forward and making us both groan with need.

I rock right back, and every nerve ending inside of my body catches fire, burning so intensely that I could pass out from the satisfaction. I slowly find a rhythm, leisurely riding up and down on his cock as though I have all fucking night to torture him with my body.

Colton tries to take over, thrusting up into me, desperate to break my torturously slow rhythm in fear of not being able to hold on. But I shake my head and dip my lips to his. "Slow," I tell him, making a pained grunt rumble through his chest.

"I want to fuck you all night, Jade. If you don't start moving, I'm going to come."

I lick my lips, the sound of his satisfaction urging me on. "You'll wait," I tell him, reaching behind me and taking his hands in mine. "Just like you make me wait."

"Babe," he groans, desperate for his release.

For a brief moment, I consider taking pity on him and ending his torture, but it's been a long day, and I want to take my time, enjoying every little second. I slow my movements even more and reach over to his bedside table before yanking his phone charger out of the wall socket.

Colton meets my eyes, his brows creasing with confusion, though it doesn't last long before he figures out my plan.

I bring his hands up to his headboard and loop the charger cable around one of the posts before tying up his hands. My tying skills aren't up to scratch, so he could free himself if he really wanted to. Judging by the look in his eyes, the brief moment of distraction has given him the time he needed to get himself under control, and he's more than prepared to let me run the show.

He tests his hands against the charger cable, and it instantly becomes loose. I raise a brow, clenching everything below the border and getting his immediate attention. "Are you going to behave?" I question, leaning forward and tightening it again. "No hands."

"That depends," he tells me, his eyes dark and inviting. "Are you going to keep playing with me, or are you going to fuck me like you mean it?"

I lean into him, kissing the side of his neck and teasing his warm skin with my tongue. As I finally make it down to the base of his neck and gently bite, a small gasp of surprise tears from within him, urging me on. "Why can't I do both?"

His lips pull into a grin, and before he has the chance to take over, I rise up off his excruciatingly large cock, and shimmy my way down his body. Licking my lips, I let him know exactly what I want. After all, I've been thinking about making this whole dessert before dinner thing a bit of a trend around here.

His eyes all but roll into the back of his head, just imagining how good this is going to be as I look down at the mammoth of a cock that's begging me to take it deep into my mouth. It glistens with my wetness in what little light that comes from the cracked door, and I find myself anxious to get started.

I peek up at him through my lashes, watching as he's already pulling on his wrists, wanting to grab hold of me and tie his hands around my hair. "No hands," I remind him.

Colton nods, and with that, I close my lips over the tip of his cock, instantly tasting myself on his skin. I lower myself down, taking him until I feel him in the back of my throat before roaming my tongue over his tight length. Every muscle in his body clenches, and I can't help but take a second to look up at him and watch the desire cut across his handsomely rugged face.

My pussy pulses with need, flooding with heat until I'm dripping wet. I'd give anything to climb back up his body, release his hands, and shove my ass up in the air so he can fuck me until the sun comes up, but this is too good, the tension, the desire, the need. It's all too much but so fucking perfect.

As my mouth and tongue work up and down his cock, teasing his tip and giving him the ride of his life, his sheer size leaves me no choice but to get both hands involved. I keep it slow and torturous, and although I know what he *wants*, I also know what he *needs*.

My tongue runs over his tip again, and I watch as he pulls on his binds and growls low, wanting to touch me. "Fuck, Jade," he groans, his words speaking to the vixen living deep inside of my soul and urging me on.

I pick up my pace, twisting my hands up and down as I go. My tongue works him as my mouth clamps down around him. I go deeper, testing my limits and feeling him right there in the back of my throat, somehow managing not to gag. Though something tells me that he'd like to see the tears in my eyes as I struggled on his cock.

I move up and down again, and just as he hits the back of my throat, all his muscles tense. He groans in pleasure as hot spurts of come travel down my throat. I take every last bit of him, swallowing until there's nothing left to give, and only then do I pull him out of my mouth and use my thumb to put on a show of cleaning myself up.

Colton watches me as I lick my lips, showing him just how much I enjoyed playing with him. He pulls against his hands, assuming I'm done, but I haven't even gotten started. I shake my head, climbing back up his body, and by the time I lean into him, he's desperate to get my lips on his.

"Do you have any fucking idea how agonizing that was not to touch you?"

I grin against his lips. "I was counting on it."

With one quick pull, Colton tears his hands free from the cable and rolls us until he's hovering above me. "Is that really the game you want to play?" he questions, moving down my body, kissing every inch of me as he goes.

I squirm under his touch, and just when I think it's about to get good, he keeps going, straight off the end of the fucking bed. "What are you doing?" I pout in protest, watching his naked ass as he struts across the room.

Colton looks back over his shoulder, smirking as he makes his way over to a set of drawers. He opens the second one down, and I raise my brow as he pulls out a spreader bar, something I thought I'd only see in movies like '50 Shades of Grey.'

I stare, unable to comprehend what I'm seeing, but damn, I'm so down for this.

Colton makes his way back to me. "You know what this is, right?"

"Mmhmm."

"Ever used one?"

I shake my head.

"Just say the word, and I'll put it away right now," he comments, raising a brow as he reaches the end of the bed.

I shake my head. "Have you ever known me to say no?"

Colton kneels on the end of the bed, trailing his fingers down my legs until they're at my ankles. "Only when you're being stubborn."

I can't help but laugh and find myself propped up on my elbow, watching as he straps my ankle into the little cuff before reaching for the other. I'm intrigued, watching his skilled fingers as they work the little buckles. He's done this before. He exudes confidence, the kind of confidence that a rookie wouldn't be able to rock.

"You want to tell me where you learned about this shit?"

Colton meets my eyes, and as he smirks at me, he spreads the bar wide and my legs open, exposing every inch of myself to him.

Fuck me, this is going to be fun.

He pushes the bar up the bed, forcing my knees up and somehow managing to expose myself more. He walks back to his closet and comes out a second later with two ties that I'm sure are made of the most expensive silk.

My wrists are bound just like his were except there's no way that I'll be getting out of this.

By the time Colton makes his way back to the end of the bed, I'm a mess filled with a nervous anticipation. I'm more than experienced when it comes to being a little kinky, but this is certainly different. I can't say that I've ever done anything like it before but fuck it, I'm so down. In fact, I'm already excited about telling Milo all about it.

Shit. Milo? Why the hell am I thinking about Milo at a time like this?

Focus, bitch. You only get to experience this shit for the first time once.

Colton climbs up the end of the bed until he's kneeling between my legs. He looks down at me … all of me, and the hunger in his eyes has me almost coming on the spot. I instantly start squirming, unable to help myself as the need intensifies within me.

He better touch me fast because there's no way in hell I'm going to last very long. Hell, I could probably just think about coming and throw myself off the freaking edge.

Taking pity on me, Colton drops his fingers to my knees, slowly trailing them down my inner thigh, watching the movement with fire deep in his eyes. He's looking at me as though he's been thinking about doing this since the second he met me.

His fingers finally find my center with the softest brush over my clit, and my whole body flinches, needing so much more. I'm so sensitive, so attuned to his touch.

He does it again, grinning as my body trembles under his touch, only this time he doesn't stop. His fingers travel south until he finds the promised land, and he instantly pushes them deep inside me, finding me dripping wet and more than ready.

His fingers curl, moving in and out as he teases me, hitting the right spot and sending me insane with pleasure as I pull against my binds. My whole body squirms as I have no choice but to completely give myself up to him. It's intoxicating, riveting, addictive, I could do this until the end of time. I've never felt anything so intense. At least, I thought so until he drops his mouth to my clit and makes me scream out his name.

My body convulses, trembling with every swipe of his tongue. His fingers are relentless, hitting the spot over and over again with perfect precision.

I'd give anything to wrap my legs around his head and squeeze, but the fact that I can't and am leaving every ounce of my pleasure in his hands is leaving me completely breathless in all the right ways.

"Fuck, Colton," I yell, not giving a shit if I were to wake his sisters. "Yes, FUCK."

He keeps going, adding pressure to my clit, and then in a blinding flash of pleasure, my orgasm slams through me, making me come on his fingers while calling out his name. My eyes clench, and I throw my head back, arching my back off the bed as my orgasm rocks through me.

Colton doesn't relent, continuing his torture on my body until my every nerve is completely numb.

My breath comes in short, sharp gasps as I struggle to take a deep breath, feeling as though I've just run a marathon.

My head falls back against the mattress, and I meet his heated stare. "You've been holding out on me," I comment, wondering what other tricks he has hidden up his sleeve.

"Baby, you haven't seen nothing yet."

With that, Colton grabs the spreader bar and flips me onto my stomach before pulling me up to my knees. I squeal out in pleasant surprise as he presses his large hand into the center of my back and forces my chest down until my ass is high in the air, all his for the taking.

Colton moves in behind me and just like that, fucks me until we're both collapsing into an exhausted heap in his bed, completely and utterly spent.

CHAPTER 26

My fingers trace circles against Colton's chest as I listen to the soft, rhythmic beat of his heart. It's the first thing in the morning, and my eyes are heavy with the need to sleep. After the night we shared together, I thought sleep would have come easily, but the second Colton drifted off, everything else came rushing back.

I knew I should have told him last night, but we had such a great night together that it would have been a shame to ruin it with my new reality. How am I supposed to tell him that I'm not a free woman and in possibly more shit than I was before? It'll crush him, but I'm done with the lies and secrets. No more. The second he wakes up, I'm laying it all out for him, and then we can make a plan together.

I intend to have Colton in my life for as long as he will have me. I'm kinda hoping that's until one of us is laying on our deathbed, you know, in sixty years, not tomorrow when Nic realizes what the hell is going on. For that to happen, we need a clean slate where the trust can go both ways. After Colton killed Marco DeCarlo, I asked for complete honesty from him, and it's only fair that I do the same for him.

As my mind swirls, while trying to figure out the best way to break it to him, my hand pauses on his chest, which makes his tighten around my waist. "Why'd you stop?" he grumbles. "I was enjoying that."

"Sorry," I murmur, picking up the movement again. "I didn't realize you were awake."

"I've been up for a while," he tells me on a yawn. "Your thoughts are so loud that I can almost hear them. What's going on? You barely slept all night."

"Did I keep you up?"

He shakes his head and pulls me closer into his chest. "You're fine, Jade. What's bothering you?"

"It's the Wolves," I tell him.

Colton lets out a heavy breath and starts rubbing his hand up and down my back. "You don't need to worry about them anymore. Russo let you go. They're not your problem."

My face pulls into a twisted cringe. "That's not exactly what happened."

"What do you mean?" he questions, sitting up in bed and twisting until he's meeting my eyes. "That was the deal I made with him. He gives you your freedom in exchange for his business."

I shake my head. "He just told you what you needed to hear so he could get his ass out of there," I tell him. "He didn't let me go. Instead, he stood down as leader and slotted me straight into the spot."

His face scrunches, and he looks at me as though I'm speaking another language. "What the fuck are you talking about? You're not the fucking leader of the Wolves. Stop bullshitting me."

"You don't know how much I wish that I could start running around here saying 'gotcha' but I can't. He made the announcement last night, and I had to face down a hundred Wolves who didn't think that some knocked up, teenage kid has enough balls to lead them, and honestly, I had a hard time believing it too."

Colton throws himself out of his bed, gaping at me like some kind of stranger. "What the fuck, Ocean. You're only just telling me this now? You had all fucking night."

"I know, but I wasn't willing to ruin our night. It was too good," I say, peeling myself off of his bed and walking around to put myself right in front of him. My hands fall to his biceps and I hold onto him tight, forcing him to take a few calming breaths. "It's okay, Colton," I whisper. "I'm right here, and I'm okay. I handled the situation last night, and I have the Wolves on my side. It's not exactly a great position to be in, but it's better to have them standing at my back than stabbing a knife into it."

Colton shakes his head, not liking this one fucking bit. "Jade," he murmurs, meeting my eyes and looking fucking sick about it. "What do we ... fuck. I can't even think right now."

"It's okay," I tell him. "I'm still struggling to wrap my head around it too. But right now, we don't need to do anything. Though eventually, I need to make a move to prove that I'm worthy of their loyalty, and the sooner I make my move, the better. Each and every one of them got on their knees and vowed that they'll follow me, but they're going to expect something great to come of this."

"Like what?" he grumbles, beginning to pace the room.

"What do you think?" I murmur. "They want Nic."

"And you promised to hand him over."

I nod, taking a deep breath. Colton drops onto the end of his bed and instantly pulls me down into his lap, nuzzling his face into my neck and breathing me in. "Could you do it?" he questions, holding me a little tighter. "Because I don't want to see what happens if you don't come through."

I nod again. "Out of everyone," I whisper, curling my arms around his neck. "I'm the only one who could even get close enough to try."

"That's not what I'm asking, Jade," he tells me, his voice low and filled with concern. "When it comes down to it, do you really have what it takes to finish it? This is Nic, the guy you grew up with, you shared your life with him, and a huge part of your heart still lives with him."

"I ..." I shake my head. "I honestly don't know. Could I stand in front of him and pull a trigger? I don't know, but could I hand him over to the Wolves to protect my family? You bet your ass I would. Nic needs help, he needs guidance, and he needs someone to pull his head out of his ass and help him to see that everything he's been doing is wrong. He's so drunk with power that he's completely lost himself. I miss the guy that he used to be."

"How can you be sure that the old Nic is still in there?"

I press my lips into a tight line, refusing to believe the worst. "Because I have to. It's the only hope I have of getting through this. To find that he's no longer in there and the Nic that I once knew is gone .. that would crush me."

Colton nods before taking my chin and forcing my stare back to his. "You realize that if you hand him over to the Wolves, they're not going to give him the chance to get better. He'll be dead within seconds."

My gaze drops to my hands. "I know," I murmur. "But what choice do I have? If I don't hand him over, I'm a traitor, but if I do hand him over, I'll be condemning him to death. Even after killing both of our fathers, I can't help but still feel for him. All I can hope is that during all of this, I can somehow get Kai, Sebastian, and Eli out of this."

Colton shakes his head. "You know that's not possible," he tells me. "While Nic is still at war, they won't rest, even with you wearing the crown of their enemy."

I let out a breath and climb off his lap before collapsing into my pillow. I hate it when he's right like this. The boys will stand by Nic until the last possible second, even if it means giving up their lives in the process. They're a stubborn bunch, and I hate them for it.

"I had a call from my lawyer," Colton offers, making my head snap back up to meet his eyes. "He said that they were able to spin some self-defense bullshit and that Nic will be getting out at some point today."

My eyes bug out of my head. "Self defense?" I gape. "It was a gang war. How the hell did your lawyer manage to spin that shit?"

He shakes his head. "Trust me," he says, his voice losing its edge. "Those fuckers don't get paid that much to sit around and twiddle their thumbs. There's a reason they're on my team. I only have the best there is to have."

I nod. "So, he's really getting out?"

"The cops are still digging deeper, but unless they can pull something out of their asses by 5pm this afternoon, then yep, the fucker's getting out." His words rock me with a wave of devastation, making me realize that while Nic was locked away, he wasn't able to get to me. No phones to harass me, no chances at a random school drop-in, no turning up at my home. I was safe, and now that he's coming out, we're back at square one.

I drop back down to the pillow, and my traitorous thoughts instantly begin to take over, making the time tick by without either of us really noticing.

Both Colton and I remain lost inside our own minds until I finally pull myself up and lean back against the headboard, much like Colton had been when I walked in here late last night. "What?" I questioned, my voice low and whispered. "You're being far too quiet."

"I, uhh ..." he says, glancing back over his shoulder before spreading out on the bed and propping himself up on his elbow to meet my eyes. "I don't exactly know how this is going to affect you now that you're in charge, but I made a deal with Russo. If he didn't let you go, I was going to look into his business deals and get every bit of dirt on him to destroy him. I want you to know that I still have every intention of following through with that."

I nod, realizing that taking down Russo could possibly be hurting me, but I can't find it within myself to tell him no. "Do what you have to do," I tell him, watching the way his eyes scan over my face, making sure he takes note of every tiny little emotion that flashes on my face.

"Are you sure?" he questions. "Because once I start, I won't be stopping. I could uncover things about your father in all of this. I really don't know what I'm going to find. I just know that the things I've already seen are enough to chill even you to the fucking bone."

"Just do it," I tell him, knowing damn well that he's going to find something, and when he does, no one is going to like it. "Just be careful, I don't want you getting hurt in all of this."

Colton scoffs, a grin stretching across his face. "Please," he laughs. "I can handle myself. If anyone needs to be careful, it's you."

I can't help but laugh. "In case you've forgotten, this bitch can be as dumb as she wants when she has a whole army of Wolves at her back."

Colton rolls his eyes while shaking his head. "Way too fucking soon, babe."

I can't help but laugh as I scoot across the bed and put myself right in front of him, biting my lip as a wave of nerves settle over me. "Look, while we're talking," I say, making his brows drop, knowing damn well that whenever I start a sentence like that, it's never good. "I wanted to talk to you about the whole bun in the oven thing. We really haven't had a chance to talk about it."

"You've got that right," he says with a soft scoff. "To be honest, I really haven't known what to say about it because I don't know where your head is at. I have no idea if you even want to keep it."

"I, umm … I honestly still have no idea. It's such a big decision."

He reaches out across the bed and takes my hand. "I know, which is why I don't want you to rush it. I don't want you to feel pressure to make a decision in haste and end up regretting it later."

I nod. "Well, I've already worked out that I can't get rid of it. That's just … it's not an option for me, but I don't know where to go from there. Jaren, the guy who works behind the bar in the Den kinda mentioned something about adoption … and … well, I haven't really had a chance to think about it yet, but it's something I want to look into more."

"And if it is mine?" he questions.

"Then that's your decision too," I tell him. "All I know is that if I'm going to be around the Wolves as more of a permanent thing, I can't have a baby with me. I … I don't even know how I feel about it yet, but I just know that having a kid … there'd be a target on it's back, and I can't do that to an innocent baby."

Colton's brows pinch as he focuses on me. "What are you saying, Jade?"

"I guess… I don't really know, but if it's yours and we keep it, I think I should give you full parental rights so that it can't be linked back to me. A baby won't be safe with me."

"What?" he grunts, staring at me blankly. "That's fucking insane.

You're not giving up your rights to your child. If we have this baby together, we're doing it right. No one is going to put a target on it's back because I will make it impossible to do so. No one will ever get near this baby, we're going to love it, and we're going to give it the life it deserves. Just as I'm going to do for you."

"What are you talking about?"

"You're going to college, Ocean. Even if you're the leader of the Wolves. If there's a baby around, we'll get a nanny, and you'll still get the chance to do everything you wanted. I'll make sure of it. I'm not going to let you put your life on hold because of all of this, and there's no reason that you should have to."

I cringe, meeting his eyes and loving how much he cares. "I just … I don't know. I don't think college is going to be possible anymore."

"It will," he tells me. "Even if you have to put it off for a year or two or do it through distance learning. You're not giving up on yourself and giving everything over to the Wolves. They don't deserve one hundred percent of you. Only you do."

"And what about you?"

"Well, I get a hundred percent of you no matter where you are."

"You're an idiot," I laugh. "But speaking of my future …"

His eyes narrow, watching me cautiously, knowing that with me, this could go either way. "What about it?" he questions, warily.

I glance out his bedroom window, watching the clouds in the morning sky. "I, um … I kinda had a thought, you know, assuming the whole college thing does happen."

"Go on …"

"Well, the other day when you were telling me about Luca DeCarlo and how he'd stolen all those kids and sold them to despicable people all around the world. It got me thinking." I glance down at him to find his eyes on mine, wondering where the hell I'm going with this. "I think once I know what I'm doing and obviously am qualified to do the job, I'd like to start a foundation or … I don't really know what to call it, but something that locates and saves the kids that the rest of the world has written off or forgotten about. Maybe there could be facilities in each state that take in these kids who have nowhere else to go so they don't end up snatched off the street by dickheads like DeCarlo and hurt. I don't know, I used to see these poor homeless kids and foster kids who'd run away in the streets of Breakers Flats. It was horrible, and I want to do something about it."

Colton grabs me around the waist and rolls us so that he's hovering about me. "Have I ever told you how much I fucking love you?" he murmurs, dropping his lips to mine and kissing me deeply. "You're the most selfless and incredible woman I've ever met, you know that, right?"

I grin against his lips. "Incredible? Yes, but selfless … that's not a word I'd use to describe myself."

"I would," he tells me, rolling us again so that I straddle his waist and look down at him. He reaches up and brushes my hair off my face. "You're everything, Ocean." I can't help but stare as I look down at him, feeling his warmth spread right through me. "Are you serious about starting a foundation?"

I nod. "I've been thinking about it since you first told me about

Luca. It's been on my mind ever since, and every day that need to do something just gets worse. I have to do it. I just don't know how to make it happen."

"Then I'll get it set up for you. We can start it right now and get the best technology and detectives in the world fighting for this cause. You could have a rescue team, an office team. Everything. You can overlook everything as it builds from the ground up, and once you finish college and have the degrees you need, you take over and flourish."

I shake my head. "I can't ask that from you. That's too much. What if I fail, and it's all a big waste of money?"

"If you have the right people on your team and the best technology there is on offer, then you won't fail. Not having this shit at your back is only going to hold you back."

"Are you sure?"

"Of course, Jade. Besides, having the Carrington name attached to a project like this is only going to improve my brand. We both win here."

I narrow my eyes. "So, does that make you a business partner, a sponsor, or my boss?"

"It makes me a boyfriend who wants to see his girl fly."

I roll my eyes but can't help the wide, beaming smile that tears across my face. "That was cheesy," I tell him, holding back a laugh. "So, we're really doing this? We're saving the world one kid at a time?"

"Hell yeah, we are," he says, grabbing hold of me and pulling me down until my lips are on his.

My phone rings on Colton's bedside table, but we ignore it, way too caught up in our moment until it rings a second time and then a third. I groan and roll over Colton until my hand curls around the phone, only to find Christian's name flashing on the screen.

Is this what my life is going to be like from now on? Interruption after interruption.

I bring the phone to my ear with an annoyed groan. "What?" I say, deciding a cheery good morning isn't called for right now.

"Where are you? I've been calling you over and over again."

"Bed," I snap, not needing to explain myself to him. "What's going on? You didn't burn the place down while I was gone, did you?"

Christian ignores my jab and gets straight into the reason for his call. "We got him," he declares.

My eyes widen. "Really?" I rush out. "Already?"

"Yep. Now get your ass down here and tell us what you want done."

Christian ends the call without another word and as I turn to look back at Colton, I find him watching me with a curious stare. "What's going on?" he murmurs, taking in the calculating expression tearing across my face.

"Come on," I tell him, pulling myself out of bed and dragging him up behind me. "You're not working today. I need you to come with me."

"What? Why?" he asks, letting me pull him up.

I glance back over my shoulder and meet his eyes. "You have a threat to come through on and I'm about to make it happen."

CHAPTER 27

"Why are we here?" Colton asks as I tell him to pull up outside the Wolf Den. He glances around nervously, even more so when I reach into his center console and pull out his gun.

"Just trust me," I tell him, handing it over and watching as he expertly takes it and checks just how many bullets are in it. "I have a feeling you're going to be pissed if I was to do this instead of giving you the pleasure."

His brows crease, looking back at me with so much more than just confusion on his face. "What the fuck are you talking about?" he grumbles, opening his door before sliding out.

I follow suit, climbing out of the Veneno, meeting him around the front, and slipping my hand into his. "They're not going to like that I brought you here."

"You think?" he scoffs. "Maybe you've forgotten that it was only two days ago that I stood with the Widows and blasted bullets towards their heads. I highly doubt that they've had enough time to forgive and forget."

I raise a brow, shaking my head. "And I highly doubt that they even realized it was you."

"Right," he grumbles, making a hint of guilt sink heavily into my gut. Christian sure as hell knew it was Colton but luckily for me, he's kept quiet on it, though I don't know how he's going to feel about me having Colton walk right into his home.

We get to the door, and being the gentleman that he is, he opens it for me. I step through before him, instantly getting the eyes of every Wolf in the Den. They think nothing of it until Colton follows me through the door, and suddenly a hundred men are getting to their feet.

I roll my eyes, holding up a hand and putting a stop to their bullshit before it can get any further. "He's with me," I tell them, slowly glancing around the room and trying to catch each of their eyes and doing my best to look like the kind of bitch they only see in their worst nightmares. "A shot against him is a direct shot against me. Anyone who has an issue with that will have me to deal with. Is that clear?"

Grumbles sound all around the Den, and I hear grunts and curses under breaths saying that this isn't how we do things around here. I'm the boss around here now. Bringing an outsider into the mix might be against their rules, but fuck it, I make my own goddamn rules.

Colton follows me through the Den as I lead him toward the bar to where Christian is sitting with Jaren having a murmured conversation. "Took your fucking time," Christian says, standing and looking straight at Colton, who clearly doesn't appreciate his stare.

I discreetly slide myself between the two men and raise my chin to meet Christian's hard stare. "Cut the bullshit. Can we just get this over and done with? I'm missing school."

Christian rolls his eyes as though the prospect of going to school is so beneath him that it's almost comical. Either way, he doesn't back down and raises his eyes back to Colton. "You have a lot of balls walking in here after you shot at my brothers."

Colton scoffs. "And you fuckers had a lot of balls going in there and shooting at them."

Christian looks down at me. "Your boyfriend isn't loyal."

"My boyfriend is a lot of things, but disloyal isn't one of them. He was there trying to save my best friends, *my brothers*. He knew what it would do to me if they were to get hurt."

Christian holds his ground a little longer and then finally relents, backing down and letting out a slow breath. He glances around the room and raises his voice so every fucker in the Den can hear him. "You heard the girl," he tells them. "Let's get down to the basement and get this shit over with."

Christian looks back at me and tilts his heads, inviting us to follow him, and as we do, the rest of the Wolves fall behind.

"I don't like this," Colton murmurs beside me. "What the fuck is in the basement?"

I shake my head, knowing one thing that we'll find down here, but as for what else lives down there … that's a mystery to me. "I don't know. I didn't even know this place had a basement," I tell him. I guess I'd assumed that they had a factory or warehouse like Colton does when it comes to this stuff.

Christian glances back at us, a smirk playing on his lips. "Trust me, this place has more horrors than you could ever imagine."

A cold shiver runs down my back, and I find my hand slipping back into Colton's. As we creep through the hallway and down a flight of flimsy stairs, my blood begins to run cold. It's creepy as all hell down here.

There's a chill in the air, which only seems to make it worse, and as we reach a large metal door with a heavy lock and chain on it, I find myself glancing up at Colton. He doesn't seem to be affected by this and I'm reminded of the fact that his soul is just as covered in darkness as mine is, perhaps even more.

The soft rumble of footsteps behind us quiets down as we wait for Christian to undo the lock, and just before he pulls the heavy door open, he glances back at me. "Are you sure about this? Once you walk in there, you won't be able to go back. The things you'll see … they're not for the faint-hearted."

I grin up at him, feigning confidence. "And pussy out with all these men at my back? Yeah fucking right."

Christian nods and glances back at Colton. "Suit yourself."

With that, the door is pulled open, and a gust of cold air comes rushing out, smacking me in the face. "The fuck?" I grunt as Christian walks in. I follow him through with Colton at my back and realize that it's some kind of a freezer in here.

"This is messed up," Colton mutters under his breath, staying close by my side.

I follow Christian, and as we walk deeper into the large basement, he walks over to the side of the room and turns on the clinical lighting above.

I suck in a breath.

There are three men scattered throughout the room, one I was expecting, and the other two a complete mystery. They dangle from the roof, their tippy-toes barely meeting the ground as the massive meat hooks hold them up by their wrists.

It really is like a horror movie in here.

I keep my attention on the man in the very center of the room.

Vincent DeCarlo.

Within seconds, understanding begins to dawn on Colton, even more so as Vincent glances up to find Colton and instantly starts thrashing in his binds, desperate to get free. After all, I was there the day that Colton made him a very specific promise, one that I'm sure lingers in the front of his mind every second of every day.

I don't need to look up at Colton to know that he knows exactly why I brought him here. While he probably had his own brilliant plan set in place, he doesn't seem too displeased with mine. Though, to be fair, I thought it'd take the Wolves a little more than one night to find the bastard. I have to give them credit for that.

I make my way across the room with the Wolves at my back and Colton still right by my side, not willing to risk letting me out of his sight for one second.

The Wolves begin to crowd around Vincent and as they do, I turn to face them, waiting until every last one of them are here and ready.

Russo moves through the Wolves until he has a front-row seat, still looking like absolute shit as he leans against a cane, his eyes quickly scanning over Colton. "Why have you brought us all here?" he demands, cutting to the chase and looking as though he could tear Colton apart where he stands.

I stare him down, making a point that I don't like being rushed. I mean, if it also rubs dirt into the wound that I currently have his men at my disposal, even better. He made his bed, and now it's time for me to fuck all over it.

I tear my gaze away from Russo's, letting him know that I'll be doing things my way and not allowing him to try and run my show. "You've all been waiting for me to make some kind of move, well here it is," I tell them. "I'm assuming that many of you have heard of the DeCarlo family."

"Yeah," one of the Wolves in the front says with an arrogant grunt. "What of it? Every fucker around here knows of them. The whole fucking country knows them. So what? They have nothing to do with us."

"I know," I say, sending a glare his way. "They have nothing to do with us because they have everything to do with the Widows. They're their main source of income right now. Dominic struck a deal with them last year, now every cent of their illegal businesses run through the Widows. Without them …"

I let the thought linger in the air and watch as understanding beings to dawn on their faces, and along with it comes respect. They're no longer seeing me as just a dumb girl, but someone with brains, a chip on my shoulder, and the overwhelming need to prove myself.

Christian steps in closer, his eyes narrowing as he looks over my shoulder at Vincent. "They'd have nothing without this fucker. No cash flow, no access to weapons or drugs. They'd be out of business within weeks."

I nod. "I mean, I'm sure they'd find other connections and make more deals, but this would be a massive hit. This would set them back years, and they'd never fully recover, leaving the Wolves as the only major players in town. Dealers will have no choice but to run their drugs through us, weapon dealers, and everyone else in the fucking game is ours for the taking."

I glance back at Russo to find his brow raised, looking somewhat impressed as his men grin, looking as though they're already prepared for a massive payday.

"Alright, then," Christian says, pulling out his gun and stepping up in front of Vincent. "Say no more."

"Hold up," I say, reaching out and taking the gun right out of his hands, only to have him gaping at me as though I just committed some terrible, offensive crime. "That's what Colton is here for."

I hand the gun back to Colton, and Christian instantly tenses, not trusting him for one second. Ignoring him, I continue, not about to let this bullshit come to light, especially while we're down here. "A few months ago, Vincent had his sons come through Colton's home, my home. They terrorized us, destroyed our home, and killed a good friend of mine. Colton made a promise that night to destroy the whole DeCarlo name and so far has sol,ely been responsible for dealing with every single one of them. Now, there's only one left. Call it two birds, one stone."

The Wolves all glance around, unsure of letting Colton in on this shit, but with me in charge, they have no choice. I let my words sink in, giving them the information they need to know that Colton isn't here to play games, letting them know just how capable he is to screw them over if they were to mess with him.

A moment passes before Christian finally steps back, and Colton takes his place, looking back at me. "I don't want you to watch this," he tells me, meeting my eyes and knowing damn well that I'm going to be seeing this moment over and over again in my sleep until something equally as bad takes its place.

I shake my head. "Don't worry about me," I murmur. "I won't look weak in front of these guys. No matter what the cost. Just do it."

He watches me a second more before walking over to Vincent and stepping right in front of him, meeting his stare. "I trust that you remember exactly what I said that I was going to do to you."

Vincent's only response is to spit at his feet, and I raise a brow before stepping into Colton's side. "Hey," I snap, waiting just long enough for his eyes to flash up to mine before nailing the fucker right in the nose and listening to the satisfying crunch of his bones breaking beneath my fist. "That was for Maryne."

Colton meets my eyes, and as I shake out my hand while trying my best not to curse out in pain, fire burns in his eyes. "Fuck, you're hot when you take charge."

I can't help but grin despite the bleeding man making a mess of blood at my shoes. "Really, now? How'd you like me to take charge when we get home?"

"You're fucking on, Jade," he tells me before turning back to Christian. "Get him on his knees." Christian doesn't like it, but he does what he's asked.

Everyone watches with wide eyes as Colton steps toward Vincent and presses the tip of the gun right against his spine. "Let's hope this doesn't kill you," he says, bending down to murmur into his ear. "I'd love nothing more than to watch you spending the rest of your life as a vegetable, watching as I take every last thing from you."

Vincent struggles against his binds, but with one devastating BANG, his body goes limp. The only sound echoing through the room are the chains as they dangle above his head, slowly coming to a stop.

Colton's gaze sweeps to mine, checking that I'm not about to start freaking out, and I watch as he wipes his fingerprints off Christian's gun and wordlessly hands it back to him. He never takes his eyes off mine. "You good?" he questions, walking around to me.

I nod before turning back to the Wolves and watching as one by one, they make their way out of the basement, leaving just me, Colton,

Jaren, Christian, and Russo.

Jaren instantly starts working on releasing Vincent by pressing a button and letting his body drop heavily to the ground. Blood splatters around his fall, and I have to look away.

If anything, I should be looking at Colton to try to ease my mind, yet I find my stare digging into Russo's as he looks back at me with that same consideration he was watching me with yesterday. "Why?" I ask. "Why put me in this position? Is this just some big joke or some kind of 'fuck you' to Colton?"

Russo glances at Colton at the mention of his name, and realizing that I'm not going to get any answers with him standing right here, Colton leans into me. "I'll be waiting by the door if you need me." I nod and watch as he walks away before focusing my stare back on Russo.

He looks around before coming back to me and letting out a heavy breath. "The truth is, Colton is going to destroy me whether or not I let you go. So, yeah, the fact that this grates on his every nerve is the fucking icing on the cake, but the real reason I put you at the top is because you're the only one here who's strong enough to handle it."

I raise my brow. "You're fucking with me, right?"

"Not at all," he tells me. "Your boyfriend was going to start digging into my business whether I let you go or not, so long as I'm going down, why should I let you go, especially when you have so much potential? You're a lot like your dad. Do you know that? He was a fucking stubborn asshole, but he was a leader, just like you."

I shake my head. "No, I'm nothing like my father."

"Believe what you want to believe, that's your business, but I say it like I see it, and I'm never wrong," he says, getting back on track. "I give Carrington two months tops before he has the FBI knocking on my door, and dragging me away in chains. I need to be prepared for when that happens."

"So, why not give it to Snake?"

Christian scoffs, pretending not to listen to our conversation but unable to help himself. Russo glares at his son before bringing his attention back to me. "In case you haven't noticed, Snake is a loose cannon. He moved into your father's position once he was killed, and it's a decision I've regretted ever since. He's not ready. He'll never lead my men because with him in power, my men will all be dead within two seconds."

"Okay, so Christian? I'm sure he'll do a much better job than I ever could."

Russo narrows his eyes, wondering why I'd suggest Christian when their relationship is strictly on a need to know basis, but seeing that I know what hasn't actually been said, he gives me the benefit of the doubt. "Because my son will never lead my men while I am still breathing."

"So, you just figured that you'd throw it at me."

He nods. "I needed someone strong and who wasn't going to sit back and take my men's shit. I needed someone who thinks outside the box and who actually gives a shit about human life. That person was you, and while I hate how quickly my men are accepting this change, it's for the best. The Wolves are a sinking ship. Within a year, they're all going to be dead or in prison, but you can turn it around."

With that, Russo simply turns and walks away, leaving me gaping at his back as Christian looks on in disbelief. "Did he really just say that?" I ask, glancing up at him.

"Trust me, that fucked with my head just as much as it did yours," he tells me. "Now, let's get out of here before these other guys start talking shit."

I glance at the two other men he's referring to, the two still dangling from the large meat hooks as he leads me toward the door. "Who are these guys?"

Christian nods toward the guy in the far corner. "That one raped Snake's mom. He's been here for two months already. I can't imagine that he'll be around much longer. And the other guy," he says, nodding in the other direction. "He's a traitor. Gave up three of our guys to save his own ass."

I nod, not wanting to get into any of it, but as we walk out of the door, I can't help but look back into the basement. I take it all into consideration, pressing my lips into a firm line. "From now on, all this gets handled somewhere else. This is our home, and you don't bring shit home with you, you leave it at the door."

"Couldn't agree more," he tells me.

"Besides, if the cops come storming in here and raid the place, we're all fucked. Have the guys deal with it."

Christian nods as he pulls the door closed, locking it just as it was before. "Done. Anything else?"

I find Colton standing outside the basement and walk straight to him as Christian falls in beside me. "I want to go to school," I tell him. "I can't be here everyday running all this shit."

"Are you planning on going to college?"

I nod. "Thinking about it."

"Right," he says, as Colton takes my hand. "Then I'll do it. I'll run the day to day bullshit and overlook everything with Jaren while you make the big calls. Go to school and have a life like a normal teenage girl."

"It sounds like you're trying to faze me out."

Christian glances down at me with a nervous hesitation in his eyes. "Would that be such a bad thing?" he questions, unsure how this is going to go.

I shake my head, a grin stretching over my face as I finally begin to see the light at the end of the tunnel. "Not at all."

With everything done and dusted, Colton gets my ass out of there as soon as he can. With Christian overlooking everything, I finally feel like things are going to start turning around. "I got a call while you were talking to Russo," Colton tells me as we drop down into his Veneno.

My brow raises, and as he starts the engine, I can't help but glance his way. "And?"

"Nic just walked free and is no doubt just learning that you're the new leader of the Wolves. You need to be ready, Jade. He's going to retaliate, and I don't think he'll be taking prisoners."

CHAPTER 28

I stand at the altar in the most stunning gown I've ever seen, watching as my mom walks down the aisle, looking absolutely radiant. I've never seen her so happy. It's not every day that a child gets to witness their mother's wedding day.

She looks incredible in her custom designer gown, and just by looking at the speechless expression on her face, this is more than just a dream come true. This is everything to her, and I can hardly believe that it's happening.

Tears well in my eyes as the music flows through the church. She's absolutely breathtaking, and judging by the way Roman is watching her, he considers himself to be the luckiest man that ever walked the planet.

Mom's eyes come to mine, and a blinding smile takes over her face. Her cheeks fill with the sweetest blush, looking both overjoyed and embarrassed by having all this extravagant attention on her. It's a great look on her. It suits her well, and though it'll be a big change for her life, she'll quickly settle into it and thrive like she's never thrived before.

I can't believe it's only been three weeks since we sat in that restaurant, watching as Roman got down on one knee and proposed to Mom. I mean, I understood that it was going to be a quick engagement but when Colton and I returned home from ending Vincent DeCarlo two weeks ago to find Mom and Roman sitting in the living room with the most expensive and extravagant wedding planner I'd ever seen, I knew it was only a matter of days before they said I do.

Hendrix went nuts the second a date was made, and the very next day, she was dragging me along to dress fittings and making sure that everything was going to be perfect. I have to admit, it's all been a great distraction from the Wolves, but it's not going to last forever.

Nic has been biding his time. He hasn't made a move, and while it makes me feel as though I'm walking on eggshells, I'm grateful. It's given me this time to truly enjoy being with Mom. We've gotten to make all these crazy decisions together and live a dream that neither of us thought we'd ever get to be a part of. I mean, when we flew out and personally met with the designer, it was a dream come true. I didn't think that making a dress in two weeks was possible, but she came through. She must have had an army working on it day and night. Though, the excessive check Roman wrote her probably had a little something to do with it.

I'm not fooling myself though, I know Nic is coming. It's just a matter of time.

Just as promised, Christian completely took over everything with the Wolves. Every few days, I get a call from him, letting me know what's been going down or if he needs my approval to make a move on something. In all honesty, I always leave the decision up to him. I don't know right from wrong when it comes to gang activity, and I fear that I'm going to bury us under a pile of shit that we won't be able to get out of.

Having Christian taking the lead has been a massive relief. It was like having a weight lifted off my shoulders, and while Russo isn't exactly thrilled about our little arrangement, it's working, and that's all that matters. I think I've been there maybe three times in the last two weeks, and every time I show my beautiful face, the mood and vibe I receive inside the den becomes easier and easier to deal with.

Drix discreetly steps into my side and nudges me with her elbow, so much excitement bubbling up within her that she can barely keep herself contained. "She's coming," she squeaks, pointing out the obvious.

"I can see that," I laugh, trying to keep my amusement on the down-low, only making her roll her eyes and squeal again.

I smile wide and instantly look back at Mom as she reaches the end of the aisle and steps into Roman's arms.

He holds her so tenderly, as though she's the most precious creature that he'll ever lay his eyes on, and I absolutely love that for her.

They take each other's hands, and as they whisper little nothings to one another, I can't help but glance back at Colton sitting in the front row.

His eyes are already on me, looking at me as though he's just waiting for the day that we get to do the same thing, and honestly, the thought doesn't completely suck. I've never taken myself as the kind to get married young. Hell, I never even considered marriage at all. It's always been a piece of paper that tied me to someone else, and the whole concept scared me, but with Colton? I don't know. I might be open to persuasion.

His eyes roam over my body, taking in the soft silk that drapes over me. He follows the line down over my breasts and past the soft curve of my stomach which thankfully isn't showing any signs of my impending doom. His gaze drops lower to where the top of my thigh peeks out of the high slit. As his eyes leisurely travel back up to mine, he runs his tongue so slowly over his bottom lip, sending an electric pulse shooting right through me. 'I'm going to fuck you in that dress tonight,' he mouths.

My thighs clench as the desire rocks through me, making it nearly impossible to even stand under his intense stare.

"Holy shit," I breathe, reaching out and clutching onto Hendrix's arm to avoid falling on my face and making an ass out of myself during Mom's big day.

I tear my eyes away from him. The look in his eyes too much to focus on for long. Not unless I plan on stripping him naked and riding him like a cowgirl in the middle of the most beautiful cathedral I've ever had the pleasure of walking into. I mean, this place looks like it's been pulled right out of a history book, and judging by the way Roman is looking at my mom, if that's what she asked of him, then he would have made it happen.

Just as the priest begins welcoming all the guests to the wedding, four deliciously suited men silently walk through the doors. They hover in the back of the church, not wanting to be noticed, but damnnnn. Four sexy as sin Widows in suits is not something that any woman could skim over.

Sebastian, Kairo, Elijah, and even Nic remain standing with their backs right up against the far wall. Silently they watch the ceremony, being here solely to support me and my mom. Despite everything that's been going down between us, I've never been so happy to see his face.

His eyes come to mine, and even from so far away, I can make out the words on his lips. 'You look beautiful.'

Fuck, it's been too long. I haven't seen his face since the hospital parking garage.

My heart swells as I look into his eyes, so full of love, while every other part of him is swimming in regret. The fact that he's here doesn't change anything. We're still at war, still enemies fighting for the win. But even with a gang rivalry between us, nothing can stand in the way of the bond we've developed over the last few years. We can still forget everything else, put it all aside just so Mom can have the day that she's always deserved.

'Thank you,' I mouth, letting him see just how much it means to me that he's here.

Nic nods and I scan my eyes over the other guys who all give me warm smiles, reminding me that while we're all currently serving a lifetime in our own personal brands of hell, that they're always going to have my back, just like amazing brothers should.

Feeling too much emotion swelling inside of me, I bring my gaze back to Colton, and seeing the happiness in my eyes, he turns back and takes in the boys standing at the back of the church. He brings his gaze back to mine and nods, letting me know that he's happy that if even for the next hour, everything in my life can be perfect, even if it's only an illusion.

'I love you,' he tells me.

'Love you too, asshole.'

He grins wide, and as the priest gets on with the ceremony, I turn my complete attention back to the front, not wanting to miss a single second of it. I focus on every little bit of what's being said, and forty minutes later, tears are running down my face as Mom and Roman say their vows, declaring their undying love for one another and proclaiming a lifetime spent at each other's side.

I've never seen anything so raw and beautiful. To me, what I have with Colton is as raw as it gets, yet looking at Mom so completely in love just proves that it can always get deeper. And while Colton and I have never felt so close, we're still just teenagers, and there's so much that we still don't even understand about ourselves.

The priest announces Mr. and Mrs. Jennings for the first time, telling Roman that he can finally kiss his wife. With a sigh of relief, Mom falls into his arms, and he kisses her deeply while Hendrix is screaming in my ear, cheering them on. "FUCK YEAH, DAD. GET

IT!"

Laughter bubbles through the church, and although Mom would be in a world of embarrassment, she's secretly loving every second of it.

Warmth spreads through me, and as the joy settles into my soul, I can't help but look back at the four boys standing at the back of the church. Only as I do, all I find are their backs as they make their way out.

Devastation pours through me. I would have loved to run into Nic's arms just once and tell him that even though Colton and I have more between us than he and I ever did, he'll always be a brother to me. I need him to know how much he's hurt me, but I also need him to know that whatever happens between the Wolves and the Widows, I'll always love him.

He's hurting, and I know deep down inside that he regrets taking my father's life because, in the end, it was the catalysts that drove me out of Breakers Flats. I try to remind myself that them being here was already a massive risk on their part, and asking them to stay would be stupid.

I'm the leader of the Wolves, for fuck's sake. If anyone found out they were here, my loyalty would be put into question, and I guess the same could be said for them.

Mom and Roman get busy signing the registry, and before I know it, they're making their way back up the aisle with their guests on their feet applauding for this new part of their lives.

The bridal party begins making their way up the aisle, following the bride and groom. As I pass Colton, he instantly falls in step with me. His hand drops to my lower back, discreetly gliding over the silk of my gown until it's firmly over my ass.

I lean into his touch, wanting it so bad but as I raise my chin and smile up at him, the words out of my mouth have his eyes bugging out of his head. "The priest is watching you."

Colton's hand falls away from my ass so fast that it's comical. "Oh, fuck," he grunts, his eyes wide and face filled with horror. He instantly glances back over his shoulder to where the priest still stands in the center of the pulpit, sure enough, with his eyes on Colton. "I'm going straight to hell."

Hendrix laughs behind us as Charlie falls in beside her, his arm dropping around her waist. "I don't know about hell," she tells Colton. "But I have a feeling that I know where else you two will be going. I caught what you told her at the beginning of the ceremony."

"What'd he say?" Charlie grumbles as Colton turns to me with fire in his eyes. He grins wide, and while he doesn't say anything, he doesn't need to. I know exactly what he's thinking, and damn it, I'm more than thinking it myself.

We break free from the church, and I instantly find Mom sinking into Roman's arms and kissing him blindly. The thought that I should give them a moment of privacy enters my mind, but fuck it, I'm too excited.

I barge into mom and pull her away from her new husband. After all, he gets her for the rest of his life, and all I'm asking for is a quick hug. I'm sure Roman will manage without her for two seconds.

Mom instantly pulls me into her arms, squeezing tight and holding me there for a lot longer than the two seconds that Roman would have been willing to give. But nonetheless, I hold onto her with everything I have. "Oh, honey," she says, desperately trying to hold back her tears of joy. "That was one of the most spectacular moments of my life."

"I know," I breathe, struggling with my own emotions. "It was beautiful. I'm so happy for you. You have it all."

Mom pulls back, taking my shoulders as she glances at Roman, who's currently holding his daughter as though she's the most precious thing in the world. Feeling Mom's stare, he glances up and gives her a warm smile that instantly hits his eyes. "I really do," she tells me. "Now, how are you feeling? That was a long time to be standing on your feet in your condition. Are you feeling alright?"

I roll my eyes. "Mom, I'm only ten and a half weeks, I can handle standing for a while. Besides, you shouldn't be worried about me today. This is all you. Today is your day so tell me what I can do to make it even better? Would you like me to grab you a glass of champagne so we can start celebrating?"

Mom's eyes light up. "You know what," she says. "That sounds like a great idea."

With that, I scurry off and two hours later, photos are done. We're standing inside the most magnificent and glamorous manor this town has to offer, surrounded by impeccable gardens and manicured lawns.

Fairy lights cover the roof, creating a chandelier pattern as the rest of the hall is completely decked out and looking like an absolute fairytale.

Mom and Roman stand out on the dance floor, and as the music changes to an upbeat song, I can hardly resist the hand that Colton offers me. I know that tonight is going to be one of the best nights of my life.

Colton leads me out onto the dance floor, and as all the other couples come to join us, I fold into his arms and let him sweep me away. I desperately wish that my boys could still be here to enjoy this incredible night with me. But as it is, I have everyone else I could possibly need.

Milo and Spencer are hiding in the bathroom getting it on. Hendrix is running around after Charlie, stopping him from telling all the wedding guests about how he screwed her while we were supposed to be doing photos. Jess has been flirting with some guy who looks like an investment banker, and who could possibly be old enough to be her father. All while Casey and Cora are taking advantage of the open bar.

How could anything ever get better than this?

It's bittersweet because I know that once this is all over and my world returns to normal, things aren't going to be quite so easy. Nic is coming for me, and it's going to be an all-out war, so why not enjoy these last precious moments that I have with the people I love before it all turns to shit?

CHAPTER 29

I sit in the doctor's office, my knee bouncing with nerves as he goes on and on about the ins and outs of the paternity test. I can't believe that it's already been eleven weeks. This whole thing is already going so fast, and it's only freaking me out more. I mean, with the wedding a few days ago and all the lead up to it, I've hardly had a second to actually take it all in.

I still have no idea what I want to do. I'm hoping that I'll just lay down one night, and it'll all just hit me like some kind of epiphany, though I doubt that I'll be that lucky.

This test should help me, though. If it's Colton's baby, then it's simple, we keep it and work out how to be parents. But if it really is

Jude's, it's going to make everything so much harder. Am I capable of loving a child who was the product of rape? Am I able to look at his or her little face and see past Jude's features, or will I resent it and end up doing more harm than good?

Maybe it's better off without me. Maybe Jaren was onto something about adoption. I'm sure there is an incredible family out there somewhere just waiting for their little bundle of joy to come along. But will I regret giving it up?

Fuck me. This is too hard. Why can't someone else just make the decision for me? I miss being a child and having everything sorted out for me. I've never had to worry about such massive things like this before. What if I make the wrong decision?

The doctor fastens a tourniquet around my arm and asks me to start pumping my fist. I try to look anywhere but at the needle he's about to poke through my veins. Why does taking blood always have to suck so bad? It's not even that bad, yet no matter what, it always seems to be the worst thing that could ever happen. That and getting a shot, I hate it.

Colton squeezes my hand, and the only thing that keeps me going is the knowledge that he's next in line for the DNA stab. Though, knowing my luck, he'll probably handle it like a pro.

An unexpected yawn tears through me as the doctor does his thing, reminding me that even though the wedding was two days ago, I still haven't had a proper chance to catch up on all the lost sleep. It was such an incredible night. We partied well into the morning, way after the bride and groom had already called it a night and had gone off to bed.

I still can't get over it. The night was magnificent.

I feel a slight pinch in my arm, and I jump while trying desperately not to move and end up with a needle poking out of my elbow. I try to focus on anything that will distract me.

Ahh, the alphabet backwards.

Z, Y, X … um, W, U … V? Fuck, it's V then U. Why is this so hard? It really shouldn't be.

"Okay, Oceania. All done," the doctor says, quickly pressing a cotton ball to my arm and holding it there to stop any bleeding. He grins at me with a teasing smirk. "That wasn't so hard now, was it?"

I scoff. He wasn't the one trying to do the alphabet backwards. I bet he couldn't just recite it like his breakfast order at McDonalds.

I get a pretty pink bandaid to place over the tiny pin prick, and as the doctor writes all my information on the vial, I find myself nervously bouncing my leg again. "How long is it going to take to get the results?" I ask.

The doctor glances up at me before focusing back down at the vials of blood. "It can take anywhere between two days to a week, depending on how busy they are at the lab."

Colton raises a brow, catching the doctor's gaze. "I'm assuming they can be persuaded to put a rush on it."

"They could," he says. "But you'll then receive a rushed result. I'm assuming in this instance, you're wanting a result that has been thoroughly checked and checked again."

Colton nods and awkwardly looks at me, not liking when his

money doesn't get him what he wants, and I can't help but laugh. Colton is such a badass, always on point and at the top of his game, but when he's sulking, it's the cutest thing I've ever seen.

I really hope this baby is his.

We finish in the doctor's office ten minutes later, and Colton gets me to school just in time for the bell to ring. I rush in after giving him a quick kiss and have to bypass my locker to make it to my homeroom in time.

The day drags on, and by the time lunch rolls around, I've had two missed calls from Christian and three texts telling me that Nic was seen by our men in Bellevue Springs. So, I'm not surprised when I walk out to find him standing in the school parking lot, leaning against his car as though absolutely nothing has changed between us.

The second Nic lays his eyes on me, he pushes off his car, and my heart begins to race. I was expecting plenty of things today, but having Nic show up at my school wasn't exactly one of them.

Glancing back over my shoulder, I check that no one is around before I slowly start making my way toward him. This could be a huge mistake, but he won't hurt me. At least, I don't think he would. Surely, after everything we've been through together, he still feels that need to protect me. Though, he sure as hell didn't feel it when he left me covered in bruises after dragging me down three flights of stairs.

"What are you doing here?" I ask, creeping towards him while making sure to keep my distance. I fight the urge to throw myself into his arms, no matter how much I wish that everything could be as it was before. That can never happen now, way too much has gone down between us. Not to mention, the fucker killed my father in cold blood.

Nic takes a step toward me, his eyes dark and deadly, no sign of the man he used to be. "Call it off, Ocean," he tells me.

I shake my head, realizing that this is a business meeting, not a social call. "I can't do that," I tell him. "And you made sure of that."

His lip twitches ever so slightly, the only hint that our situation is affecting him. "You don't know what you're doing. You're going to get yourself killed."

"Like you give a shit about that," I snap, though deep down, I know he does. If he didn't care, he wouldn't have shown his face at the wedding, and honestly, hating him would have been so much easier if he hadn't come to show his support.

Nic scoffs, just as I knew he would. "You know that's not fucking true," he spits back at me. "I'm the only fucking one who's had your back, right from the start. I was going to fucking marry you."

"Oh, come on," I all but laugh. "Now you *know* that's not true. You haven't had my back since the second I moved to Bellevue Springs. You've been against me, always fighting, resenting me for moving on and allowing Colton into my life. Oh, and have you also forgotten that you killed my father because I sure as hell haven't. I'm pretty sure that someone who had my back wouldn't even consider hurting my family like that, no matter who they are."

He takes a big step toward me, putting him right in front of me and becoming the leader of the Widows, not the Nic I grew up with. "Call. It. Off."

I stand tall, raising my chin in defiance and refusing to back down. I don't just stand here for myself anymore. I represent every Wolf who got down on one knee and vowed their loyalty. I will not be weak, not anymore. "No," I tell him. "If you want to prove that you truly have my back, then you call it off. Be the bigger person, prove to me that you're still a good guy."

"Good guy?" Nic scoffs. "Where's your fucking loyalty? Was it fucking easy turning your back on the boys? Do you have any idea how much you've hurt them?"

I press my lips into a firm line. "Probably about as much as they've hurt me."

"So, that's it then? This is all about payback. Hurting us because we hurt you."

"No," I tell him. "This is about making things right. The boys hurt me, but you did so much more than that. You killed me. The Ocean you used to know, she doesn't exist anymore. She's dead. I'm a Wolf now, and you can sleep well knowing that you're the one who pushed me to it. They're my family now."

"They're not your fucking family," he growls. "Russo is just using you to get to me. You're a fucking pawn to them, and you're letting them walk all over you."

"Just like you used me to keep tabs on my father?" I say, before realizing what he actually just said. My brows crease, and as I look at him, it hits me. A sick grin twists across my face, and I step in even closer, my skin brushing against his as I raise onto my tippy toes. "You don't know, do you?" I whisper, taking a step and circling him.

Nic keeps his eyes straight ahead, refusing to get caught up in my little intimidation tactics. "Know what?" he spits, his voice low and careful.

"Russo stepped down," I tell him, stepping around him more so that I can see the surprise on his face. "There's a new leader now, someone else calling all the shots."

"What the fuck are you talking about? Russo wouldn't step down."

"Oh, but he did. Didn't the boys tell you? I bet they would already know all about it. After all, it happened while you were spending those two cozy nights in a cell. How was that, by the way? I'm sure you had a great time."

I come full circle, and as I place myself right back in front of him, Nic grabs me and spins me around until my back is against his car. "Fucking spit it out already," he growls. "Who's your new leader?"

I laugh to myself, hating how much my next words are going to hurt. "Damnnnn, the boys really didn't tell you. I bet that one stings."

Nic slams his hand down on the car right beside my face, and I flinch before reminding myself that I'm supposed to be right at the top of the food chain now. So, despite the way he has me pinned against his car, he still allows me room to breathe. I push up onto my tippy-toes before pressing a soft kiss to his warm cheek and then leaning into his ear. "You're looking at her."

Nic rears back, taking three large steps and looking at me as though I just told him that I fucked his mom in the ass with a power drill. "You're lying."

"You keep claiming that you know me the best, that you're my family. So, ask yourself, would I lie about this?" I question, taking the three big steps with him and keeping right in his face. "I'm as serious about this as you are about the Widows. I'm the fucking bitch at the top so keep that in mind when you decide to make a move against the Wolves. A move against them is a move against me."

Nic's jaw clenches. "I don't give a fuck who you are to me, if you hit against the Widows, I'll fucking hit back."

I grin wide. "You mean directly taking a hit against the Widows by doing something like taking out Vincent DeCarlo with a clean shot through the back of his spine?"

Nic's whole face drops, and anger tears across his face, knowing just how fucked he is without the last DeCarlo still breathing. He goes to step into me, but as he makes his move, a voice sounds behind me. "Hey," Miss Davies snaps, her tone low and deadly, something that not even Nic is stupid enough to argue with. "Step away from my student before I'm forced to call for reinforcements."

Nic's eyes swivel around to Roni, and recognition flashes before a wicked grin stretches wide over his face. Miss Davies reaches out and curls a hand around my elbow, yanking me back from Nic, not wanting me anywhere near the guy. But how did she know he was here? There's only one logical explanation, but it can't be true. Christian wouldn't risk reaching out to his sister just to look out for me. The Wolves' loyalty is strong, but it couldn't be that strong.

Nic straightens and turns to face Roni as though she's the bigger threat out of the two of us, and honestly, after her upbringing, she might just be. She doesn't squirm under his stare, and the way he watches her is filled with curiosity. "If it isn't little Veronica Russo," Nic murmurs, roaming his eyes up and down her body as though she's about to be his afternoon snack. "I've been waiting for my chance to get at you. I couldn't believe my luck when Ocean mentioned her guidance counselor was a Wolf. I couldn't resist doing my homework. Both the Widows and Wolves have been looking for you for a very long time."

Nic goes to grab her, but she yanks her arm away, evading his vice-like grip. She steps into him, not fearing him one bit. "Touch me, and it'll be the last thing you do."

Nic's lips lift into a smirk, and the way they drop is almost seductive. What the fuck is going on here? Is he trying to get into her pants or kidnap her to use as bait against the Wolves? "Have you always been this brave, or have you just been away too long?"

"What I've been doing is none of your goddamn business," she spits, looking at him with a deep hatred in her eyes. There has to be something else going on here, something deeper. Maybe they have history. They both would have grown up around the same time, perhaps gone to school together. "Now get off my school grounds.

I won't be asking again."

Nic laughs as if she were a child having a tantrum. "I'll leave when I'm ready," he tells her. "So be a sweetheart and take that fine ass back to wherever the fuck it came from. Ocean and I were in the middle of a talk."

"You and Ocean were finished. You have no right to enter school property and speak with a minor."

"Tough shit. She's not a minor anymore. I'll talk to her whenever the fuck I want to."

"Alright," I snap, done with their back and forth bullshit. "This is ridiculous. Nic, she's right. You need to leave. I'm done with ... whatever this bullshit is," I say, waving a hand between us. "Nothing has changed. You killed my father, you forced my hand, and I won't be stopping until you've paid for what you did. I don't even care how much I have to hurt myself to make it happen."

Nic glares, his eyes digging into me like two lethal laser beams. "You're going to be responsible for the end of the Wolves, you know that right?"

I step out of Miss Davies' shadow, reminding him just who he's talking to. "Bring it on, Nic. You know how much I love it when dickheads like you underestimate me. It only pushes me harder."

Nic scoffs, and I see the change in his eyes. He's ready to go in for the kill, and as he goes to make his move, the familiar sound of a bullet being loaded into the chamber of a gun sounds through the dead parking lot. "You've been asked to leave twice now," Colton says, his gun aimed right between Nic's eyes, the same way Nic had done to him as we were leaving the hospital. "You don't want to find out what it looks like when I have to ask you a third time."

Nic slowly raises his eyes to Colton, not afraid of his gun in the least. "You don't want to do that," he warns him.

"You see, I think I really do. More now than ever."

The two remain locked in a heated stare until Nic finally slices his gaze back to me. "You're making a mistake, O," he tells me, keeping his eyes locked on mine for a moment too long. His unrelenting stare is too intense, almost as though it's filled with a million messages. Six months ago, I would have been able to read those messages as if they were my own thoughts, but now, I get absolutely nothing.

Nic finally tears his gaze away, and with three quick steps, he's back at his driver's door. He drops down into his car and revs the engine before screeching out of the student parking lot and finally giving me a chance to take a deep breath.

Miss Davies sags in relief beside me and drops down onto the hard pavement before letting her head sink into her hands. "Holy fuck," she breathes. "That was too much."

I stare at her in shock before dropping down beside her. "Are you okay?" I ask, my eyes wide and concerned.

"Yeah, I just … I haven't seen Dominic for a very long time. He's worse than I could have ever expected."

"I …" I press my lips together, unsure why her statement bothers me so much. Why am I still so desperate to defend him? I feel as though I should be running my mouth and telling her about all the good he's done for me over the years, but I don't. I let her opinion sit, knowing that she might just be right. "Yeah, he's certainly changed."

She shakes her head, and I watch as a single tear falls down her cheek. "I'm sorry, I need to go," she says, shakily getting back to her feet. "Will you be alright?"

"Yeah, I, um …" I glance back at Colton, who stands back, giving us this moment. "I'll be fine."

Miss Davies nods and then practically runs away, leaving me more confused than ever. I don't get it. She was so tough before, so in charge and ready to face down the enemy, and now she's an emotional wreck? What's going on? There must be more to it, something that I'm missing.

Colton steps into my side, and I instantly curl into his chest. "Thanks," I murmur, curling my arms around him as he holds me against his chest. "I wasn't exactly expecting that today."

"It would have been better had you not provoked him," he grumbles. "You're just lucky that Christian called me when he couldn't get through to you. He panicked, thinking something was about to go down."

"Nic would never hurt me," I tell him.

"Right," he says with disbelief. "Just like you thought he'd never kill your father or lie to you. Nic really isn't the guy you've always believed him to be."

"I know," I murmur. "Just let me pretend for a little while longer. It's easier than knowing the real Nic is a monster who gets off on other people's pain."

Colton rolls his eyes and starts pulling me toward the front of the school where his Veneno is parked. "Like you can talk. You get off on my torture all the time."

I shove my elbow back into his ribs, unable to help the laugh that bubbles from deep within my stomach. "That's different, and you know it."

"What can I say?" he questions, shrugging his shoulders as his hand trails down my back until it's cupping my ass. He gives it a tight squeeze. "Do you wanna go and get off on my torture now?"

My, oh my. It seems my day is already starting to turn around.

I grin up at him, my eyes sparkling with excitement. "I thought you'd never ask."

CHAPTER 30

I barge through the door of the pool house on Friday night and come to a screeching stop as I find Mom filling every moving box that she could possibly get her hands on. I gape at her in horror. What the hell does she think she's doing? I knew the whole getting married thing meant that she'd be moving in with Roman, but to start packing without even giving me the heads up … holy hell, I was not prepared for that.

"What do you think you're doing?" I demand, walking into the pool house and feeling my heart beginning to grieve for how much I'm going to miss her when I can't just walk into a room and find her smiling back at me.

"Just getting a head start on the packing," she tells me, climbing up onto the kitchen counter to reach the top shelves, oblivious to the world of panic currently soaring through me. Am I seriously going to be living without my mom? Usually, the kid gets to decide when they're ready to move out, and the parent cries about their baby being all grown up and moving on. Not the other way around.

Fuck this. I don't like it, but damn it, I was the one who told her that she should follow her heart. What in fresh hell was I thinking?

"Wha ...why. What do you mean?" I demand, my arms flailing about as I stare at her unbothered back. "You're not supposed to be going anywhere until you get back from your honeymoon?"

"Oh, I know," she says, grabbing the vase that sits in the top of the cupboard, the one she'd received from her mother the year before she passed. "Here, grab this for me," she says. "I don't want to drop it."

Is she kidding me? Does she have no idea that the essence of her womb is currently having a moment?

I let out a huff and walk through the kitchen until I have the vase safely in my hands. I place it down on the counter, being extra careful, knowing how special this is to Mom. "Umm ... hello? This is a bit extravagant for just 'getting a headstart' don't you think? Your honeymoon is for like ... I don't know. Is it five weeks long? Six? You can pack when you get home. Better yet, I'll pack up while you're gone, so you don't have to worry about it. You're making it too real."

Mom glances down at me and finally gets a look at the devastation on my face before bursting out into uncontrollable fits of laughter, which only has my jaw dropping to the ground. "Excuse me," I scoff, watching as she tries to climb down from the counter. "I don't find any of this funny."

"I'm sorry," she howls, wiping the tears from her eyes. "I shouldn't be laughing. You're the leader of the West Side Wolves, and you're getting your panties in a twist because Mommy is getting organized. Surely you must see the humor in that."

I scowl, crossing my arms over my chest while trying not to pout my bottom lip. "Nope. I really don't."

"Come here," she laughs, pulling me into her arms and holding me tight. "I'm your mother, and I birthed you after seventeen agonizing hours of labor with no pain relief. So I'm entitled to laugh at your quirky little ways."

"No, you're not," I grumble, unable to resist her hug and wrapping my arms around her back, holding her close.

"You're such a brave, tough girl, but deep down, you're still my sweet baby who hated when her peas touched the carrots."

"They're different colors. They can't touch. It's absurd. It's like a little vegetable massacre if they're not all in their little sections. I can't handle the chaos."

"Yet you mix your peas into your mash potatoes," she says, pulling back and raising a brow, giving me a smug grin.

I roll my eyes, pulling out of her arms. "Don't get me started on you," I tell her, grabbing the vase and wrapping it in bubble wrap, only to have Mom come over and undo everything I just did to do it again her own way.

"What's going on?" she asks, glancing back at me. "This is the last thing I would have taken you to get emotional about. Is everything alright?"

"Yeah, it's fine. I guess I'm just stressing about the whole Nic thing, and then there are all these ridiculous pregnancy hormones. They're making me an emotional wreck. Yesterday, a butterfly flew past me and its wings just fluttered so peacefully, and it didn't have a single care in the world as it passed, and I couldn't help it, I burst into tears. Colton panicked and called 911. He thought I was hurt and was in the middle of demanding an ambulance by the time I was able to actually get the words out that I was alright. It's insane."

Mom bites down on her bottom lip before studying the bubble wrap very hard, fighting the smile that's desperate to tear across her face.

"Mooooom," I whine, walking around the pool house and flopping down on the couch, studiously ignoring the amusement on her face.

"I'm sorry," she says. "It's just funny. It'll pass, and soon enough, your body will learn how to handle it all. It gets easier. Just be thankful that you don't have absurd morning sickness like I did. I was throwing up in my shoes while riding public transport with you. It's still one of the most humiliating moments of my life."

I gape at her, horrified. I'd die of embarrassment if that were me. "Are you kidding? I've never heard that story."

Mom smirks. "And there's good reason for that. You never would have let me live it down."

I laugh. "Yeah, you're probably right," I tell her, watching as she gets back to her packing.

The heaviness instantly comes over me again, and I sink back into the couch, wishing there was some way for me to hold onto her forever. Though, I don't know why it's hitting me so hard. She's only going to be two minutes down the road, and it's not like I can't just visit her whenever I want.

Mom glances up, pausing midway through wrapping the photo frame of us with dad, the very last family photo we had together before Nic decided to ruin everything. "This is really bothering you, isn't it?" she asks, her brows furrowing as she watches me.

I press my lips together and gently nod my head as I let out a heavy sigh. Mom instantly comes around the counter and joins me on the couch. "You can always come with me," she reminds me. "Roman said it was an open offer. He's already got a room for you right beside Hendrix's. All you have to do is say yes."

I shake my head. Mom and I have already been over this, and she knows damn well that I'm not moving away from Colton. Not now. Things are too real between us, too serious. He's my forever, and while I'll never actually say the words to Mom, she knows it just as well as I do. "Why can't Roman move into the pool house?" I question, smirking at the thought of the billionaire moving from a ginormous mansion into a small, two-bedroom pool house. "Drix and I could get bunk beds."

Mom laughs. "And have to share a bathroom with that girl? You know that would drive you crazy. I've walked past her room in the mornings and nearly suffocated from the fumes that came out of there. The perfume, body sprays, deodorant, and hairspray. It's honestly the most horrendous thing I've ever seen."

I can't help but laugh knowing exactly what she's talking about, after having to suffer through it once with her. I never agreed to stay the night again.

Mom takes a deep breath and curls her arm around me before tugging me in beside her. "You can always come and visit when you're missing me," she tells me. "I'll never be far away."

"Except for when you're on your year-long honeymoon."

"Six weeks is hardly a year," she grumbles, rolling her eyes.

"Feels like it," I say before sitting up. "Just do me a favor and leave the packing for now. Just get yourself ready for your honeymoon. Drix and I will do everything else while you're gone."

Her brows crease. "Oh, honey. That's sweet, but I can't ask that of you. It's too much."

I give her a blank stare. "Mom, we hardly have any possessions after the bank took it all. It's fine, really. Besides, you're not asking. I'm offering."

Mom groans and lets out a loud huff before finally agreeing. "Fine," she says, preparing herself for the list of rules and regulations that Drix and I will have to abide by if we're going to start messing around with her things. Only she never gets the chance to voice them before Colton barges through the door.

"What happened to you?" he questions, reaching up and grabbing hold of the top of the door frame, making his shirt ride up above the waistband of his jeans, showing off his perfect V and making me drool. "You were supposed to be getting dressed so we could go? I warned you, Spencer will start the party without you."

My eyes bug out of my head, and I cringe. "Shit, I kinda got distracted."

"Yeah, no shit," he grumbles, a smirk pulling at his lips. "Now unless you'd like me to come over there and force your sweet ass into your closest, then I suggest you hurry up and do it yourself. Otherwise, you're going to end up in that skimpy red dress and those boots that come halfway up your thigh."

Mom's mouth drops. "Excuse me?" she demands, gaping at me. "What boots? They sound like hooker boots to me."

Colton grins, his eyes sparkling with mischief. "Oh, they are."

That fucker.

I groan, pulling myself off the couch. "Alright," I say, rolling my eyes. "I'm going, but I'm driving, and just so you know, I'm taking the Veneno and driving like I just stole every last cent you had."

Without giving him a chance to get another word in, I strut away while shaking the ass that my momma gave me.

Half an hour later, I drive the Veneno down Spencer's long-ass driveway and gape at his home. How have I never been here before? This is ridiculous. I mean, it's not as ridiculous as Colton's mega-mansion, but it's definitely one of the more impressive homes in Bellevue Springs.

It's after nine at night, so it's hard to see all the finer details of the home, but from where I'm sitting, it looks as though it's been pulled right out of a novel. It's a beautiful white manor home with massive pillars around the whole building stretching right up to the third story. Just like every other mansion in Bellevue Springs, there's a stunning staircase that leads to the front door, and I'm left speechless. I'm going to have to come back during the day to get a proper look at this place, maybe sneak in through the service entrance to give myself the grand tour.

Colton glances over at me as we pass the tree-lined driveway with each of the trees lit up with their very own spotlight. I mean, what else do you do when you have too much money? Give your trees lights. It leaves me wondering what other little treasure this place is hiding.

"Why do you look like that?" he asks me, staring at me as though I've just gone a little insane.

"Look at his place," I screech, taking my hands off the steering wheel to point it out. You know, in case he can't see the absurdly huge building right in front of his face. "This is insane. Why have I never seen this before?"

Colton dives over and puts his hand on the steering wheel, way too precious about his special little car, but I have to admit, every time I drive this thing, I think I come a little. "Will you concentrate on what you're doing?"

"I can't help it. I think I'm in love."

Colton rolls his eyes, but can't help grinning back at me, still thinking it's cute when his world manages to surprise me. "Yeah, you've met Spencer's dad. He's all about appearances and has expensive tastes. This place took him nearly four years to build. Just wait till you see inside."

"Why?"

He shakes his head. "Spencer will have the lights down, so it won't be as good as if you were looking during the day, but every single inch of the place has been planned out. I wouldn't even be able to describe it. You just have to see it for yourself. I'll bring you back tomorrow, and you can have a proper look at it."

Excitement bubbles through me. I'd like nothing more, I don't know why though. I should be secretly hating the place. After all, Spencer's dad is a bit of an arrogant dickwad.

We finally reach the top of the driveway, and I have to be careful not to hit any of the guests that are all pouring in. There must be hundreds of people littering the property, some already drunk and dancing to music that isn't there, while others scramble up the massive staircase, wanting to get to the real party inside.

I bring the car to a stop and am instantly greeted by a valet driver. I grin to myself as I open the suicide doors. I could definitely get used to this kind of treatment, though to be honest, I think I'd get annoyed with it after a while. I don't like the idea of people doing things for me, especially when I'm more than capable myself. To some people, it's a benefit and something to take advantage of, but to me, it just makes me feel lazy.

Colton meets me around the front of his car and takes my hand, lacing his fingers through mine. As we start walking toward Spencer's house, Colton can't resist glancing back over his shoulder and watching as the driver takes off with his car, driving in the opposite direction of the rest of the valet drivers.

My eyes bug out of my head and I tug on Colton's arm just in case he hasn't quite figured it out yet. "He's stealing your car."

Colton laughs. "He's not stealing it," he says, finding way too much amusement in my confusion. "There's a certain … hierarchy around here, and some people have priority over others and …"

"And let me guess," I say, getting way too familiar with this place. "Your car gets special undercover parking where it'll probably get a spit shine during its stay, it's own personal butler, and a complimentary tire rotation?"

A guilty expression crosses his face, but he can't help but look smug about it. "There's no fucking butler or tire rotations going on, but yes, the Veneno will be parked in the Vanderbilt's private showroom.

"And the spit shine?" I ask as we reach the stairs.

He rolls his eyes, the smugness returning once again. "I don't know about the spit shine, but I'm not going to lie, I have walked out of a few of these parties with a polish, but they're not usually very good. At most, it's a rushed job. A party this big though, I doubt it. The valets would be pretty busy all night."

I shake my head, choosing not to comment on that as we walk up the stairs. The closer we get to the door, the louder the party inside becomes. Excitement bubbles through me. I haven't been to a great party where I can relax and have a good time in ages. I can't drink tonight since I'm knocked up with a Devil spawn, but I can tell it's still going to be a great night. I can feel it in my bones.

The second we walk through the door, Milo barges into me, grabbing me by the shoulders and spinning me away from Colton, who just keeps walking, knowing there's no point in trying to wait for me now that I'm in Milo's clutches.

"Where the hell have you been, skank? The party started ages ago. I've been waiting to take shots off your perky ass."

I laugh, looping my arm through his. "Sorry," I tell him. "I got distracted and then couldn't figure out what to wear."

He gives me a blank expression. "Bitch, you have all of three outfits. How hard could it be to choose something?"

"I have more than three outfits," I grumble, trying to change the topic to avoid telling him that the reason I couldn't figure out what to wear was that everything I own is starting to get a little tight.

"Bitch, please. I'm going to take you on a shopping spree and fill your closet with everything. I can't wait. I've been planning it since the day you got here, but your skank ass is always too busy trying to avoid gang wars and getting jumped."

"Yeah," I laugh. "That always tends to slow things down a bit."

Milo gets distracted and drags me through the bodies before finally bringing me to a stop in front of all our friends. Drix squeals and throws herself at me, clearly already drunk, while Jess sips on her cocktail through a long straw with a dreamy look in her eyes, appearing to not even know where she is.

Colton stands with Spencer and Charlie talking shit, and after peeling Drix off me, I barge my way into their circle and jump at

Spencer. "HAPPY BIRTHDAY," I yell, instantly stumbling over the many pairs of feet.

Spencer catches me with ease and sets me back on my feet, while Colton watches me with wide, horrified eyes, probably only two seconds away from marching my ass out of here and giving me the big speech on what's safe during pregnancy. But seriously, unless he's the one who has to carry it, then he doesn't exactly get a say.

Spencer thanks me and says something else, but I can't make out his words over the sound of the music blasting through the room. There are so many bodies that just one person passing through causes a chain reaction of people shuffling around, and for the first time in a long time, it makes me miss my home in Breakers Flats. Whenever we partied back home, it was always insane like this. We never had a mansion to do it in or the expensive alcohol, but it was still fun.

Milo barges into our group with a tray of shots, and everyone grabs one. I curl my fingers around the glass and toss it right over my shoulder. I'm not really ready to spill the beans on my pregnancy yet, so I make a big show of the alcohol burning down my throat.

Everyone else laughs and instantly dives in for a second shot, and to be honest, the majority of them are already drunk enough that they don't even notice when I don't go for another. After all, this is the good stuff. If I can avoid wasting it, then I will.

They all take their shot, and as Colton steps in behind me and starts swaying me to the music, I lean back against him, not realizing just how badly I needed this.

The night flies by and despite my feet aching and the yawns that keep tearing through me, I refuse to go home. Milo stumbles into me, taking my shoulders and pulling me away from Colton. "Tonight is the best freaking night like ... ever," he cheers, his voice somehow traveling over the music.

"I know," I laugh, trying to catch myself when Drix bumps me with her ass, trying to be sexy for Charlie.

Milo glances back over his shoulder, smiling as he watches Spencer. "It could be better, though."

"Huh?" I grunt, but it's too late, he pulls away from me and crosses over to Spencer before whispering in his ear. Spencer instantly pulls back and looks at him as though he's lost his mind, and when Milo nods eagerly, Spencer shrugs and yells out. "HELL YEAH! LET'S DO THIS."

My brows furrow as I watch the two of them walk over to a table and start climbing up onto it. They hover over the party, and Spencer grabs Milo's elbow, keeping him steady on the table.

Partiers begin noticing them, and as the cheering starts, more and more eyes turn their way. The music is turned down just enough that when Spencer puts both of his hands in the air and calls out, everyone can hear him perfectly. "I'M SICK OF HIDING. FUCK THE HATERS AND FUCK THE STATUS QUO," he calls over the party, slipping his hand down until it's clutched into Milo's. "MY NAME IS SPENCER VANDERBILT, I'M GAY AND I'M FUCKING IN LOVE WITH THIS INCREDIBLE MAN."

My mouth drops before a wide grin spreads across my face. The whole party cheers for them, and as I watch in disbelief, Spencer grabs Milo's face and kisses him deeply. The two of them run full bolt out of the closet, finally claiming who they are with pride.

When they finally break apart from one another, the guests are chanting their names and showing their acceptance. The smiles on both of their faces is exactly what I never knew I needed.

The music is turned right back up, and within seconds, Milo holds out his arms, turns around, and drops down into the bodies to crowd surf. When he runs out of space, they drop his ass to the hard ground as he snorts with laughter.

All I can do is shake my head as I watch in astonishment, never being so proud of anyone in my whole life.

At this moment, I realize that I have everything I could ever need right here. Yet for some reason, it all feels so far away, like I'm grasping onto it and struggling to keep hold. It could all be torn away from me so quickly, and I'm terrified of losing it. I've gained so much since coming to Bellevue Springs, and if I was to lose all of this, it might just break me more than Nic and the boys ever could.

CHAPTER 31

Traffic flies past me as I sit on the side of the road, unable to take my eyes off the little envelope that seems to have been staring right back at me since the second it landed in my hands. How is it possible? It's just a piece of paper, yet if I concentrate enough, I think I might be able to feel a pulse and hear its little whisper telling me my worst nightmare is about to come true.

The doctor called me first thing this morning to tell me that the results had come in. Within seconds, I was in the Audi racing to get to him despite only getting home from Spencer's party less than three hours ago. Yet now that I have the results here in my hands, I can't possibly avoid it more.

I hate this.

This moment is going to define everything that happens from here on out. This moment defines my future. This stupid envelope holds more power than it should ever be allowed to hold. It's insane.

I should just tear it open and get it over with, though I'm also certain that I won't understand any of the medical terms that are in the report. The doctor offered to go through it with me, and for a brief second, I was about to say yes. Then I realized that if it is Jude's baby, that my reaction is something that should definitely happen in private.

God, I'd do anything for this to be Colton's baby, to know that it was his DNA growing inside of me. Both of our lives would be so much easier. The thought of still having something of Jude living within me ... no. I just can't.

I take a shaky breath and flip the envelope over before sliding my finger under the seals and slowly ripping it open. Nausea sets in hard, and I throw the envelope to the passenger seat as I scramble for something to throw up in.

I hurl into the empty slurpee container Milo had left in here during the week, and while I was hating on him for leaving a mess behind, I can't fault him for it now.

I get myself cleaned up with the baby wipes Mom insisted that I start carrying around for these 'just in case moments,' and with a cup full of vomit and a disgusted scowl on my face, I get back to learning my fate.

Please be Colton's. Please be Colton's. Please be Colton's.

I wonder if I chant the whole way through and promise my soul to the devil that I could magically manifest what I want to see. It's a long shot, like a really, really long shot, but it's definitely worth a try.

My hands begin to shake as I grab the envelope off the passenger's seat and let out a slow, calming breath. Why did I choose to be alone right now? Maybe it would have been better to just let the doctor deliver the news, that way he could have just ripped it off like a bandaid, and I wouldn't be sitting here making myself sick with the anxiety.

My fingers slip into the envelope and I feel the papers inside, the ones that are either going to tell me the best news I've ever heard or have me wishing for a time machine to send me back to kill Jude before he ever got the chance to touch me.

The papers get stuck on the edge of the envelope, and I accidentally tear the corner off. But my anxiety is riding too high to bother worrying about it. I just hope it's not the little bit of paper with the actual result on it. Now that would suck.

My fingers can hardly move as I turn the papers over and begin unfolding it. There must be at least ten pages here, and I have a good feeling that I won't understand any of it.

Remembering that I'm supposed to have balls made out of steel, I pull my shit together and realize that the sooner I get this over with, the better.

My gaze drops down to the pages, and I find my name and information at the top. There's a whole lot of stuff, explaining what the test was for and how to read the attached graphs.

I scan over it all, searching for the one thing I need.

I flip through the pages. There are graphs, charts, everything, but nothing that actually says what I need to see.

I continue flipping the pages until finally, the very last page gives me a report on everything that I just skipped through. There are a whole bunch of numbers that I don't understand. One column is labeled 'CHILD' the other 'ALLEGED FATHER' and at the very bottom of the numbers are the results, followed by a detailed explanation.

I begin scanning, my eyes traveling over the words faster than I've ever read before.

Combined paternity results: 0

Probability of Paternity: 0%

The alleged father is excluded as the biological father. Based on test results obtained by analysis of DNA collected, the probability of paternity is 0%

No. no, no, no, no.

This can't be happening. Colton isn't the father.

I feel like I'm trapped inside a bad 'Maury Povich' episode.

I scan over the results again and again as the tears begin welling in my eyes. They drop furiously down my face, splashing against the papers and smudging the results. It takes three seconds before the painful sobs begin tearing up my throat, and my world starts closing in on me.

Jude is the father.

I have his DNA living inside of me. My child will have his face, his genes, his eyes. That slight bit of hope I'd gotten, telling me that it could have been Colton's was dangerous because now it only hurts that much more.

I can't… I can't do this. How am I supposed to raise a child who came from rape?

Brutal visions of that night slam back into my mind and start overwhelming me, making it difficult to breathe. I need air. I need … I need out. I need this to be over.

I push the car door wide and struggle to breathe as the fresh air flows through the car. Is this a panic attack? I've never had one before, but it sure makes sense if it is. I drop my head to the steering wheel and take slow, deep breaths, willing myself to calm down.

I'll go home, break the news to Colton, and then we can make a plan. I'll start going through my options and maybe look into the whole adoption thing a little more. Jaren insists that it was the best decision he ever made. Could it be the same for me?

Fuck. This is too mu—

A flutter in my lower abdomen has every thought dissolving from my mind. What the fuck was that? My eyes drop to my stomach, along with my hands. I've experienced butterflies in my tummy before and it sure as hell wasn't that. Was it the baby? Was that what it feels like when it moves? Did I just feel my child?

The tears stream faster down my face, dropping onto my hands that rest against my hardening stomach.

My child.

Am I seriously considering giving up a piece of me? This is too overwhelming. I've never felt so lost and confused in my life. Am I a bad person for wanting to give up my baby? Does that make me a monster? What if I regret it in years to come. What if the kid comes looking for me, demanding answers. What am I supposed to say then?

I swallow back the lump in my throat, maniacally wiping at the tears that just keep coming back. How am I going to break this to Colton? Every day, I see the hope growing in his eyes. I see the way he's planning for our future, planning on being this child's father, but I can't do that to him. I can't dump this child on him knowing it's not his.

Fuck.

I hate this. I fucking hate this so bad. It hurts.

My chest tightens, and I force myself to keep breathing despite wishing I could just end it all. I'm too young for this, too inexperienced to be making these kinds of decisions. I just need someone to come and tell me what to do, someone to make it all right again.

I could always contact Jude's parents and offer it up to them, but … no. That doesn't seem right, that seems like the worst possible option. They're horrid people and wouldn't give this baby a good life, but what better could I do?

Shit. Someone, please make it stop.

Thirty minutes quickly turns into an hour, and when my phone starts going nuts on the passenger seat, I realize that I can't waste any more time. I have to get home and deal with it. I just need to be in Colton's arms, where he can tell me that it's all going to be okay.

I fold up the tear-drenched papers and lean over to the passenger side before shoving them into my bag. As I straighten up and reach out of the car, ready to close the door, a black bag is violently shoved down over my face.

I scream out, grabbing the black material and desperately trying to pull it off. I feel hands at my body. My seatbelt is unbuckled, and then people are pulling at me. I fight and claw against the hands on my body, screaming for someone to come and help me as I hear the scuffle of feet on the pavement beside the open car door.

A hand covers my mouth between my face and the material, desperately trying to muffle my cries. I bite down, getting a mouthful of the material, and the hand pulls away. I take the opportunity to yank up the material, ready to run for my fucking life, but the hand reaches around my face, which is when I see it.

A fucking tattoo on the guy's wrist of a black widow spider.

Nic. It's not his exact tattoo. This is someone else, but it's his doing.

The hands sure as hell don't belong to him, I'd recognize them anywhere. He sent his fucking henchmen to come and grab me off the street. He's a real big fucking man to do that. The boys are going to be pissed when they hear about this.

I barely have a second to fight back before the material is pulled back over my face and the hands finally get hold of me. I try screaming again as my body is pulled out of the Audi, fighting against the men who hold me off the ground.

I hear the distinct sound of a van door sliding open. Immediately, I'm thrown into the back of the vehicle, my ribs slamming against the hard metal floor as my back crashes against the side.

The door slams shut with a loud thump, and two seconds later, someone comes in after me. My hands are bound behind my back, and my whole body is thrown off balance when the van takes off, screeching through the streets of Bellevue Springs.

CHAPTER 32

Disorientation swirls through me as a rusty smell fills the cold room. I think it's large, like some kind of warehouse. Judging by the way each footstep that comes toward me seems to bounce off every wall, it seems so much worse. My guess is that this place is empty, which means that it serves for one purpose and one purpose only.

Torture.

And I just became Nic's newest victim.

I don't need to see his face to know that this is Nic. He'd never let any of his men touch me. You know, apart from dragging me off the street and stuffing me into a van for two hours.

I can sense him, the sound of his footsteps as he transfers his weight from one foot to the other, the gruff sound of his leather jacket as his arms swing past his body, and that smell. It's the smell of my teen years, the smell of home. That familiar smell was once a comfort to me. It told me that Nic was near and that everything was going to be okay. Now, it means something much, much worse, something sinister and devastating.

I try to prepare myself. The echoes bouncing off each wall are making it impossible to pinpoint just how far away he is, which makes any form of preparation useless. What am I going to do? Wait until he rips this thing off my head and then run? Where? I have no idea where the door is, and my hands are still bound behind my back, probably somehow tied to this stiff, wooden chair.

I'm screwed. I just have to hope that Nic won't take it too far. Maybe he's just trying to scare me or use me as bait to lure in the Wolves.

Either way, I'm fucked.

With every step he takes, my heart breaks just a little bit more. How did it come down to this?

I feel that same flutter in my stomach, and I find myself holding my breath. Why does the little rape reminder have to come up and give me all sorts of feels right now? There's no time for this. Though one thing is for sure, now that I can feel it, it seems so much more real, and with that comes a whole new level of momma bear protective bullshit. I don't know if I want to keep this baby, but I sure know that nobody is about to hurt it, and if they do, they'll be more than fucked.

The footsteps grow closer, and when I feel a soft breeze brush over my skin, I know that I'm out of time. Nic walks around me, not saying a damn word and only making this so much worse.

My hands clench into fists, and I tug against my binds, a loud grunt of frustration pulling from deep within me. I spent two hours in that damn van with my ribs aching, and who the hell knows how many hours I've spent in this ridiculous chair. My ass is aching, my stomach growling, and I need to fucking pee. I'm not the bitch anyone wants to be dealing with right now.

I squirm in my chair, desperately pulling and trying to free myself despite knowing damn well that I'm not going anywhere. This isn't Nic's first rodeo. He knows every last trick in the book by now and being my first time in this situation, I'm sure that dealing with me will be as easy as taking candy from a baby. You know, one of those babies that don't know any better, not the ones who hold onto shit for dear life.

Despite having Nic at my back, I sense him lean into me, although he doesn't touch an inch of my skin. Call it female intuition, or maybe I just know Nic well enough to know what he's going to do before even he knows. Let's hope it's the second option. At least that way, I might have the slightest hope of getting out of here.

"Stop fighting it," Nic murmurs, his breath rushing past my ear, his voice low and deadly. "You're not going anywhere."

"Give it up, Nic," I growl, slamming my head back and cracking him in the face, getting the slightest satisfaction out of his grunt of pain. "This shit isn't funny. Untie me and let me walk out of here.

Otherwise, you're going to have every single Wolf on your doorstep, tearing this place to shreds."

"I highly doubt that," Nic laughs, though I hear the pain in his voice. "Is this how you want to play this?" he questions. "You're down for petty threats and pain because baby, you know damn well that I'd love to play along."

"I'm not your baby," I snap, always hating how he's never been able to stop calling me that, even now. "Take this fucking bag off my head. If you're going to try and hurt me, then at least have the balls to do it while looking into my eyes."

"You don't think I will?" he questions, his hand dropping to the top of my head and peeling the bag off.

I blink into the room as I adjust to the brightness, but in reality, it's not actually that bright. The room is dark except for one low hanging light bulb gently swinging above my head. Nic moves around me and steps right in front of my face, letting me see him. "Really?" I laugh. "You want to use the light bulb bullshit to try and intimidate me? You think that this is going to work because you know everything about me, but maybe you've forgotten that the door swings both ways. I know all your dirty little tricks, Nic. It's not going to work."

A brilliant smile stretches over his face, pulling at his dimples and taking me back to the good old days. I haven't seen that smile in months, and I'm only now just realizing how much I missed it. "Do you honestly think I've brought you here to hurt you?"

I raise a brow, pointedly tugging on my bound hands. As the light bulb gently swings, it sends shadows soaring across his face, quickly flickering and drawing attention to the bloodstains on the concrete floor. I try not to think about all the things that have gone down in this exact spot. Slowly, I raise my gaze back to Nic's. "You're kidding yourself, right?"

He shrugs his shoulders and walks back into me before pulling out a small pocket knife. The shiny blade glistens in the swinging light, and as he creeps closer, I wonder just how far he'll go. He leans down over me, placing his hands on either side of the wooden chair, looking right into my eyes. "You've been crying," he tells me, the blade way too close to my skin for liking. Yet for some fucked up reason, I still find myself completely trusting him.

"So what if I have?"

A growl rumbles through the back of his throat, and I can't help but breathe him in, still wondering if the old Nic still exists in there. "Why?"

I scoff. "Like you care."

His eyes glisten with a deep, genuine concern that tears at every piece of my soul. "Try me."

I keep my glare locked on his. "Really?" I say with a laugh, trying to shrug off my emotions, knowing all too well how they keep coming up and betraying me at all the wrong times. "You don't talk to me for weeks, you show up at my mother's wedding, and then come storming into my school making demands, and you chose this exact moment to catch up on the ins and outs of my life. Are you crazy?"

"Answer the damn question, Ocean. Why were you crying?"

I roll my eyes. Why am I giving in to what he wants? "If you must know," I say with a frustrated huff. "Just before your dickhead Widows decided to drag me out of my car, I'd just received the paternity results."

His brow arches and for just the briefest moment, all signs of intimidation fade away. "And?" he questions, appearing to actually care.

"What do you think?" I snap. "I'm not going to be sitting in my car sobbing like a fucking baby if it was Colton's."

Nic lets out a heavy breath and leans even closer, dropping his forehead to mine. "Fuck," he grumbles. "I'm sorry, O. What are you going to do?"

I pull back, not liking his closeness, not in the way that I used to. "I'm going to get the fuck out of here, that's what I'm going to do."

As if remembering where he is, Nic stiffens and pulls back from me. "I'm sorry, baby, but you're not going anywhere."

He walks around me again with the knife still in his hands. Nerves begin to flutter through me as I lose sight of him at my back. I feel as he steps into me and presses the very tip of the knife against my shoulder. He slowly trails it down my arms, not pressing hard enough to cut my skin, but just enough that I'm more than aware of what he's doing.

The knife travels right down to my wrist, and then in one lean slice, my wrists are freed, and I throw myself out of the shitty wooden seat, instantly launching for the door.

I run at full speed, racing for an exit. When he doesn't come after me, suspicion pulses through me, only I'm not stupid enough to hang around and figure out why. I don't know where I am, but I'm assuming Kai, Sebastian, or Eli would be close. All I have to do is find someone with a phone and I'll be alright.

I finally find a door handle, and as I reach for it, a loud BANG startles me just as a perfectly round bullet sails past my face and sinks into the metal door. My eyes go wide as I suck in a breath, coming to an immediate standstill as shock rumbles through me.

I turn, my eyes instantly zoning in on Nic as he stands under the flicking light. I should be trying to get through this stupid door, yet I find myself moving back toward him, not afraid of the gun that's still pointed my way. "Tell me that you didn't just shoot at me?" I demand, my strides large as I race back at him. I storm right into him, shoving the gun away and slamming my hands against his chest. "What the fuck, Dominic?"

"I told you," he says, not looking the least bit sorry, after all, we both know his aim is near perfect. If he wanted to actually hit me, he would have. "You're not going anywhere."

"The hell I am," I demand. "How many times do I have to tell you? I'm not yours anymore. You can't order me around, and you sure as hell can't hold me against my will. I'm the leader of the fucking Wolves now. This isn't just some high school, possessive ex-boyfriend shit anymore. You're playing games that you don't want to get your men involved in. So yeah, I'm fucking leaving and if you want to stop me, then you better not miss this time."

Nic laughs. "In case you have noticed, this isn't a negotiation. This is a hostage situation, and unless you'd actually like to test my aim, then I suggest you sit your sweet ass back down."

I step back into him, refusing to let his gun and attitude defeat me. "Where are the boys?" I ask. "Do they know you have me locked up in some shitty warehouse, waving your fucking gun around like a psychopath?"

"They know exactly where you are, and you know what, they fucking approved of my plan."

I scoff, dropping into an exaggerated curtsey. "Congratulations. That's some first place bullshit if I ever heard any. How would you like your trophy engraved? World's biggest douchebag or just straight up liar?"

"Sarcasm?" he grunts. "That's the way you're going to deal with this?"

"Then tell me oh wise one, I skipped out on 'how to escape psychotic kidnappers 101' last week. Whoops. How do you suggest I should be dealing with this?"

"How about sitting your stubborn ass down, so you don't end up getting yourself hurt."

"We've been over this, Nic," I say, grabbing his hand that holds his gun and pressing it right against my temple, watching as his eyes narrow, unsure of how I'm about to play this. "You wouldn't do it. You can't hurt me. You're all talk and no game. And despite how much you wish you could, you'd never even try. I'm too important to you, and it's killing you that I'm standing with the Wolves and not with you. You hate that you love me, but no matter what, you can't stop. To hurt me would be to hurt you too, and we both know that you're too selfish to do that."

"You're wrong," he tells me, pulling the gun away and turning it on himself. He raises it to his temple, keeping my hand firmly in his grasp. I suck in a terrified breath. "I'd hurt myself every fucking day of the week if it meant keeping that goddamn fucking smile on your face."

His hand doesn't shake, as steady as the baddest motherfucker in town. "Don't you dare," I tell him through clenched teeth. "I'll never forgive you."

"Take it then."

Without hesitation, I tear his hand off the gun, keeping it tight on my own, yet I find myself unable to lower it. I mean, I am in a hostage situation after all. "Where are the boys?"

A grin pulls at his lips, and for a moment, I truly fear the darkness in his eyes. "They're busy."

"Call them. I'm getting out of here."

He laughs, not bothered by the gun I still hold at his head, knowing I wouldn't pull the trigger just as much as he wouldn't. "I told you, they're not coming. They're more than happy for me to keep you away."

My brows dip. "What the fuck is that supposed to mean?"

"What do you think it means, baby?" he questions. "We've been over this. There's not a goddamn thing I wouldn't do to keep you safe."

"Safe? Safe from what?" I ask, panic beginning to rise within me. I step into him, really pressing the gun against his head in the same way he'd done to me. "What did you do?"

His smirk is terrifying, and for a brief second, I see the real him, the one that he usually tries to keep concealed. "Nothing, just dealt with a little wild dog issue that I've been having."

Terror settles into my chest, and I clench my jaw, my breath coming in sharp, jagged gasps. "What. Did. You. Do?"

Nic leans into me and lowers his voice to a whisper. "Shhhh," he says, holding his hand to his ear as if trying to listen carefully. "If you're really quiet, you might be able to hear them scream as they burn to ashes."

Fuck no. My eyes bug out of my head, and I turn for the door, only Nic instantly blocks my path with a wicked grin stretching across his face. "Move," I shout, desperate to get to Blaxlands Grove and make sure it's not true. "I swear, Nic. If any of my guys are hurt …"

"You'll do what?" he laughs. "Come on, baby. You're way out of your league here. You can't handle this shit, so I handled it for you. No more Wolves, no more fucking problems."

I shake my head. "You're fucking sick."

"And you're fucking stubborn," he shoots back. "Just go and sit your ass down, and it'll all be over soon. I'm not about to let you go running in there to save the asses of douchebags who don't deserve you."

As if remembering the gun in my hand, I raise it back to his head, this time aiming right between his eyes, my hand steady as fuck. "Move."

"Do it," he says, almost daring me. "If anyone around here has got the fucking guts to do it, it's you, baby girl."

I clench my jaw, feeling as though I'm about to be sick, but what choice do I have? Either take him down or let over a hundred of my men burn. There is no fucking choice. One life to save a hundred others. It's simple math.

BANG.

Nic's eyes go wide as though he can't believe that I pulled the trigger, and not a second later, his body collapses heavily to the ground. Tears instantly well in my eyes, and I race into him as he stares up at me in shock.

I drop to my knees beside him as blood pours from his thigh and instantly pull the bandana from his head. "I'm sorry," I cry, my hands shaking as I fumble, trying to wrap it around his leg then pulling it tight like a tourniquet to stop the bleeding. "I can't let you do this."

He grabs hold of my arm. "Don't do this, Ocean. Don't go."

"I have to. I can't let you senselessly kill all these people. Why can't you see that I've been trying to save you?" I cry, desperately wishing for the old Nic as he groans in pain beneath my hands. "All of this is changing you. You're becoming someone that I don't even recognize anymore. I want the old Nic back, the one who would be sick at the thought of ending another's life. Let me save your soul. Why do you think I went to the Wolves in the first place? I needed to stop you, not hurt you. You need help."

Nic shakes his head. "My soul can't be saved, Ocean. It died a long time ago. Worry about saving yourself. No one can help me now."

"I can't do that," I tell him, pulling tight on the bandana and making him groan in agony. I reach into his pocket and find his phone and car keys before jamming them into my pockets. I know damn well that he's going to try and call someone to get me, but he's also going to need an ambulance.

I lean forward and press my lips to his forehead. "Please forgive me, Nic. I never meant to hurt you, but you murdered my father, and I'll never move past that. I hate you so damn much, but a part of my heart will always be yours. Which is why I need you to stop this. Step down from the Widows. Be a good man again, be the man I know you can be."

"Ocean," he snaps, desperately trying to cling onto me as I pull away. "Don't… you'll get hurt. It's too fucking dangerous."

I get to my feet and race to the door, tucking his gun in the back of my jeans. I look back at him, helplessly bleeding out on the ground. "I'm sorry," I tell him again. "I'll call you an ambulance as soon as I get out of Breakers Flats."

With that, I throw myself out of the door and race toward Blaxlands Grove with fear pulsing through my veins and tears staining my cheeks, hoping to God that this isn't true.

CHAPTER 33

I race down the street in the same car I learned to drive in, way too familiar with all the little ins and outs to need to concentrate on what I'm doing. I throw Nic's phone down at the floor space on the passenger side of his car after calling an ambulance and letting Colton know exactly what's been going on.

I hardly got three words out to Colton before he was already in his Veneno racing toward Blaxlands Grove. He told me that he's been calling all afternoon, worried sick about where I've been. He knew that I was collecting the paternity results this morning, and figured that I just needed time to myself.

What a big fucking joke. The fact that this baby is Jude's seems so pitiful compared to the bullshit that's going on now.

I turn one last corner, and as I race closer and closer to the Wolf Den, I finally see it.

Thick, dark smoke billowing up into the sky. My eyes instantly go wide.

No. No, this can't be true. Surely I'm seeing things. I push Nic's piece of shit car faster.

A familiar car comes screeching down the opposite side of the road, and I gape at it, instantly recognizing Kairo in the driver's seat with both Sebastian and Eli in the car. As they pass me, all three stare at me in horror, realizing that not only some shit must have gone down for me to be in this car, but that I'm more than prepared to throw myself inside the Den to save as many men as I can, even fucking Snake and Scarface.

When someone gets down on their knee and vows that they'll follow me, then they sure as hell have my respect and deserve to be saved. Nic does not get to decide their fate. Nobody should have that power.

I fly past the boys, not wanting to deal with them right now, and instantly watch as Kairo's car tailspins, and he chases after me. I push myself faster. I will not let them pull me away.

I pull up into the Wolf Den less than thirty seconds later, and as I fly out of the car, I realize that all the doors and windows have been boarded up. There's no way for the smoke to really escape except for out of the burned roof.

I hear them all screaming, desperately trying to save themselves from within. I run for them, but the boys fly out of Kairo's car right behind me, immediately coming for me.

I turn on them, not hesitating for a second as I grab Nic's gun and pop off two shots, bringing them to an immediate stop as the bullets smash into the concrete at their feet. "Get out of here," I yell. "Don't make me fucking shoot you like I did Nic," I spit, so disgusted in each of them. "I swear, I will not hesitate. Nothing will stop me from saving their lives."

Their eyes go wide, and seeing the desperation in my eyes their hands instantly raise. "Is Nic alive?" Kairo asks, his voice low and terrified, something I've never heard from him before.

"Yes, he's fucking alive," I demand. "I called an ambulance. Now either get the fuck out of here or help me save their lives. Either way, you need to fucking move."

The boys glance at each other, and with a cringe, Eli and Sebastian run for the doors while Kai backs up. "I have to check on Nic."

"Just go," I spit, turning my back on him and racing for the Den.

The boys struggle with the chains on the door while I go for the massive roller doors. There has to be a way to get in there. I push against it, trying to find a weak spot, but I'm five foot nothing. What am I going to do? The Wolves are dying in there. If the flames haven't got them, the smoke will.

Fuck.

I panic, looking around for some kind of way to help them.

Sebastian and Eli haven't had any luck and while I hear the sirens in the distance, they're still too far away.

I glance back at Nic's car and before the idea has fully formed in my head, I'm already running toward it.

"OCEAN. NO, DON'T," Sebastian calls out, running for me, but it's too late. I back up as he tries to get a grip on the door handle, more than ready to yank me out of here, but I'm going too fast.

What does it matter if something happens to me? Sacrificing my life to possibly save a hundred others? It seems like a good way to go.

Putting the car back into drive, I pull on my seatbelt and hit the gas, curling my hands around the steering wheel. My knuckles instantly turn white while I tense every part of my body, knowing that this is going to hurt. My jaw clenches and my eyes squint as my face twists into one of fear.

I race toward the roller door, knowing that someone could be standing right behind it and hoping to God that I don't cause more damage, but at this point, how much damage could I really do? I'm sure they'd be happy to sacrifice their roller door if it meant they got to live for another day and go home to their loved ones tonight.

The car hurtles toward the roller door and in an instant, I crash right through it. My body is jolted forward, and I smack my head against the steering wheel, rebounding back into my seat as a sea of glass rains over me, cutting up my arms.

My head instantly begins to throb, and as I try to blink through the thick smoke that comes crashing into the car, I feel the blood start trickling down my face.

Fuck. I don't have time for cuts and bruises.

I try to force my way out of the car as bodies begin rushing toward me, some coming for me while others escape out of the gaping hole in the roller door. All I see is a red glow, the bodies being nothing but a black silhouette against its brightness. As my head finally stops spinning and the thumping begins to ease, the noise becomes louder.

Men are shouting for help, some laying on the ground not moving, while others drag lifeless bodies through flames in a desperate attempt to get people out.

Someone pushes me out of the way and dives into Nic's car, instantly putting it into reverse and getting it out of the way, making a bigger space for the Wolves to get through.

I stare around in horror, watching as the building quickly starts to crumble around me while men shoulder past me, gasping for fresh air.

Christian comes storming back through the roller door, pushing his way past people with urgency, making me realize that it was him who'd moved Nic's car out of the way. "Snap out of it," he tells me as Eli and Sebastian come rushing in. "Either help get your men out of here or get outside and help the guys who can't breathe. Don't just fucking stand there."

Fuck. He's right. It's one thing slamming through the roller door, but standing here gaping at everything isn't helping anyone. It's only going to make everything worse.

The boys all take off, going for guys who are struggling on the ground, and knowing that they'll be okay, I focus on what I can do. I squint my eyes into the Den and raise my shirt over my mouth before running in. Heading for the rooms in the back, I know I don't have long.

The smoke is thick, and flames are licking their way up every wall. I hear loud cracks as the foundation of the building begins to shake, and the fear that settles into my stomach is like nothing I've ever felt before.

The heat instantly has me in a sweat, but I push through as I race down the hallway. After learning the hard way just how hot door handles are, I slam my foot against every door, checking that no one is getting left behind.

I kick down the door after door, quickly losing count until I get halfway down the hall and hear desperate banging coming from behind one of the doors.

"MOVE OUT OF THE WAY," I yell, not waiting a second longer before busting down the door.

I come face to face with Snake, and he stares at me for a second too long before grabbing the hand of some girl and pulling her out of the room. They take off down the hallway without even looking back or asking if I need help, and I instantly shrug it off. I can deal with that later, as for now, there's still another five doors to kick in.

My leg instantly starts to hurt, and by the time I get another two doors down, my lungs are screaming as they fill with thick smoke. I have to get out now or become one of the many casualties. Risking not checking behind the last three doors, I run, needing to save myself.

As I get back to the main part of the Den, I find the firefighters have cleared most of the people to safety. Relief filters through me. Feeling better for needing to run, I make my way toward the roller door, but as I run, struggling to see through the thick smoke, I trip over a body and crash down onto my knees.

I feel around, my eyes beginning to sting as I search for the person I just tripped over. My knees ache, but I put the pain aside as I find an arm and feel my way up his body. The guy is face down, and I grab hold of him, using everything I have left to turn him, and as his limp body falls down on his back, Jaren's perfectly handsome face stares up at me.

I suck in a breath and instantly regret it as I start choking on the smoke.

"JAREN," I yell, slamming my hand down on his chest when he refuses to even look at me. I tug on his arm, desperately trying to move his heavy body. "QUIT FUCKING AROUND. WE HAVE TO GO. GET UP."

He doesn't move, and the tears instantly begin streaming down my face again. "COME ON."

I try pulling on him, fearing the worst, but as arms curl around my waist and pull me off the ground, I scream out. "NOOO," I cry, recognizing Eli's tattoos as his arm tightens around my sore ribs, holding onto me and pulling me out. I claw at his hold, refusing to take my eyes off Jaren. "SAVE HIM," I beg. "GO AND GET HIM."

Eli doesn't relent, just keeps pulling me until we're out in the hot sun. "SEBASTIAN," he yells. "TAKE HER."

Within seconds, Sebastian is at Eli's side and grabs me out of his hold only to lock me in another tight grip. I fight against him, desperate to go back in as Eli races back through the roller door, leaving me praying that he's going after Jaren.

He can't be gone. I refuse to believe it. He's too good. He was the first person in the godforsaken place that I didn't instantly hate.

Agonizing seconds tick by as I wait for Eli to come back through the roller door, and I take a moment to look around me. Bodies lay all over the driveway of the Wolf Den, some motionless while others struggle to breathe. Wolves race around with water, ventilators, and inhalers, listening to every word that the many paramedics are throwing their way.

Police surround us while the firemen do their thing, trying their best to save everyone inside before they can even start putting out the flames.

The Wolves are covered in soot, their faces smudged with black charcoal as ash litters the ground. It's like a scene out of a horror story. I can hardly believe what I'm seeing.

A slumped figure emerges from the broken roller door, his body bent under the weight of another man slung over his shoulders. They stand for a moment in the hazey doorway, two faceless silhouettes against the flames at their backs. Brothers at first glance, clawing their way to safety. The face of a wolf is barely visible under the streaks of ash, painted across Jaren's forearm with pride, and a stark contrast of the widow's ink wrapped around the arm gripping him. I can't help but gasp at the sight. I've never seen anything quite as poetic as a man saving his sworn enemy

The second Eli clears the burning building, Sebastian instantly lets me go. I race toward them and nearly beat the shit out of Eli when he refuses to put him down and keeps hauling him away from the burning building.

When he finally stops moving, Sebastian calls over a paramedic. I drop to my knees and press my fingers against his neck, trying to find a pulse like they do in all the movies. But I have no fucking idea what I'm doing. Am I even feeling in the right spot?

A paramedic moves in, and I get booted aside, but I stay right by Jaren's head, keeping him protected. Christian moves in beside me with wide, horrified eyes, shaking his head, clearly seeing what I'm refusing to believe.

The paramedic looks up and seeing Christian as the guy in charge, she meets his eyes before shaking her head. "I'm sorry," she says with sad eyes. "He's gone. There's nothing I can do for him."

Christian nods, and as the paramedic moves on to the next guy, I break. "NOOOO," I cry, throwing myself down onto Jaren. He didn't even get a real chance to live. He was stuck working a rundown bar for a bunch of gang members. Surely, he had so much more to do with his life.

"Hey," Christian says, pulling me up. "You don't get to break down yet. I know you're hurting, and seeing all of this is a lot for a kid like you, but you're the leader here. These guys are counting on you. Get in there and help until every last man has been checked, every wound stitched, and every flame is gone. You have a job to do. You can cry when you get home."

I nod my head, getting back onto my wobbly feet with Sebastian at my side. I fucking hate that he's right … again. But I have no choice. These guys are counting on me to be their voice of reason, to bring them back from making a drastic move, and to put forward a plan to make this right, but before that, there's still a crisis to handle and chaos to fix.

I turn to Sebastian while also taking in Eli over his shoulder. "You two get out of here before the rest of them realize who you are and take revenge into their own hands."

They nod, and just like that, they're gone, not stupid enough to hang around longer than necessary.

I make my way over to one of the many firemen and pull on his arm until I have his undivided attention. "I kicked in all the bedroom doors in the west corridor but the three at the end. Make sure someone checks those. I want every single one of my men accounted for, is that clear?"

The fireman gives me a strange look, wondering who the fuck I am to be giving out orders but seeing the look in my eyes he nods and instantly speaks into his radio. "Last three bedrooms in the west corridor have not been cleared. I repeat, the last three bedrooms in the west corridor have not been cleared. Over."

A crackly voice comes back through the radio, and I listen intently. "Heading there now. Over."

Confident that they have it under control, I focus on the men struggling on the ground until every last one of them has been tended to. Men are driven off in ambulances while others are treated on-site by their own brothers.

The police make their way around, trying to take statements, and just as they've been trained, no one gives away anything. It's like an unspoken rule that everyone claims that they don't know how it happened.

Someone points me out as their leader, and just as the cops are taking my name, two firemen come walking out of the flames carrying one last body. Only this one is different and hasn't fallen like the rest.

Mikhail Russo's lifeless body is laid down on the ground beside his fallen brothers as the remaining Wolves stare in horror. Unlike the others who have fallen through smoke inhalation and burns, there's a perfectly round bullet hole right through the center of his skull.

Christian drops to his knees, the grief instantly taking over him, and as the rest of the Wolves drop to their knees in respect of their former leader, one man remains standing with a twisted grin on his face.

Snake.

I catch his eye from a distance and watch as he turns on his heel and runs, telling me everything I need to know and giving me another target. I look back at Christian and for a brief second, I wonder if now is the time to tell him before Snake can get too far. But with the cops and the grief heavy in the air, I save it for another day knowing that the Wolves will be able to track him and won't stop until they have Snake right where they want him.

An eye for a fucking eye.

As everybody grieves, I turn to face the burning Den, wondering what my next move will be. Like Christian said, they're all counting on me, and this next move has to count.

I don't know what I'm going to do or how I'm even going to do it, but what I do know is that Nic was right. From now on, I won't bother trying to save his soul because, as of now, his soul is fucking dead to me. No longer is this about trying to save Nic and hoping that he can somehow find himself on a good path and start earning forgiveness. This is about cold, hard, revenge.

Dominic Garcia is going down for what he did here today.

Mark my fucking words.

CHAPTER 34

Thirteen men.

Thirteen fucking men lay dead at my feet. One of them being Jaren, a friend, and another being Russo, Christian's father, and a leader. Miss Davies' father.

How am I supposed to handle the fall out from this? I'm just an eighteen-year-old girl. The Wolves are going to want answers, and they're going to want them now. If I'm not careful, we'll be starting a whole new war with the wrong people.

The whispers are already going around with everyone assuming the Widows are responsible for Russo's death, but I won't let that fly long. I don't care how many times I have to scream it from the rooftops, we will not be starting another war with the Widows when they're innocent of this crime. The real culprit will be paying, and he'll be paying with his life.

As for Nic, I still don't know how I'm going to go about that, but I will handle it, even if it's the last thing I do. I can guarantee it.

I drop down onto the soot-covered floor, my ass instantly getting wet from the water that's flooded through here over the past two hours. Sadness settles heavily into my heart as a feeling of failure washes over me.

I've been their leader for two seconds, and already thirteen men are dead. How will I morally ever be able to live with myself? What was Russo thinking when he put me in charge? Sure, I might be strong enough to tell a dickhead when to get fucked, but dealing with the pressures and heartaches of the reality of this world? It's too much.

My head falls into my hands, and I sit there with my heart on my sleeve until the familiar rumble of the Veneno vibrates through the ground. My head snaps up just in time to see Colton bringing his car to a stop, and as I get to my feet, the tears begin staining my cheeks again.

I run to him.

As my body crashes against his, the heavy sobs come tearing out of me. Colton wraps his arms around me, sliding his hand up to hold my head tightly against his chest. "It's going to be okay," he whispers, his chin dropping down over my head as he stares at the devestation before him. "I've got you."

I cry into his chest, this time not caring about how weak I appear to the Wolves. I'm human and entitled to break down every now and then. All that matters is how quickly I get myself back up again, stronger, wiser, and more determined than I was before.

After a minute, Colton's hands slide down to my arms, and he gently pulls back, looking deep into my eyes. "Are you okay?" he asks, his eyes full of concern.

I shake my head. "How could I ever be okay?"

"I mean physically," he amends. "Are you hurt? Did the paramedics check you out?"

I shrug off his concern. "I'm fine," I grumble, glancing back at the men still on the ground, some still struggling to breathe but refusing to take their asses to the hospital. "Besides, the paramedics have more to worry about than checking in on me. These guys are stubborn and need all the help that they can get. Who knows how long they were breathing in smoke and fumes before I got here."

Colton looks up over my shoulder, really taking a second to take in the scene before him. The police are still scattered around, helping where they can while the firemen are putting out the last of the flames and checking over the condition of the building. I'm almost certain that someone is about to come and tell me that the building needs to be torn down, but I'm hoping against it. This is the Wolves' home and while fire damage is one thing, actually having it taken away is another.

Nic won't get away with this. I can't let him go without punishment, and up until now, I've been hoping that his form of punishment would be to get the help he needs to turn things around. I've always had hope that the old Nic still lived inside of him, but he doesn't. That Nic I once knew is long gone. A bullet to the thigh is not nearly enough to make up for the devastation he's caused today.

What if I had been in there? What if it was me who lost my life today? How would he feel then? Would he just shrug it off and call it a shitty day in the office, or would it kill him like he's always told me it would?

I can't believe a word he says anymore. I should have let Colton handle it in the beginning like he'd wanted to. Look at all this devastation my actions have brought down over us. I have to do something to make it right, and this time, I won't be talked out of it. I'm going to stand tall and give him exactly what he deserves.

From now on, Dominic Garcia is as good as dead.

Colton's hand travels down my arm until it's firmly grasped in mine, our fingers laced, and his grip tight. "Jade, please tell me that hole in the roller door didn't come from you ramming Nic's car into it."

I nod my head. "You would have done the same thing," I tell him. "The doors were chained and boarded up. They were suffocating in there. I did what I had to do."

Colton lets out a heavy breath, not liking the idea of me putting myself in danger like that. But honestly, ramming the car into the door was the least dangerous thing I'd done today. "I know you did," he urges. "Taking out that door ... fuck, Jade. You must have saved countless lives today."

My head falls back against his chest. "Just not all of them."

"You did everything you could," he murmurs. "Don't hate yourself. You got here as soon as you could, and the Wolves rallied around you to get everyone out. You should be proud because even during this tragedy, you're still thriving. You're going to get back up, you're going to end the Widows, and you're going to rebuild this empire as your own, cleaning out all the bullshit as you go. This is a chance at a new start for the Wolves. The slate has been wiped clean."

"Russo is gone," I murmur. "A bullet right through the head."

"Yeah, baby. I see that," he murmurs, his voice low and strained as he pulls me away. "Come on, let me take you away from this for a minute. You need a second to figure out what you're going to do because I can guarantee that those men are going to need your leadership. You need to come in strong when they start demanding results."

I let him lead me over to his Veneno, and I climb into the passenger seat, staring out the window at the wreckage as he makes his way around the car. He drops down into the driver's seat and as his door closes, shutting out the devastation across the road, a peaceful silence settles over me.

I reach over to him, putting a hand on his thigh as the engine rumbles to life. "Don't drive away," I tell him, nodding out the window to where I find the Wolves watching my every move. "I don't want them to think that I'm abandoning them."

Colton nods, collecting my hand off his thigh and holding it. "Whatever you need, Jade."

I continue staring out the window, taking it all in and watching as the Wolves rally around one another, helping their brothers. They're doing everything they possibly can to keep their spirits high. I bet they haven't taken a hit this big in a very long time, I'm sure it's crushing them.

"What am I supposed to tell the families?" I ask him, nodding toward the thirteen bodies that lay across the dirty ground as paramedics begin placing them into body bags. "They're going to want answers, and I don't know what to tell them."

"You tell them that you did everything that you could to get them out of there. You tell them that they died with their brothers at their side. That they were strong, courageous, and loyal. And then you tell them that you're going to make it right and ensure that Nic won't be able to hurt anyone else because that's what they deserve."

I nod, knowing he's right, but the thought of having to face these men's loved ones is tearing me to shreds. What other high school senior is dealing with this kind of bullshit? I should be home complaining about not understanding my calculus homework.

I fall back against the chair, hating that he's right. I have to suck it up, and while it'll probably be the hardest thing that I'll ever have to do, it needs to be done. They deserve that respect.

Silence falls through the car as Colton pulls me across the center console and helps me onto his lap. I find myself staring out the window, mindlessly rubbing at the red marks on my wrist from where Nic had me bound.

Realizing what I'm doing, Colton drops his hand over mine and rubs his thumb over the red mark. "You're really having a shitty day," he comments.

I can't help but scoff. "That's an understatement if I ever heard one," I tell him, dropping my head against his chest. Unwanted images come to mind, being dragged out of the Audi, having the black bag shoved over my head. I was terrified. I've never felt anything like it. I don't know what I would have done had I not seen the Widow's tattoo. Knowing that I was going to Nic eased my panic, but for a few terrifying moments, I wondered what other enemies the Wolves have. How many people do I need to be watching my back around? "Today has been horrendous. Did I tell you that I got the paternity test results back?"

His brow raises. "To be honest, with everything that's been going on right now, I'd completely forgotten about that."

I press my lips into a tight line and scoot back on his lap so that I can look at him properly. I keep his hand in mine and decide that ripping it off like a bandaid is the only way to do that. "I'm really sorry," I tell him. "I know you were excited about the idea of this baby being yours, but it's not. It's Jude's."

Colton's head drops back against his seat as devastation pours through him. He takes a deep breath and slowly lets it out as he pulls me back into him. "It's okay," he murmurs, the pain in his voice tearing me apart. "I knew there was a good chance that it wasn't mine. I just didn't expect it to sting so bad."

I crush my face into his chest, hating how hurt he is. "I'm sorry," I cry. "I wanted it to be yours so, so bad."

"I know," he murmurs, his hand coming up my back and tangling into my hair. "But it doesn't change anything. If you want to have this baby, then I'll be right there by your side."

I shake my head. "I can't ask you to raise someone else's kid. That's not fair."

Colton pulls me off him, a hand on either side of my face as he looks deep into my eyes. "Any child of yours is a child of mine. No matter what. I'm with you, Ocean, and nothing is going to change it. You and me … we're in it for the long haul, so if you decide to keep it, just know that this baby will have a father. I'd sooner lay down my life than let you do this alone."

The tears well in my eyes again, and I lean into him, brushing my lips over his as his love wraps around me, completely overwhelming me with emotions. "I love you," I whisper, my lips gently brushing against his. "But the more I think about this, the more adoption is looking like my best option. I know that with you, we'd be able to give this child a great life, but I just … every time I think about it, all I can see is Jude forcing himself onto me. I think any child we have deserves so much better than that. My baby deserves unconditional love and I just don't think I could fully give it to him … or her."

Colton brushes the dirty hair off my face and swipes his thumb over my bottom lip. "You know that whatever decision you want to make, you have my complete support. But have you really thought about this? I don't want you to get a few years down the track and realize that you regret giving up your baby."

I shake my head. "To be honest, too much has been going on that I haven't exactly had a massive chance to really think about it, but so far, that's what I'm wanting."

"Okay," he whispers. "You still have time to think it through. There's no rush. Why don't you sit on it for a few weeks? If you're still feeling that way then, we can start looking into adoption agencies. We'll find the baby a perfect family that will love them like never before."

I nod, my heart shattering while knowing deep down that it is truly the best option. "I'd like that," I say, leaning into him only to pull back as a knock sounds on the window.

I glance up to find Christian standing over the car, staring down at us. "It's time," he says, nodding back over his shoulder to where the Wolves all stand in a group, their eyes on me.

I watch as the paramedics pack up their ambulances, and within moments, they're gone, shooting down the street with all of our fallen men. The police are long gone, leaving just the Wolves, anxious to figure out a plan. My eyes trail back to Christian's, and I nod. "I'm ready."

With that, he opens the door and offers me his hand as I climb off Colton's lap. I get both feet down to the ground, and I stand with my shoulders back, and my chin raised, more than ready. Colton climbs out behind me and with his hand on my lower back, we walk toward the group of pissed off, anxious, and broken-hearted men.

"What's the plan, boss?" one of the guys says, making a rumbling sound through the group as all eyes stare at me.

Colton stands at my side, his hand always on me. "Has anyone gone in?" I ask, nodding back to the burned warehouse. "Where are we at with weapons?"

Christian shakes his head, his lips pressed into a tight line. "All gone," he says. "All we have left is what we had on us, in our cars, or at home. It's not looking good. We can't stand against the Widows like that."

"Then we won't," I tell them, watching as each of them pulls back, ready to start arguing, but I get in before they have a chance. "Dominic needs to be stopped, and not a single one of you can get anywhere near him without your head being blown off. We can't go to them as a group, so I go alone. I'll end this on my own."

They all shake their heads, not liking the idea at all. Colton's hand moves from my back to clutch onto my elbow, more than ready to grab my ass and shove me into his car, taking me home where he can lock me up and never let me out of his sight. "Nah," Christian says with a grunt. "You'll be shot on sight. I'm not risking it."

"I don't care what you are, or what you're not prepared to risk. I'm the only one who could even get remotely close to him. This morning Nic had his guys take me off the street. I spent hours in one of his many warehouses, and after he told me what was going down, I shot him right through the thigh. So, if there's a chance for me to get at him, it's now. Nic will be taken out, and Kairo will step into his place, ending it. We've already taken his funds, and once I take his life, it's over."

The guys shake their heads, not liking it one bit, but when it comes down to it, they don't have a choice. This is between me and Nic. Besides, they have other things to worry about now.

"As for you guys, while we wait to figure out what's happened with our home and rebuilding our empire, you're going on a manhunt."

"What?" someone grunts. "For who?"

"For a traitor," I say, raising my chin and taking a step forward. "It was one of your brothers who shot Russo today."

Christian grabs me, pulling me back into him as he meets my eyes. "Who?" he demands, anger radiating off him and making me feel like a bitch for not having spoken to him about this is in private.

"Look around you," I say. "Is anyone missing?" The Wolves begin glancing around before Snake's name is whispered on all of their lips. "That's right," I tell them. "Snake did it. The second Russo's body was brought out here and you all dropped to your knees, he looked right at me, grinned, and then ran. If that's not an admission of guilt, then I don't know what is."

"You're only telling us this now?" Christian spits. "You let him get away."

"No," I snap, grabbing his hand and forcing it off me. "I allowed you a moment with your brothers to mourn the loss of the man who had led you for the past twenty years, knowing damn well that once I shared this information, you'll stop at nothing to make it right."

Christian clenches his jaw, the anger pulsing through him, but as the seconds tick by without breaking his stare, he finally begins to relax. He knows I'm right, and while he'd never admit it, his slight nod is all the thanks that I'll get.

Christian turns back to the Wolves. "Right," he says, pointing out a group of guys. "You guys hit up his place. He'll be long gone, but there might be something there." He turns to another group. "Check the bars, clubs, whore houses, and then join the streets with the rest of us. We do not rest until that fucking Snake is dead in my hands. Got it?"

"Where do we go?" one of the Wolves questions, looking back at the burned Den behind him. "We can't exactly come back here."

Colton steps in beside me, looking around at the Wolves. "I've got a place."

Christian meets his eyes, and the two of them remain locked in a stare until Christian finally tears his gaze away. "Right. You heard me. Get the fuck out of here."

The Wolves instantly break away, and I don't doubt that with the heartache sitting heavily on their chests, they will not rest until this is done.

With everyone walking away, Christian looks back at me, lowering his voice with warning. "You made them a promise to take out Dominic. I don't want to be the one to tell you what will happen if you don't come through."

"I know," I say, my jaw clenched as I look up at him with finality. "I won't fail."

CHAPTER 35

My head rests against Colton's arm as he holds me, his body curled around mine like a big spoon, keeping me as close as possible. I stare into his dark bedroom, unable to close my eyes as every time I do, I'm hit with the visions of men screaming on the ground, engulfed in flames. Their pained cries will live with me forever, the feel of the smoke in my throat, the struggle to take a deep breath as men lay lifeless on the ground around me. I never want to feel it again.

Today was easily the worst day of my life, yet as I lay here, I can't help but feel that it's not over.

Colton took me home, and for the two-hour car ride back into

Bellevue Springs, he begged me not to do it and said that he'd take my place. He'll be the one to finish Nic and that I won't have to have that burden resting on my shoulders, but I wouldn't be able to live with myself if anything happened to Colton. Especially while he's out there cleaning up my mess and trying to protect me from myself. He's too good for me. Nic wouldn't hesitate to shoot him and I won't risk that.

I told him over and over again that I couldn't let him do it and that I'd give it a few days before making my move. We spoke at each other the whole way home, neither of us really listening to what the other had said, just desperate to get our point across until we had nothing left to say. The car fell into silence, neither of us willing to give in.

We got home, and he took me straight upstairs. We showered, and I washed the ash out of my hair while trying to come to terms with what I have to do. I don't think I have what it takes, but thinking of those men who died of smoke inhalation and severe burns, I have no choice.

I have to end it, and I have to look him in the eyes as I do it. Nic can't get away with this. He needs to be punished for his actions, and after giving my word to the Wolves, I need to keep strong.

If only Colton knew what I was thinking right now ... fuck. He'd never let me go.

The movie Colton had put on when we climbed in bed continues playing on a loop. This is the fourth time that it's starting again. Neither of us watched a single second of it, and while I know I should turn it off, I can't bring myself to do it. The noise helps to dull the thoughts that are screaming in my mind.

The clock reads just after 11 pm, and despite how tired I am, I know sleep will never come. In fact, sleep won't come until this is over. Though, the question is, how will I sleep afterward, knowing I killed a man I once loved?

My stomach twists into knots. What are the boys going to think of me? If I pull that trigger, they'll never speak to me again. Is that a risk I'm willing to take? Hell fucking no, but do I have a choice? No.

That familiar flutter begins tickling inside of me, and my hand instantly falls to my lower abdomen. Why does it have to choose now to remind me that it's there? Doesn't it know that I'm already struggling with something else? I don't need to be reminded that this baby may or may not have a momma. Fuck, I couldn't do that either. If I didn't find a good enough family for it before it's born, then I sure as hell will be taking care of it until I do. The thought of giving it up to sit in some rundown foster home for the first few months of its life makes me feel sick.

I take a few slow, deep breaths. I can imagine the baby telling me to grow the fuck up and go and do what needs to be done. I'm an adult now. If I'm old enough to get knocked up and become the leader of the Wolves, then I'm old enough to handle my shit.

I just have to suck it up. I have to go into the pool house and find Nic's gun that's hiding in my underwear drawer, and then I'll take my ass into the garage and get into the car. It's not that complicated. You know, except for the whole shooting him with his own fucking gun thing.

Picturing the way that I'll squeeze the trigger and seeing the look of betrayal on Nic's face has my stomach beginning to squeeze. I throw the blanket back and dart across Colton's bedroom before flying into the bathroom. I only just get enough time to close the door behind me before all the contents in my stomach begin coming up.

I throw myself down to my knees in front of the toilet and only just manage to get my head over the bowl before chunks of my dinner splatter all over the white porcelain.

I heave over and over again, getting every last bit of it up until my cheek rests against the cold toilet seat while my stomach cramps with the excessive vomiting.

Once I'm confident it's all gone, I lay back on the cool tiles, sinking into the feel of their coldness on my sweaty body. What kind of idiot overthinks something so fucking much that she makes herself hurl?

When my stomach finally begins to settle, I peel myself off the bathroom floor and rinse my mouth in the sink. There's nothing worse than vomiting, but over the past eleven weeks, I've started to get pretty used to it.

Fuck this pregnancy. I don't understand all those women who say that it was the best time of their lives, because so far, all I've felt is sick and sore. I've cried over everything, and become a raging fucking bitch at the same time. The next six months are really going to test me, but it's the whole pushing it through my vag thing that's scaring me the most. Watermelons just aren't made to be squished through tiny spaces.

Beginning to feel better, I pull my head out from under the faucet and walk back toward the bathroom door. As I open it and take in

Colton, still fast asleep in bed, I find myself pausing. What's the point in going back to bed and staring into the dark?

I shake my head, letting out a sigh, unable to take my eyes off Colton's peaceful face. If I'm going to get any chance to sneak out of here, then now's the only time.

Taking a shaky breath, I feel the nerves instantly rising. I creep across the room, snatching my phone off the bedside table, and slip into a pair of jeans. Before I know it, I'm opening his bedroom door just a crack and sliding through it.

I glance back at him, making sure that he's still asleep before gently closing the door and dashing down the stairs with the help of the flashlight app on my phone.

I take myself out to the pool house, and the second my hand curls around the gun in the back of my underwear drawer, that same sickness takes over me. But with my stomach already empty, there's nothing for me to do but forge on.

It's either now or never, and I'm done playing games.

I pull the gun out, and it feels heavy in my hand, but before I can talk myself out of it, I slip it into the back of my jeans and walk straight back out of the pool house.

I go the long way around the house, not wanting to risk walking back through it and waking anyone up. As I come around front, I find the Audi already parked by the grand entrance stairs, right where Colton's security had left it.

Getting in the car, I instantly hit the gas, buckling my seatbelt while I'm already flying down the drive, not giving myself a chance to back out.

The two-hour drive back to Breakers Flats is the hardest two hours of my life. My hands shake on the steering wheel, and the whole way here, I have to convince myself not to stop and throw up out the car window.

Yawns tear through my body just as they've been doing all night, but I ignore them, desperate to get this done.

By the time that I bring the Audi to a stop outside Nic's apartment complex, there are tears in my eyes, and my whole body is in a cold sweat.

I can do this. Just take a deep breath and shoot.

I get out of the car and glance up to the fourth floor. I find Nic's apartment with every single light on, telling me that the stupid fucker didn't take himself to the hospital like he was supposed to. My guess would be that when the paramedics arrived, they treated him on site, and gave him enough painkillers to last a lifetime, and then Nic threatened their lives and sent them on their way.

I stand out in the deserted street, and as I look up at his apartment, I pull out the gun and raise it up into the air.

I take one definitive shot and my arm instantly jumps back as the bullet is freed from the chamber.

The sound is deafening but it does exactly what I need it to do. My heart races and my palms begin to sweat, knowing that this could either be the end of me or of Nic, but either way, only one of us is walking free from this tonight.

With the sound of the gunshot echoing through the streets of

Breakers Flats, Nic appears in his window, instantly looking down. Only two seconds later, Kairo appears, then Elijah, and right after that, my sweet Sebastian.

Fuck. I can't do this with them here.

The boys instantly disappear from the window, no doubt on their way down here as the tears begin falling from my eyes.

How could I be so stupid? Of course the boys are here. After everything that went down today, they'd all be talking it through. Trying to work out their plan to keep their men alive and making sure that Nic doesn't do anything else stupid.

I nervously glance back at the Audi. I wonder how far I could get before they catch up with me? Maybe I'd be able to get into Blaxlands Grove and seek protection from the Wolves, but how would they protect me? All their weapons are gone.

I'm a sitting duck, and I can guarantee that each of the boys have a gun on them somewhere, all with much faster reflexes than mine.

It's four against one, and I'm at a loss. No matter how strong I look on the outside, they will always win. They know me too well. They know how to break me.

It feels like forever as I wait for them to come down, when in reality, Nic breaks through the door of his complex so fast that Sebastian and Elijah are rushing to keep up with him. Kairo takes his sweet ass time though, acting like nothing is about to happen. He wasn't there today, so he couldn't understand just how badly this tore me apart.

Nic comes storming toward me with fury in his eyes. He tries his best not to limp, pretending that the bullet hole through his leg isn't bothering him, but I can already see the blood seeping through his jeans from here. He probably just tore his stitches wide open.

The boys instantly fall in behind him, flanking him like I've seen them do so many times, only I've never been the one standing on the opposite side.

They get a few feet away when I raise the gun and point it straight for Nic's head, my hand steady while the rest of me is in a fearful, desperate panic.

All four of them come to an immediate stop, all eyes on me.

"Don't move," I growl, standing my ground and letting them see just how serious I am.

"What do you think you're doing?" Nic spits, acting like this is all some kind of joke. "Here to shoot me again?"

"That's exactly why I'm here," I say, having to physically remind myself why I need to hate him so much. "You killed twelve of my men today."

A grin pulls at his lips and he holds back a laugh. "And they sent you to finish me off?"

I shake my head. "I told them to back the fuck off so I could do it myself," I tell him proudly. "After all, I'm the only one who could get close enough, and besides, I want to see the look in your eyes when you finally pay for everything you've done."

Sebastian's hands fly up, the first to grasp onto just how serious I am. "Okay, guys. Let's just chill. This is getting out of hand."

I turn my gaze on Sebastian. "I suggest you step aside," I tell him. "Unless you'd prefer to be covered in your boss' blood."

"Ocean," Eli says, his voice low and filled with warning. "Put the gun down, girl. We don't want to hurt you."

I scoff. "Really? So you weren't on board with the whole 'kidnap Ocean off the side of the road, throw her in the back of a dirty van, and chain her to chair in the middle of Nic's dirty little murder house' plan?"

"The fuck are you talking about?" Kairo grunts as Nic's jaw clenches, his dirty little secrets being aired for the world to see.

I raise a brow, turning my stare back on Nic. "So much for having their approval, huh?"

Nic raises his chin, not sorry at all. "I did what I had to do to keep you safe."

"You had your men put their hands on me. You held a gun to my head. How is any of that keeping me safe? You're fucking delusional, Nic, but now your time is up."

Nic takes a step toward me, and my hand instantly begins shaking, even more so when the tip of the gun presses against his chest. I feel my heart breaking, dread sinking into my stomach, and the little voice inside my head telling me that I'm not strong enough to pull this off. "You think you have the balls to shoot me?" he questions, leaning in and forcing me to hold my arm out stronger. "We've been here already once today. Let me bring you in on a little secret; you don't."

"Really?" I laugh, dropping my eyes to his leg. "How's that bullet wound feeling?"

He grins. "Peachy," he says. "But you know damn well that's not what I'm talking about. You couldn't take a kill shot, so what the fuck are you doing here if not just trying to waste my time? You want to shoot my other leg? How about mixing it up and going for an arm?"

"I already told you what I'm here for," I say, flinching the gun to show just how serious I am, done with his bullshit attitude.

I feel the boys' eyes on us, watching with caution, and as Nic takes in the seriousness deep within my eyes, his brows pinch as betrayal washes over him. He looks at me like I'm some kind of stranger, unable to truly comprehend what's happening right in front of him. "You're really serious," he questions, his eyes bouncing over my face, taking me in, hardly able to believe what he's seeing. His voice breaks. "You've come here to end my life after everything we've been through?"

Tears well in my eyes, but I hold my ground as my voice drops to a broken whisper. "You need to be stopped," I tell him, fighting the tears as they begin to drop. "I've tried so many times. I've begged you, I've forgiven you, I've let you back in, but it never works. I've done everything that I can to turn this around, but you just keep hurting me. I can't let it go on anymore. Don't you see how bad you've become? You're as bad as Kian was, and it's only getting worse. Killing my men was the final straw. They were good guys with families at home who loved them. You're not the Nic I once knew, you're nothing but a cold-blooded murderer."

Pain twists across his face, his eyes dropping with disappointment as the boys secretly move around us. "That's what you really think of me?" he says on a whispered breath, disbelief and hurt in his tone. "That I'm just like my father?"

I nod as the tears roll down my cheeks. "I've been trying so hard to hold onto that love I once had for you, wishing that I could somehow bring you back, but you're gone. This world has changed you, and it's on me to stop you. I can't let you go on hurting people the way that you do."

Nic stumbles back a step as if finally seeing things through my eyes, and when Sebastian takes a step toward me and turns to face Nic, the tension rises. "I'm sorry, bro," Sebastian says, his voice deep and pained. "She's right. This has gone on for too long. You're going to get us all killed, and I can't stand back and watch you destroy yourself."

Nic looks at him as though he's never quite felt pain like it, but when Eli moves into my other side, it only gets worse. "I'm sorry, Nic," Eli grumbles. "It kills me to stand against you like this, but this road you're traveling down. I can't … I joined the widows for the brotherhood not to become a killer."

Nic scoffs and then looks back at Kai. "What about you?" he grunts, saving the worst for last. "Are you turning your back on me too?"

Kai shakes his head. "You're my best friend, bro. None of us are turning our back on you, and you know damn well that we'd follow you to the ends of the earth, but something's gotta give. You're going to get us all killed over a bullshit war that you could have ended. Your selfish need to always be at the top is tearing us down, and I'm afraid that once you finally reach the top, you'll have no one there holding you up."

Nic glances around, looking at the boys before finally coming back to me. He stares at me for a long, drawn out moment before stumbling back a step, almost as though the weight of the moment is too much for him to bear. "I have. I've turned into my fucking father," he says with a whisper, a hint of disbelief and horror surfacing in his tone. "You're fucking right. I did the one thing I always said that I didn't want to do, but I'm just like him. Right down to the fucking core."

I clench my jaw, my hand still shaking as I watch him. How am I supposed to continue through with this now?

"O," Nic murmurs, his voice low and broken as he looks at me with those eyes that have tortured me for far too long. Betrayal flickers through them, and it tears me to shreds, only making the tears fall faster. "I get it now, but don't do this to yourself. You might be strong enough to pull that trigger but what do you do afterward? I can't have that burden sitting on your shoulders for the rest of your life. It will tear you apart."

"Don't," I demand, the desperation getting all too much as he starts playing with my emotions. I clench my jaw, flinching the gun and forcing myself not to break. "Fight back. Don't make this harder than it needs to be."

He shakes his head, truly realizing that this could be the end. His eyes soften, and he steps right into me, wrapping his arms around me and holding me tight, his hands traveling up and down my back as the gun gets squished between our bodies. "It's okay," he murmurs, his head dipped and his lips brushing across my neck. "I understand. I've killed countless men, I've tortured women, I've played twisted fucking games. I knew it was only a matter of time before it all caught up with me. This day was coming, I just didn't realize it was going to be so soon. Though I have to admit, I'm glad it's you. You're the only one that I'd even be okay with pulling the trigger. Just do me a favor and make it quick."

Sobs pull from deep within me, and Nic holds me tight, giving me this moment. "It's okay, my sweet angel," he murmurs over and over again. "It's going to be okay. I forgive you. I know you have to do this. I love you so goddamn much."

"The fuck are you doing?" Kairo grunts, watching Nic in horror.

Nic ignores him and steps back out of my arms, and I instantly hold the gun back up, aiming right between his eyes as the sobs continue tearing out of me. I try taking deep breaths but the lump in my throat makes it nearly impossible.

I struggle to hold myself together, and when Nic holds his arms out wide, begging for me to take the shot and end it all, Sebastian and Eli gasp in horror as Kai runs out in front of the gun, blocking my shot. "Don't you dare fucking shoot him."

"MOVE," I demand, the tears washing down my face like waterfalls. "I have to."

"Ocean, don't," Sebastian begs, the panic rising in his tone. "Please, baby. We'll figure out a way. Don't take him from us."

The tears stream down my face, and as I take a deep breath and bring my finger over the trigger, a firm hand comes down on my shoulder. "Jade." His soft, velvety voice breaks through my inner turmoil before his body presses against mine. "Stop."

CHAPTER 36

"Listen to your friends," Colton says, his voice wrapping around me like a silky caress, commanding me like never before. "Don't do this. It'll destroy you."

Unable to help myself, I lean back against Colton, knowing he's right but still struggling against what I have to do. The Wolves need this. I need this. Nic has to be stopped.

His hand travels along my outstretched arm until his hand hovers over mine. He presses down, forcing me to lower my arm, bringing the gun to my side. I drop the weapon, listening as it clatters to the ground.

Colton holds me up, and weakness overwhelms me.

I crush myself into his arms as I hear the soft sighs of relief coming from all four of the guys. Nic drops down onto his knees, breathing heavily before falling back onto his ass and letting his head hang as the emotions overwhelm him.

Kai walks to his side and presses his hand against his shoulder. "Come on, man," he says. "We'll get you whatever help you need."

Nic shakes his head before looking up at Colton, knowing damn well that what he's about to ask is going to be refused by the others. "Call the police," he says. "It's time to hand myself in."

Colton nods, and as he digs his hand into his pocket and pulls out his phone, I pull out of his arms and make my way toward Nic.

I hold out my hand, still struggling against the tears and sobs that continue coming, one after another.

Nic instantly takes my hand, and instead of allowing me to help him up, he pulls me down into his lap and curls his arms around me. My face is pressed against his chest, and I breathe him in, knowing that this is going to be the last time I see him for a while. "I'm so sorry, O," he murmurs. "I knew I was hurting you, but I've never been able to see past my own needs. I've been so fucking selfish. I don't deserve you in my life. You've stood by me time and time again when I never once deserved that loyalty from you."

"I'm not going to pretend that it's okay, because it's not. The things you've done to me and the people around you are ... they're awful, Nic, and it's going to take us all a really long time to learn to forgive you."

He nods. "I understand," he says. "But just know that no matter what I've done or how I acted, I've always loved you. I always will, and despite what you might think, everything I've done has been to protect you."

"You have a weird way of showing it."

"I know," he says. "Just do me one favor."

"Anything."

"Get yourself out of the Wolves. You should be living back in Bellevue Springs with your rich boyfriend and perfect life. Put all of this behind you and find real happiness. I want you to have the world, and it's taken me a really long time to figure out that I couldn't give it to you."

I nod, already down with the idea of leaving the Wolves behind. The second I can, I'll be out of there and leaving it to Christian to take over.

We hear the sirens in the distance, and Nic cringes. "Shit. This is really happening," he says, looking like the kid I first met when he was only seventeen years old.

"Yeah, it is," I murmur, pulling back to meet his eyes. "I'm sorry that it had to come down to this, and I'm sorry that I stood here with a gun, intending to kill you. If I could have it any other way …"

Nic nods, not needing me to finish off that thought, and instead of prolonging the moment, he looks up at Sebastian, Kai, and Eli. "Here, help me up," he says, holding a hand out to Kai.

I quickly scramble off him, knowing he must be in extraordinary amounts of pain after being shot less than twelve hours ago.

Kairo takes his hand and after he pulls him up, Nic instantly wraps his arms around him. "Widows are yours now," he murmurs. "Take care of them better than I did. Get rid of all the bullshit, and make it a brotherhood like it was always supposed to be. Watch your back, though. They won't all agree with that."

"You sure, bro?" Kairo asks, his brows rising. "It's not too late. I can get you out of here."

"Yeah, I'm sure. I have to do this. Just try and avoid gang wars. They tend to fuck things up."

Kai laughs, and as Nic moves onto Eli, I can't help but watch every last second. "I don't know how long I'm going to be put away for, but from now on, you're my eyes and ears out here. You need to keep Kairo grounded. Make sure he doesn't fuck it up like I did."

"You got it, bro," he says, folding him into his arms and clapping Nic on the back. "I'll move your mom into my building. She'll be taken care of too."

They hold each other for a second longer before Nic turns to Sebastian. "I don't know where I'd be without you, bro," he tells him. "I need you to look out for O, make sure she's keeping out of trouble, and keep this rich fucker in line."

"You know it," Sebastian says, glancing back at me with a bittersweet smile.

The boys hug it out, and as the sirens get louder and louder, Nic finally turns to Colton, and holds out his hand. Colton takes it, and they meet each other's stare. Nic's hold tightens on Colton's hand, but it's nothing he can't handle. "If you ever hurt her," Nic says, his voice low and terrifying. "I will hunt you down like the fucking animal that you are."

"If I ever hurt her, I'll welcome it."

The boys remain locked in a heated stare, and then finally Nic nods, and their hands drop back to their side. "So, what now?" Nic asks, looking down at me.

"Now we wait," I tell him as the siren begins to deafen me. "You tell the cops exactly what you've done, and you pay for your crimes, giving justice to the people who need it most. Maybe even meet with a therapist while you're in there. God knows you need it."

"That easy, huh?"

I nod. "Yeah, it really is."

Sebastian scoffs from behind us, walking into Nic's side. "Just don't bend over in the shower," he tells him. "And I highly suggest not acting like a bitch in there. You know there's bound to be some Wolves."

Nic grunts, not fazed at all. "And plenty of Widows. Don't worry about me, I'll be good."

The cops turn the corner, and suddenly the deserted street is lighting up with blue and red flashing lights. The cops get out and walk toward our small group as Eli discreetly kicks the discarded gun under the Audi, trying to make this transition as peaceful as possible.

Nic instantly stands taller and faces them with his hands out, ready to be cuffed. "It's time," he tells them, already knowing each of them by name. After all, they were all investigating Kian before he died, and that investigation then fell onto Nic's shoulders. "I'll tell you whatever you want to know."

The cops don't hesitate and instantly step into him, cuffing him behind his back and reading his rights. They start pulling him away, but Nic stops and looks back at me with love shining through his eyes. "While I regret it all, I'll never regret you," he tells me. "Maybe once this is all said and done, we could work on going back to how it used to be."

A small smile pulls at my lips as Colton steps into me and curls his arm around my waist. "Yeah," I whisper, longing for that day, though knowing that it may never come. He'll be locked up for a very long time. "I think I'd like that."

Nic nods and not wanting to drag this moment on, he starts walking toward the cop car ready to make amends for everything he's done and finally pay for every single one of his crimes. It'll be a long road, and who knows how long he'll be in there for. I just hope when he comes out the other end, he'll finally have become a better man, someone that we can all be proud of.

It's bittersweet watching him walk away but deep down, we all know it's for the better. With me in charge of the Wolves and Kai now taking over the Widows, this world is going to be a much better place. We can finally begin to turn everything around, and my hometown can start to be somewhere that doesn't need to be feared.

Nic is put into the backseat of the cop car, and not three seconds later, the cruiser is pulling away, and Nic is driven off into the metaphorical sunset. It's not exactly a horse and carriage, but for now, it'll have to do.

"Come on," Colton tells me, gently pulling on my waist. "Let's get out of here. I need to prepare my lawyers. They're going to have their work cut out for them this time."

"Okay," I tell him, glancing back at the boys. "Just give me a second."

Colton nods, and I turn back to the boys, who all stare at me with big puppy dog eyes. "Don't," I say, feeling the guilt washing over me. "Please don't hate me."

Kai shakes his head. "We could never hate you," he tells me, pulling me in for a big hug. "Am I a little surprised that you tried to shoot him down? Sure, but is it anything that the rest of us haven't done before? Not exactly."

Sebastian hijacks our hug and throws his arms around the two of us. "It's for the best. Nic is going where he needs to be, and hopefully, he'll seek out the help that he needs to find the old him."

"Yeah, what he said," Eli adds, joining in on the group hug. "Now, get your ass out of here before any of our guys see us fraternizing with the enemy."

I roll my eyes and pull away from them, knowing that this isn't goodbye. "I'll catch you dorks later," I tell them. "Try not to burn down anyone else's homes for a while."

"We make no promises," Sebastian calls after me.

I can't help but laugh, hating how easily those idiots can make me forget about the heaviness of the day. I make my way back to Colton, knowing that either the boys or Colton's security will take care of the Audi again, and as I go to open the car door, my phone buzzes in my jeans pocket.

I hover in the open door, feeling the eyes of the guys on me as I read over the text.

Christian - Consider Snake handled.

I raise a brow as Kairo calls out. "What's that about?"

I glance up, meeting his gaze as I try to cover my surprise with how quickly the Wolves get shit done. "Wolf business," I tell him.

Kai shakes his head, unable to help his grin. He winks and the little gesture fills my chest with happiness. Assuming my message is about some form of payback, he raises his chin. "Bring it on, pretty girl. I'm looking forward to it."

I roll my eyes, and drop down into Colton's car, and as he takes off down the street, leaving the Audi behind, I work on my reply.

Ocean - Nic got arrested and will be locked up for a very long time. I know that's not exactly what you had in mind, but as far as I'm aware, the war is over. You can all sleep soundly tonight. Then tomorrow we figure out how the fuck I'm supposed to faze myself out and leave the Wolves under your command.

After hitting send, I drop the phone into my lap and look over at Colton. His hand instantly slips into mine, and as he glances at me, I can't help but feel like shit. "Sorry for slipping out of your room like that."

He shakes his head, squeezing my hand, and rubbing his thumb back and forth. "Don't worry about it," he tells me. "I had the security set up with an alert. I knew you were going to go, I just hoped that you didn't. But it's all over now."

"It's all over," I confirm. "All the threats are gone, no more Widows, no more Nic." That thought instantly sends a pang of guilt soaring through me, but in the end, it's where he needs to be.

"You're going to be alright, Jade."

"Are you sure about that?"

"I'm fucking positive."

Christian's reply comes in a second later and has the last piece of the puzzle finally sliding into place.

Christian - Sounds like a good fucking plan to me.

CHAPTER 37

Charlie flies through the air, screaming out as he curls his body into the fetal position, only to go crashing down into the pool, sending a wave of water slamming down over all of us.

Drix squeals and instantly goes in after him as Casey and Cora screech, trying to protect their hair that they just dropped a bomb on at the salon yesterday. Though if I have to be blatantly honest, their hair looks no different than how it did when they first walked in there. They seem to love it though, and that's all that matters.

Jess steps toward the edge of the pool and instantly starts shaking off the water that drips off her arms, and I watch as Drix ducks down under the water and swims right to the edge. As Jess is distracted, Drix comes up, wraps her hand around Jess's ankle, and yanks her into the water, sending yet another cocktail flying to the bottom of the pool. She hardly has a chance to scream before she crashes down into the water.

I can't help but laugh as I sip on my drink, absolutely loving this day. It's so perfect. I wish I could have had this all along. The past five months have been the worst kind of roller coaster, but at the same time, I've come out the other end with these new, incredible friends who I couldn't live without. It's just a shame that other friendships had to be tested along the way.

Two warm arms circle my waist, and before I know it, Colton's lips are teasing the sensitive skin of my neck. "What do you think you're laughing at?" he grumbles, his arms suspiciously tightening around me as his voice gets lower and lower.

"Don't even think about—AHHHHH, PUT ME DOWN YOU BIG, FAT COCK-SUCKING, DICKWAD," I screech as Colton yanks me off my feet and bounds toward the water, laughing like a freaking hyena, refusing to ease up on me.

I scream, scratch, hit, flail, trying everything in my power to free myself, but nothing stops Colton from flying through the air, sending us both out into the center of the deep end.

We crash down into the water, hopefully sending another wave of water over Jess, and we instantly swim right back up to the surface. I suck in a deep breath, more than ready to bust the fucker, but Colton is nowhere to be seen.

I glance around, my anxiety instantly coming up and sending me into a panic. Where the fuck is that little turd? I look around, unable to find him anywhere, so I do whatever any girl would in my situation; I swim as fast as I can.

Bodies start dropping into the pool from every direction, and getting away seems almost impossible. I kick my legs as fast as they'll go, knowing he's bound to be up to something. As I finally come into the shallow end of the pool without being dragged back, I finally start to relax.

Ha. Fucker. Whatever his plan was, he missed me.

I can't explain why that makes me feel like such a badass boss bitch, but it does, and I freaking love it.

I come up into the shallow end, and as I come up for breath, I smack face-first into a hard body and end up swallowing a mouthful of pool water as I try to gasp in surprise.

Ah, shit.

Colton looks down at me, a shit-eating grin across his face. "Looking for someone?" he questions, stepping into me as I hastily try to back up. I don't know what he thinks he's going to do to me, I'm already in the pool. It's not like he can throw me in all over again.

"Don't know what you're talking about," I say, taking another step back.

A sparkle hits his eyes, and I scream before diving back under the water. Colton instantly comes after me, his strength in the pool like nothing I've ever witnessed before. He catches me in seconds, and his hands curl around my waist, twisting me until we're swimming together.

We get down into the deep end, both of us right down at the bottom of the pool. I'm quickly running out of oxygen, but I don't care. Not now that his eyes are on mine.

His fingers trail over my face as my hair floats out around me like a massive brunette halo. As he winks, a smile cracks across my face, letting the last of my oxygen bubble up in front of me.

I push up off the bottom of the pool, and within seconds, I break through the surface with Colton coming up right behind me. His hands never leave my body, and somehow, I still get a thrill out of his every touch. It will never get old.

Colton pulls me in, only giving me the slightest chance to fill my lungs before crushing his lips to mine and kissing me deeply.

"Ugh," Casey whines from across the pool, sitting on her sunbed and soaking up the rays in her new bikini that she insists on showing off every chance she gets. "Would you two get a room already? I swear, if we weren't here, you'd probably be screwing right now."

Colton reluctantly pulls back from me and glances up at his little sister. "Actually, I've already fucked her in here. There are too many surfaces to get through to bother doubling up."

Casey's eyes go wide as Cora's face scrunches up in disgust. "Wait. What do you mean? Are you making your way through the house? Where else have you fucked her?"

Colton grins, his hand slipping into mine as he pulls me back to the shallow end. "Everywhere," he tells her as Milo booms with laughter. "We hit that particular sunbed just last week."

Casey flies up off the sunbed slamming a hand over her mouth.

"AND YOU LET ME SIT ON IT?" she screeches, grabbing her towel and wiping it all over her as though that's going to help get the DNA off. "You're so gross."

"Actually," I laugh, turning my gaze on Cora. "I'm pretty sure it was that sunbed."

Cora flies up right behind her sister and crashes into her, sending the both of them toppling into the pool as the rest of us howl with laughter. So much for their expensive salon trip.

I finally get myself out of the pool and drag my tank over my head before twisting it in my hands, wringing out all of the water. I mean, I'm already in my bikini. Would it have been that hard for Colton to just let me pull it off before tossing me into the water?

Damn. Boys can be assholes, but usually in the best kind of way.

As I grab my towel and dry off, Milo comes over to me with a new drink after mine … actually, I have no idea where it ended up. One second it was in my hand and the next. Poof. It was gone.

I glance down at the mixture and cringe. knowing Milo, this would be filled with every spirit he could get his hands on. My drink before was just juice but everyone had assumed that I was drinking right along with them. I haven't exactly gotten around to telling them about the little bun in the oven. I know I won't be able to hide it much longer, and an explanation will be demanded.

"Thanks," I grumble, giving him a warm smile and wondering how I'll get away with accidentally losing another drink.

Milo grins before looking out at Spencer, watching as he fucks around in the pool, looking happier than I've ever seen him before.

"So," he says, bumping me with his hip. "What's going on with all the Wolf shit? Have you tried to kill any of those bastards yet?" My eyes go wide as I look over at him, and as he meets my gaze, he sees the cringe twisting across my face and gasps. "Spill it, bitch. What else could have possibly happened?"

I bite down on my bottom lip, feeling the same guilt sweep over me. It's only been a few days since everything happened with Nic, and so far, the guilt isn't going anywhere. It might take a little while to be okay with everything that went down.

"So, umm … I didn't try to kill any of the Wolves," I tell him. "But does Nic count?"

"What?" he gasps, his eyes wide as saucers. "I know he's been a real douche lately but dammmmnnnn. What would possess you to try and hurt that sexy piece of demon meat? He's too pretty to be wasted like that. I mean, girllll, those tatts and that body under that silky smooth skin. I'd be his bitch any day."

Spencer scoffs from across the pool. "Please, a guy like that would have you shitting your pants, running scared. Now, Sebastian, he's more your speed."

Milo has the audacity to look offended. "Excuse you, sir. I could handle him."

"Uh-huh."

I gape at the two of them, wondering how the hell we got onto this topic. I don't particularly want to be thinking about any of the guys like that, though I'm not going to lie, a Widow sandwich would be sexy as hell.

"Speaking of Nic," Colton says, coming over to me with his phone in hand before stopping and meeting my eyes. "What's going on?" he asks. "You look like you're thinking too hard."

"Nothing," I grin, glancing at Milo, who grins right back. "Just thinking about a Widow sandwich and what exactly that would involve."

"Girl," Milo grumbles, his voice low. "If you need any visuals, you just let me know. I've got them all stored up in this perfect head of mine. Every position, every angle, anything you need."

"Alright," Colton says, shoving Milo off towards Spencer. "Get out of here before she decides one dick ain't enough for her."

I can't help but laugh as I pull my towel tighter around me, but seeing the seriousness come over Colton's face, the laughter fades away. "What's going on?"

He holds up his phone. "I just had an update from the lawyers. Nic is playing it smart and only confessing to the crimes that would have him serving a lesser sentence."

I let out a sigh, but honestly, I'm not surprised. Nic is a very 'in the moment' kind of guy. He may have had a conscience with a gun to his head, but he's had some time to think it over. Apparently, his newest plan doesn't include spending the rest of his life behind bars. One thing I know about Nic is that he's not stupid. He's going to play the system as well as he can.

I meet Colton's eyes. "What's he looking at?"

"Worst case scenario, he's looking at twelve years, but my lawyers are pretty fucking good. They'll do what they can to get it reduced, and obviously, with good behavior, he'd probably be out sooner. My guess is maybe he'll be out after ten.

I nod my head, lost in thought. Ten years is a long freaking time, but in the end, is that ten years enough to make up for what he's done? Probably not.

"You okay?" Colton murmurs, hooking his arm around my waist and pulling me in so that he can press a kiss to my temple.

"Yeah," I say with a sigh. "I guess it's better than the alternative."

He nods, knowing I'm referring to having to put a bullet through his head, but nothing else is said on it when Harrison comes striding out the door with burgers.

"Lunch anyone?" he announces, placing the burgers down so we can help ourselves.

Fuck yeah. A wide grin stretches across my face, and I drop my towel to the ground before practically barging Harrison out of the way and grabbing a burger. I've been so hungry lately. I could eat a supermarket out of groceries right now.

I start chowing down on my burger, shoving it down as though this is the last meal I'll ever eat. Everyone starts getting out of the pool, and as they start making their way over to grab their own burger before I clear them out, Milo stops and stares.

"What?" I grumble around my full mouth. "Quit staring, bitch."

"Dude, what the fuck is wrong with you? Slow down. I'm all for loving every body shape, but girlllll, you're putting on a little pudge down there."

"What?" I grunt, my eyes going wide as I glance down my body, taking in the tiniest little baby bump that was poking out just a bit this morning. I guess after adding four glasses of juice and my non-stop eating, it's all sticking out just a little bit more.

Fuck. There's no avoiding it now.

My eyes swivel to Colton's, and he watches me with a raised brow. He's all for making the announcement so I don't have to tip-toe around anyone, but for some reason, I've been keeping the whole baby thing close to my chest.

I put my burger down, swallowing what's left in my mouth, and glancing up at everyone now staring at my 'pudge'. "So, umm … I kind of have something to tell you guys." The twins and Drix instantly suck in deep breaths, catching on a lot sooner than the guys. "But," I continue, cutting them off before they get a chance to get excited. "It's not exactly what you think."

All four of the girls glance around at each other in confusion while the guys just stare, having absolutely no idea what's going on.

"So, as you know, a few months ago, after the masquerade party we had here, I was attacked by Jude." Drix instantly starts shaking her head, figuring it out too soon for her own good, but I continue on, knowing that if I stop now, I won't be able to get the words out. "He got me pregnant that night, and I found out a few weeks ago."

"What?" Casey gasps as Milo watches me with wide eyes, completely speechless. "So … you're having a baby?"

"I, umm … technically, I guess."

Charlie narrows his eyes, still as confused as ever. "What's that supposed to mean."

I let out a sigh, and as Colton steps into my side, I find the strength to say the words out loud. "It means that once this baby is born, I'll be giving it to a family who's been wanting this a lot more than I do. I only just turned eighteen, and right now, the thought of being someone's mom is kinda terrifying. I'm not ready and the fact that it's half Jude's ..."

"Don't," Milo says, stepping to me and pulling me tightly into his arms, knocking Colton right out of the way. "You don't need to explain or justify your decisions to us. Just know that we support you completely. Whatever you want or need is yours."

Spencer steps in and joins the hug, and before I know it, every single one of them are crowding around me, huddled in and squeezing me tight.

Charlie's amused laugh comes from the back of the group and I can't help but hear the nervousness in his tone, probably doing the math to make sure it's not his. "No wonder she's been such a moody bitch lately," he chuckles, immediately followed by a low groan when Colton's fist slams into his arm.

Drix's head pokes over my shoulder, and I narrow my eyes at her shit-eating grin. "So, I'm just putting it out there that Hendrix is a fucking awesome name, you know, if you felt that way inclined."

I laugh as the others all start making their own suggestion, offering their names up like a Thanksgiving turkey. "I don't think I get to pick the name," I tell them. "That would be up to his or her new parents. I wouldn't dream of taking that away from them."

A sniffling sounds behind me, and I look back to find Mom standing with Roman at the back door, watching us all huddled together. She instantly gives me a warm smile, and as the pride shines through her eyes, I find myself walking straight into her arms. "That's your final decision?" she asks. "You want to adopt?"

"Yeah," I say a little nervously. "I hope you're not upset with me."

"Not at all, sweetheart. I'm proud of you. You gave yourself time to really think about it, you considered all your options, and then you made your decision based on what would be best for the baby. You're giving a gift to a family that they will never be able to repay. You're so selfless and loving, and I'm so damn proud to call you my daughter. Your daddy would be proud of you, and so will your boys, even Nic."

Tears well in my eyes, and I crush my face into her neck, her words meaning the absolute world to me. I stand in her arms, both of us clinging onto one another until we're finally ready to pull apart.

Mom gives me a wide smile, before clutching my chin between her thumb and pointer finger. "Look at you getting me all emotional when I was supposed to be coming out here to brag about the incredible honeymoon that I'm about to go on."

I can't help but laugh. "Sorry, stealing the show has always been a gift of mine."

"Don't I know it," she laughs.

"Ugh," Drix grumbles from behind us. "Are you old farts still here? Get lost. Go and celebrate your honeymoon already so we can party in your house and trash it every night for six weeks."

Roman's eyes go wide, looking at his daughter first and then at me before going full circle and gaping at his new wife.

Mom instantly laughs. "Oh, chill out," she tells him. "Hendrix stirs you up so easily, and you fall for it every time."

Roman shakes his head, playfully glaring at his daughter, but the love shining out of his eyes is unmistakable. "Alright," he says. "You kids behave. I'm stealing my wife and getting out of here before you get yourselves in trouble, and I have no choice but to stay. You have my international numbers and the neighbor's. Call them if you get yourself in trouble, and if in doubt, you can always check in with the security or call the police. Stay safe, you hear me?"

"Yes, Dad," Drix grumbles.

Mom looks at me. "That goes for you too, young lady."

"Mom, I'm more than capable of taking care of myself." Colton scoffs, and I roll my eyes as Mom chuckles at his reaction. "Fine. I'll be a good little girl who sits at home and watches Netflix every single night. I'll have absolutely zero life until you get home."

"That's more like it," she says, going in for another hug, only Roman pulls her away and throws her over his shoulder.

"No more of that," he tells her, slapping a hand down over her ass and making her giggle like a schoolgirl. "We have a cruise to catch."

Roman disappears inside with my mother, and just before the door closes between us, I hear her voice calling out. "I LOVE YOU."

I can't help but laugh. "I LOVE YOU TOO. DON'T GET DRUNK TATTOOS. THEY'RE NEVER A GOOD IDEA AND REMEMBER, EIGHTEEN IS TOO OLD TO BE HAVING LITTLE BROTHERS OR SISTERS."

And just like that, my mother and Roman are gone, leaving us here with nothing to do but have an amazing time, live our lives, and party until we can no longer stand. Which is exactly how my dumbass ends up right back in the bottom of the pool.

CHAPTER 38

Colton's hand slips into mine before he loops his arm over my shoulder, keeping me right by his side as we walk up the stairs. A yawn tears out of me. It's well past eleven at night but after the parents disappeared and everyone was celebrating, it sort of turned into a bit of a party.

Besides, what's not to celebrate? I'll be giving a family a baby, I'm on my way out of the Wolves, Nic is going to be behind bars where he can't hurt anyone, and I have the most incredible people in my life. Not to mention, Colton only just finished telling me how the paperwork for our new foundation just got finalized, and starting next week, we'll start putting together a team and working on the plans to get this thing off the ground. Hopefully, it won't take too long because there are children out there who desperately need our help.

There was a stage where I thought finding this happiness was never going to come. I was so filled with dread, pain, and regret that I could hardly see a single step in front of me. Without Colton there to guide me through, who knows where I'd be now.

I have to admit, I've made a few mistakes along the way, but this is it. I've finally reached the finish line, and to be here with Colton right by my side is so much more than I could have ever asked for.

Hell, for a while there, I thought that I'd never get my happy ending. I was so close to having it all, and then bomb after bomb just kept getting dropped on me, but here I am again, and this time, there are no bombs left. There's nothing stopping me from having the future I want and deserve. You know, as long as I work my ass off for it.

I've been speaking to Miss Davies about which courses to take once I go to college after this baby pops out. She's been helping as much as she can, always smiling at me like she's so damn proud, and honestly, I kinda love it. Though, she keeps asking me about Christian and if I accidentally let any more details of his life slip out, he'll probably hang me in a meat locker and use me as a human pinata, poking me until all my insides fall out.

We finally reach the top of the stairs and the exhaustion is creeping in so thick that I can hardly hold myself up anymore. But once we finally reach his bedroom door and it closes behind us, a new energy sinks into my bones, something that I only ever experience with him.

There's just something about Colton that I can't get enough of.

He walks over to the side of his bed, pulling his clothes off as he goes, ready to sink into the sheets and call it a night, completely oblivious to the thoughts running through my mind. He grabs hold of his belt buckle, and I'm mesmerized, watching as he undoes it. The muscles in his arms and abs flinch with each movement, and for a brief second, I have to make sure that I'm not drooling.

He's absolutely everything. How is it possible for a man to look like that? It's as though he was carved out of stone, so perfectly incredible.

He drops down into his bed and looks up at me, still standing by the door, my eyes hooded as I bite down on my lip.

I reach behind me and turn off the light, sending the room into darkness. As my eyes adjust, I find that I can see perfectly well with the moonlight streaming in through Colton's bedroom window.

How could anything be more perfect?

I take full advantage.

I walk around to his side of the bed, putting myself right in front of him where he won't be able to miss a thing and put on a show fit for a king … my king. I do a slow spin while taking my time peeling off my bikini top. I feel Colton's eyes on me, watching, wanting.

His hand reaches out and skims over my skin as I turn my back on him. I glance over my shoulder, unable to resist watching how his eyes flame with desire. That look is everything to me, it spurs me on and gives me the power to feel invincible.

Colton is so strong, and the fact that he lets me stand as his equal, lets me make my own mistakes while having my back, and always supports me is the biggest turn on I've ever felt.

This thing between us is solid. It's unbreakable. It's forever.

Keeping my eyes locked on his, I hook my thumbs into the side of my bikini bottoms and slowly draw them down my legs. I bend low, slowly taking them all the way down to the ground and feeling the goosebumps rising all over my skin.

There's something so sexy about exposing myself like this. I love the feel of his eyes burning into my skin, seeing what's his, but nothing compares to when he tastes it.

I hear his low growl just moments before his soft fingers brush over my ass. I close my eyes, loving every little bit of it.

The blankets rustle, and not a second later, Colton is standing behind me, his hard cock already out and resting heavily against my ass. He presses his hand on my lower back, keeping me bent over as his other hand trails over my ass.

My skin is cold and sensitive from spending the day in and out of the pool, so just the softest brush of his fingers sends my nerve endings into overdrive.

His fingers brush over the curve of my ass and stop at the base of my spine before making their way straight down.

I can't help but suck in a breath as he passes my hole, biting down on my lip in anticipation as he continues down.

I'm already dripping wet for him, more than ready to go, but as his fingers glide over my center and find my clit, he's more than happy to spend a few minutes playing with his favorite toy.

He rubs small, lazy circles over my clit as he kicks out my foot, forcing me to spread my legs, opening me up wide and giving him exactly what he wants. A low moan slips from between my lips. If he's not careful, I'll be coming on his fingers though I'm sure that's not a problem for him. A guy like Colton Carrington is more than happy to start all over. He aims to please.

Colton drops to his knees behind me, and my eyes roll into the back of my head in anticipation.

Holy hell. In this position, I'm bound to come before he's even really touched me.

His fingers trail back to my entrance, and he slowly pushes them into me once, twice, three times, making me groan out his name. He pushes a little harder, and the movement forces me to put my hands down on the soft carpet, stopping me from toppling over. I use the leverage to push back against his fingers and take them deeper. Only they're not there for long as he replaces them with his mouth, eager to taste what's on offer.

His fingers travel back up my ass, and I feel as he spreads my wetness, making me crave so much more. As his tongue roams over my clit and his lips work my body, his fingers find my hole. He gently pushes them in, and I suck in a desperate breath before pushing back against him, letting him know that I'm ready for more.

He reads my body like a fucking book and instantly gives me exactly what I want.

With my legs spread wide and my head down near the ground, groaning like a bitch in heat, I have a perfect view of Colton behind me, and more importantly, the way he grips his cock and slowly works his hand up and down.

I fucking drool.

I finally get why men love watching women touch themselves. Seeing him working his cock is the most erotic thing I've ever seen. It's so big, hard, veiny, and long, pulsing with need and then as his thumb circles the top … holy fuck. This is my porn right here.

With this perfect view, it's only seconds before I come on his tongue, and it tears through me like an explosion. Colton waits until my pussy has finished pulsating before he finally gives in and pulls away, but I don't let him go far.

With him down on his knees, I instantly turn and push him back until he's leaning against the side of the bed. I step into him, placing a foot on either side of his thighs and looking down at him. Colton watches me with stars in his hazel eyes, looking at me as though I'm some kind of goddess, and it makes me feel like the most wanted woman on earth.

My hands fall to his shoulders, and I sink down onto his cock, completely filling myself until I feel him in my fucking throat.

His hands fall to my hips, and he squeezes as we both get used to the feel, that is until I start moving. I ride up and down his long, thick cock, listening to his body, and giving him exactly what he wants. He groans, murmuring my name over and over again. His fingers dig in and as my body inches toward another earth-shattering orgasm, I keep myself moving, not daring to come again before he gets a chance.

"Fuck, Jade," he grunts as I slowly pick up my pace, riding him right to the tip of his cock before dropping back down until he's balls deep. Over and over again.

His hands tighten, and then finally he comes. Hot spurts of come shoot deep inside of me, and the feeling has me clenching down around him and as he murmurs my name one more time. I let go and come harder, calling out his name.

After peeling ourselves off the floor and taking a needed hot shower together, we both go crashing down onto his bed. As he pulls me into his arms, I know that nothing will ever have the power to tear this away from us.

Colton Carrington is my end game.

He's my ride or die, and I'll never have it any other way.

His hand falls to my waist, and his thumb rubs back and forth over my skin. "You know the day you walked into this house was the best day of my life."

"If only you knew it back then."

His laugh rumbles through the room. "I fucking did, babe. You're the one who didn't know."

I roll my eyes. "What can I say?" I laugh. "I'm stubborn like that, but you love me anyway."

"I sure fucking do," he says, dropping his lips to my forehead.

"Will you still love me when I'm nine months pregnant with stretch marks and a fat ass?" I ask, glancing up at him, knowing the question is ridiculous but loving how he always insists on reassuring me.

"Fuck no," he says, trying hard to fight the smile that tears across his face. "You know me, I'm shallow as fuck, but you might just win me over if those perfect tits of yours keep growing at the rate they are."

"You're an asshole," I laugh, snuggling into his side. "But I love you anyway."

"I know," he murmurs. "I'm irresistible. Now, go to sleep so I can wake you up early and eat that delicious pussy all over again."

My, oh my. How is a woman supposed to say no to that? So, like a good little girl, I close my eyes, knowing damn well that I'll be having sweet, sweet dreams tonight.

EPILOGUE
Four Months Later

My leg bounces with nerves as I listen to the doorbell ring. "It's going to be fine," Mom says from the doorway of the formal dining room, as Colton sits beside me, doing his best to keep me calm. "They're going to be perfect, and if you don't like them, just send them on their way."

"I know," I murmur, listening to Harrison's footsteps as he goes to answer the door. "But what if they're just putting it on and only look good, but behind closed doors, they're assholes? How can I be sure?"

My hand drops to the seven-month baby bump that's hidden

beneath the table as Colton's hand falls to my thigh. "You have a sixth sense for picking out assholes, Jade. You'll be fine," he tells me. "Besides, I might have had a background check done on them before they got here."

My eyes widen. How can I be surprised by this still? "And?" I prompt.

"And they're everything that I wish I had growing up."

My heart instantly swells, and I suddenly feel a million times better. That is until I hear Harrison at the door, followed by their voices. There's a man and woman, just as I expected. The woman has a kind voice while the man is firm but not demanding.

I hear her heels against the floor, and as they get closer, I stand, taking a deep breath and slowly blowing it out. Colton stands beside me, slipping his hand into mine as Mom discreetly moves to the back of the room, wanting to be here as a voice of comfort but not wanting to overstep. This decision is completely up to me, but she's fooling herself if she thinks that her opinion isn't going to help.

The couple arrives at the entrance of the formal dining room, and I straighten my back, not wanting them to think any less of me for making the decision to give up my child. As the woman lays her eyes on me and drops her gaze to my swelling stomach, tears instantly fill her eyes.

Her husband steps in closer and curls his arm around her waist in the same way that Colton does to me, and just like that, I know this couple is the one. But I'm not stupid enough to announce it to the world until I've had a proper chat with them and get a feel for who they are. All I know is that by looking at the way they stand together, I can tell they love each other in the same, all-consuming, forever and for always kind of way that Colton and I do.

What more could I ask for the child growing inside of me?

"Miss Ocean," Harrison says, putting on his professional hat for our guests. "May I introduce Rebecca and Bryson Bates."

I give them a warm smile, trying not to be too over the top and keep my cool. "It's a pleasure to meet you," I say. "May I offer you any refreshments? Tea, coffee, water?"

"Oh, no, dear," Rebecca says, walking deeper into the room with her husband at her side. She offers me her hand, and I instantly take it. "I honestly don't think I can drink anything. I've been so nervous about meeting you that I'll somehow embarrass myself."

I can't help but laugh. "Trust me, that's not possible around here."

Bryson offers me his hand next, and I get the warmest feeling from him, the same feeling I used to get with my dad growing up. Though unlike my dad, I'm sure this guy isn't hiding any horrible secrets. "It's a pleasure," Bryson says. "I just want to thank you for taking us into consideration and giving us this opportunity to meet with you today. This means the world to Becca and I."

"Of course," I say as Harrison discreetly moves around the room, wanting in on the action and finding every excuse under the sun not to walk out. But in all honesty, once they're gone, I'm going to be asking his opinion on them too, so he better be ready with a full report.

Rebecca and Bryson take a seat on the couch opposite me, and I do some quick introductions. "As Harrison said, I'm Ocean, and this is my boyfriend Colton," I say before leaning around Colton to seek out Mom in the distance. "And this is my mom, Maria."

They give warm smiles as Bryson glances at Colton, clearly knowing who he is. After all, his face is splashed on every news channel and magazine in the country. "Thank you for inviting us into your home."

Colton nods. "Of course, but now that we've gotten the introductions over and done with, why don't you share a little bit about yourselves. What brings you here today?" he questions, sounding as though he's interviewing for a new lawyer.

Rebecca takes the lead, glancing back at me and quickly dropping her gaze to my stomach with longing before realizing what she's doing and looking back up at me. "My husband and I met as children, and before I knew it, we were high-school sweethearts. Everything was happening for us, one thing after another. One minute we were dating, then he was taking me to prom. Soon enough he was down on one knee, and as if I blinked, the next thing I knew, we were happily married and buying a big home to raise all our children in, but then everything stopped. Our world slowed down. One year turned into three, and before I knew it, nearly ten years had gone past, and there were still no children filling those rooms. We would try every month, I would go to the doctor and get the right medications, and every single month without fail, my hopes and dreams would crumble."

Rebecca glances at her husband, who takes her hands, giving her the strength to continue. A single tear rolls down her cheek. "Two years ago, we looked into IVF, and after three failed attempts, I finally fell pregnant. Then at sixteen weeks, we found that my little baby boy no longer had a heartbeat. Due to complications, I was told that I wouldn't be able to try again and had to come to terms with the fact that I would never be able to birth a child of my own. It crushed me and took quite some time to move on from."

She goes to continue but struggles to get the words past the lump in her throat, which is when Bryson takes over. "Last year, we started looking into our options, which is how adoption fell onto our radar. We put our names down, had every single check and application form handed in, and every single day since then, we watched the phone, waiting for the call to say that we might have a shot. Then you called."

"And then I called," I repeat, feeling the baby starting to kick. Tears fill my eyes as I look at the two sitting before me. I've met with four other couples, but these are the only ones who give me this feeling I can't describe, but somehow I know that these people are the right parents for my child. They've fought for this and I know that they're going to adore this sweet baby.

"Look, I, um … I don't want to get your hopes up or anything, but the baby is moving, and I was wondering if you might want to feel?"

Rebecca's eyes fill with tears, and she nods, instantly throwing herself to her feet. "Are you sure? I really don't want to make you uncomfortable in any way, or overstep."

I shake my head. "I'm not uncomfortable in the least," I tell her, taking her hand and gently placing it over the foot that's sticking out just above my belly button. "That's his foot," I murmur, knowing in my heart that this woman will be a mommy in two months. "He gets really active once I've been sitting down for a while. I think he finds it soothing when I'm moving around."

Rebecca's bottom lip quivers. "He?" she questions, hopeful.

I shrug my shoulders. "I don't actually know, I just have a feeling."

Another tear rolls down her cheek, and I can't help but look back at Mom, who gives me a proud smile, tears of joy in her eyes, clearly seeing what I'm seeing. She gently nods, telling me that it's okay to trust myself, and as I glance up at Colton he does exactly the same thing before pressing a kiss to my forehead.

I place my hand over Rebecca's, moving it around as the baby moves inside of me. "I have an appointment for a check-up this afternoon, and the doctor was planning on doing another ultrasound. I was wondering if maybe you had some time and would like to come along? I know there are some things that we would need to discuss first, but I wouldn't want my child's mother to miss seeing him."

"Your child's …" she sucks in a gasp, her eyes going wide as Bryson steps into her back, placing a hand on her shoulder. "Are you saying … do we… is this my child? Am I finally going to be a mommy?"

"Yeah," I whisper. "I would like it very much if you two would be the parents of my child."

Rebecca breaks into sobs and throws her arms around me, instantly sending a wave of emotions crashing over me. Bryson steps into Colton and offers him his hand only to pull him right in and clap him on the back. "Congratulations," Colton says to the both of them. "You're going to make incredible parents. This baby is lucky to have you."

Two Months Later

My fingers nervously drum against the cheap plastic table as I watch all the guys in orange jumpsuits come through the door in chains. Their wrists and ankles are cuffed, and I can't help but stare.

I see this stuff in movies all the time, but nothing prepares you for the real thing, especially when it's someone that you care for.

Nic walks into the room with a guard at his back, and I watch with wide eyes as he does exactly what he's told, being on his best behavior as his wrists and ankles are freed. As I watch him, I can't help but notice the way that he holds himself. It's almost as though I'm seeing a new person. The Nic I saw six months ago was haunted, he was jumpy and nervous, but the guy I'm looking at now is strong, proud, and healthy. He looks almost familiar, almost like a carbon copy of the old Nic that I once knew, and I can't help but wonder what his time in here is doing for him. Is he finally at peace and forgiven himself for the horrible things that he's done, or is he just living life in denial?

Once Nic is free from the chains, he begins scanning the room, trying to figure out who brought him here, and as he does, nerves pulse through me. I haven't seen Nic since I was sitting across from him in court, watching as he confessed to a jury about all the things that he's done. Well, by all, what I mean is just a few things that meant he wouldn't get life in prison. Though, just as I knew it would happen, the judge made an example out of him and gave him ten years behind bars. His only hope is that he behaves and can apply for early release when the time comes.

Nic's eyes come to mine, and I watch carefully as surprise flashes across his face. I've been so nervous that he's been blaming this all on me, and well, honestly, for some parts of it, he'd be right. I am responsible for putting him here, but he's the one responsible for the things he did that lead him down this path.

Nic instantly starts making his way toward me, and I quickly glance around at the other inmates, trying to figure out what's the correct protocol here. Am I allowed to touch him, or do I just sit still and wait for him to come to me?

Nic laughs as he makes his way to me. "Don't make it so obvious that it's your first time here," he teases, giving me a brilliant smile that warms me.

"I just … am I allowed to give you a hug?"

"Of course you are," he tells me, walking around to my side of the table and offering me his hand.

I take it greedily, and he helps pull me up. The second my bump becomes visible out from under the table, Nic's eyes bug out of his head. "Holy fuck, Ocean. I knew you were fucking pregnant, but damn. I guess I'd lost track. You look like you're about to explode."

"Gee, thanks for the reminder," I grumble, stepping into him and curling my arms around him, squeezing tight as he tries not to do anything, fearing that if he squeezes enough, the baby might just pop out.

I quickly return to my seat, not wanting to get in trouble with the guards, and as Nic does the same, he keeps his eyes on mine. "Fuck, I missed you," he says, his eyes shining bright. "How are you? I'm assuming Richy Rich ain't far away?"

I shake my head. "He's sitting out front waiting for me. Do you have any idea how hard it was to get him to be alright with me coming here? If he could sit here beside me, he would, but he knew I needed this time alone."

Nic nods. "So, what took you so long?" he questions, a seriousness coming over him. But seeing as though we only get an hour, it's probably best to get all the bullshit questions out of the way.

I press my lips into a tight line. "Honestly," I murmur. "A part of me was still very angry with you. It took me a while to even wrap my head around it all, and by the time that anger had started to fade, months had gone by. But for the most part, it's the guilt. I hate that you're here and that I had a part in putting you here."

"Don't do that," he tells me. "I'm the only one responsible for putting my ass here. I had a choice, and I did what I had to do. And to be completely honest, I get plenty of sleep, I get fed, someone else does my fucking laundry, and I don't have to deal with other bastards' problems all fucking day. Life's pretty good."

"You're such a liar," I laugh. "It fucking sucks in here, and you know it."

He grins wide, and I shake my head, appreciating that he at least tried to make me feel better about it. "What's going on with you?" he asks, glancing down at the bump. "What did you decide? Are you keeping it?"

I shake my head, knowing he would be happy with this decision. "No," I tell him. "I found a couple who are going to be the new parents. They're great. I mean, they're certainly not your cup of tea, but as far as amazing parents go, they're going to give this baby the world."

"Good," he says. "I'm glad. But what else? I'm assuming the Wolves are pleased that you're giving it away?"

I give him a tight smile. "I honestly don't know what the Wolves think. After your arrest, I spoke with Christian and handed him the reins. He took over everything and Colton handed over the deeds to a new place, they've been rebuilding ever since. He promised that he was going to deal with all the rotten eggs and turn things around, just like Kai's been doing with your Widows."

Nic rolls his eyes. "Don't get me started on Kai," he says, a smirk pulling at his lips. "He'll have my men prancing around in fucking tutu's with girl guides, knocking on doors, and helping sell those fucking charity cookies. I thought I told you to keep him in check."

"Nope," I grin. "You practically told everyone else to watch me while telling me to watch myself."

"Yeah," he grumbles. "That sounds about right."

I can't help but laugh, and before I know it, a buzzer sounds through the small room, and the inmates start getting to their feet. "Why don't you come back every now and then?" Nic suggests. "It might make my time in here pass a little quicker."

I give him a warm smile as I stand up and walk around to him, throwing my arms around his neck. I can't help but laugh. "Sure thing," I tell him. "But you better make it worth my while. Next time, I want a full rundown of the guys you're in here with and what fucked up shit they did to get themselves locked up."

"You've got yourself a deal," he tells me, and just like that, he walks away.

I watch as he goes and gets himself locked back into the cuffs, and as the guard bends down in front of him, the fucker gives me a dirty wink, making me snort so loudly that not only do I scare the people around me, but I scare myself too, jumping and making my fucking water break all over the floor.

Colton speeds through the streets, trying to get our asses back to Bellevue Springs. I had a plan. I was supposed to get induced at the hospital next week with Rebecca and Bryson at my side. I was going to get all the drugs in the world and push this baby out like any other September day. But noooo, here I am on the freeway, screaming at my boyfriend to drive his multimillion-dollar car faster because my fucking vag hurts.

"Fuck, babe," he says, glancing at me while desperately trying to keep his eyes on the road. "It can't go any faster."

"Then what kind of moron pays that much for a car that can't teleport a bitch to the fucking hospital?"

"I know, I know. I swear, in the next car I get, that's going to be the very first feature that I have installed."

"You fucking better," I cry as another contraction tears through me. What the fuck is this? It's supposed to take hours. I was having pains all through my visit with Nic, but I assumed it was just the Braxton hicks contractions that I've been getting every few days. I'm not sure yet. I still have another week. How was I supposed to know that it was go time?

Either way, my doctor told me that most first time moms have a really slow process, but fuck, I feel like the head is already poking out. Why are these contractions coming on so quickly? I should have had plenty of time instead of being here, destroying Colton's car.

"Fuck," I grunt, moving around on the seat and struggling to get comfortable, feeling as though I should at least be a little concerned for the expensive seats that I'm sitting on, but fuck them. Colton's going to have to get the whole thing detailed after this. Technically we both knew that this was a possibility, so we should have taken one of the other cars. You know, the ones that don't have a ridiculous price tag on them.

Realizing that there's nothing we could have done, I take slow, deep breaths and try to relax. I lean back into the chair, focusing on my breathing just like I was taught in the classes that Colton insisted I go to. Only another contraction comes just thirty seconds later.

Holy fuck. That's not good. I look over at Colton in a panic. "They're too close together. We're not going to make it."

His eyes are wide as we race down the road. "We'll make it, babe. I'll fucking get you there." He reaches over, taking my hand, but I instantly yank it out of his grip, desperately needing to move myself around.

I shake my head, knowing he's just trying to calm me. He's been at all the doctor appointments and knows exactly what to look for. He's not stupid, he knows as well as I do that he's about to be delivering this baby on the side of the road, and honestly, I don't know why he isn't freaking out with me.

"Call Becca and Bryson," I say through a clenched jaw, the contractions coming up and squeezing the fucking life out of me, literally. "They can't miss this."

"They're already on their way to the hospital," he tells me in a too calm tone that instantly grates on my nerves.

"No," I snap, a harsh glare flying his way. "They need to meet us here. I'm telling you. I. Am. Not. Going. To. Make. It."

Colton's face twists with a cringe, and I see the exact moment his calm poofs into non-existence. "Fuck, okay," he says with urgency, instantly bringing up their number over the bluetooth speaker.

Bryson's voice comes through the car, but in all honesty, I don't hear a word either of them are saying. I'm too busy screaming at the pain tearing through me. This isn't how it's supposed to go. I need to be in a hospital doing this with drugs. I want the fucking drugs.

We get another five minutes down the road when my hand slips down between my legs, and I feel something there. The need to push sails through me, panic instantly pulsing through my veins. We're really going to do this. I'm delivering on the side of the road without the parents to see.

Fuck. This is not how it was supposed to go.

I instantly start pulling at my leggings, sliding them down my legs as Colton gapes at me. "Please, baby, just hold on. We're only ten minutes away."

"The baby is fucking coming," I panic, struggling to get any more deep breaths. "I can't wait any longer. IT'S COMING."

"Like … RIGHT FUCKING NOW?" he asks, his eyes wide and terrified.

"YES. PULL THE FUCK OVER."

"FUCK."

Colton careens off the road, brings the car to a screeching stop, and sends a cloud of dust flying up behind us. He dives out of the car, racing around and helping me to get my door open. He takes one look at me, his gaze sweeps down between my legs, and his face instantly turns white. "Oh, fuck. Okay … umm."

Colton searches around, trying to figure out how this is going to work before peeling off his shirt and laying it down on the dirty ground. "Here," he says, offering me his hand. I instantly take it and squeeze the living hell out of it as another contraction rocks through me.

Getting out of the car is easily the worst pain that I've ever experienced, and after everything that I've been through over the past year, that's saying a lot.

Not being able to bend to get down to the ground, Colton has to pick me up and physically lay me down. The second my back is flat, the pain eases, but not by much.

"Okay," I say, meeting his eyes over the top of my wide open legs. "What do we do?"

He shakes his head, looking panicked until he swan dives through the car and grabs his phone to call for an ambulance. He gets the operator on the phone, who instantly starts talking him through it.

Colton's hands reach down between my legs, and I honestly can't even think about what he's telling me. All I know is that when the next contraction tears through me, I start pushing, grabbing into my thighs, and desperately trying to get this thing out of me.

I scream out, never having felt anything like it before. "Keep going, Jade," Colton encourages. "Harder."

He starts counting to ten, and I listen to the sound of his voice, following exactly what he's telling me to do as I tear my body apart. I take a quick breath and then push all over again as my eyes and jaw clench, in complete agony.

"Okay, okay, okay," he rushes out. "Stop, stop. stop. The head is out. Now what?"

The guy on the phone tells him exactly what to do, and as I lay here panting, we hear a car coming to a screeching stop before two people start rushing in toward us.

Bryson and Rebecca suck in shocked gasps but instantly fall in beside Colton, doing anything and everything they can to help. Rebecca takes my hand, letting me squeeze it until she loses feeling while Bryson somehow finds a water bottle and a cloth and presses it to my face.

Colton checks the cord isn't wrapped around the baby's neck, and when he glances back up at me, there's nothing but pride shining through his eyes. "Alright, Jade," he murmurs. "You're nearly there. On the next contraction, you're going to get this baby out."

I nod and as if on cue, the contraction comes back, and I give another devastating push. Pain rockets through me, and with tears in my eyes, I finally bring Rebecca and Bryson's new baby into this messed-up world.

Tears stream down Rebecca's face as Colton holds this precious little baby in his arms, looking somewhat shocked that this just happened. He glances around holding the baby while trying to figure out what the hell to do with it. It's covered in all sorts of shit, but all I can do is gape. That thing just came out of me.

Bryson is quick to jump into action, peeling off his own shirt, and helping Colton to wrap the baby. Then in a moment that equally kills me while also filling me with the most incredible amount of love and joy, Colton hands the baby to Rebecca.

With the cord still attached, Rebecca has to move closer to Colton, but I don't mind as it gives me a better view of this perfect little angel that just came out of me.

She takes it eagerly, and I struggle to take my eyes off them. "Is it a boy or a girl?" I whisper.

Rebecca shakes her head, having absolutely no idea. She adjusts the baby and shuffles around Bryson's shirt before a bright smile tears across her face. She glances back at me. "You were right," she whispers, her bottom lip quivering. "It's a little baby boy."

Colton reaches out and takes my hand, wanting to give me all the love in the world. "You did great," he says as we hear the familiar sound of the ambulance in the distance.

"You really did," Bryson says. "We'll never be able to thank you enough for this incredible gift. It's … I have no words to describe just how thankful we are."

I give him a tight smile before looking back at the little boy who I've just spent the last nine months with, knowing that I did something great. "Just give him an incredible life, and if it's not too much to ask, maybe a photo on his birthday."

"Of course," Rebecca says with tears of joy in her eyes as she holds her sweet little boy. "Every year on September 20th, look out for an email. I'll send you a whole collage with videos included."

A wide smile spreads across my face and as Rebecca leans down to show me his perfect little face, tears fall from my eyes. "Does he have a name?"

"Yeah," she says so softly that even I feel soothed. "Meet Jackson Bryson Bates, the most cared for and loved child this earth is ever going to come across."

I reach out and brush my fingers over his tiny little hand. "It's absolutely perfect," I tell her, knowing now more than ever that I made the right decision.

Bryson walks around on his knees beside Rebecca, having a few moments together as they celebrate their brand new family, and as they do, Colton moves in beside me, instantly pulling me into his arms as the bittersweet tears roll down my eyes. "You were amazing," he tells me as his lips press against my temple. "So fucking strong. You're a goddamn queen. I love every single little thing about you."

I don't say anything, just rest my head against his chest, listening to the sound of the ambulance as it quickly gets closer.

Rebecca glances down at me with a nervous expression on her face. "Would you like to hold him? Say goodbye?"

Tears instantly form in my eyes, and I look up at her. "Would that be okay?"

"Of course," she says, leaning in and passing him to me before showing me just how to hold him.

Rebecca instantly takes a step back with Bryson and gives us this moment of privacy, and as I look down at the perfect little boy that I've created, I know that this is for the best.

I slip my fingers into his hand, and as I do, Colton discreetly brings out his phone and captures the moment on video. He knows that one day, I'm going to want to look back at this moment, and treasure it until my dying days.

I look down at his little eyes that look so much like mine. "I'm so sorry," I murmur. "You don't know how desperately I wish that I could have the strength to be your mother, but you deserve so much more. You need parents who are ready to take on the responsibility and give you the life that you deserve. They're going to love you so much, treasure you, and give you the world so you can flourish and become the best man this world has ever seen. You're so strong, and I don't need to see you grow up to know that." Tears stream down my face, even more when I hear his tiny little cry for the very first time. "Please don't grow up hating me for giving you up. I want you to know how hard this has been for me to make this decision, but I know that it's right. And just know, that one day, if you're ever curious about me, that I'll be standing there with open arms, ready to tell you all about it."

Colton's arm slips around my waist, and as the ambulance pulls in behind the Veneno, my heart shatters into a million pieces. "I love you so much," I tell my sweet little baby boy, fearing the moment that I have to hand him back to Rebecca. He squeezes down on my finger, and for just a small moment, I can imagine that he's telling me that he loves me too. "I will always love you, my beautiful boy."

The paramedics rush in and quickly check over Jackson before looking over me and then finally cutting the cord. They help me to finish delivering the placenta, and before I know it, it's time to hand the baby back to his brand new parents.

I'm put into the back of the ambulance with Colton by my side.

Rebecca and Bryson follow along with little Jackson, getting him straight to the hospital to give him exactly what he needs to have an incredible start at life.

As we drive, I know that this isn't the end. I know that one day, I'll see that little boy again and be honored to watch him grow up and become the guy he was always destined to be. Hell, who knows, maybe even one day, Colton and I might have a little bundle of our own.

Dominic

Six Years Later

Two thousand, three hundred, and eighty-two days.

I know it's only been six and a half years in the slammer and technically, I still have just under four years left of my sentence, but fuck it. I've done enough time. I'm over this.

My Widows need me back. It's time to get back on top.

At first, I was all good to spend a few years behind bars. I had too many enemies, too many people coming after me that being locked up was the safest place for me, but those enemies are gone now, and it's time to take it all back.

Sure, it kinda sucked leading Ocean to believe that I had turned a new leaf and that she had somehow saved my soul, but it was a means to an end. I do love her though. I hate that she was hurting for being a part of putting me here, but she wasn't wrong. The time in here did do me good. I was able to put my life into perspective and make amends for the crimes I'd committed, well, at least the bare minimum that I actually admitted to.

I'm done with that now. The time has come to rise up again. The time has come to claim back what's mine.

I walk through the hallway, a cocky as fuck smirk on my face knowing that this is going to go off exactly how I had planned it. I'm not going to lie, there may have been a few extra bonuses along the way.

Today is the day. We've been waiting for this for so long, planning every little moment right down to the end.

I'm going to have to go underground, going to have to keep silent, keep my head down. I've even been toying with the idea of an alias, but I can figure that shit out later.

I look left and then right before slipping through the door of the infirmary. It took me weeks to get on the cleaning roster for this room, and now that I'm here, I won't be wasting a single second. This has to go perfectly.

The infirmary is cold. It's always fucking cold, but lucky for me, I haven't had to come in here often. I'm usually the one putting dickheads in here in the first place. The room is empty, just as I knew it would be, but I don't have long. The old Doctor is due back from his lunch break in twenty minutes.

My hand slips into the front of my pants and stepping out of the line of cameras, I pull out the key that leads through to the back room. As the camera scans, I make my move, running to the door and slipping inside the room before the camera comes back around.

I duck down, hiding behind the window, and I have to crawl like a fucking toddler to get through to the next door, but when I do, it's so fucking worth it.

Right where I knew it would be is the black body bag of the dickhead I'd put in here only two days ago.

The room is freezing, but I put that to the back of my mind as I walk over to the body bag, grinning as I take hold of the zipper, and slowly drag it down, revealing the face of Ocean's nightmare.

Jude Fucking Carter. I've been waiting for the day that I got to take his life, and it was fucking perfect. The fact that it worked well with my plan was just the cherry on top.

"Good afternoon," I say, grinning down at the fucker. "I trust you're having a nice little rest in here, but unfortunately, it's time to fuck off."

I grab his heavy body and glance around. Now, where the fuck am I supposed to stash this? There's a supply closet where his body will start decomposing quickly or the freezer. Hmm, choices, choices.

I take the supply closet. The fucker can rot for all I care.

I throw Jude's body into the supply closet before looking back at the black bag and cringing. This is the part of the plan that I wasn't all that thrilled with, but I do what I have to do to get back on top. It will just never get spoken of again.

I climb in and zip it up, sending my world into darkness as I do my best to try not to breathe in the stench of Jude's dead body. I hold back vomit. I have to be careful. If I get caught in here, I'm fucked.

An hour ticks by before I hear the door finally open, and I listen carefully, not moving a fucking inch. The table starts moving, and I'm rolled out a back door to where I hear the familiar sounds of a transport van. There are birds, the sounds of men working in the yard, chains and gates, but the one thing I don't hear is the alarm.

The roller table that I lay on is pushed right to the back of the van and I feel as the tags on the bag are all checked. I hear a familiar voice who confirms numbers with the guard in charge of the transport, and after double-checking that this is indeed Jude Carter's body bag, the whole bag is grabbed and carelessly thrown into the back of the transport van.

The engine starts, and soon enough, the van is driving out of the gates, stopping at every checkpoint to have the van searched. I hold my breath every time. I can not get caught, especially after getting this far.

When the van finally makes it out onto the road, I let out a breath of relief, and before I know it, the zipper is yanked down and light floods in through the fucking dirty ass bag.

"Hey, brother," Kairo grins, looking down at me. "Long time no see."

He instantly helps me out of the bag and claps me on my back before tossing a pair of clean clothes at me. "Here, take these. You fucking stink like death."

I quickly get myself dressed, and within seconds, the van pulls off the side of the road and we bail out, leaving everything behind and making our steps from here on out untraceable.

The second my ass drops into the backseat, the car is already moving. I look up front to find Sebastian and Eli looking back at me with wide grins across their faces. "Fuck yeah," Eli cheers as Sebastian races down the road, determined to put as much space between us and the prison before they figure out where they fucked up and put out a statewide manhunt.

"Where are we going?" Sebastian asks, glancing up at me through his rearview mirror.

I grin. "One stop, Bellevue Springs and then it's back to business."

Knowing exactly what I'm referring to, Sebastian hits the fucking gas and within an hour and a half, I'm standing at the big ass door that's brought me so much grief, love, and pain in the past.

The boys hang back at the bottom of the stairs, giving me this moment, and after banging my fists against the heavy fucker, I stand back and wait.

Ten seconds.

Twenty seconds.

My heart races. She has no fucking idea that we planned this escape, and now that her life has moved on and she's doing her thing, I don't want to bring her back down, but there's no way in hell that I'm about to let her find out by seeing my face splashed across every news outlet in the country.

The door finally opens, and as I take in her face, I'm fucking blown away. She'd be twenty-four now, and she's just as perfect as she was when I met her as a kid.

Her mouth instantly drops and she stares at me wide-eyed before gaping over my shoulder at the boys. "What the actual fuck?" she breathes before finally believing what she's seeing and throwing herself out the door.

Ocean crashes into me, and I hold her tight for a long, drawn-out moment but knowing that I'm on a timer, I pull back and make it quick.

"I couldn't go into hiding without seeing you first," I explain.

"But … what?"

I laugh. "We kinda planned a prison escape," I explain. "Figured that I'd done enough time."

"You're an idiot," she tells me before looking down at the boys and calling out. "You're all fucking idiots. You're going to get caught, you know that, right?"

I shake my head. "Nah, I'm too good for that."

"Who's at the door, Mommy?" comes a sweet little voice from just inside the door.

Ocean glances back and holds out her hand, and the tiniest little princess walks straight into her side. "Hey, my sweet girl," she says, curling her arm around her baby and holding her close to her side. "You know all those stories I tell you about your Uncle Nic? Well, this is him," she explains, making my heart swell as I look down at the girl who wears a much younger version of her mother's smile.

Ocean looks back at me. "I can't tell you how long I've been waiting to introduce you to my daughter," she tells me. "Nic, meet my baby girl, little Storm."

My mouth drops and I instantly drop down onto one knee before the little girl, loving the way she looks at me with such love already. Her mother's stories must have made me out to be some kind of hero. "Hi there, I'm—"

Storm crashes into me, throwing her little arms around my neck as Ocean watches on with tears in her eyes. I can't believe I didn't know about this. I can't help but glance back at the boys, who all cringe. They have some serious explaining to do, but that's not what's important right now.

I pick up the little girl and hold her in my arms as I look back at Ocean. "How are you?"

"Good," she tells me, holding up her hand and showing off the magnificent ring that would be visible from space. "We're getting married in a few months, but I'm guessing that you won't be able to attend?"

I shake my head. "I'm sorry, girl, but you have no fucking idea how happy I am for you."

Little Storm gasps, her eyes wide and for a moment, I wonder if I've hurt her until she bursts into laughter. "Uncle Nic said a bad word."

My eyes bug out. "Oh, shit. I did."

"And you just did it again," Ocean laughs.

The sweet baby girl falls back into her mother's arms, and I take a step back. "What have you been up to? Did you go to college like you always wanted?"

"I sure did," she tells me. "I graduated just last year and finally got to take over the foundation. We've saved nearly a thousand kids from online predators and monsters since starting six years ago. I mean, you have no idea how many kids go to bed each night without a roof over their heads, but we're slowly helping them, and the more children that we return to their parents, the better."

"You really are incredible," I tell her. "I always knew you would be."

"Yeah," she scoffs in disbelief. "And you're out of prison."

I suck in a breath, deciding it's time to get serious. "People are going to come asking you questions about me."

She nods and steps back into me before pushing up onto her tippy-toes and pressing a kiss to my cheek. "I've got your back, just as I always have," she tells me. "If anyone comes looking, I never saw you."

I wink and turn back to the stairs before taking the first three, feeling her eyes on my back. I turn back, knowing she's still watching. "Did I remember to tell you how much I love you?"

Ocean laughs and waves her hand. "Get lost before I have every cop in the state busting down my door, you big idiot."

I laugh and make my way down the steps, heading back to my boys. As they look up at me with shit-eating grins on their faces, I realize that not a damn thing has changed since the days of sitting in my busted up car, hotboxing the fucker with my best friends at my side.

I get to the bottom step and instantly take the keys out of Sebastian's hand before dropping into the driver's seat and taking off like a fucking rocket. I leave the three fuckers behind, gaping at the back of the car as they realize they're stranded. That'll teach them to keep such a massive secret from me.

As for now, it's back to business.

I have one more score to settle, and this one is going to be my favorite by far.

<u>Rejects Paradise Series Playlist</u>

Game of Survival - Ruelle
I'm Gonna Show You Crazy - Bebe Rexha
Nightmare - Halsey
Never Tear Us Apart - Bishop Briggs
Bird Set Free - Sia
Helium - Sia
Dusk Till Dawn - Zayn feat Sia
Heaven - Julia Michaels
Graveyard - Halsey
Bad Bitch - Bebe Rexha
Love Drug - G-Easy feat Halsey
Hurricane - Tommee Profitt
Unloveable - Delacey
Power - Isak Danielson
Cruel Intentions - Delacey feat G-Easy
Not Afraid Anymore - Halsey
Unstoppable - Sia
Monsters - Tommee Profitt
Can't Help Falling In Love - Tommee Profitt
Angel Cry - G-Easy feat Devon Baldwin
Bad At Love - Halsey
Creep - G-Easy feat Ashley Benson
In The End - Tommee Profitt
Wicked Game - Daisy Gray
Haunted - Beyonce
Gasoline - Halsey
I Feel Like I'm Drowning - Two Feet
Twisted - Two Feet
Wild Horses - Bishop Briggs
The Fire - Bishop Briggs
Killer - Vallerie Broussard

Thanks for reading!

If you enjoyed reading this book as much as I enjoyed writing it, please consider leavinge a review.

www.amazon.com/dp/B08HR8V5NH

For more information on Rejects Paradise, find me on Facebook or Instagram –

www.facebook.com/SheridanAnneAuthor

www.instagram.com/Sheridan.Anne.Author

<u>Other Series by Sheridan Anne</u>

www.amazon.com/Sheridan-Anne/e/B079TLXN6K

<u>Young Adult / New Adult - Romance</u>

The Broken Hill High Series (5 Book Series + Novella)

Haven Falls (7 Book Series + Novella)

Broken Hill Boys (5 Book Novella Series)

Aston Creek High (4 Book Series)

Rejects Paradise (4 Book Series)

<u>New Adult Romance</u>

Kings of Denver (4 Book Series)

Denver Royalty (3 Book Series)

Rebels Advocate (4 Book Series)

<u>Urban Fantasy - Pen name: Cassidy Summers</u>

Slayer Academy (3 Book Series)